LIGHT ON BONE

KATHRYN LASKY

LIGHT ON BONE

Woodhall Press
Norwalk, CT

woodhall press

Woodhall Press, 81 Old Saugatuck Road, Norwalk, CT 06855
WoodhallPress.com

Cover design: Jessica Dionne Wright

Layout artist: Amie McCracken

Library of Congress Cataloging-in-Publication Data available

ISBN 978-1-954907-04-1 (hardcover)

ISBN 978-1-954907-06-5 (electronic)

First Edition

Distributed by Independent Publishers Group
(800) 888-4741

Printed in the United States of America

I've been absolutely terrified every moment of my life and I've never let it keep me from doing a single thing that I wanted to do.

—Georgia O'Keeffe

Prologue

Just outside Ghost Ranch, Abiquiu, New Mexico, July 1934

The damn cassock was really a nuisance. Even worse, he was almost out of gas after becoming hopelessly lost in this desert country. And these roads, gouged with arroyos from the violent summer downpours, made driving almost impossible. So before he drove another inch, he wanted to make sure he had finally found the right road after somehow missing the turnoff for the ranch. Supposedly an animal skull marked it, but tourists often took the skulls, some sort of macabre souvenir. Apparently this one must have been plucked off the road. But right now, he was trying to find any road that would help orient him. This was difficult work to do, here in the wilds of the American desert—in the thick of the night and the sand sifting in these bloody, improbable sandals—with only a map and a mission.

It had begun to rain. Softly. Not one of those clattering lightning-filled storms that in these godforsaken brown parts of the earth sometimes rose up out of nothing, or so it seemed. He thought of the hours he had spent as a child huddled with his family under umbrellas when a picnic had been wrecked by rain. But his mum's eternal optimism: "It's brightening, children; I truly believe it is." What would one say out here? "It's blinding, children. Dodge the lightning!"

He saw a flickering light ahead. Perhaps a house. He stopped and took off his hat—a friar's hat—and fanned himself. He must look like Friar Tuck, he thought, but he was far from Sherwood Forest. This costume, however, was what he had been told was the local style—Franciscans had founded this diocese, the largest in New Mexico, part of the European conquest over the heathens.

A pale moon was just beginning to rise. It would be a full moon when it got up there. And then the dawn, with that fragile lavender he already had found so enchanting. A whisper of a wind chafed against the rocks and scraped his scalp, which had been tonsured in the style of his brethren.

But there was something else he heard. A sound that did not belong to the desert. A metallic click. A new darkness began to slide over him—a long shadow. *That's not right ... moon's not up enough for shadows to be cast.* Then a whistling sound.

He gasped. And clutched the base of his neck, where a knife was now embedded. Why? Twenty years of service never a scratch, and now? Unendurable pain as a rising tide of blood began to choke him. No air. *Drowning in my own blood.* He knew it was over. "For God, king, and country," he tried to murmur as the blood gurgled up in his throat and his congealing eyes settled on that rising moon.

Chapter 1

Georgia O'Keeffe woke up, as always, an hour before dawn. She inhaled deeply that scent of sagebrush and adobe. There was simply nothing comparable to these desert fragrances. Swinging her legs over the edge of the bed, she let her feet touch the floor and rest a minute, maybe two. Under her soles she felt the smoothed grains of dirt and flour mixed with water that was often used in these desert homes. She marveled at how close to the earth it made her feel. She was happy that the Ghost Ranch had not finished the floors in this particular casita she had rented. In this space, this landscape, she felt planted as she had never quite felt in her life. Her body had acclimated beautifully since she had arrived at Ghost Ranch three months earlier. It was almost as if something had been rekindled deep inside her.

The light in this high wild country was infinitely fascinating. And she had become attuned—deeply attuned—to its endless shifts. There was a point, perhaps an hour before the dawn, when the darkness frayed into a silvery dust, bleaching the last of the stars. And that is when she rose from her bed as she did now, went outside wrapped in shawls, and climbed the ladder leaning against the adobe casita to the roof and into the sky. She could smell the rain that had passed through earlier in the night. The earth always smelled different after these nighttime showers.

She looked toward the Pedernal. They called it a mountain, but it was in fact a mesa. The word itself, *pedernal*, meant "flint." She had filled a sketchbook with drawings of it. The sketches had become increasingly spare, distilling the image in her mind. She began to think of it as her private mountain. She thought if she painted it enough, it would belong to her. It seemed, during these months at the ranch, that this single mountain anchored her after the tumult of the previous year with Stieglitz. The mesa was steadfast and loyal. Somewhat ironically, however, it was said to be the birthplace of Changing Woman, the daughter of Earth and Sky. Clad in white shells, turquoise, and abalone, she represented the cycle of the seasons and that of woman as child, daughter, mother, and grandmother. *Well, I have certainly changed out here*, Georgia said, almost aloud. *Yes, indeed.*

She set herself down, leaning against the chimney with a cup of tea to immerse herself in this moment between night and dawn. Looking to the east, she caught sight of a vulture's jagged wings. *Something's died out there*, she thought. She'd wait a bit and not rush out to paint. She'd let the vultures do their business. They would have cleared off by the time she loaded the Model A with her easel and paints.

She was eager to collect a horse skull she had spotted the other day but forgotten about until she was halfway home. She planned to bring it back and paint it on the patio—never in the studio but against the bright blue sky. She really needed the light on the bone. She might put the horse's skull against a faded old American flag she had. No stars—they would only distract from the shape. Even though she had already begun to think of it as her American painting.

America—God only knew what would happen now with that monster Hitler on the rise, and then of course the Fascists in Italy. But people, including herself, resisted looking east. They muffled any instincts to shudder. The Great War was only some sixteen years past, but its wounds were unhealed. Roosevelt, president less than two years, was mostly focused on the Depression and did not seem at this point overly concerned about idiots abroad, but when she could bear to listen to the news on the radio, she heard warlike anger that made her shudder, even in this landscape that seemed beyond such conflict.

She hugged her shawl more tightly. *Here comes the lavender!* she thought, and felt the thrill of sheer ecstasy as she watched it seep across the land. A few more minutes and she would go down, get dressed, and have more tea, a banana, and a muffin. That would set her up fine until she came back for lunch. She was excited about the horse head. *Imagine*, she thought, *to be excited about the skull of a horse's head!* Many things excited her, but out here in the vast seeming emptiness of desert, there was room for more to be found. Nothing got in the way—at least not the way it did back at Lake George with Stieglitz and the constant parade of family members, artist friends, and clients. Nothing intruded to disturb her peace or her concentration. This was her place, her retreat. It was unassailable, un-shareable, if there was such a word.

There had been words, clinical words, to describe her state before she came here. It had taken the psychiatrists a few attempts. In the beginning she had heard the term "mood disorder." But that hardly described it. To her it suggested that the lighting was somehow wrong in a room. The doctors eliminated "manic depression," thankfully. She found those words terrifically offensive, as if suggesting a wild woman with flying hair and flailing arms sinking into despair. They had finally settled on "major depressive disorder." Despite the verbiage, it sounded tidy to Georgia. However, it didn't really explain much. Not the abortion that Stieglitz had insisted she have years before that had begun to haunt her anew, nor his ensuing romantic escapades. She had been a complete mess.

For years after the abortion those words the doctor had spoken had tormented her: "You are no longer pregnant." That child by now would have been in high school. But she had trained herself, disciplined herself, not to think about the child. She had been successful until her breakdown. But her anger with Stieglitz came back, roared back. The musings about the child, the fetus returned; the deep wonder about the possibility of becoming a mother recurred as well. But now she was done with it all.

Not done with Stieglitz. Not done with Lake George or New York, just done with being a mess. She finally, after three months in a clinic in New York, and now three months in the desert, felt unassailable. She was a fortress, but an odd one. A bastion through which light and shadow and all hues of color could once again flow. And not simply colors but shapes. She felt them—their forms, their contours—gathering around her, nuzzling, and, yes, gently goading her back to work.

When she came back down the ladder and walked into the kitchen, she cast a glance at the stack of letters from Stieglitz. One arrived every day, telling her how much he missed her. Amusing descriptions of life at Lake George with the endless flow of guests and the smothering abundance of Stieglitzes and their games of croquet and charades. Charades must mean his daughter Kitty, fragile and demanding Kitty, was there. No mention of swimming. But of course he wouldn't say "nude" swimming if Dorothy Norman was splashing about with him. This confirmed her suspicions that perhaps Dorothy was there, as he often talked about how hot the summer had been. There was no way that Stieglitz would skip swimming in such heat. It was likely that Dorothy was there, despite the loving terms and endearments he threaded through his letters to Georgia: "My Faraway One ... Dearest Little One ... Dearest Runaway ... My Sweetest Heart ..."

But now she reveled in the desolation of this place. Lake George was anything but desolate. There was the Shanty of course, as she called her studio there, a burnt wooden brown shack that stood in contrast to the colors of the landscape. It offered an escape from the distractions of the boisterous Stieglitz family. It was perfect, with a wonderful view of the mountain-rimmed lake. But when she was there, she rarely painted outdoors. It was often cloudy and rainy and chilly. So she watched that world and painted it from the windows of the shanty. Her palette was cool—greens, grays, blues. It was when she came to the Southwest for the first time that her palette grew warmer with oranges and reds and yellows and even brown—not "shanty brown," as she now thought of it, but rich with hints of red. She began to realize that she had been yearning for light—the kind of light that had enriched her palette since she had first come out here five years before.

At Lake George she had been completely intrigued by the geometry of the long band of lake water, then the stretch of mountains above. Of course here it was almost the reverse. The sky dominated and then a narrow band of desert. And there might be a distraction in that narrow band—a wild hollyhock suddenly sprouting up or the bleached bone of an animal. Her favorite bones were the weathered horse skulls or the bleached pelvis of a cow. The sky was so vast, so uninterrupted, that one had to sometimes view it through the aperture of one of those weathered bones. Unlike the shanty back at Lake George, her adobe casita blended in with the desert. Out here she was as well camouflaged as a chameleon. And she liked it that way. Almost every day a letter came from Stieglitz. *"When are you coming home, My Faraway one … ?"*

Just yesterday Georgia had written him a loving letter, though not one of forgiveness, to simply say that she planned to stay on at Ghost Ranch longer and perhaps divide her year in half between the East Coast and this enchanting place.

A half hour later, as she drove down the long winding road out of Ghost Ranch, a fragment of a Schumann piano sonata floated through her head. She had listened to it the night before on her own Victrola, and she began to hum. She looked in the rearview mirror and watched as her casita receded in the distance. *Tawny,* she thought in this light. *Tawny with shades of ochre.* Her adobe house was on a far corner of the ranch, away from the other guest casitas and the Hacienda, where folks gathered for meals, lectures, endless evenings of bingo, and occasional musical performances if there was a musician at the ranch.

She pressed on the accelerator. She wanted to drive fast by the Hacienda, where all the fancy guests gathered. Fancy and celebrated. At least one heiress—she was not especially inclined toward heiresses, as Stieglitz's most recent mistress, Dorothy Norman, was a Philadelphia one. Then there was Robert Wood Johnson, heir to the pharmaceutical company, and his wife, Maggie. Also, the occasional Rockefeller, and there were rumors that Charles Lindbergh and his wife would be arriving soon, still seeking to escape the press after the terrible kidnapping and murder of their baby two years before. Georgia had no desire to mingle with any of them. But since her exhibit had opened seven months before in New York and had sold out, two of those buyers had been at the ranch, and her whereabouts was known. So avoiding people was a bit more difficult than usual.

Carmelita, the manager and activities director, had come out to Georgia's casita two days before to announce that Georgia was "in demand." "Come—just have a glass of wine, Georgia. You don't have to stay long—you know the Johnsons bought one of your paintings." Of course she knew it. At forty-five hundred dollars, it was the largest amount of money she'd ever received for a painting. Enough maybe to buy her casita on Ghost Ranch. She only hoped she could convince Carson Powell, who had just bought the ranch, to sell her this one small parcel with the casita she was now renting. She would be a homeowner! It would be all hers. Not like the apartment at the Shelton in New York or the house at Lake George. This casita would be hers and hers alone!

She turned off from the ranch road onto a narrow rutted one that could barely be considered a road. She patted the dashboard of the Ford. "Come on, dearie. You can do it." The road had deteriorated to a two-wheel track. Her painting "studio," which she hauled in the back, rattled about, but she had double-tied her easel to some brackets. She peered at it in the rearview mirror, narrowed her eyes, and muttered, "Don't you move a damn inch!" Scowling, she began to descend a steep slope. Ahead was a majestic valley and on its horizon an undulation of rosy pink hills, almost flesh colored in this light, which made her think of a reclining nude stretched against the sky.

She reached the bottom of the slope and continued for another quarter mile before she pulled over to the side of this "implied" road, as she thought of it. She got out of the Model A, loosened the bolts of the front seat, then swiveled it around. Next she propped up the canvas. That was for a bit later, when it would get too hot to paint outside. But right now she wanted to fetch that horse's head. The vultures must have finished their business with the other thing. There might be coyotes, but she could shoo them away if need be. Clapping her broad-brimmed black hat on her head and grabbing her rattlesnake stick, which she also used as a walking stick, she set out. Ansel Adams had called her Friar O'Keeffe every time she put the hat on when he'd come to visit. With her face cast in the deep shadow of the brim, she picked her way carefully over the rubbly ground toward where she remembered the horse head was.

She saw something black perhaps fifty yards ahead on the trail where she thought the skull would be. She took a few more steps, then stopped abruptly. She sensed that something was … out of *order*. Those were the words that came to her: *out of order*. A cold feeling began to creep through her. She blinked and emitted a small gasp. Ahead was an odd configuration. She tipped her head to one side and squinted.

It made no sense. A bad joke if anything. A hat had been blown by the wind and fetched up right atop the horse's skull. It was black, like her own hat, and tilted downward at an almost jaunty angle over the place where the horse's forelock had once grown.

She walked quickly over and picked the hat up from the skull. A stampede of thoughts raced through her head. This was the real thing, not at all like the hat she'd bought in Taos five years before. The crown of this one was more rounded and not as high. A real monsignor or friar or priest had worn it. Did this hat have an owner? She looked up, as if to ask the hills, the same ones she had painted just yesterday. But her eyes seemed to stumble before they reached the hills.

A hundred or so feet ahead, there was a dark heap. A lava rock? But there were no lava tubes around here. The old flows were mostly to the east in the ancient volcanic fields. And rocks didn't billow in the wind. She slowed down. This was not rock but cloth, cloth that swelled on the gusts that swept the mesa. On the pile of fabric a vulture perched, pecking delicately at something pink and shiny. A coyote crouched patiently near the desiccated hub of a wagon wheel, and, perhaps oddest of all, a hollyhock bloomed, slightly out of season. A dazzling white hollyhock blossom—whiter than the bleached horse skull.

Waving her snake stick, she rushed toward the vulture. "Scat!" she roared, setting the bird into flight. The coyote scatted as well. She walked up carefully, the way one might approach a sleeping baby. But this was no baby. It was a man, a man with a perfectly shaved bald spot in the center of his head. There was a fringe of dark hair encircling the bald spot. But the vulture's claws had incised deep gouges. It looked as if the man's eye had been torn out by the vulture she had just shooed away. A flap of skin still attached to the scalp fluttered in the draft of the vulture's wings as it took off.

Georgia swallowed. It wasn't so much the blood but rather the sight of that quivering flap of pale skin—and the thought of a vulture flying through the sky with this man's eye—that horrified her. She swayed a bit and clamped her eyes shut. How could this be happening out here? *Not here! Not here!* a voice shrieked in her head. She had found such tranquility out here and carefully, so delicately, pieced herself back together. Would she shatter again? She willed her eyes open and turned her head toward the body. The blowflies with their metallic blue-green bodies were swarming in now to feast on the blood, which would be dry in another hour. The man's head was at an odd angle that suggested his neck might be broken. But then she saw that his throat had been slashed deeply, almost to the bone. She put a hand over her mouth for fear she might vomit. One glassy eye stared up at her.

The garment was not black as she had first thought, but brown. A cassock the color of the Franciscan order that was prevalent throughout New Mexico. This she knew. And then there was the corded rope around his waist with three knots. One for poverty, one for chastity, and one for obedience. A large dark stain had saturated the ground where the man had bled out. She scanned the area. Was there any sign of a weapon? The shells from a gun? No visible tears in the cassock, but still he was face-down with his head turned at a strange angle so she could see that one eye; the other that was a bloody mess. There was a great deal of congealed blood around his neck. However, she could not clearly see the wound itself, just the blood, and she didn't want to disturb the body in any way.

As she crouched down she was startled to hear the ragged croak of her own voice: "Who did you disobey, my friend?" Where had he come from?

She looked up. On the horizon the sun was trembling like a bloodied egg yolk against the sky that was pressing down on it. The glare within seconds was so harsh at this angle that she had to look down. She knew that moment. The moment of the weight of the sky. She could feel it on her shoulders, on her back. How often had she painted that nearly treacherous moment? Light so crushing that it had to be abstracted. She kept her eyes on the ground for another several seconds and scanned the rubbly dirt.

Ahead just a few yards there were some footprints in the softer sand. She rose up and walked closer to the prints. She followed them for perhaps a quarter of a mile and then saw, looming behind a sandy mound, the shiny roof of a car. The car must be his. He must have walked from it, trying to find something. He certainly hadn't staggered out into this desert like some biblical prophet. She approached it with her stick, as cautiously as she would a rattlesnake. When she was close enough, she peered under the car to see if, in fact, one was hiding in the shade. She walked once around the car and then stepped closer and looked in. There was a valise on the backseat with a tag attached. She craned her head to read the tag: MSGR. A. CASTENADA. On the front seat next to the driver's was a map, partially opened. She reached in through the window, took out the map, and squinted at it. There was an *X* that marked the road to the Ghost Ranch. Then an *X* with an *H*, for Hacienda, she supposed. Then she saw another *X* that must mark the wranglers' bunks up by the corrals. West and north of the Ghost Ranch almost to Chama was another *X*. Coming down from Chama to the White Place she saw one more marking. She traced the road back to the Ghost Ranch, where she saw a very tiny *x*, with some seemingly indecipherable letters. She squinted more, then gasped as she read the tiny letters printed next to the *X*: *G. O.*

The initials screamed at her. This was her house that had been marked exactly at the turnoff from the main Ghost Ranch road. Why would this murdered man, this murdered priest, have a map with her initials on it? She felt a sudden wave of nausea. She opened the door and sank onto the seat. *How scared should I be?* she thought. What the hell would have led a priest, and his killer, to come to her in the desert? New York was where murders happened, not here.

"I'm a fool ... a goddamn fool," she murmured. She felt a peculiar sensation of fear and disgust. Disgust at herself for chasing this silver chalice, this Holy Grail of peace, escaping everyone she knew, every landscape she had painted, into the uncompromising clarity of the desert. Three months she had spent in that damn hospital. She was supposed to be well, healed. But with a murdered man just yards from her home, and with his killer still in these hills, might she unravel again? *Unraveled*—that was Stieglitz's word for what had happened to her because it did not sound as noisy or as catastrophic as a breakdown. A breakdown was destructive, clamorous, with pieces scattered and mending perhaps impossible. Unraveling was what the cuff of a sweater did after moths nibbled away at it. Still, she hated the word. Stieglitz had no use for mess. He was one of those people, one of those men, whose mothers always cleaned up after them. Stieglitz had a million euphemisms for what had happened to her: *Oh, she's just a bit undone ... nerves a little frayed, you know. A little shaky.*

And sure enough, here she was, sitting in a car, shaking as the temperature outside the car was rising to close to ninety. She set her jaw in what Stieglitz often called a line of grim defiance. She had to go back to her car and drive it to the Hacienda and report this murder. It wasn't simply a body. It was a murdered body. And once upon a time, she thought, that body had been a priest. She would go back to the Hacienda, report it like a responsible citizen, and that would be the end of it.

But there was the tiny niggling detail of her initials on the map. Probably nothing. She could have read it wrong. But less than two minutes later those initials—her initials—were blinking in her head like neon. She got out of the car. A harsh wind had started to blow. A haboob. She knew she had to wait it out. It took twenty minutes before she could get back to her own car. The footprints, including hers, had been erased, and she was chewing grit. She could only hope there wouldn't be too many guests milling about in the lobby of the Hacienda. How she loathed engaging with guests. Her solitude had become precious. Few people knew she had rented the casita up the hill for an indefinite period of time, and that was just the way she liked it.

Chapter 2

A quarter hour later, she staggered into the lobby of the Hacienda, the sand and dirt grating in her shoes. Behind the desk, Carmelita was speaking to her assistant manager, Joaquin. "Monsignor Castenada is quite late. Must be that haboob that just blew through," she was saying.

"He won't be coming," Georgia said in a rather loud voice.

Carmelita looked up, startled. "Miss O'Keeffe! You look like you've seen a ghost."

"Not a ghost. A dead man." Georgia swayed a bit, and Carmelita and Joaquin scurried out from behind the desk.

"I'm fine … I'm fine. Really. You need to call Santa Fe. The police."

Joaquin took her to an easy chair in the corner of the lobby and brought her a glass of iced tea. He set it down on the small table beside her. "Anything to eat? Lupe just baked some fresh cookies, Miss O'Keeffe."

"No, this will do fine."

Nevertheless, Carmelita came out with a plate of cookies and pulled up a chair. She settled into it. *Oh dear,* Georgia thought. She really didn't want to talk about it. She just wanted the police to be called so she could leave this to the authorities and go home.

"Did you see what had happened? How he was killed?"

"No, Carmelita."

"Blood, I suppose?"

Georgia didn't answer. She was good at silences. Carmelita wasn't. "I suppose it must have been quite upsetting."

Of course it was, you idiot. But she didn't say that. She just turned to her and in a very weary voice said, "Carmelita, I need to be alone with my thoughts. As you can imagine, this was terribly upsetting; the police will be here, and I must remember everything I saw and how I found him."

"I could take notes. That might help you," Carmelita said gently and had the audacity to pat Georgia's hand. *Goddammit,* this woman was intent on driving her crazy. "No, Carmelita. That is very kind of you, but let me just sit here a while and think."

"Yes, I'm sure that will help you be more ... more objective." Carmelita nodded approvingly at the wisdom of her own remark.

Georgia hated the word *objective*. So often during her teaching years, she had told her students, "Objective painting is not good unless it is good in the abstract sense." She would go on to tell them, "A hill or a tree cannot make a good painting simply because it's a hill or a tree. Lines and colors are put together so that they say something. It's the intangible that can clarify. So what is intangible here? What are the lines and colors I have to put together to make sense out of this?" With that, she tipped her head back against the headrest of the chair and closed her eyes.

She was thankful to hear Carmelita's retreating footsteps. She heard other footsteps too, of guests coming and going, all their talk about going to Anasazi ruins, Pueblo villages for pottery, horseback riding. "You must have Joaquin make you his special drink. He calls it a margarita. It's made with tequila and lime juices—it's delish." Georgia hated the word *delish*. And she realized in that moment that any one of these guests could be a murderer. Even the person who'd said "delish."

It took more than an hour for the police to arrive. They made a caravan of three cars and an ambulance. Georgia rode in the first car with the sheriff, Ryan McCaffrey, to the scene. He was a large man with a fairly ample belly, but he did not strike her as fat—just solid. He had a nick on his chin from shaving. Georgia could still see a trace of blood. This prompted her to remark upon the vast amount of blood she had seen on the ground. "A lot of blood, but I couldn't exactly see where it had come from. The wound, you know. But I think maybe his neck."

"You didn't touch the body, did you?" he snapped.

"No, of course not. Why would I do that?"

"I couldn't say, but some people do. They have aspirations—amateur detectives."

"I have no such desires. I am a professional painter." She winced at her own words. It sounded so tacky to call yourself a professional painter. Which of the two of them was she trying to convince? "No amateur gumshoe aspirations whatsoever," she growled in a low voice.

When they pulled off the road to take the short hike to the body, the sheriff pulled something off his dashboard that looked similar to a phone. "Florence, this is the sheriff calling in. Now at the SOC. I guess we have to walk in a quarter of a mile. Parked at side of road. Can you maybe send Jeremy out here? We'll need a photographer on the scene. I believe he's just getting back from Taos."

As she and McCaffrey stepped out of the sheriff's car, a woman emerged from the ambulance. With her gray curls piled on top of her head and her pince-nez, she certainly didn't look like a cop.

"Hello, Coroner," the sheriff called out to her. The woman strode over. "Miss O'Keeffe, meet Dr. Bryce, county coroner."

"Pleased." Bryce held out her hand and shook Georgia's and then immediately began to put on rubber gloves. Rubber gloves withstanding, Emily Bryce was about as prim and proper-looking as a woman in trousers could look. She wore a man's tie with her khaki shirt and she carried an umbrella—a rare sight in New Mexico.

"My, my, I don't think I've ever met a woman coroner," Georgia said, sounding nervous in a way that made her own ears almost wince.

"How many coroners have you met, Miss O'Keeffe?" There was the lilt of a lost Irish brogue in Bryce's voice. *Cork!* Georgia thought. Her own father had come from near Cork. The familiar singsongy, melodic, long *i*'s gliding into *o*'s as Dr. Bryce now replied, "So I'm your first one?"

"Uh, none…. Yes, you're my first one." How could she be so stupid?

"Good for you!" Dr. Bryce declared. Georgia blinked. She would not have thought of this as an accomplishment, but she supposed it was.

"It's not far from here. Half mile at the most."

Georgia took the lead. The others followed. What they saw first were the dark wings of vultures flapping around the body, rowdy and joyous at this sudden banquet.

"Damn vultures," Dr. Bryce said. "Nothing like that middle talon of theirs for tearing skin. Better than a scalpel."

McCaffrey regarded the body, its sprawled position, the blood-darkened neck, the exposed places on the scalp that the birds had bored into, the brown robes windblown and dusty. "So this is just how you found him, Miss O'Keeffe?"

"I told you I haven't disturbed a thing here. Are you implying that I moved him somehow?"

"Of course not. But was anything different?" He gave her a squint as if to say, "Don't be so touchy." *Touchy* was another word that irritated her.

"The vultures. I shooed them off. They'd done what they could. Until I came."

"Shooed them off, did you? And now they're back." A slightly accusatory tone was creeping into his voice. "How'd you figure that?"

"How did I figure what?" Good lord, this fellow was annoying.

"How'd you know that nothing has changed now since you first found the body?"

"Well, I'll tell you, sheriff. I walked up to the body and I saw that his scalp had been torn. Torn by claws, talons. There was a flap of skin waving in the breeze. I saw the vultures circling." Was she playing Sherlock to his Watson? That would certainly annoy him to no end.

"So the birds left but were still circling about." He scratched his chin and looked at her as if scrutinizing the inscrutable inner thoughts of an artist, as if she were a different species entirely. The pause that stretched into almost half a minute as he regarded her and kept scratching his chin—these gestures seemed very choreographed. Was he trying to unnerve her? Well, he wouldn't, goddammit. "You know birds and talons, Miss O'Keeffe?" He said this with a deliberate casualness and flicked something off the cuff of his shirt.

This fellow was impossible. She took a step closer to the man. "Well, Sheriff McCaffrey, I'm not an ornithologist, but I was pretty sure it wasn't a paring knife that had done this or, for that matter, a vegetable peeler."

She heard a snort emanate from Dr. Bryce.

"All right, all right. No need to get testy." He growled.

"Miss O'Keeffe wasn't getting 'testy,' Ryan," Dr. Bryce said. "*Testy*, not a nice word. Used mostly in reference to women, unfortunately."

Georgia burst out laughing.

Two more vultures had the audacity at this moment to come down and settle near the corpse's head. The flapping skin was gone, however. They must have gotten down to the bone.

"Okay, you scoundrels, party's over," the doctor bellowed, racing forward, waving her umbrella. The birds scattered. "Avian scum of the skies," she murmured, then turned to Georgia. "You can't imagine how many crimes scenes they've wrecked, Miss O'Keeffe." She crouched down close to the body. "They like the head, especially a bald one. They get frustrated with fabric." Georgia imagined that this woman was full of such fascinating details.

Dr. Bryce looked up from the body. "Killer used something like an H-W commando knife, I believe." Her face was no longer ruddy, but drained of color. This seemed odd for a coroner, Georgia thought. Hadn't she more or less seen it all? "See that cut? The incision suggests that the blade must have beveled where it went in. Those knives should be outlawed. As dangerous to the owner as to the victim. But this fellow." She paused. There was a bit of a twinkle in her eye. "Could be a gal, of course. Whoever, but they knew how to use it. Anyhow, I'm reckoning this person threw it from a short distance and truly hit the mark. They came up to retrieve it and finish the monsignor off by slitting his throat."

She looked at Sheriff McCaffrey, who was standing on a mound crowned with a small clump of sagebrush. He was in a surveyor pose, as if measuring the horizontal angle with an invisible transit. He annoyed her immensely. She shifted her gaze and noticed that the hat on the horse skull had blown off during the haboob and settled about twenty feet away. Georgia walked over to pick up the skull.

"Don't touch the crime scene!" a young sergeant shouted.

She pointed at the monsignor's hat. "This is the man's hat. I wasn't going to touch it. I just … just wanted the horse skull." Now the two officers, the coroner, the other policeman, and the ambulance driver were all staring at her.

"You what?" asked the sheriff.

"I like bones. I paint them."

"You mean," the younger officer asked, "you paint them, like pretty colors?"

"Oh, no, no! Not at all. I paint them against a landscape." How to explain this? "I like to paint them against the sky or the mountains."

The sheriff stepped forward. "Well, Miss O'Keeffe, can you restrain yourself for a bit? We'd like to leave the crime scene absolutely untouched until we have examined everything." Georgia felt the shadow of a cringe building inside her. Should she tell them now or later about the car, the map with her initials on it?

"Poor fellow. Okay! I've finished up here as much as I can for now. Rodney! Jeff!" Dr. Bryce called out to the two men who had arrived with her in the ambulance. "Come collect the body."

Two young men hurried over, holding a stretcher. Georgia supposed they needed to work fast, as the heat was beginning to rise. It could easily reach over ninety by noon. It had always disturbed Georgia that as a soon as a person died, they became a "body." Nonexistence was instantly conferred. She remembered this with her own parents, when the funeral director had come to discuss burial. They talked of "the body," "the deceased." Anything that even suggested that the person had a name, a history, was erased. She longed to yell at the funeral director: "She's not the body! She's my mother. Dead or alive, she'll always be my mother."

"May I sit over there on that wagon hub, sheriff?" she asked softly.

"Sure, ma'am. Need any water?"

"That would be nice."

"Joseph, get one of the canteens." The four police officers started walking a grid they had marked out, scouring for evidence. "Dr. Bryce," the sheriff said; "you say the knife was thrown from a short distance." He looked to his two deputies. "Any footprint evidence that might tell us how far away the knife thrower might have been?"

"Nothing, Boss," one replied.

"Nada," said the other.

"But there are," Georgia said softly.

"Huh?" said the young man.

"I mean there were," Georgia replied.

"Can you explain yourself, Miss O'Keeffe?" the sheriff asked.

"The haboob wiped the footprints away. But they were here, and I followed them to his car—or I guess it was his car, the monsignor's car."

"Car? Where?" the sheriff looked around.

"About a quarter of a mile over that way." Georgia pointed. She waited a beat. She saw the sheriff looking at her. "And yes—" She began to speak then stopped.

"Yes what?"

"I disturbed the crime scene." They all looked at her now as if stupefied.

Sheriff McCaffrey removed his hat and appeared to be studying the brim with what Georgia considered undo intensity.

"That's a crime, I guess—to disturb a crime scene." Georgia looked around. "Maybe a felony, seeing as we're on federal land here, I think," she added.

"Miss O'Keeffe, are you asking me to arrest you?"

"No, just confessing. I mean I just saw the footprints and thought I should see where they led. I thought this might be considered useful information."

The sheriff replaced his hat. "It is, Miss O'Keeffe. It is. But may I ask, did you touch the car?" There was an icy expression in his eyes.

"Well, actually I sat in it."

"You what!"

"Jesus Christ," one of the deputies muttered. But she also heard a half snort, and it didn't come from the horse skull but from Doctor Bryce. She seemed to be enjoying this.

"Why the hell would you sit in this man's car—if indeed it belonged to the victim?" the sheriff asked. "You're a nosy little thing, aren't you?"

This made Georgia seethe. Again, it was the kind of insult a man would only make to a woman. It infuriated her. Stieglitz had done this too. How furious he'd been when she told him she might buy the casita at Ghost Ranch. *"Dammit, woman—it's because of me that you have money to buy it."* "I earned the money to buy it!" she had replied. "You just brokered the deal." And Stieglitz accused her of being coarse because, apparently, artists were not supposed to use such vulgar terms as "brokered" and "deals."

"I sat in the car because it was getting hot for one thing. I needed a bit of shade. I had—if I may remind you—just seen a dead man. His scalp flapping in the wind. I didn't want to faint."

The sheriff's eyes narrowed as he looked at her. He cleared his throat. "You don't strike me as the fainting type."

"What type is that, sheriff?"

"Never mind."

Oh, grumpy now, are we? Georgia thought.

The sheriff turned to another young man. "Joe, you go over and take a look at the car. Dr. Bryce, can you check if the victim has the keys in his pockets?"

"No, Sheriff. He left the keys in the car."

"Oh!" he said brightly. "Did you take it out for a spin?"

What a card, Georgia thought. "No, sir. I was having too much fun disturbing the crime scene!" She heard a loud chortle from the deputy behind her.

The sheriff walked several yards away from her up a small slope then turned around. "From this vantage, if the fellow—"

"Or gal," Dr. Bryce added.

"Or gal, if good enough." Sheriff McCaffrey nodded. "The knife would have gotten some extra propulsion. Downhill, after all." He scratched his cheek, his eyes casting slowly over the ground. Suddenly Georgia realized as she looked at this man that despite his outrageous condescension, in an odd way there was something intriguing, bordering on appealing, about him. Sheriff McCaffrey was perhaps slightly exotic in his own way. No one could be physically more opposite from Alfred Stieglitz, who was skinny as a rail. The sheriff had a definite belly. It hung over his belt by a couple of inches. His salt-and-pepper hair was thick, well cut, and brushed straight back. When he'd removed his sunglasses, she'd been surprised by his eyes. Were they gray? Blue? There was definitely something uncompromising in them.

His name, Ryan McCaffrey, suggested pure Irish. But she felt she was looking into a Pueblo face. Could be Navajo or maybe even Apache. There were more than twenty tribes in New Mexico alone. For a man of his size, he was fairly nimble. He scrambled down from the mound and sprang across a dry creek bed toward another spot, near where another hollyhock, which Georgia had not noticed before, had burst into bloom.

"Huh," she laughed softly.

"What's that, ma'am?" He looked across at her.

"Oh, nothing. Just noticing that hollyhock beside you. Another one out of season, or so it seems."

"Happens when the rain comes this time of year," the sheriff replied. "The notion that some flowers are finished blooming by this month gets a second chance with rain. Rebirth, if you believe in such malarkey."

Malarkey, thought Georgia. What a great word. One that would never come out of Stieglitz's mouth. A glimmer of a smile seemed to ghost across her lips as she tried to imagine this. "I'm going to stay out here with the sergeant," the sheriff called out. "The rest of you can go back. Eddie, you give Miss O'Keeffe a ride back to Ghost Ranch, okay?"

"Sure thing, Sheriff."

Georgia got up and dusted off the seat of her pants.

"Thanks for your help, Miss O'Keeffe." The sheriff tipped his hat. It seemed a rather courtly gesture considering the circumstances. What was she supposed to answer? *No trouble? Think nothing of it? Happy to do it?*

"Fine," she said, turning her back and walking away.

When she walked into the lobby, Rosaria rushed out to her.

"Here." She thrust a cold glass of yerba buena, "good herb" iced tea, into Georgia's hand.

"Rosaria, dear, so kind." She took two deep swallows. "Wasn't this for someone else?"

"It was for them." Rosaria tipped her head toward the terrace, where Georgia saw a small group gathered. *Them* were the Lindberghs. She recognized him from the back of his head. Unmistakable. The reddish-blond hair covering a perfectly proportioned head, like the head of a Greek sculpture—of a god, no less. He was very still. Indeed, still as a statue. But the woman, his wife, Anne Morrow Lindbergh, was quite animated. She gestured with her hands and moved about in her chair, soft peals of laughter sometimes issuing forth. Her hair was reddish brown and slightly wavy, but not nearly as curly as her husband's. She radiated an aura not so much of sadness but of resignation. And despite this, she appeared to be laughing at something. *Poor woman*, thought Georgia. A maverick notion streaked through her mind. Laughter was a very good camouflage for grief, Georgia knew. *Despite her laughter,* Georgia thought, *she is the one grieving. She's grieving alone.*

"You heard about ... the murder?" Georgia asked.

"Yes, Carmelita told us not to say anything. Doesn't want to upset the Lindberghs."

"Well, I can certainly understand that, after what they've been through."

"*Sí*—." Rosaria cast her eyes toward the celebrated couple.

"Have you met them yet?"

"I took them to their casita. It's on my list for housekeeping."

"Are they nice?"

Rosaria shrugged. There was a wariness in her eyes. "Yes, sure," she said automatically. "You want some more tea?" she asked.

"No, this will be fine."

"I'll be over tomorrow to clean, and I'll make you some enchiladas. You can take them when you go out to paint."

"Oh, what would I do without you, Rosaria?" She patted the young woman's hand. "And how is Clara?"

"Ah, not so good, you know. Nightmares. Doesn't want to go to school. School's out now. But who knows what will happen when fall comes." Rosaria sighed. "Even though it's been almost a year since our mother died, it's still tough, you know."

"It must be. Here you are, barely seventeen, and trying your best to raise your sister. How old is she now? Eight?"

"Ten."

"Bring her with you tomorrow. I'll give her some paints and paper to fool about with. She'll enjoy it."

"Oh, *señora*, you are too nice."

"Don't be silly, Rosaria. Nobody can be too nice." Georgia let her gaze drift over to Mrs. Lindbergh, who had reached out to pat her husband's hand. He did not move. Not one scintilla. She might as well have been touching stone.

Carmelita now rose from the table where she had been sitting with the newly arrived guests. She bustled over to where Georgia sat on the couch, sipping the iced tea.

"You poor thing," she said, grasping Georgia's free hand. "How was it?"

"How can it be? There's a dead man out there. Well, not now. They took him back." Georgia shook her head wearily. "I've seen dead people, of course, but never murdered people."

Carmelita lifted her finger to her lips. "Not too loudly. You know they"—she nodded toward the Lindberghs—"are still recovering. Even though it's been two years."

"Of course." Georgia nodded.

"The priest had reserved the casita two doors down from them— Casa Tranquila!" Carmelita said in a low voice. "Can you imagine if it happened here? Near them?"

"No, I cannot imagine it," Georgia said.

"But I must tell you something so exciting!" Now Carmelita wiggled like an impatient child. Though middle-aged and plump, the Ghost Ranch manager often reminded Georgia of an exceedingly enthusiastic little girl.

"What's that?"

"Mrs. Lindbergh just about collapsed when she heard you were staying at Ghost Ranch."

"Collapsed with joy or what?"

"Georgia." Carmelita slapped her hand playfully. "What do you think? She worships you. A woman artist who knows her own mind. You're a hero."

"I don't want to be anybody's hero, and I definitely don't want to be worshipped."

"Won't you come over and meet them? It would be such a treat for them."

It would be such a treat for Carmelita, Georgia thought. "Not now, Carmelita. Remember, I just saw a dead man, and the blowflies were having themselves a feast—not to mention the vultures, which pecked the priest's eye out."

Carmelita turned a tawny gray. Guiltily pleased with herself, Georgia got up to leave. "Maybe some other time," she said. But the last thing she wanted to do was socialize. When she thought about her initials on the map—the *G*, the *O*—they seemed to radiate a terrifying heat. That murderer could have been anybody. It could be a guest here at the ranch. Did she really want to sit down and have a cocktail with a possible murderer? But on the other hand, did she want to be alone in her casita? What was she to do? Lock herself up for the rest of her time here? Never go out to paint? It was unthinkable. She refused to imagine her retreat as her prison. Her refuge as a cell. But had she gone from one sanitarium at New York Doctors Hospital to another in the desert of the Southwest?

Chapter 3

As she drove back home along the dusty road from the Hacienda, Georgia suddenly remembered that she had left the horse skull at the crime scene. Well, it would be there tomorrow. She was too exhausted now to do much of anything. She'd take a nap and then a shower, or maybe a shower and then a nap. She certainly didn't feel hungry. Always another day for the skull. Then she caught herself. *Not if you're Monsignor Alberto Castenada.* Carmelita had told her his full name. It was curious that the monsignor had reserved the Casita Tranquila. At fifteen dollars a night, it was one of the most expensive casitas at Ghost Ranch. There were three casitas on the same road. The staff referred to the road as the Camino de Oro.

"So much for poverty," Georgia muttered. She wondered how Castaneda had been doing with his chastity and obedience vows.

Ahead she saw Lanny Powell, the Ghost Ranch owner's wife, walking alongside Peter Wainwright, the Powell children's tutor. Lanny and Peter were laughing at something. The three Powell children were trailing behind them. The children looked hot and bored. The adults appeared deep in conversation. Georgia slowed down.

"How ya doin', kids?"

"Not doing anything," Elsie, the oldest, said grumpily.

Lanny turned around and flashed a dazzling smile. "Another wonderful archaeology lesson with dear Peter."

"Not true," Elsie said.

"Not true at all," Peter Wainwright echoed with a laugh. "It was Chuckie who found an arrowhead."

George Powell, Chuckie's twin, spoke up. "Mom and Peter buried it! They do that all the time. They go out at night and bury archaeology stuff. Kind of like cheating."

Lanny now came up to the car window. "It's a marvelous experience the children are having out here." Elsie's grimace was actually funny. Georgia had to suppress a laugh. "We are so appreciative of Peter. By September the little schoolhouse will be completed, we hope, and of course we'll open it up to all the ranch help's kids and other children in the area. It will be much closer than going over to the Chama school."

"That's nice," Georgia said.

"Why don't you come over to the Hacienda tonight and have a drink with our illustrious guests, the Lindberghs?" Lanny asked. She often seemed to want Georgia to join her for some activity, if not cocktails then a hike or a ride into Santa Fe. It had struck Georgia just a week ago that she was most frequently invited to join Lanny when Carson was around. It was as if she needed company beyond her own family. She did not apparently relish being alone with her own husband. Georgia knew other people like that. Rebecca Strand for one. Beck, as everyone called her, couldn't stand her husband, Paul Strand, couldn't abide being with him without a passel of friends around. Georgia knew Beck well and understood that, as a painter, she was jealous of her husband's fame as a photographer. For his part, Paul grew weary of her constant need for attention. He worshipped Stieglitz. The Strands immersed themselves among the acolytes at the Stieglitz altar, perhaps so they wouldn't have to deal with each other. Beck had had a brief affair with Alfred. Her husband didn't seem to mind. Was this what Lanny was looking for? A method for enduring her marriage? There would be a fair amount of money at stake and three children. Or maybe, however improbably, she saw Georgia as an artistic celebrity and wanted to feel artistic herself in her company, as if the artist could adorn the heiress's desert-getaway salon.

"Not tonight, Lanny. A bit tired." Obviously, Lanny and Peter had not heard yet about the murder. Murder was not exactly a subject she wanted to bring up in front of the children. A horrible image flashed through her mind of the children out digging for arrowheads and encountering a dead body instead.

She was about to start off again but cut the engine. "Hey, Lanny, I do have one question of ask you."

"Anything for you, Georgia dear."

"You and Carson know how interested I am in buying the casita where I'm staying. Might you mention it to him again?"

"Not a good time, Georgia. Sorry."

"Oh, really?"

"Really! Carson is absolutely furious with Rosvinski."

"Who?"

"Roosevelt. His pet name for him. He hates the guy." She gave an ugly little smirk that Georgia read as one of disapproval.

"Why? The president is dragging us out of this depression. The New Deal and all that."

"Yeah—he blames it on Morgenthau. Stupid!"

"Morgenthau is secretary of the treasury. Why would he blame him?" Lanny gave a soft laugh. "Some say Morgenthau is so rich he's actually financing the New Deal." She sighed deeply now. "In any case, Morgenthau's father is a big New York real estate mogul and banker. Carson went to him for a mortgage on the Ghost Ranch and the conservation projects he wants to do out here. Supposedly the Morgenthaus have funded some agricultural conservation projects in New York State, but Carson was turned down flat."

"Oh dear!" Georgia said.

"Oh dear is right. Overnight he's turned into a grouchy old man."

Ten minutes later, Georgia was home and standing in the shower. She wanted to scrub everything away. The sand from the haboob. The image of the fragment of scalp flapping up from the bone of the man's skull. Her own initials on that map. But what was she to do? Barricade every door and window? She had to stop thinking this way.

The harder she scrubbed, the more the images flooded her mind, bringing with them a tide of resentment. This was supposed to be her place to heal, to paint. She had wanted to wallow in the remoteness of it all. The Hacienda and that crowd were annoying, but she had become skillful at insulating herself against all that, somewhat in the same way she had become skillful at avoiding the gaggle of Stieglitz's relatives who would descend on Lake George in the summer. She was adept at decluttering her life not just of relatives but also of all the knickknacks and furnishings that Hedwig, Stieglitz's mother, had stuffed into the Lake George house. If she never saw a fringed lampshade again, it would be too soon. When she moved into this casita, it had hardly any furniture. For a dining table, she'd found a piece of plywood up at the wranglers' bunkhouses and asked if she could take it and a couple sawhorses. There were only two light bulbs in the house. For the most part she used kerosene lanterns. And right now, as she stepped out of the shower, even as she was clean in body, she felt the threat of a kind of encroaching clutter—the clutter of this crime. Her life was becoming complicated again, and she felt that resentment building, gathering in her. She wanted to turn her back on it all.

The *X*'s haunted her. Had she really been marked for something? She was trying to remember exactly where those other *X*'s were on the map. Hadn't one of those on the Ghost Ranch property marked the Camina de Oro? She closed her eyes and tried to recall the map she had found in the car. It was impossible to chart it without a map. Then she remembered she had a map in her own car. She put on a bathrobe and ran out to get it. Her door squeaked. She must remember to oil the hinges. Then she remembered that she had no oil. She'd pick it up the next time she went into Abiquiu.

She spread the map on the kitchen table. Almost immediately she recalled the locations of the *X*'s. They rose like an afterimage ghosting in from somewhere deep in her eye. Someone had once told her that when this happened, it was a chemical reaction generated from the original image, the stimulus that had disappeared. This idea fascinated her. She wondered what other visuals her mind could summon.

Unfortunately, with that stimulus came the fear again. It flooded through her as she gripped a pencil and methodically marked all the places where an *X* appeared on the priest's map—from the Hacienda to the wranglers' bunkhouse, including her own house, and the *X* on the Camina de Oro. Was that *X* where the Lindbergh casita was? There were at least three, maybe four casitas on the *camina*.

She examined the rest of the map and recalled the *X* on the old Chama road as well, near the White Place. What did it all mean? Were people on these sites marked for death? What did the priest with the curiously expensive tastes want from her?

"Stop it," she muttered. She knew she was being overly dramatic. She folded the map neatly and slipped it into a kitchen drawer.

She put a record on the Victrola of the Bach cello suites. Pablo Casals was playing. She had heard him at Carnegie Hall perhaps two—or was it three—years ago, and Stieglitz had given her the album for her birthday. The natural resonance of that beautiful instrument began to fill the casita. Soothing, pure, natural. The melodic nature of the opening seemed to cradle her and allow her mind to play. Images floated up from some unknowable depths like bubbles of colors she had never imagined. "Draw what you hear," her teacher, Alon Bement, would say to the class at Columbia Teachers College. Then he would always put a record on for the students to listen to as they drew or painted. The music, she discovered, freed her from the superficial details of creating art. It moved her toward abstraction.

Her own footprints in the sand and those of the priest had been swept away by the haboob. But what else might have been left—camouflaged now by new sand, perhaps to be revealed by the shifts of a new wind or shifts of light? The clatter and clash of light like mute cymbals, the brass of the noon sun—what might that reveal? She let her mind drift as she floated in the music that filled the casita. She'd go back tomorrow. She needed to see it all again in a different light, a different time, with the music still in her head.

Sheriff McCaffrey opened the valise of Alberto Castenada. There was nothing unusual on the surface. Some underwear, socks, some slippers, a toilet kit tucked into the side. He slipped his hand beneath some more formal-looking garments—priestly wear, he supposed, until his hand met with metal. Carefully he removed the layers and tossed them aside. He blinked. *Most un-priestly!* he thought as he peered down at the barrel of a Beretta 418. Small, elegant, efficient. Yes, it could easily fit under vestments, but why? He reached for some rubber gloves he kept in his office drawer and put them on.

"What the devil," the sheriff muttered. There was a small canvas pouch. He assumed it would contain bullets. He opened it. Yes, bullets but … *Oh, my.* Two packages of condoms! *Whoa! Talk about un-priestly!*

"This takes the cake," he murmured. "Or the wafer!" He took a deep breath. "Joseph!" he called out.

Joseph Descheeni, the young deputy, stuck his head around the door. "What's up, Boss?"

"Take a look at what I found in Monsignor Castenada's bag."

Joseph let out a low whistle as he took in the pistol and the package of condoms. "Looks like the friar was prepared for all occasions." He watched as the sheriff walked away from the valise, shut his eyes, and pinched the bridge of his nose. This was a familiar posture. It indicated that the sheriff had stepped off into another world in which the usual protocols dissolved. He was totally silent, no uh-huhs, yeps, maybes. All anyone could hear was thinking, the effort to compose some sort of logic out of these disparate elements.

Finally, Sheriff McCaffrey looked up at the deputy. "You've seen that map, right?"

"Yes, sir, but not closely."

"Did you see that there were a few *X*'s on it? Take a look over there on my desk."

Joseph walked to the desk where the road map was unfolded. "G.O.— Georgia O'Keeffe."

The sheriff's gloved hand put the Beretta and the condoms on the desk. "I think I'll drive out and drop in on Miss O'Keeffe."

"Protection?"

"I'll ask, but I don't want to alarm her."

Despite anxiety over that damn *X* on the map, Georgia was not going to miss the day's sunset. The air seemed rinsed from the rain the night before. She took out a cream silk crepe dress she had made earlier in the summer. It had pin-tuck pleats in front and a tuxedo-style collar with a bow. She went outside to where the ladder leaned against the adobe wall and climbed once again into the sky. A sky that was alive with color. There was an intense river of pink hovering just above the horizon, and above that an orange glow, and then over that a gauzy band of clouds. The hills appeared bruised as the shadows crept over the land—this vast land. There was no wind.

She saw a whirl of dust. "Oh dear," she whispered. "Company? I hope not." But it was. She got up from where she was sitting with her back against the chimney that was still warm from the day's sun. As the car came closer, she realized it was a police car. "What now?" she muttered as she looked down from the roof. No one ever really came to visit her except for Rosaria, her housekeeper. That was part of the beauty of this place. It was completely different at Lake George. The innumerable stream of guests that Stieglitz invited, the seeming infinity of Stieglitz relatives, thought nothing of tracking her down in her studio. Knocking or perhaps not knocking on the shanty's front door and just coming in to chat—chat about anything. A skinned knee a child had suffered. An angry complaint about another family member. A request that she please join in for after-dinner charades. Here at Ghost Ranch it was almost as if she had put an enormous Do Not Disturb sign on her door. She was left alone.

She looked down and saw the sheriff climb out of the car. He went to the rear, opened the trunk, pulled something out, then looked up.

"You come to arrest me for disturbing a crime scene, sir?"

"Naw, I'll let you off this time. I brought you something, Miss O'Keeffe." In one hand he held a stalk of hollyhock. In the other he held the horse skull.

"My goodness. And here I forgot all about it."

"Well, murder can do that to you," he said in an exceptionally jolly voice.

The remark caught her off guard. Georgia tried not to laugh. She would never have taken him for having an ounce of humor. "You can set it down by the walk right there. Want to come up? You don't mind climbing?" Her own words surprised her. She was not one to issue spontaneous invitations, but he had brought her the horse skull.

"'Course not. I'm fat, but not that fat."

As the sheriff stepped onto the roof, he looked around. There was the bite of sagebrush in the air. He took a deep breath and seemed to inhale the beauty, the stillness, and did not talk for several seconds. "So ..." he finally said, softly. But nothing followed.

"I'm sorry I don't have chairs up here," Georgia said, breaking the silence. "I usually just sit with my back against the chimney."

"I'm not picky."

"Didn't think you were."

They both walked over to the chimney and settled down. Georgia tipped her head up toward the sky. She saw the glimmer of the first stars, baby stars, crawling out of their crib of low violet clouds.

"So, as I was saying. We've run into some ... how should I put it? ... strangeness ... with Monsignor Castenada."

"Strange? In what way."

"Well, he's kind of ..." He hesitated again for several seconds. "He appears to be trackless."

"Trackless?"

"He arrived from nowhere. He's a will-o'-the-wisp."

"But a reservation was made for him at the ranch."

"Yeah, true. A letter was written perhaps six weeks ago. But Carmelita couldn't find it when I checked in at the Hacienda. She said she thought it came from California."

Should she ask him about the map? There was no way he could have missed it, as she had replaced it on the seat. Had he seen her initials by the *X* where the road branched off the main Hacienda road? If she didn't mention it, could she be accused of concealing vital information? Not telling the whole truth and nothing but the truth? Forget it. Missing it would be their fault, not hers.

He cleared his throat now and began to speak. His valise had some odd items. Uh ..." He was hesitating.

Oh dear, here it comes, Georgia thought. *He saw my initials. He wants to warn me.*

"Like what?" Maybe she had dodged a bullet with the map.

The sheriff hesitated a moment. "Phantasma condoms and a gun."

"Phan-what condoms?"

"Phantasma condoms—expensive."

Georgia couldn't help herself. She snorted. "Considering the alternative, maybe not so expensive." Folding her arms across her chest, she chuckled softly. "I don't quite know what to say." She settled her gaze on a jackrabbit crouching behind one of the numerous sagebrush clumps that erupted between the flagstones of the patio below. Jackrabbits' ears were larger than most rabbit ears. On this particular evening, with the sun so low, the light caught the ears, making them glow. They were almost transparent. She could see the tiny veins branching like minuscule tree limbs. Georgia turned to the sheriff.

"Sheriff."

"Oh, please, just call me Ryan."

"All right, Ryan. Why would a condom maker call a condom Phantasma?"

Ryan McCaffrey slapped his hand against his forehead.

"Oh my God, Miss O'Keeffe."

"Oh, you can call me Georgia. I know that *phantasma* is a word that suggests apparition, shadowy things or ghosts. And here he's reserved a casita, the most expensive one at the ranch. Kind of curious, isn't it, for a man who is a Franciscan? It seems as though he is the apparition." She paused again. "I think in literature they call that pathetic fallacy." She emitted a harsh laugh. "A ghost priest with a libido."

"Well, it's pathetic, all right." Then the sheriff sighed deeply. "I never in all my born days thought I'd be sitting on a roof in the middle of New Mexico with a famous painter discussing priests, condoms, and—"

"Murder," Georgia chimed in. "Don't forget that." She paused. "But you're right, Sheriff—I mean Ryan. None of this exactly adds up." She hoped to God she wasn't getting drawn into this. She couldn't be considered a witness—or could she? She wanted to be at her easel and not on a witness stand. Extricating herself from long boring family lunches at Lake George took a bit of finesse, but a homicide investigation, how did one wriggle out of that?

"None of it adds up. Not at all, Georgia. Not at all." He paused and took a deep breath. "One more thing. There's the condoms and the pistol. But there's the map, Georgia."

"Yes." She cleared her throat a bit. "Uh … I know where you're going with this. My initials were on that map."

"Indeed they were."

"And you think I might be scared."

"I didn't say it, you did."

"Well, I've spent a lifetime being scared about things. But nothing really ever works. I mean you can't get rid of your fears. You just have to live with them."

She thought back to the most recent phone call with Stieglitz. There was only one phone at the Hacienda, in Carmelita's office. But at least Carmelita had the consideration to step out as Georgia's voice rose in anger. It was a conversation she and Stieglitz had had at least three times since she had been at the Ghost Ranch. It always began the same way, about how the prices was going up on her paintings. And the annoying phrase "high for a woman. The highest ever. Here or in England or France." Then it would go on: *"This is your moment, love. You need to come back. Back to New York. Six months ago I got you almost five thousand dollars."*

"I know," she had replied. *"It was R. W. Johnson, and he's out here right now at the Ghost Ranch and not in New York. Maybe I could get him up to ten thousand?"*

"That's not the point, Georgia. And don't be crude." She had absolutely cackled at that.

"What are you laughing about?" Ryan asked.

She looked at him directly. "My fears." Then she shook her head. "But no, I don't need protection. I don't think I could paint if I thought I was being watched all the time. So, don't trouble yourself, Ryan. Besides it could have been some other G.O."

"Like who?" he asked.

She thought for a moment. "Glenn Olsen."

"Who's that?"

"The only other G.O. I know. A chicken farmer. Specializes in Rhode Island Red chickens in Sun Prairie, Wisconsin. My hometown. I almost went to a prom with him."

"Almost? What happened, an emergency hatching?"

Georgia poked the sheriff in the arm. "Ha-ha! What a wit you are. No, I almost went to a lot of proms. I had a habit of backing out."

By the time they came down the ladder, the sky was a pale green with a touch of blue and the moon looked white in the arc of the sky. White as the hollyhock blossom stuck in the eye socket of the horse head the sheriff had brought.

"Looks nice, that hollyhock in the eye socket," Georgia said. "Flower arranging is another of your talents, Ryan?"

"Seemed fitting. Still can't quite imagine why you'd want an old horse skull."

"As I said, I like bones." She reached down and picked the hollyhock from the eye socket. "What I really like are the interesting holes in the bones."

"Holes?" the sheriff asked.

"Yes, sir. Pick that skull up and hold it to the sky." He picked it up. "What do you see?"

"Sky."

"You see a piece of the sky. You know sometimes it can seem that one has more sky than earth in their world. Helps to contemplate things—to frame them." Sheriff McCaffrey lowered the skull and, holding it in both hands, studied Georgia.

"You're a wise woman, Miss O'Keeffe. Maybe you should be a detective."

"Not on your life. As I've said before, I'm just a painter, Sheriff."

Chapter 4

More sky than earth ... The words lingered in Ryan McCaffrey's head as he drove back to Santa Fe from Georgia's house that evening. In this case, what exactly was he seeing? There were too many disparate elements. His mind was filled with scattered fragments, bits and pieces that did not come together to make a whole but seemed, if anything, to contradict one another. He had to find a focus. So far, he had a priest—not just a priest but a monsignor. That in itself, he supposed, could be significant, since the title indicated the priest had distinguished himself in some manner and thus had been honored by the pope. He doubted if a priest carrying condoms would qualify for such an honor. But would the pope actually know about each monsignor he honored? Of course Sheriff McCaffrey wouldn't have to go as far up as the pope. The bishop of the diocese of Santa Fe would know. Bishop Claudio Peterson. He had presided at McCaffrey's wife's funeral.

Mattie had been the "functioning Catholic" in the McCaffrey household. They had a very egalitarian system, with each taking on the chores and tasks they did best and most enjoyed. Mattie was not especially religious. But she liked Mass and ritual. Ryan like cooking and working in the garden. Mattie liked playing bridge and the piano. Ryan liked carpentry and crossword puzzles. Mattie like reading English novels set in large houses with lots of heirs arguing over their inheritance. She also loved children's books, as she was a librarian and in charge of the children's room at the Santa Fe library.

Ryan also liked sewing. His mother had been a seamstress. It was the process that appealed to him in sewing—planning the designs, making the patterns, working the treadle on the old Singer sewing machine, one of a few in their house. His mom had discarded the old treadle ones when the first electric ones came out around 1890. He found tranquility in sewing. In a certain way, sewing wasn't all that different from detective work. It was all about trying to grasp the whole design yet keep an eye out for the telltale details. Maybe like looking at the sky through the bone hole, as Georgia had shown him. And Miss O'Keeffe's cream dress had not been lost on him. The pin-tuck pleats, no more than three-eighths of an inch wide, were beautiful. He had made all of Mattie's clothes. Even her wedding dress.

In high school, when he and Mattie started dating in their junior year, he had made her prom dress. How he had been teased about that. Teased until he had punched Gilbert Esposito in the face and broken his nose. No one teased Ryan about sewing or anything else after that. Miss O'Keeffe—Georgia—he felt a small flutter in his stomach. Mattie had been dead for almost three years. In the thirty-five years of their marriage, he had never been attracted to any other woman. It was unimaginable. But now … He let the thought drop. He had to keep his mind on this murder. Something was just all out of whack about it. But then his mind wandered back to Georgia. He wasn't really attracted to her. No, not in that way. What did he mean by "that way"? Not like Mattie? *Christ almighty, concentrate, Ryan!* These endless conversations swirling about in his head were getting him nowhere.

He turned off the highway onto the Agua Fria, the road that led into the center of Santa Fe. It had been a long day. The stars were rising. The tip of Orion's sword scraped the cross on the tower of San Sebastian. It looked as if there was a light on in the sanctuary. "Why go to Rome when the bishop is still up?" he muttered to himself. He hadn't seen Bishop Peterson, at least not in church, since Mattie's funeral. He pulled over to the side of the road and got out of the car. Then he thought he should be more discreet. If people spotted the sheriff's car right out in front of the church at this hour, they might become curious. There were not that many folks around, but he decided to pull into the drive and park behind the church by the parish house, where the car would be less visible.

Just as he opened the car door, he saw Bishop Peterson walking out of the presbytery toward the rear door of the church.

"That you, Sheriff?"

"Yes, Your Excellency."

"What can I do for you? You haven't come to pray, I take it."

"I guess not. That was Mattie's department."

The bishop held up his hand as if to stop Ryan from saying more. "No problem there. I know that's not your bailiwick. But thank you for that altar cloth you repaired so beautifully."

"You're welcome. It wasn't a hard fix. I'm here because I have some questions. There's been some trouble."

The bishop motioned Ryan to follow him into the church and his office.

"Take a seat." He gestured to a leather chair on the opposite side of his desk. "Trouble, you say? Law kind of trouble?"

"I guess that's what you'd call it." Ryan paused. "Murder."

The bishop's thick black eyebrows hiked up toward his skullcap. "Who? Where?" Mattie had said those eyebrows always reminded her of caterpillars. *Leaping caterpillars*, the sheriff thought. He felt a deep twinge. Sometimes it was almost as if he were ambushed by his loss. All those tiny things he missed about her.

"Found a body out there near the southeast corner of Ghost Ranch, just past the sandy basin before the turnoff to the road into the ranch. We found the car. He must have gotten lost. Maybe stepped out to see if he could find the road." Ryan sighed as he pictured the poor fool stumbling around in the night, looking for a road that was almost invisible in the daytime. "This is when I wish New Mexico required driver's licenses."

"We don't?" the bishop asked.

"Nope." Of course, how would the bishop know? He didn't drive. "Only thirty-five states require them."

"Any identification at all?"

"Just a business card with his name and church, or rather monastery."

"Monastery, so he was clergy. Do you have the card with you?"

"No. It's in the evidence folder."

"What did it say?"

"Said he belonged some monastery in Monterey, California. Called the Franciscan Friars of the Atonement."

"Wha-a-a-at?" the bishop exclaimed as his caterpillar eyebrows took another hike.

"Surprised?"

"Mildly, yes, but let me get my directory out."

He reached for a large book on the shelf behind him, licked his thumb, and began to quickly turn the pages. "Okay, here we are. First of all, that monastery shut down twenty-five years ago after a kitchen fire got out of hand. The friars fled the fire!" He looked up with a sparkle in his eye. "I don't mean to make a joke out of this, but I'm addicted to alliteration. Extra points for puns with alliteration."

"Is this a confession, Bishop?"

"Of sorts, but you're in the law business, not the absolution business."

"Yep, you got that right."

Bishop Peterson shut the book and put it aside. He put his elbows on his desk and, lacing his fingers together, rested his chin on his hands. "So, tell me more, Sheriff."

This was what Ryan had been dreading. He wasn't sure why. It wasn't confession or anything. And he was sure the bishop had heard worse. He took a deep breath. He supposed he didn't have to give the brand of condoms.

"Uh, condoms and a gun." He paused. "We found them in his valise."

The bishop blinked. "What kind of gun?"

"Good question." Ryan replied with almost visible relief. At least he didn't ask about the brand of condoms. "A Beretta 418."

"Foreign?"

"Yes, Italian."

"No Colt or other American-made firearm?"

"No, just this Italian Beretta. I don't think, at least in my time on the force, we've ever come across one."

"And how did he die?"

"Knife—a military-style knife from the looks of it. Maybe used during the Great War. Thrown at possibly a fair distance with pretty much deadly accuracy."

"Thrown at a distance? Not like he was tackled or anything? And how could you identify the type of knife?"

"Coroner. She'd seen similar wounds before, apparently. I think Dr. Bryce served as a medic in that war. Apparently, it's a knife designed for throwing—very aerodynamic. But she thinks the attacker finished him off in close contact."

"Emily? Emily Bryce?" the bishop asked. Ryan nodded. "She's head of the altar guild, you know. If I weren't a priest—" He let his words hang as he reached down and pulled out a desk drawer. He brought out a bottle of mescal and two tiny ceramic cups.

"Not me, thank you. But if you weren't a priest, then what?"

"Oh, you know we all think about how our lives might have been—if we had married, had children, raised a family. It's not unusual to have such thoughts." He sighed.

Was this a confession of sorts? Ryan wondered.

"Sure you won't have a touch of this mescal? Very good stuff." Ryan shook his head. "Technically still on duty, I suppose."

"Yeah, and it's not good for my stomach."

That was a lie. He and Mattie used to sit on their patio having a nightcap of mescal and watching the stars rise. They had planted a peach tree in the center of the patio on their first anniversary. They would watch over it in every season. It was almost as if that tree was like a child—a child they had never been able to have. In March they would watch the buds forming on the tree. By early May the blossoms would burst forth like miniature supernovas. Mattie had a sense of smell that rivaled a hunting dog's. She could pick up the peach scent when the fruit was still hard and green, not much bigger than a ping-pong ball. They'd start picking at the end of June. By the Fourth of July, they'd have them on ice cream. By late August, Mattie would start canning them. He could easily become lost in this reverie of peaches—the scent, the taste irrevocably entangled with memory and Mattie and mescal.

"So!" the bishop clapped his hands on his knees. "Not sure where to go from here, now that we know that this place, the monastery, no longer exists. And this priest, what was his name again?"

"Castenada. Alberto Castenada."

"Sheriff, this friar is most likely not a friar at all." His brow knotted and he drummed his knuckles on the desk. It was almost as if Ryan could read his thoughts. *He's anxious. He has a diocese to protect, after all. If this news spread, it could hurt a lot of plans.* Since Pope Pius IX had created the Vicariate Apostolic of New Mexico in 1851, before statehood, there had never been a New Mexican cardinal. Ryan knew from Mattie that the bishop was, as she had put it, salivating for such an appointment—and the archbishop in Albuquerque was frail. If the archbishop died, Bishop Peterson would most likely be elevated. And in the Vatican there was pressure for another American to become a cardinal. If Al Smith hadn't been defeated by Hoover six years earlier, after much controversy, it could have happened. At least that was what Mattie had said. She had also told Ryan that there had been financial woes for the diocese, that Bishop Peterson was having to spend an inordinate amount of time down in Albuquerque pleading with the "money guys" at the cathedral.

He looked at the bishop and decided to push a bit.

"But why was this Castenada here at the Ghost Ranch and with a reservation for one of the more expensive casitas? Maybe I should go up to Albuquerque and have a talk with the archbishop?"

"I wouldn't!" A grimace flashed across the bishop's face. Ryan noted the excessive fierceness of his reply. Bishop Peterson immediately began arranging some papers on his desk. Ryan was practiced in the art of waiting silently. Put the burden of speaking, explaining, on the other person. He could tell, already read the regret in the bishop's reply. "I didn't mean to suggest you shouldn't go. It's just that …" He began to fumble slightly for the right words. He finally met Ryan's steady gaze. "I just mean I think it would be a waste of time. Let's just say there's a lot of confusion over there in the seat of the diocese. They're consumed with financial problems. And something like this could cause some bad publicity. And … and … we're trying to get a little help from … well … you know."

"No, I don't know." Ryan said flatly and looked at Peterson, who now reached for his pipe and began an elaborate process that involved knocking out the old tobacco and tamping in the fresh. Finally he looked up at Ryan with a steady gaze. Was this checkmate with not a king but a bishop?

"Maybe you should just talk to Father William." The bishop sighed.

Just talk, the word *just* was the key. A kind of code perhaps. *"Don't go to the big guys in Albuquerque. Stick with the small fry in our diocese."*

"Who is Father William?"

"A Franciscan, but he became an ordained priest perhaps ten years or so ago. He still wears the cassock he wore over at the Acoma Pueblo. He came over here maybe three years ago when Abiquiu and the whole San Juan Basin were reestablished as a bona fide parish. They were no longer simply a mission church when he was named the pastor. St. Francis is the church." The bishop took a sip of mescal. "Would he be likely to have heard about the murder yet?"

"Not officially. But you know, word travels. Georgia O'Keeffe—"

"The painter?" the bishop asked.

"Only person I know named Georgia O'Keeffe. She discovered the body and came rushing into the Hacienda at Ghost Ranch to call the police station here."

"Goodness sakes! Poor woman. What in the world was she doing out there?"

"Painting."

"At night?"

"No. At dawn."

"She paints out there?" The bishop seemed to have relaxed. Ryan was accustomed to this reaction. The tension was seeping away. This was a nice neutral subject—why would a distinguished painter, a woman, be tromping around alone at dawn in the desert?

"Yeah, she likes bones. Bones and sunrises, I guess. Not relics, Bishop, bones—horse skulls, cattle bones. Stuff like that." He paused. "Creatures that die naturally in the desert."

"Really?" The bishop swallowed his last drop of the mescal. He looked at the bottle as though he was considering pouring himself another tot.

"I think she likes churches too. Have to admit I don't care for her church paintings." The bishop added. "Seen any of those, Sheriff?"

"I don't think I have. What's the problem?"

"Dark, very dark; gives the wrong impression of the Church."

"In what way?"

"Makes it seem oppressive, powerful."

Well it is, Ryan thought

"Powerful in a wrong way," the bishop continued. "Seems more of a political statement to me. Wouldn't be surprised if she's a bit of a Commie."

Ryan pressed his lips together. He was not going to comment. But he found the bishop's attitude disturbing. *Commie! What a crock of shit!* He couldn't help but think of the cardinal in Rome who had more or less spearheaded an agreement, a concordat, with the German Holy See and the Third Reich. The Vatican said it was merely made to protect Church interests. When he had read about that in the *Albuquerque Journal,* he was certain that Mattie must be turning in her grave.

"Father William is the priest of St. Francis out in Abiquiu. He might be helpful. I could arrange for you to speak to him. You want me to give him a call?"

"No," Ryan said firmly. It was always better to show up unexpected in these situations. But he didn't want to tell Bishop Peterson that. Having a cop call was never an easy event. Better they didn't know in advance. People, innocent or guilty, had less time to anticipate, to plan.

"Hey," the bishop said with new energy. "I heard that Lucky Lindy—" He paused. "Well, guess we can't call him Lucky anymore after the tragedy with his child, but I heard that Lindbergh's staying out there."

"Yep, he and his wife were there when Miss O'Keeffe came bursting into the Hacienda."

"Hope it didn't upset them, after what they've been through."

"I doubt that she came in yelling the news. At least I don't think so. She's a soft-spoken person." He thought of her again on the roof in that lovely cream-colored dress with the pin-tuck pleats. The hem barely stirring in a low breeze. She was all angles, actually, but there was a softness to her. There was something about her standing on the roof that reminded him of those clouds one saw on crisp winter nights. Too faint to be seen in the daylight, they stretched across the upper atmosphere, tenuous and wraithlike. They were called noctilucent clouds, and that was exactly how Georgia O'Keeffe had appeared on that rooftop. A noctilucent cloud that had deigned to come down at sunset.

Chapter 5

Just past midnight, a flare of sheet lightning bleached the bedroom. Georgia woke with a start. She sprang from her bed and raced to the window. The night was shattered by shards of lightning. They weren't mere bolts. They were bones—sky bones, as if all the ones she found in the desert had suddenly taken flight into the night and begun a jangling skeletal jig, dancing madly until they splintered and re-splintered. How she loved this crackling electrical dance, with the boom of thunderous explosions underscoring it all. She pulled her rocking chair closer to the window and watched the performance of the bright zigzagging flashes of light that peeled back the skin of the night. This indeed this was the clatter and clash of light, no longer mute. What might have shifted out there where that man had died? She would go tomorrow—at just sunrise—and see what the alchemy of rain, wind, and breaking light might disclose.

It was as if this casita on the ranch gave her a front-row seat to the universe, not that tiny shanty window that had been so miniscule on Lake George. How tame and cloistered the lake seemed in comparison. Summers there were like being folded into a plush green velvet bag. She didn't really feel the wind there or feel the sky in the same way. This was where she must stay for at least half the year, but maybe longer. Stieglitz and his silly little mistress were mere specks of dust on the far edge of this cosmic dance.

She stayed up until just before dawn. She wanted to see that first squeak of light on the horizon. It almost sizzled in those earliest seconds. She got dressed, pulling on her jeans and an old flannel shirt. She stepped into her heavy boots in case there was mud from the storm the night before. Then she wrapped her hair into a low bun and tied a kerchief round the whole business.

She thought briefly of the friar's hat, and this led her to reflect again on her conversation with the sheriff. She had to chuckle. Who'd have ever thought she'd be discussing condoms with a sheriff? There was something so fetchingly peculiar about the whole thing that she was tempted to write Stieglitz. She wondered what else the sheriff had found out about Castenada.

Just as she was about to leave, she saw that a large brown envelope had been slipped under the door. She bent over and picked it up. There were still damp rain splotches on the envelope from the downpour. No name on the outside to suggest who it came from our where, or even if it was for her. No postage stamp. Nothing. She opened it and gasped. It was a poorly reproduced photograph of one Stieglitz had taken of her years before. Her hand was splayed between her exposed breasts.

EXPOSED—the word flared in her mind. So did the *X* on the map. They knew where she lived, but who would do this? Why? She understood that when she agreed to let Stieglitz photograph her nude, there was a certain cost in terms of her privacy as an individual and as an artist. But he'd taken those photos thirteen years before, and not here—but so far away from New York, why now? She felt completely defenseless, absolutely vulnerable. More so than she ever had when the exhibit had opened years before at the Anderson Gallery in New York.

She drew her face closer to the coarse reproduction. Her breast had not been cut then. That would happen seven years later for the removal of a benign cyst. She felt panic well up in her. Was the person who slipped this photograph under her door the same one who had marked the *X* on the map? She couldn't tell the sheriff about this photo. She had laughed at him when he had offered protection. If she told him this ... well, she didn't even want to think about it.

Stieglitz had limited the sales of the photographs. Several photos had been displayed in galleries. She didn't dare call Dorothy Norman to go through the files, nor Stieglitz. Stieglitz would go absolutely berserk, race out here, and yank her back East in a heartbeat. With trembling hands she took the photograph to the sink and tore it up. Then she lit a match to the scraps and washed them down the drain. She turned around and walked to the corner, where she grabbed the snake stick and marched out the door.

The snakes would certainly be out this morning. They always emerged after heavy rains. She headed out toward the Pedernal in the Model A. The roads were worse than ever, but she got there as the grayish light of night began to leak away. *Dishwater down a drain*, she thought; she stepped out of the car and began walking briskly toward the mesa.

Ahead perhaps five feet, no more, there was a bright glimmer of black and gold in the gray veil of morning as a diamondback rattler glided across the path, blocking her way. It was a gorgeous creature, with tawny diamonds that merged into bold black and white stripes. She sneaked up with her snake stick, one end of which Rosaria's brother, Tomas, had honed to the sharpness of a blade. A single quick motion and the snake's flat head was severed. She kicked the body to the side then carefully lifted the head, which was impaled on the point of the blade, its jaws still snapping. There was a stunned look in its eyes, as if to say, *How could you?* The jaws might snap for as much as a quarter of an hour after its death. A doctor once told her that this peculiarity was attributed to snakes' low metabolism. A snake's nervous system, he had explained, was quite primitive. Didn't sound so primitive to Georgia. She doubted her jaws would keep snapping. But he further explained that the brain was still alive even if disconnected from the rest of the body. The conversation had taken place at a cocktail party at Mabel Dodge Luhan's home in Taos. She remembered clearly the doctor describing all this as he held a martini in one hand. "You see, Georgia, the eyes in the severed head can even follow movement. The pupils can expand and contract in response to light. In short," the doctor said, almost triumphantly, "their nerve tissue is very tough."

This snake looked fairly dead to her, but she wasn't taking any chances. She took out her multi-tool knife and walked quickly up the path to where the snake's headless body lay. In one stroke, she sliced the rattles off the tail and put them in a small cloth bag she always carried in her pocket. She was getting quite a collection. The rattles varied in hue from ivory to a deep metallic gray. She liked to play Chinese checkers with them.

In another five minutes, she forked off the trail she had been walking and headed out toward the sandy basin. She wasn't sure what drew her to the place where she had found the priest's body scarcely twenty-four hours before. Would it tell her anything about how her initials showed up on that map? Unlikely. Was this just a fruitless act to prove to herself that she wasn't afraid? That she didn't need protection, as the sheriff had suggested? Or was it her way of claiming this desert, this landscape, as her own in some way? That, goddammit, she was going to paint.

As if to answer her, straight ahead she saw that half a dozen hollyhocks, ranging in color from yellow to pink to a deep claret red, had opened up since yesterday morning to greet her. There were jimsonweed flowers as well. These mostly were pale lavender. Perfect match for the coming dawn. But she wanted to find one that was white with the elusive green that edged the petals. The petals were spiky, which led to the other name for jimsonweed—witch weed. How she would love to paint one of the white ones in the light of a full moon. It was an image that haunted the palette she thought of as her dream palette. So often colors, shapes, streamed through her sleep. But they were fragmentary, as dreams often were—illogical, with tangled narratives. Now she wanted to see things differently, aside from how these flowers had changed in the shifting landscape of wind, rain, and breaking light.

She remembered now how she had fallen asleep with the image of the hollyhock blossom the sheriff had stuck in the eye socket of the horse. Both white but different shades. The blossom was so white that it almost made the bone look yellow. Two such incongruous pieces of this world, and yet together they struck a rare harmony. That was so often how her paintings evolved in her mind. They grew bit by bit. Pieces she would pick up as she walked would become part of the painting. Of course in this case, it was Ryan McCaffrey who had done the picking up.

Ahead was the wagon-wheel hub where the coyote had lurked and she had sat while the police examined the crime scene. She walked over to it and took a seat. The moon was still up, large and pale, but sinking rapidly like a silvery balloon behind the hills, which were now a cool violet. There was one bright star left in the sky that reminded her of a teardrop. For the dead man? She doubted it. But she wondered if anyone cried for that man. Who was he? Alberto Castenada—not a friar or a brother. But what? She waited quietly for several minutes, then turned east. With the moon at her back, her figure cast a long shadow as she sat on the wagon wheel, but it would not last long; the sun—that first squeak of light— was coming.

A thread of gold illuminated the blade of the Pedernal. She waited for the moment when both sun and moon would be visible. She swung her head from moon to sun and back again. It seemed as if light were smashing around her, shattering into sharp fragments. It was a prismatic moment. *But I am the prism.* It was exhilarating but, at the same time, frightening. She felt caught in the crosshairs of slivered light. She shifted her gaze down. Something caught her eye—a glint suddenly ignited by this radiance. She got up and walked toward it. Bending down, she saw that it was a penny. She picked it up.

"Well, not any penny," she murmured. "Not Lincoln, but George!" She recognized King George the Fifth on a farthing. *For heaven's sake.* And she realized she was standing perhaps ten feet from where Castenada's body had lain.

How had the police missed this? How had she missed it? It was as if those mute cymbals had been unmuted and clashed. And all she had to do was come back—back in a different light—when the wind and the rain had been left to go about their business. The palette changes and new things emerge.

She was anxious now to get back and call the sheriff. But she would have to go to the Hacienda to do that, as there was no phone in her casita. She didn't relish the thought of the Hacienda. Carmelita would accost her again about coming for dinner with the Lindberghs. The woman was tenacious when she got an idea in her head. Georgia fully expected to be bombarded with gracious notes over the next few days requesting her to come up to the Hacienda for dinner or a cocktail. Wouldn't all the guests be agitated about the murder and be peppering her with questions? She immediately decided not to call from the Hacienda to tell the sheriff. Instead she would drive into Abiquiu and make the call from Goetz's general store.

There was another very good reason to drive the extra mile—she often had the feeling that Carmelita listened in on her calls from another extension. The woman was a preternaturally nosy person. Georgia wouldn't give her the opportunity. The general store was always very generous with their phone. She needed some milk anyway. And perhaps some peaches. There was nothing better than a New Mexico peach. *Forget Georgia*, she thought, even if she shared the name with the peach-growing state.

By the time she arrived back at her own casita after her walk, she could tell that Rosaria was there. She had forgotten it was her cleaning day until she smelled the bread baking. As she came into the kitchen, Rosaria greeted her with a big smile.

"I'm going to make you some more muffins too."

"Oh, thank you, dear. I've got a pork loin marinating. Too much for me, so you take some home for yourself."

Georgia caught a glimpse of a shadow in the corner of the kitchen.

"Oh, my goodness! Clara, honey. Almost missed you there. Quiet as a mouse." *Too quiet*, thought Georgia. The girl had changed somehow over the course of the three months Georgia had been at Ghost Ranch. "Come here, darling, and give me a hug." Clara seemed to hesitate, then walked stiffly over to her. Never lifting her eyes, her face was tight as a fist. Georgia embraced her, but it was like hugging a splinter of flint.

Georgia felt a chill run through here. What was it? She shouldn't pry. The Indians here were reticent by nature. But this was not simply a matter of being quiet. Georgia pushed her back gently, still holding on to the child's thin shoulders. The little girl would not meet her gaze. She was about to say, "Let me take a look at you" or "My, how you've grown." But something stopped her. Instead she said, "How would you like to mess about in my studio? I have to go into Abiquiu and get some stuff at Goetz's, but I have some fun things in my studio, you know. Come, follow me." She took the girl's hand and gently led her into the white-washed room. In one corner was a kiva-style adobe fireplace. A chill still clung to the morning. "I can light that for you if you're cold."

Clara said nothing, but shook her head slowly. Gathered on the mantel-piece and windowsills around the room were myriad gifts from the desert—gnarled branches, more bleached animal bones. There was also a small round table covered with stones polished by wind, sand, and weather.

Georgia went over to a plywood plank on sawhorses, where her paint-brushes rested upside down in a can. Next to the can was a wooden box holding tubes of paint. There was also a shelf with drawing paper for sketching and several boxes of pastels. Next to the pastels was a large coffee can for charcoal.

"You can pick your tools, Clara. I've got watercolors too. Right here in that flat metal case. I can set up a palette for you as well with some oils."

Again, Clara shook her head. But her hand crept toward the coffee can holding the charcoal. *Yes!* thought Georgia—*a sign of life.* She quickly pulled a whole tablet of drawing paper from a shelf and set it before Clara.

For the first time, Clara turned toward her and looked at her. It was as if the child were asking permission. "Draw anything you want. See? This is why the table faces toward the Pedernal. It's my window on the world." Clara was silent, but the words of her question almost seemed to form in the air. Georgia waited. *What was she trying to say?*

Georgia reached for a piece of charcoal and, gripping it between her thumb and index finger, dragged the large chunk across the paper in one bold stroke. Clara glanced from the paper to the window. "No, I'm not looking outside at the mesa. This is an image in my head from last night. Images stored up in your head can be as good as looking out a window at a landscape. That electrical storm last night. All the lightning." She paused and glanced at Clara, whose eyes were riveted on the thick dark mark. Again, she could almost read Clara's mind. "You don't see the lightning, do you?" Clara shook her head just a bit. "Well, look how I can fix that." She reached for a tool that had a pointed eraser on one end. Georgia began making long sweeping strokes through the charcoal, revealing the white paper beneath the heavy dark marks. "Look at that. Lightning, presto!"

"Huh." The sound came softly, but it was the first utterance from Clara. Georgia handed her the piece of charcoal. "You have yourself a good time. Use as much paper as you want, charcoal too. Plenty more."

"Thank you," Clara said, but she kept her eyes on the sheet of paper.

Georgia stood there for a moment, studying the child. She was so still but not calm. Quite the opposite. Her slight frame radiated tension. Stillness and tension—what an odd combination. She almost wanted to reach out and touch her shoulder. But she dared not.

Chapter 6

As she drove into Abiquiu, Georgia could not get Clara out of her mind. Some essence had been scraped from her. It was as if she were a shadow cast by what was once the light of a real girl. But where had that light gone? Clara had always been shy, but she had been a smiling girl who laughed and loved to catch the chickens for Alicia, the cook up at the Hacienda. She often rode a pony out into the desert with her big brother, Tomas, who was a rodeo rider. Rosaria had told Georgia that Clara kept a picture of Bertha Blancett, a bucking bronco champion, tacked up over her bed. She practiced her roping skills with her brother at least twice a week when he had time off his job. He worked as a wrangler at Ghost Ranch and as a mechanic in Santa Fe.

Georgia sighed and shifted her thoughts to the farthing in her pocket as she pulled up to Goetz's general store.

Otto Mueller's wife, Nina, was behind the counter.

"Good morning, Miss O'Keeffe." The tiny woman nodded. "What can I do for you?"

She spoke English with a heavy German accent. If Stieglitz had been with her, he could have told her exactly the region or federal state in Germany she came from. Although Stieglitz been born in Hoboken, New Jersey, he had spent his high school years in Berlin because his parents felt he could receive a better education there. His mother came from Offenbach, his father from Saxony. Alfred himself had an ear for language and dialect.

"I was hoping to use your phone if possible," Georgia replied.

"Certainly, but at the moment I believe Otto is on it. Not for long. Calling a supplier in Albuquerque. Two minutes most." Then she smiled bashfully. "We have some happy news."

"Oh, really!" Georgia said knowingly. No matter what the language or the accent, there was only one kind of news that people delivered in that soft way that brimmed with happiness. She could not help but think of the abortion Stieglitz had forced her to have.

"*Ja, ja,* a baby on the way." Then she giggled. "All the way from Germany."

"Oh, you mean you're adopting?"

"Yes, baby is expected in January. I cannot have baby."

She came out from behind the counter. "I ... I ..." With both hands she began making small gestures around her stomach. "My womb is ... is ..." She appeared to be struggling for a word. Georgia hoped this was not going to get too gynecological. "*Gebärmutter versiegelt!*" she blurted out. "Shut! Baby eggs can't ... can't ..."

"Swim?" Georgia said."

"*Ja, ja,* swim upriver to womb."

Georgia felt herself squirming. It was getting gynecological and a little geographical as well, not to mention a strange thing for a woman to share just seconds after announcing she would indeed have a child.

The bell on the store's screen door tinkled, and Georgia turned around. The sheriff walked in.

"Well, if it isn't Miss O'Keeffe."

"Goodness, you saved me a nickel. I was about to call you."

"I'm flattered."

At that moment, she also was tempted to tell the sheriff about the photograph that had been slipped under her door. But she resisted. It was odd, but in her mind, that photo had suddenly become something it never had been before—salacious. Stieglitz had not shot it that way at all. The lighting was masterful. The genius of the photograph was how Stieglitz had capture the light—the light on the partially open cotton shirt, on her breasts and her hand with the long fingers that splayed across the skin. A black-and-white platinum print had conveyed so subtly the nuances of skin and light and shadow. She simply could not show him this picture. It would be like undressing in front of a stranger—well, he wasn't really a stranger, but he wasn't a doctor either. He was a cop!

"I found something out there."

"Out there? Where?"

"My, my," she sighed. "How quickly one forgets." She hesitated for a moment. What should she say in this case? *The body? Monsignor Castenada?* "Perhaps we should step outside and I'll show you." She turned to Nina Mueller. "Congratulations, Frau Mueller."

"*Danke,*" she murmured softly and watched them leave.

"Take a look at this." Georgia dug into her pants pocket, taking out the farthing.

"What's that?" the sheriff asked.

"Not a nickel." She paused. "A farthing."

"A what?"

"A British quarter penny. That's George on the face."

"George who?"

"King George the Fifth."

Sheriff McCaffrey whisked a handkerchief from his back pocket.

"I've already contaminated it with my own fingerprints," Georgia said. "You know how I like to disturb crime scenes and tamper with evidence."

"True, but it doesn't need my prints in the mix. You found it out there, near where the body was? How near?"

"Ten feet or so."

"We must have overlooked it." Ryan McCaffrey took a step back and gazed up at the sky. It was blue and flawless. He made a sound halfway between a huff and a chuckle.

"What's so funny?"

"I need one of those bones of yours—the kind with a couple of holes."

"Why?"

"Well, as you said yourself, I think I've got more sky than earth here. Or in this case, more earth than sky. I need a bit of focus."

"You going to let me get into my automobile?"

"Sure." He stepped back and opened the door. There was something almost courtly in the way he stood beside it.

"So, what are you doing out here?" Georgia asked.

"Came to talk to this fellow, Father William, pastor at Saint Francis. You go there?"

"Do I look like a churchy type to you? I paint them. I don't go into them. But why do you want to talk with the pastor?" She tipped her head in the direction of Saint Francis. It was down the road less than a quarter mile.

"I was talking to the bishop in Santa Fe. This fellow Castenada, according to a card in his wallet, was associated with a monastery in Monterey called the Franciscan Friars of the Atonement."

Georgia rolled her eyes. "These names!" she muttered.

"What about the names?"

"Where I came from in Wisconsin, there was a church named Saint Mary's of Precious Blood. They need to tone it down a bit."

"You want to write to the pope?" His eyes crinkled at the corners as he smiled.

"What a card you are sheriff!" She chuckled warmly; she liked a man with a sense of humor—even a gun-toting one.

"In any case, the monastery burned down more than twenty years ago."

"It burned down, and the fellow claimed to be part of it?"

"Well, he only had a card in his wallet. I'm not sure it was a 'claim.'"

"Yes, but these pieces ... the condom, the gun, now this card."

"And don't forget the farthing. Or maybe his farthing? All the way from Great Britain to here!" She paused. "But you know, um, maybe I could go with you when you visit Father William?"

"Why?" She wasn't sure what to say. She hadn't wanted to become involved. At least she thought so. But a man had been murdered, and then there were those initials on the map. Her initials, no one else's. Didn't that give her some right, some reason to have an interest? She actually found the sheriff's question slightly annoying. She refrained from voicing her thoughts: *Look, I found the body. My initials were on that map. Why shouldn't I be interested?*

"Uh, just think of me as one of those holes in a bone. Might help you focus, Ryan."

"And how am I supposed to explain your presence to Father William?"

"Just tell him the truth. Tell him I found the body. I called you from the Hacienda. I think I have a right to be curious. Someone murdered so close to my home—where I walk out in the desert every morning and every evening."

"Okay, you don't have to convince me. Let's get into my car."

"It's a two-minute walk, for crying out loud. You're going to drive?"

"We go in a cop car," he said abruptly.

Of course, she thought. *The authority of the law. Church and state here.*

As they turned into the drive of the church, they passed a Model A pickup.

The sheriff took note. "Guess now that this church has been reestablished as a parish, they throw a car into the deal."

"Looks newer than mine," Georgia commented. "This fellow's a Franciscan?"

"Yep."

So much for poverty, Georgia thought for the second time in less than forty-eight hours. They saw a figure in a garden, hoeing. He was dressed in a cassock and wore the broad-brimmed hat of a friar. The hat cast a huge shadow on the ground. It gave Georgia a start. She recalled the hat she had seen fetched up on the horse skull. Again she was stirred by some sense of disorder. The man in the garden stopped hoeing, looked in their direction, then waved. Ryan quickened his stride. Georgia followed. Some chickens were pecking around a small enclosure just off the house.

"Brother William," the sheriff said, extending his hand. "Or rather Father William. Sorry about that."

"No matter." He smiled broadly. "A title is but a shroud for an occupation, as the body is simply a shroud for the soul."

Oh boy! thought Georgia as he extended his hand to shake the sheriff's.

"I'm Sheriff McCaffrey out of Santa Fe and this is Miss O'Keeffe," Ryan said.

"Ah, the illustrious painter! What an honor."

Oh dear, Georgia thought. She didn't like being fussed over. Maybe she shouldn't have come.

"We'd like to talk to you."

"Certainly. Tell me what I can do for you?"

"I think it would be better in your office."

"Of course. I was just finishing this last row of broad beans. Trying to squeeze in one more crop before first frost."

"That's some time off, I'd say," the sheriff replied.

"Perhaps I'm used to the Acoma planting schedule, where I was before I came here to reestablish the parish. Much higher altitude there. You can get a frost very early. But follow me."

The hem of his cassock was dusty; his feet, bare in his sandals, were too. Had she not noticed Monsignor Castenada's shoes? She must remember to ask the sheriff about them.

They went into the parish house, just behind the church.

"Humble but nice," Father William said as they entered. "They wanted to expand the parish house, make it larger, with more modern conveniences. But I begged them not to. This is fine. Can I get you some water?"

"Yes," Ryan said.

"No," Georgia said at the same time.

"Good to stay hydrated out here, Miss O'Keeffe," Father William offered.

Hydrated. For some reason the word just didn't sound right. He took off his wide-brimmed hat and reached for a skullcap. Scratches were incised across his perfectly round, bald scalp. She almost gasped. Instantly she was back in that early-dawn light, transfixed by the flap of pale skin fluttering in the draft of the vulture's wings.

"An accident, I see." She spoke softly and nodded at his head, where he had just placed the skullcap.

"What?" Father William looked up at her. His gray eyes were eerily translucent.

"Your head."

"Oh, that! Yes, one of the hazards of the brotherhood. The tonsured head is vulnerable if the skullcap is not in place." He looked toward the kitchen counter. "I bent over right there, forgot that I had left a drawer pulled out, and banged my head rising up. I'd left the skullcap I wear inside by the sink when I was washing my face."

"Really?" Georgia said.

"What?" He seemed slightly annoyed by the question.

"I mean, really, that can be a hazard, I suppose … for … for those with tonsures," Georgia stammered. "I'd never thought about that before." She wasn't sure why, but for some reason she was trying to reassure him.

"Yes, yes, it can. Now tell me what brings you here." He said this briskly, as if he were suddenly in a hurry to get on with the business at hand—or back to his beans.

Sheriff McCaffrey quickly recounted the details of the murder and was just moving into what Georgia thought of as the "coda" of the story. But McCaffrey used the word *upshot*.

"So, the upshot is that the victim, though dressed as a Franciscan like yourself, had a card that identified him as a member of a monastery in Monterey, California, called the Franciscan Friars of the Atonement."

"What!" Father William blurted out. "That place burned twenty years ago at least."

"Exactly."

There was more of course—the condoms, the gun. But Ryan had warned her in the car that he was not going to mention that. Not yet.

"It's all timing in this game, Georgia," he had said. And then as a footnote of sorts: "Never say too much." He had paused. "But I don't think that will be your problem. You're not a gabber."

"Hmm …" was all she had said. She supposed it was a compliment.

Father William now turned to Georgia. "And you were the one who discovered the body?"

"Yes."

"How did you happen to come across it?"

"I like to walk." She left it at that.

"Walk?" Father William repeated.

"Yes."

"So, when you were out walking, you found him."

"Yes, at dawn. My favorite time. Got to him just as a vulture was tearing off his scalp." She paused again. "That's why I reacted when I saw that angry scratch on your head."

"It was a drawer. No anger with a drawer. Just myself." He gave a small chuckle.

"Oh, yeah," she said, "not a vulture at all." *Maybe a chicken ...* she thought to herself.

The priest blinked, as if he were about to ask another question.

Ryan McCaffrey opened his eyes wide, expecting him to say more, but the priest didn't. The sheriff turned toward Georgia, as if he were now waiting for her to say something. She shrugged slightly. In the silence of the moment, Georgia realized there was really no question about the color of the sheriff's eyes. They were a lovely deep blue—a midnight blue, she realized. Why had she thought they were possibly gray when he took off his sunglasses out there yesterday? And never noticed when he visited her on the roof of the casita?

Before they left, Father William insisted that they each take some eggs from his flock of chickens. "This is an exceptional flock, tastiest eggs you'll ever eat."

When they climbed into the sheriff's car to go back to Goetz's store, she put a hand on his forearm. "Wait up. Take off your sunglasses and look at me for a second."

He turned and did as she asked him. "What's this all about?"

"Um-hm!"

"What?"

"In Father William's kitchen your eyes were dark blue. Navy blue, I would say. Now they're more like"—she hesitated to say baby blue—"uh, sky blue."

"Baby blue," he replied. "My late wife, Mattie, always said baby blue."

Late wife? Now was she supposed to say something about her present husband?

Oh, God, even without murder, things could get complicated awfully fast.

———————

It was past noon by the time Georgia got home. Rosaria had finished her cleaning. She had left the freshly baked bread, wrapped in a blue-and-white cloth, on a wooden cutting board in the middle of the kitchen table. Next to the bread was a jelly jar full of pink trailing four-o'clocks, which bloomed in such profusion at this time of year. These people were inherently artistic, Georgia thought. Perhaps it was growing up in this spare high-desert country where color, line, and shape stood out so clearly. This reminded Georgia that she should see if Clara had drawn anything and perhaps left it behind.

She went into her studio filled with anticipation. Nothing was immediately visible, but when she walked to the plywood table, she saw that at least a third of the large tablet had been used. A block of charcoal still lay on the table, worn down to a mere nub—sure evidence that Clara had used it—and there was charcoal dust on the table. Georgia picked up the piece. She must have pressed hard, and yet not a trace of a drawing. If she'd used this much paper, Clara would have made at least twenty drawings, and yet there was no sign of them. She must have taken them home with her. One would have thought she'd have left at least one—kind of a thank-you. How very odd! Georgia searched all over the studio, pulling other tablets and paper supplies from the shelves. She looked in the wastebasket.

Returning to the kitchen, she noticed an envelope sticking out from beneath the breadboard. It was one from the Hacienda and had the Ghost Ranch logo. Undoubtedly from Carmelita.

Hello, Georgia.

The Lindberghs keep asking about you—especially the Mrs. She seems so downcast most of the time. It would be so nice if you would join them for dinner tomorrow. R.W. and Maggie will be here by then, and Lanny is coming. Carson has a cold.

Please come, Georgia—for me?

Affectionately,

Carmelita

Georgia sighed. Carmelita could be so manipulative but, at the same time, guileless. Why should she come for Carmelita? And, yes, she was sorry for Mrs. Lindbergh and her downcast state, but why should she be prevailed upon to somehow help mitigate it? Just meeting a painter would do this? She supposed she should go if only to lighten the pressure Carmelita was putting on her.

She reread the note and made a soft snorting sound. "R.W.," she muttered. "Lanny is coming." Carmelita and her social ambitions. She would never address them directly by their first names or nicknames in the Hacienda. Never call Robert Wood Johnson, the pharmaceutical heir, anything but Mr. Johnson. However, there was nothing she loved more than to do so offstage, so to speak, and create a semblance of intimacy that others could only yearn for. Alanna Powell—or Lanny as she was known among her close friends—and her husband, Carson, represented the pinnacle of the social order at the ranch. Georgia had not even been at the ranch for a week before she noticed the jockeying among guests to be invited for cocktails with the Powells and the manipulations of Carmelita. And how quickly Carmelita had decided to add Georgia to her arsenal, and not without the encouragement of Lanny Powell. Nothing like an artist on the premises to validate one's own artiness and adorn one's salon. The Hacienda was unfortunately becoming a salon.

In many ways, it was not unlike the contrivances in the New York art world to get close to Stieglitz. To be invited to his openings and, of course, the supreme invitation—to be invited to Lake George. It was harder to avoid in New York, but here it was easy.

She closed her eyes for a second as if trying to clear her head and figure out how she might wiggle out of this invitation. An unbidden picture drifted across her mind. Those horrible scalp tears on Castenada's head, pecked and torn by the vultures. "Better than a scalpel," Emily Bryce had said about the creature's talon, and then she'd taken off, waving her umbrella to scare them away. Then came the image of Father William's tonsured head with the skin still firmly attached but raked—raked not by the middle talon of a vulture but, perhaps, a chicken? Seemed more likely, she thought, than by banging one's head on an open kitchen drawer.

Chapter 7

Nina Mueller's husband had drunk himself into a stupor. He stank of liquor and sweat. He began to grope her then heaved his weight upon her and tried in his alcoholic haze to become erect. He shoved her head down to service him with her mouth. Finally, he was hard and entered her. Then the guttural name ripped the night: "Ah! Gerda!"

Two seconds later, when he was done with her, he fell sound asleep, not even aware of his deceit. This was the third time he had called out this name in his drunkenness.

She got up from her bed and went to the kitchen, where she stared out the window, the kitchen window of their living quarters at the store. It was still early, still light, no later than eight o'clock. But on evenings like this, he often started drinking as soon as he closed the store at six o'clock. As she looked out, she was trying to imagine what this baby growing in the girl in Munich would be. Boy? Girl? What would it look like? What would they name it? She had started almost immediately to make a list of possible names for whatever sex the child might be. She didn't tell Otto. She would as the time came closer.

If only she could have had this baby herself. She and Otto had tried everything, including two relatively simple operations, but to no avail. And then, because of Otto's high rank in the Party, they went through further testing for racial purity and were deemed eligible for the Fount of Life program. It was called *Lebensborn*. Even though Nina herself could not give birth, she could become the adoptive mother to a baby conceived with Otto's sperm by a young woman selected by the *Lebensborn* council. The birth rate in Germany had been falling. Hitler, the Führer, needed Aryan babies to propagate the traits that were valued by the Third Reich and assure that the Reich would indeed endure one thousand years, as he had promised.

Now, as Nina Mueller stared into the night, her eyes began to fill with tears. She pulled a small piece of paper from the pocket of her bathrobe, took a pencil, and crossed the name Gerda from the list of girl names

"I shall only see her three times," Otto had explained. "I shall not even know her name. That is one of the rules. They are all called Maria. We must not even meet except at Tegernsee." Tegernsee was the castle in Bavaria that was one of the designated breeding sites.

Otto had lied to her. They weren't all called Maria.

Even though their meetings had been brief, Otto refused to talk about the young woman who had conceived the child on his visit to Germany two months before. "Just three nights, Nina. She was nothing ... just a vessel. Very mechanical, the whole thing." A *vessel—ein Schiff.*

The word lingered in her head. A vessel: something she was not; could never be. Her womb was sealed. *Gebärmutter versiegelt.* She was one out of ten thousand women in the world who had this condition. She didn't doubt that she would love this child, but what was she to do? It was all wrong. So wrong. Should a child even be brought into this world? She knew what was coming. She knew why they were here in this godforsaken desert. But a baby would burn up alive here. A part of her wished that the baby would never be born. That Gerda would miscarry. Was it a sin to wish for that?

That evening Ryan McCaffrey began to clean up from his solitary dinner in his kitchen. It was a ritual he enjoyed, more than the lonely meal itself. He tried to wipe down the counters just the way Mattie had always instructed him, with a sprinkling of the 20 Mule Team Borax and some lemon juice. "That's the trick, sweetie," she would remind him.

He overcleaned the counters this evening and began wiping down those that weren't even dirty from his dinner preparations. The motion was soothing, and Mattie's voice hovering on the edges of his consciousness actually helped him think.

Ryan McCaffrey reflected on his two interviews, the first with Bishop Claudio Peterson and then with Father William. Should he attempt a triple play—triple ecclesiastical play, that is—and go to the big guy, the archbishop in Albuquerque? Maybe. What would Bishop Peterson do if he found out? Well, what *could* he do? One priest, one sheriff. One looks after God's children, one tracks down murderers. The twain do meet.

He got up early the next morning. Again, he decided not to call. The element of surprise was usually a benefit. He'd even polished his badge to make it shiny. Mattie used to do this; now it was up to him. A shiny badge was the best way to get past the front office, or a stubborn secretary.

Two and a half hours later he was being ushered into the archbishop's office in Albuquerque. As he walked in, he noticed the large portrait of the current pope, Pope Pius XI. *Grouchy,* Ryan thought. If this diocese was hurting for money, the archbishop's office did not reveal it. *Sumptuous* was the only word Ryan could think of. Rich fabrics. A picture of the Virgin Mary showing a discreet amount of her bosom as she nursed the baby Jesus. He wondered if the archbishop found this arousing. Maybe he masturbated under his desk. But of course next to it was some sort of tapestry hanging on the wall depicting the crucifixion of Christ. Cradle to grave, Ryan supposed.

"Your Grace, I am sorry to disturb you." He was indeed frail-looking.

"Please, please. Sit down, Sheriff. What brings you here?"

"An unfortunate matter, I am afraid." The archbishop merely nodded.

"Murder," Ryan replied.

"Murder?" The archbishop looked down and blinked. He was silent for several seconds. "Not a child?"

"No, no not a child at all." How strange, Ryan thought, that he would jump to that conclusion. "As a matter of fact, it was an adult male who ... uh ... was actually dressed as a Franciscan priest." Ryan took a deep breath. "Yes, strange. Isn't it?"

"Who? Where was he from?"

Ryan McCaffrey told the full story. The archbishop sat very still. He was rapt with attention. What impressed Ryan most was, in fact, his utter stillness. He didn't fiddle with a pipe or rearrange papers on his desk the way Bishop Peterson had.

"Most peculiar. But why, Sheriff, would a man dress up as a priest."

"Because he didn't want people to know who he really was," Ryan replied. Saying that out loud made it seem so obvious, yet remarkable. He had never exactly answered it in his head this way. He had, of course, wanted to know who this condom-carrying, pistol-toting fellow was, and yet he had not quite articulated this obvious truth to himself quite so simply. Who was this guy really? Who did he want to be and why?

The meeting with the archbishop had been fruitless except to confirm in McCaffreys' mind that the Church did not seem to be as impoverished as Bishop Peterson had suggested. He had briefly toyed with some sort of ecclesiastical motive for the murder, even though the contents of Castenada's suitcase hardly pointed to a priestly life.

The body had been released from the Santa Fe morgue the day before and driven down to the morgue in Albuquerque. So far, from what Ryan knew, there had been no next of kin located, no indication of where to ultimately ship the remains. Ryan decided to drop in on Gus Montez, the Albuquerque chief of police. They went back decades. Perhaps the cops had dug up some more information.

Fifteen minutes later he walked into Gus's office. The lanky fellow took his feet off his desk and popped up.

"Ryan, bet I know why you're here. The stiff, right."

"Yep. Got any more information?"

"Put out an APB; only thing that came in was something from Canada ..."

"And ... ?"

"It's a telegram that says the Castenada family would like the body sent to the Morgan Smathers Funeral Home in Washington, DC."

Ryan inhaled sharply. "You don't say!"

"I do say," Gus replied and nodded. "You know the funeral home?"

"Nope. Somewhere in DC, I guess."

Gus inhaled sharply. "You don't suppose the Feds could be in on this?"

"I think they would have more on their mind than us. I mean, my God, we're just now, maybe hopefully, coming out of the Depression. We're a two-bit regional police force in the middle of nowhere."

"You ever been to Washington?" Gus asked.

"Once."

"Me, never." He sighed. "I write to them all the time. The Feds, that is."

"What about?"

"Pestering them about stuff—better roads, driver's licenses."

"Damn, wouldn't that make our jobs easier. If they'd just put a goddamn license plate on a car," Ryan growled.

"You realize that New York and Massachusetts have had license plates since 1903?"

"Yes, and that's nine years before we even became a state." Ryan sighed. "Johnny-come-latelies, that's us." He paused. "Well, can't bellyache about it forever. You read my reports, right?"

"Yeah, supposedly Castenada was a Franciscan priest."

"But with condoms and a gun in his suitcase. Priest, my ass!"

"A little early for Halloween and trick-or-treating," Gus chuckled.

"I would say."

"Well, Father Castenada, or whatever we should call him, is boarding his flight now."

"Flight? You're not shipping him by train?"

"Hey, they're paying."

"Who's paying?"

"Morgan Smathers Funeral Home."

"Strange. I don't get it."

"Me neither." He paused for a long time.

"Maybe it's the Feds," Gus Montez mused.

"I don't think the Feds are that original. And certainly not the Bureau of Investigation." Ryan caught himself. "Oh, pardon me; I hear they're changing the name to the Federal Bureau of Investigation, FBI."

"Why are they doing that?"

"I don't know. They need something to do. Depression, the New Deal can't keep them busy enough, I guess. Not to mention Herr Hitler and that thug Stalin." Ryan McCaffrey paused. "You worried about them?"

"Who?" Gus looked up. "Hitler and Stalin?"

"Yeah,"

"Nah," the chief of police said. "Hey, we're barely done with the Great War."

"Not barely, sixteen years now."

"Okay, sixteen years, still a long time to carry a grudge, Ryan."

"I hope you're right," he said, getting up from the chair. "I hope."

Fifteen minutes later, heading toward Santa Fe, he saw ahead of him a car that looked an awful lot like the Model A that Georgia O'Keeffe drove. "My God, she drives fast," he said aloud. It was a perfect time for him to try out the new siren. No other cars around. This could be fun. He pressed a small switch on the dashboard. Immediately a sound halfway between a groan and a screech issued forth. He pressed the accelerator and began to close the gap. Sticking his head out of the window and motioning with his arm, he signaled her to pull over.

"What the hell?" Georgia poked her head out the window as Ryan opened his door. "Jesus Christ, it's the sheriff. What is it?"

"Are you aware, ma'am, that you have broken the speed limit?"

"Of course not. What's a speed limit?"

He leaned his head in the car and laughed.

"Lucky for you, we don't have them yet in in New Mexico. Not yet. Only in Connecticut. They have a legal maximum speed. What took you to Albuquerque?"

"Paint supplies, paper, that kind of stuff. So why are you pulling me over? Just to talk?"

He smiled and shrugged. "Just for fun, I guess."

"Just for fun! That might be a waste of taxpayer money—or something like that."

He nodded. "Yeah, I guess you're right. Something like that. But you don't drive like a woman."

"I'm supposed to take that as a compliment?"

"Yes, I think you should, actually."

"Well, actually, I don't take it as a compliment. I take it as an indictment. I'm sick of men defining standards. Coming up with this false criteria about women."

"Jesus, I don't see why you have to be so touchy."

"See, '*touchy*,' now that's a perfect example."

"What is?"

"The word *touchy*. A word, along with others, almost exclusively used to reference women. Next, are you going to tell me I've got my monthly?"

Ryan felt himself going pale. Georgia absolutely cackled at this. "Touchy, aren't you now? A woman daring to mention menstruation in front of a man. "Menstruation—M-E-N-S-T-R-U—"

"I know how to spell it, goddammit!"

Georgia roared with laughter. She turned the engine back on, leaned out the window, and hollered. "Don't take it personally, Sheriff." Then she blasted off down the road.

That evening back in Santa Fe, Ryan McCaffrey sat on his patio. The scent of the peaches ripening on the tree was just starting to thread the air. He peered into a glass with a half inch of Scotch. What would Mattie have thought? But actually he knew. She would have used one of her favorite expressions: "Oh, don't be an A-M." *A-M* stood for "ape man," dumb, crude, vulgar. Mattie would have agreed with Georgia about his behavior out there. *Damn, Mattie why'd you have to up and die! Why'd you have to leave?*

He squeezed his eyes shut. He felt the tears pressing against the inside of his lids. *"It's your own damn fault."* That's what she would have said about the scene out there on the road. But what a conniption that lady pitched out there. *"See, there you go again, Ryan. 'Conniption,' a lady word. Miss O'Keeffe wouldn't have liked it."* But now he couldn't undo it. Death had separated him and Mattie, but murder had brought Georgia O'Keeffe to his door. And in many ways, Mattie and Georgia weren't all that different. It surprised him. Actually, it shocked him because it was not at all obvious. At first glance, they were hardly replicas of each another. The similarities lay deeper, much deeper.

Chapter 8

That same evening, Georgia, obedient to the request of Carmelita to join the Lindberghs for dinner, left for the Hacienda. She was dressed in her summer uniform of immaculate white cotton. Her only jewelry was a silver cuff bracelet and a silver Navajo button she had converted to a pin to close the V-neck of her shirt, with its men's-style collar.

As she approached the Hacienda in her car, she saw Lupe, one of the maids, walking up with a bundle in her arms. She had delivered a girl about a month before, and Georgia had not yet seen the baby. She pulled over.

"Lupe, dear, nice to see you back, but even better with your baby. May I take a peek?"

"*Sí*, Miss O'Keeffe." Lupe came over to the car and folded back the pink blanket. Georgia caught her breath as she glimpsed the plump, rosy little face.

"Oh, my goodness. What's her name?"

"Alma," Lupe replied. Georgia felt a twinge. How much she had wanted the baby that Stieglitz insisted she abort.

"Alma," she repeated. "Bless you, little Alma. I'm going to make you a present."

"Ah, too kind, Miss O'Keeffe."

"No, no not at all. Just a little watercolor to wake up to in the morning."

"Very kind, Miss O'Keeffe."

"I'd better be on my way. Late for dinner at the Hacienda. Carmelita will be upset."

The others had already gathered for cocktails on the patio when she arrived. The gentlemen stood up to greet her as a beaming Carmelita led the celebrated guest to the patio. Anne Morrow Lindbergh appeared to be almost trembling with excitement and seemed on the brink of standing up herself to greet Georgia. She was an enchanting-looking woman with a heart-shaped face framed by soft wavy hair. Her eyes sloped down. She had a slightly boyish look to her face that seemed to give it a refreshing innocence.

Her husband was, of course, as handsome as his photographs in the newspaper. He too had a shy, unassuming manner. Lanny Powell's attention was focused on him entirely. "Well, I've been in Houston talking with Howard Hughes," Lindbergh was saying.

"Oh, of course. We use Hughes drills for drilling wells out here," Lanny said in a low voice as she leaned forward. It was almost as if she were disclosing an intimate secret. "Tell us more. Howard Hughes must be such an intriguing man."

As Lindbergh began to talk, all the attention was riveted on him. Georgia listened but took in each person around the cocktail table. Would anyone at this gathering be capable of hurling a knife—a commando knife—and killing Castenada? As she had threaded her way toward this table, she'd passed someone saying something about "a man dying in the desert ... a priest, apparently." This was the only mention she had caught of the murder. But the word *murder* had not been used—simply dying, as if perhaps the person had suffered heat stroke.

"Well, with Howard, it's not just tools anymore," Lindbergh continued. "He's developing a whole new company called Hughes Aircraft. It's really, in one sense, a subsidiary of the tool operation. Howard has a passion for aviation racing."

"Oh really! How marvelous." Lanny's eyes opened wide with a kind of delirious wonder, and she tilted her head in a decidedly coquettish manner. She was in her element. That was Lanny, Georgia thought. A natural-born flirt. Peter Wainwright, the young Princeton man who tutored the Powell children, seemed slightly embarrassed by his employer's behavior. Her husband, Carson, sat beside her, completely detached. Most likely he had retreated into his own world of new plans for the Ghost Ranch that reached far beyond attracting a clientele of wealthy and socially prominent guests. Georgia applauded his idealism in terms of his conservation efforts, but she could imagine the stamp of his Brooks Brothers shoes could still overrun the desert she loved just as it was. She could only take so much noblesse oblige. And his pet name for Roosevelt—Rosvinski—that definitely made her wince.

Georgia switched her attention to Lanny, still chattering away at Lindbergh, tilting her head and narrowing the space between them. Peter Wainwright's apparent mortification was increasing dramatically, or at least it seemed so to Georgia. And Carson Powell seemed wrapped in a cloud of oblivion. Georgia wondered. But now the tutor turned his attentions to Lindbergh's wife in an obvious attempt to engage her in conversation and distract her from Lanny's flirtatious exhibition. And it was an exhibition, or so it seemed to Georgia. But for whom?

Georgia recalled her encounter with Lanny and Wainwright and the three Powell children on the road that morning after she had found Castenada's body. The conversation about the arrowhead flowed to her: *"Mom and Peter buried it! They do that all the time. They go out at night and bury archaeology stuff. Kind of like cheating."* Yes, *kind of like cheating,* Georgia thought. Is that what's going on here? Is Lanny's unfettered flirting with Lindbergh designed to provoke Peter Wainwright, with whom she is cheating on Carson? She had honed her coquetry to perfection, with her hand usually touching Peter Wainwright's sleeve and her sparkling eyes advanced, aided by flashing dimples, toward Lindbergh. She was playing two ends against the middle, but what was behind this game?

Lindbergh was now talking about his work with Hughes to develop better magnetic navigation systems. He launched into a narration of a perilous flight he had experienced recently over the Straits of Florida when his compass began rotating without stopping. There was a thick haze, and nothing he could see corresponded with what was on his map. He had discussed this problem with Hughes, who was interested in developing advanced instrumentation systems and helping planes become more fuel efficient. "I think I'm going to go over to Germany and discuss it with Goering. He was quite a pilot himself in the Great War." Georgia winced. Had she heard him wrong? Thank God Stieglitz wasn't here!

Peter Wainwright now leaned in toward Mrs. Lindbergh. "I'm trying to teach Lanny and Carson's kids a bit of astronomy." It was a valiant effort to try to include Mrs. Lindbergh in her husband's conversation and distract her from Lanny's graceless performance. "The nights are so clear out here. And the Perseid showers will begin soon. Does that interest you at all, Mrs. Lindbergh? They are so beautiful. You're welcome to join the children and me on one of our viewing nights."

"Oh, yes. I actually minored in astronomy at Smith."

"Wonderful! Maybe you could give the Powell kids a lesson. I have a pretty good scope here."

"That would be lovely," she said breathlessly and turned her attention back to her husband, who appeared still to be in deep conversation with Lanny. However, Lanny was now aware that Georgia had joined the party. "Georgia, Charles here"—she gently touched his hand—"was telling us that he has been invited to Germany to meet with Hermann Goering and possibly Adolf Hitler." She glanced quickly about to see if anyone else seemed shocked or expressed the slightest dismay as to what Lindbergh had just said. Not in the least. It was disturbing.

Lindbergh dipped his chin, meeting no one's eyes at the table, and, with that small aw-shucks smile he was known for, replied, "Nothing's for sure, ma'am. But I'd be interested, of course."

Georgia found this peculiar. She tipped her head to one side. "Why would you find it interesting? That man Hitler seems horrible to me." She slid her eyes to her left, where Carson sat, then glanced toward Peter Wainwright. Nothing seemed to have registered with anyone.

"Well, ma'am, they've actually made remarkable strides since the war. You know, certain races throughout the years have demonstrated their superior abilities in the design, manufacture, and operation of machines. The Germans are certainly one of those. You can't deny it." She wasn't about to deny anything. But she had already asserted that Hitler was a horrible man. She thought she'd better just leave it at that. "We know very little about the present status of the aviation industry in Germany. They say that, in fact, they have created a plane that can take off straight up into the air—no taxiing."

Still, she couldn't quite leave things alone. "But what about this fool Hitler?" Georgia asked. "These rallies."

"Well, ma'am, to tell you the truth, I think it's lucky that Germany is between Communist Russia and the rest of Europe. France is so aggrieved, who knows what could happen if they get back on their feet again? With the extremes of government that now exist, it is more desirable than ever to keep any one of them from sweeping over Europe. But it sure can't be Communism." She remained silent for a few seconds and furtively looked about, trying to ascertain how others were reacting to this. Were there any ripples in the placid pond of luxury and privilege? Not a one. She took a deep breath.

"But surely it can't be this madman Hitler."

As she spoke, Georgia slid her eyes toward Mrs. Lindbergh. If fear had a smell, Anne Morrow Lindbergh would have reeked. A desperate light seemed to flicker behind her lovely blue-gray eyes. In that moment Georgia felt profoundly sorry for the woman. She was married to America's golden divinity. But she seemed to know of a belligerent darkness in him, an attitude not borne out of the great public loss of their child but, rather, bred in the bone.

Luckily, Carmelita soon led them into the dining room. Georgia sighed as she took her place between R.W. and Charles Lindbergh. Innocuous talk followed through the first course, a summer corn soup served cold.

Lanny looked down at the soup. "Oh, my goodness. This reminds me. I nearly forgot! Less than two weeks from now until the first of the Corn Dances."

"Corn Dance?" replied Mrs. Lindbergh, a slight quaver in her voice. "Sounds fascinating." Georgia could tell that she was not really fascinated at all, just happy the topic of conversation had changed.

"A festival in Santo Domingo and one in Santa Clara, not far from here. All the Pueblo Indians come together to dance. They wear headdresses and all sorts of costumes, and there's wonderful food."

"Is it a religious festival?" Anne asked.

"Yes, I suppose so. But perhaps it's more like Thanksgiving—thankful for the corn they have grown. Isn't that right, Georgia?" Lanny said, turning to her.

"Religious in a way. But as I understand it, it's very much tied in with the Indian legends of Blue Corn Woman and White Corn Maiden and something they call the Lake of Emergence. I suppose you could say they're the Pueblo creation stories."

The conversation went on harmlessly enough until R.W. Johnson turned to Charles and said, "You really think that France is so 'aggrieved,' as you said, that they would pick a fight with Germany after all they've been through?"

"Well, sir." Charles looked down at his plate. "I do fear that it could come, sooner or later. And I worry about the British, and I worry about Roosevelt and the Jews he has surrounded himself with." Georgia dropped her fork with a clatter on her plate. She simply did not know what to say. How had such talk become acceptable dinner conversation? He turned to her.

"Oh, I didn't mean to alarm you, ma'am."

"My husband is a Jew."

"But he's not a war agitator."

"Of course, I know that! But you have just neatly reduced the complexity of the human race to three categories and stuffed them into one goddamn sack."

She stood, balled up her napkin, and threw it down.

"Oh, ma'am." The curly-haired hero popped straight up. "I didn't mean to offend you."

"Mr. Lindbergh, you didn't simply offend *me*. You succeeded in offending two nations, a president, and a religion!"

Carmelita, who had been standing a short distance away supervising the waiters, seemed to have frozen in place.

As Georgia went by her, she whispered in a hot voice, "Don't you ever invite me to sit with that vile man again, Carmelita."

She stomped into the night.

An hour later as she undressed, she heard the roar of a motorcycle on the road outside. She looked out her bedroom window. It had to be Peter Wainwright. He was the only one who lived close to her own casita. The motorcycle was an Ariel Red Hunter. Very expensive. It was rumored that Lanny had bought it for him. They certainly raced around the ranch on it quite a bit. But tonight he seemed to be riding it alone. "Hmmm ... I wonder if someone feels scorned," she murmured.

Chapter 9

Peter Wainwright had, in fact, also left the dinner party at the Hacienda steaming, but for different reasons than Georgia's. Why did Lanny do this to him? Her outrageous flirting seemed to be her default behavior every time he told her that they simply couldn't run off together because he had to finish his thesis. "Oh, nonsense," she would say in that dismissive voice he hated. "Why do you need a thesis? Scholarship is just an excuse for not embracing real life. Real people get up and do things. I have the money—you know that." Then she would launch into how they could become the first couple of American wildlife preservation and archaeology. She had a scheme to reintroduce pronghorn, a kind of goat antelope, to the Ghost Ranch.

But in truth, it was Carson's scheme she had purloined. Peter felt that he was trapped. He wasn't sure exactly how this had happened, but it had. And, admittedly, he had been somewhat complicit. She had paid for his last term at Princeton and promised to pay for graduate work once he got his degree. She imagined herself as his research assistant. He knew for a fact that she had been rejected by both Radcliffe and Wellesley. This had propelled her into marriage with Carson, and immediately they had begun having children. She loved sex. She just didn't realize that the by-product could be boring.

He had to admit that, once he met Lanny, he loved sex too. "Pussy-whipped," he had heard a wrangler mutter once to another when he was seen with Lanny. And if they didn't say it out loud, he could tell by the looks exchanged. How could he blame them? He liked those guys, even though they teased him. He liked their peyote too, and that was where he was heading: to the grub house, where the wranglers often gathered. There was a fug of peyote in the air, but something else too. They must be smoking it in marijuana leaves. Some of the caps were merely chewed after the button had been cut from the roots of the cactus and dried.

Tomas Benally looked up as Peter Wainwright came into the grub house. He seemed nice enough but, at the same time, seemed out of place. As tutor for the Powell children, he wasn't exactly a guest, but neither was he a ranch employee. There was nothing clear-cut about him except for this Princeton thing. He never seemed quite comfortable down at the Hacienda, but he sure didn't fit in with the wranglers either. However, there was no doubt he like the peyote. Nevertheless, Tomas felt a little bit sorry for him. A phrase Tomas's mother often used came to him: *Corazon de un Huerfano,* "orphan heart."

"Mr. Tiger is here," a wrangler called out. Gentle laughter arose. Peter had a sweatshirt he sometimes wore on cool evenings that had a Princeton tiger emblazoned on it. The wranglers found this curiously amusing. And so they often called him Mr. Tiger.

"You want to smoke or chew? My sister picks the best, you know," Tomas said. He nodded at Rosaria, who sat demurely with a heap of peyote buttons in her lap. "She'll pick you some good ones."

He watched Peter Wainwright walk over to where his sister Rosaria sat. Maybe he'd been wrong about Peter, but he'd sworn the guy was coming on to him the other day when he'd agreed to take him and the Powell kids on a ride to Black Mesa.

Peter sat down by Rosaria and she picked out a few buttons. He couldn't seem to take his eyes off her as she dropped the first button in his hand.

"Chew slow, and take a few breaths every now and then," she cautioned him. Tomas could see that Wainwright savored the touch of her hand on his.

For Peter Wainwright there was something kindling in the brush of her hand as she dropped the buttons into his palm. He remembered scant hours ago how Lanny had touched Lindbergh's hand. He wished she could see him now. He peered into Rosaria's deep brown eyes. It seemed as if in their very depths, there were licks of gold.

"Thank you, ma'am." She shrugged. Her breasts moved slightly beneath the thin fabric of her blouse. A minute later—or was it an hour? Who knew, but someone passed him a joint.

As she was bending down in front of him and offering him a cup of peyote tea, there was another voice: "Rosaria makes the best tea." He could see the crease between her breasts—the furrow ... pleat ... tuck ... what was it? How would one describe this lovely groove between the two gorgeous mounds? A pleasant euphoria enfolded him. Shadows, colors, shapes began to stream through him. He could feel the colors and grasp the soft shapes. There was a pleasant prickle of straw beneath him and billowy clouds. *I am healing. This woman beneath me is healing me, in every way*, he thought, as they moved rhythmically through a landscape of the massing clouds and shimmering colors.

I am cleansed, Rosaria thought as she felt Peter Wainwright enter her. Peter Wainwright was having similar thoughts. He too felt cleansed. Cleansed of Lanny and her money. Cleansed of gorgeous tigers. She ran her fingers through his thick hair.

Neither one of them heard the thud of a sheathed knife dropping to the floor from the bed of the empty bunkhouse where they lay. A strong wind began to blow. They curled around each other, snug in the flickering light of their dreams.

Anger perhaps was the best antidote to fear, Georgia thought. The *X* on the map with her initials receded from her head as she steamed over the events at the Hacienda dinner. But Lindbergh's words still blistered: *"I worry about Roosevelt, and the Jews he has surrounded himself with."* Sleep was impossible. She finally decided to go up onto the roof. Looking straight up into the glittering canopy of a starry night often calmed her. As she reached the top and, though her rage had not abated in the least, she inhaled deeply and stood in wonder at the beautiful night. The grove of piñons to the south appeared like black embroidery against the gray of the moon-bleached landscape. Here and there a cholla cactus punctuated the half-darkness. Their twisted forms reminded her of bent old men. But mostly there was the deep silence and the empty arch of the sky. Was the sky black? Not quite, but maybe an inky blue. In the silence, in the stillness of the evening, she let the clamor of those awful words at the dinner table dissolve.

A light breeze stirred. From the corner of her eye she caught a wisp of something blowing across the patio and fetching up in a clump of sagebrush. Rosaria must have forgotten to put the top on the trash bins. She'd check when she went back down from the roof. But within a minute, it looked as if there was a small blizzard on the patio—a blizzard not of snow but of paper scraps. Georgia felt a darkness swim up within her as she walked to the edge of the roof and looked down. Instinctively, she guessed that these scraps were Clara's torn-up drawings. She went slowly to the ladder, as if to prepare herself for what she would find when she descended.

Once her foot hit the last rung, she took a deep breath then rushed into the maelstrom of torn paper She was gasping after two minutes. Her hands clutched wads of paper fragments. She went into her studio, dumped them on the floor, then bolted out the door again. She swept across the patio like a possessed bird. Two more times she went out to gather every scrap she could find. She then went into the shed that held the trash bins. It was obvious that the lid had not been secured on one of the bins, and at the bottom were a few more pieces of paper, which she gathered up. Once back in her studio, sitting on the floor, she began sorting through the scraps, piecing them together until they made some meaning or sense. It would be a long night, and that "sense" would soon reveal an incontrovertible truth.

The teeth were huge and black. The figures, always two—one small and armless, one large with three arms. At first she thought they were arms, but then she realized that the third "arm" was actually a phallus; sometimes that phallus turned into a whip that was beating the smaller figure. The smaller figure had no mouth. It seemed to float in a sort of limbo but radiated waves, as if to indicate silent screams issuing from its mouthless face. Georgia felt as though she had walked into the middle of a nightmare.

Finally, just as dawn broke and the first light began to seep over the edges of her world, Georgia, still on the floor, grasped her knees, buried her face in her arms, and sobbed uncontrollably. "Poor Clara. Poor, poor Clara."

That same moment, the newly installed phone in the stable at the Ghost Ranch rang just as Tomas watched his sister walk off with Peter Wainwright. It sounded distant, far more distant than it actually was to Tomas, who had just begun to chew a button. *Odd hour of the night for the phone to ring up here,* Tomas thought. Why would the vet be calling about something at this time of the night? Just then, Jack McKinley, the head wrangler, called out to him.

"You too far gone to take a call?"

"Did they say who it is?" *Stupid question,* Tomas thought. As if Sissy or Gwendolyn would say.

"Nope. But very fancy voice. Possible debutante. You know how those debutantes go for you, Tomas." He laughed. "Tell me, do you ever give their asses a little pinch?"

"Yeah, sure; you'd throw me be out of here on my ass if I did."

"Damn right."

"*Hola,*" Tomas said, picking up the phone.

"Got someone coming in." It was Sissy. Tomas loved her crisp English accent. He wondered if he'd ever meet her in person. But she was all-business, this one. "Has his own setup. However, check the one out at W.P. Figure out the coordinates with the latest you gave us."

"You bet." He hung up. Had to sober up fast. Water. Lots of water. He went to the bunkhouse. Stepped into a shower. He'd take his car to the house he shared with Rosaria in Abiquiu; get Flint, his pinto; and ride out to the White Place, a couple miles east of Abiquiu. He had to ride and not take a car. The last time he'd gone out to install a setup, he had the feeling he might have been followed despite his precautions.

Tomas was pleased that Sissy and company had taken him seriously when he had sent the message that he had picked up a possible outlier signal. And now, someone coming in meant they could set up another Hartley transmitter-receiver with cross bearings to pinpoint where this signal was originating. He found a unique satisfaction in the process of assembling a set—the coils of winding copper wire, the transformers, the large valves—all the parts, the guts of the radio. He had picked up the technical skills so quickly and had learned how to build the transmitters, receivers, rectifiers, and frequency meters within a matter of weeks. He loved the work the way he loved rodeo riding. Crazy, he knew. He couldn't, and of course he shouldn't, explain to anybody what attracted him to this.

An hour later he dismounted from Flint and tied the lead line to a cottonwood, although this was hardly necessary. It took an earthquake for Flint to shy. Taking his saddlebag, he walked perhaps twenty feet toward a rock that was no more than a foot across. He shoved it aside then took out his knife and gently began scraping at the dirt. There was a slightly muffled clink of metal against metal. The moon, just a sliver above, provided enough light to reflect off the metal cap, which he removed then drew out the antenna. Then he took the field radio from his saddlebag and hooked the antenna jack into the socket on the radio.

Tubes began to glow. He loved this part. It was as if a miniature city had suddenly sprouted in the desert. He put on his earphones. There was the familiar crackling. He swiveled the direction-finding antenna. There it was, the maverick signal on the 6087 MHz frequency from 245 degrees slightly north of west. He was going to need another receiver to pinpoint the location of the new station in order to set up cross bearings. But how many others were out there? Four so far. He clamped his eyes shut and imagined countless transmitting stations out there combing the air of this empty land. Listening ... just listening for a war that might never come.

Chapter 10

Georgia had lost track of time, but when she finally got up from the floor of the studio where the fragments of those awful drawings were laid out and walked outside to the courtyard, she knew one thing. She had to immediately get a bucket of cold water from the well in the courtyard and pour it over her head. She had to clear those images from whatever part of her brain they had lodged, at least for now.

"Just do that one thing," she whispered to herself. She stopped and paused as she was about to step onto the patio. No, two things she had to do. Between her and that cold bucket of water, a large, fat rattlesnake was stretched across the paving stones, basking in the first rays of light. She reached for one of her snake sticks and strode the short distance between her and the cool water. The snake was slow. Light flashed off the blade as the point went right through the head but behind the eyes. No snapping jaws this time. She got a shovel and scraped it up, then walked twenty feet or more from the patio and buried the mess in the soft dirt.

"So long, buddy," she said, stomping on the dirt.

She returned to the patio, hauled up the bucket of chilly water that came from the Chama springs, and poured it over her head, not bothering to take off her dress from the night before. That was just the first of three buckets. Did she feel cleansed? Not really. But ready to think at least. She came to a quick decision. She could not tell Rosaria. This was not a matter to be discussed with her.

Once again, Georgia had the feeling that her life was becoming too complicated, that there was a rising tide of clutter. But how could she think of this child, this violated child, as clutter? Those charcoal draw-ings jarred her out of her ridiculous hopes of tranquility, of solitude. She could not turn her back on this. Georgia knew she was often selfish, but now it was not her art that had been offended, not her precious solitude, but her sense of justice.

She drove up to the bunkhouse where the wranglers, cowboys, and guides boarded. She pulled over as she saw Jack McKinley, the head wrangler, come out. He waved at her and came over to her car window.

"Hello there, Miss O'Keeffe. Ready to ride on this fine morning?"

"No. No. Not today."

"Now you're sure?" He crinkled his eyes, and they flashed a bright blue, blue as the sky. Oh my, how the lady guests went nuts for him, she thought.

"Yes, I'm sure. I'm looking for Tomas. He around?"

"Sorry to say, no. This is his day to work at the garage in Santa Fe. He's a mechanic there. We could have used him too. We got a full house up at the Hacienda. Lucky Lindy, his wife, and a few others want to go out for a ride. And did you hear about Diego Sanchez?"

"The movie actor?"

"Yes, ma'am. They've been making that movie over there in Monument Valley, and he and his new wife are coming here."

"Oh dear." Georgia was slowly remembering. She had met this new wife four or five years before at Mabel Dodge Luhan's place in Taos. A ridicu-lous socialite, from Philadelphia no less, just like Dorothy Norman. She wasn't Sanchez's wife then. She was just out trolling for "artistic adven-ture," which included a roll in the hay with Isadora Duncan. "Art is an adventure" seemed to be her favorite line. And so was sex, Georgia guessed.

"Well, thanks, Jack."

She wasn't sure what her next step should be. Keeping Clara safe was the first thing that needed to be done. But how? Where? And who did this to Clara? She felt as if she had hit an impasse. Even the word *molesta-tion* was almost unspeakable. Actually, it *was* unspeakable. She recalled from years back that her parents had warned her not to hang around Mr. Winerick's place. Her parents had spoken in some sort of coded language that was meant to warn but not explain. Then when she was perhaps in sixth grade, there was what was called "an incident" with a child who was no more than six or seven. The family left town abruptly. A few years later there was another "incident," with a girl who was maybe thirteen. Again no one spoke of it. But several months later, the girl—Edna was her name—was found dead. She had drunk an entire bottle of weed killer concentrate. There were all sorts of rumors, not about the crime but how she had flavored the weed killer with lemonade and her father's favorite whiskey. "Lemonade." Georgia whispered the word. Tears began to sting her eyes. She looked into the mirror and blinked several times. "Damn you, Georgia." Something savage began to rise in her. She glimpsed a new light in her eyes—something feral. She was going to have to name the unnamable. But to whom? How?

When she walked into her kitchen ten minutes later, she saw another note on the table. She groaned, seeing it was on Ghost Ranch stationery. She prayed it wasn't from Carmelita. It wasn't. Different handwriting. It was from Luz, Carmelita's assistant.

Miss O'Keeffe,

A phone call came in here for you this morning from a gentleman, Simon Bowes. Long-distance—a very long distance. London, I believe. He's with some magazine, Collokwee. *He needs you to call him soon as possible. He would like to come here to the ranch to interview you.*

Luz

Collokwee? Odd name. Then it dawned on her: Luz must mean *Colloquy.* It was an art magazine in London. But as far as she was concerned, there were no emergencies in the art world. And why would he want to come here? *Schlep* here, as Stieglitz would say. Come to think of it, why hadn't Stieglitz handled this? Why hadn't Mr. Bowes contacted Stieglitz? London!

She thought. The farthing ... the *X* with her initials on that map? Well, maybe she should check into this. It disturbed her that a London art magazine could track her all the way to the desert. But first she wanted to talk to the sheriff, if he would talk to her again. He might slam the door in her face after their little exchange on the road out of Albuquerque. She could apologize, she realized. It wouldn't kill her. Stieglitz once told her that she was so stubborn that even when she was wrong and knew it, she'd never apologize. "It's not in your wheelhouse, Georgia, dear, to apologize." Well, maybe it was time to open up her wheelhouse a bit more. *I can apologize*, she thought. *Not to Lindbergh. But yes, I can do that to the sheriff.*

As she was about to leave, she wondered if she should also tell the sheriff about Clara's terrible drawings. The idea of discussing them with Ryan McCaffrey was not easy.

On her drive into Santa Fe, for some reason she began to ruminate about snakes. It was snake time out here, as the one on her patio had reminded her. Just driving to Santa Fe, one could expect to see half a dozen dead ones pressed flat on the road. She didn't like seeing them dead, but sometimes there was no choice. Particularly when they came between her and water, as the one on the patio had.

The sheriff had the phone wedged between his shoulder and ear as he looked down at a carbon copy of the shipping papers on his desk that Gus Montez had provided him. On the other end of the line was his friend Ray at the BI, Bureau of Investigation.

"Why are you calling me about this, Ryan?"

"Because the body was shipped to Washington to some nutty address that supposedly is a funeral home, and when that happens, it usually means the BI is involved in some way, shape, or form."

"You're jumping to conclusions, and what do you mean 'supposedly'?"

"Well, I can't track down the Morgan Smathers Funeral Home."

"Have you tried?"

"Of course I've tried. How else would I know I can't find it?"

"You're getting philosophical on me, Ryan. If a tree falls in a forest and no one is there to hear it, does it make a sound?"

"This is not some philosophical exercise, Ray. This is a death, a murder. It happened. I'm just trying to find out why and who the victim really is. Maybe more important, who the mourners might be." And though he did not say it, who would gain from this death. That was the real question. He sighed deeply. "Well, thanks for nothing, buddy."

"Don't go grumpy on me, Ryan."

"I am grumpy." He hung up and stared at the phone.

Sheriff McCaffrey peered down at the farthing and then the document that released the body of Monsignor Alberto Castenada for shipping to Washington, DC. Why DC? So far, nothing was making sense in this case. He had lots of random bits of information that defied logic. A monastery that didn't exist. A gun and a pack of condoms. The commando knife hurled by an expert. Why would someone pretend to be a priest? Or maybe he was a priest but just a randy one? That could explain the condoms, but not the gun. And if you were such a priest, why list as your residence a monastery that had burned to the ground decades ago?

Nothing was fitting. And Ryan McCaffrey did not like things that didn't fit. The tailor in him was coming out. He was puzzled by this ill-fitting garment. It had no shape. There was a shape lurking somewhere. He just had to find it and place the darts properly. He eased himself back in his chair and stared at the crack in the ceiling as if he expected a clue to drop from it.

"Sheriff in?" Georgia asked the woman behind the desk at the Police Department.

"What might this concern?"

Georgia was facing a slightly prudish-looking middle-aged lady. Her hair was screwed up in a knot so tight that it looked as if it might be an experiment in the revolutionary surgery Georgia had read about—face-lifts. A new kind of torture on the quest for beauty and eternal youth. If this woman undid that bun, would she suddenly have jowls? Would her eyebrows drop two inches?

How could Georgia word it? *"I'm here about the murdered fake priest with condoms"*? Or maybe *"armed real priest with condoms"*? Georgia did not do well with bureaucrats, functionaries. She tipped her head to one side and regarded the woman, who was a few years older than herself. Definitely Anglo, no Indian blood. The woman appeared slightly flustered. Georgia was not flustered in the least. She rocked back and forth on her heels, as if to suggest she was settling in. She'd seen Stieglitz do this so often when he was holding firm with an art dealer on a price. It was almost as if her feet sank an inch or so into the wood floor. She definitely gave the appearance that she was here to stay. She simply looked at the woman and blinked a couple of times.

"Florence, just tell him Georgia is here." *To apologize and to conduct related business*, she thought.

"How did you know my name is Florence?"

"There's a sign on your desk. It says Florence Gilbert. Tell him Georgia O'Keeffe is here." *What a detective I am!*

"Oh?" Florence blinked now. Her eyes, behind her bifocals, appeared magnified and lashless. The bottom eyelids were quite pink. The entire effect was one of appearing perpetually startled. She rose from her desk, walked over to the sheriff's office door, and tapped lightly on it.

"Come in."

Florence Gilbert entered—and shut the door firmly behind her.

Three seconds later, the sheriff came striding through.

"Georgia!" He seemed shocked but delighted. It had been less than twenty-four hours since their rendezvous for speeding.

Florence seemed even more startled by this warm greeting and stepped back to her desk. Georgia began to follow the sheriff but then turned back and walked over to the desk.

"Florence, thank you so much. And you may call me Georgia too. Like Ryan does."

Florence's thin lips moved, as if trying to find the shape of a word in response. Then she simply nodded.

"So, something … uh … something new?" Ryan said, settling behind his desk and indicating a chair for Georgia to sit in.

Too much new, she thought. "Well, yes. This is new for me, but I'm here to apologize for what I said yesterday."

"Oh, don't worry about it."

"But it was a problem for me. You see, I'm not that good when it comes to apologizing. Stieglitz says it's not in my wheelhouse."

"Stieglitz?"

"My husband."

"He's a nautical sort?"

"Hardly," Georgia laughed. "But, as I said, I came to apologize."

"I was going to write you a note and apologize for my behavior. My wife, my late wife, Mattie, would have called me an A-M."

"A-M?"

"Ape man—crude, vulgar and stupid, unevolved."

Georgia tipped her head. She felt a trace of a smile began to crawl across her face. "Ooh, I like that—unevolved." She spoke softly, savoring the word. "I think I would have liked Mattie."

"I think you would have, Georgia." She looked at him. His eyes were now a very soft blue. *Oh God, I've made him cry.*

"Well, I was kind of a … a jerk," she replied. She'd heard one of Stieglitz's nieces used that term. "You know, sounding off about women and stuff." She quickly backpedaled. "But then again, this women stuff, it is true, Ryan."

This somehow provoked mirth in those eyes, and he slapped his knee.

"My God, woman, you are something!" It was a compliment. Perhaps the best she'd ever received. "So what brings you here?"

"Murder, farthings, London maybe."

"You're trying to connect the dots."

Was there a just a tinge of a patronizing tone in his voice? Well, she was going to cut him off at the pass on that.

"London is one of the dots. I got a message this morning from Carmelita that there had been a call for me from London. No phones in the casitas. And I was hesitant to call from Carmelita's office—not much privacy. Anyhow, I think there's something odd about it—a call coming all the way from London."

The sheriff eased back in his chair and laced his fingers over his belly. "Odder than a priest with a gun and condoms?"

"Possibly. You see, Ryan." She paused for several seconds. "Well, those *X*'s on the map. Are they part of the dots?"

"You're worried? I can get you protection."

"No, no." This was not going the way she planned.

"Who did Carmelita say the call was from?" Ryan asked.

"A journalist for an art magazine, Simon something. I did not speak to him directly. Carmelita took the message."

Ryan compressed his lips and raised his eyebrows. His thought was implicit: *So?*

"Yes, 'So?' you might say," Georgia replied to the unspoken word. She could read faces, facial expressions, like blind people read braille.

"Yep, I was going to say that." But then Ryan leaned forward and planted his elbows on the desk. "The farthing, London, art, the *X*'s on the map."

She was glad he, not she, was saying this. So maybe she wasn't jumping to conclusions. "Yes but ... but ... ," she stammered. "And my house was marked—you know the initials and the *X*. Maybe I'm stretching this connection between the farthing and this London magazine and my initials on a map. Nevertheless, this Simon would like to come here, to New Mexico. Seems like a long way to talk to an artist."

"How'd he get hold of you?"

"Stieglitz, I presume."

"Oh, that's your manager ... uh, husband."

"Oh, yes, that he is." She paused and looked at Ryan directly. "I actually prefer the word *agent* to *manager*."

"Well, why not call your agent, Mr. Stieglitz, and ask him?" Ryan said curtly. "You can use this phone." He got up as if to leave.

"Oh, you don't need to leave." This was an awkward moment. "It's nothing personal after all … just maybe murder." She gave a weak little chuckle.

"No, that's all right. I wanted to get a cup of coffee anyway. Be back in five."

————

The phone rang five times before anyone picked up. "Hello?" Goddammit, it was Kitty, Stieglitz's spoiled, cranky daughter.

"Kitty, it's Georgia."

"Oh, finally."

"Not finally, Kitty; you and I talked last week. And you didn't give him the message."

"It must have slipped my mind."

"What mind?" Georgia was tempted to say.

She heard Stieglitz's voice in the background. "Who is it?"

"Georgia," Kitty replied dully.

"Well for heaven's sake, give it to me!" Georgia loved it when Stieglitz roared at Kitty.

"Darling!" he gasped. "Is something wrong?"

"No … no … dear. All is well. It's just that I got this message that a certain Simon Bowes had called and left a message at Ghost Ranch."

"Oh, yes, yes. I was going to call you today and leave a message myself that if he wants to schlep across an ocean and a desert to see you, he should first talk to you directly. But I feel this is a very good opportunity. I mean, there are good collectors over there, dearest."

"Who, King George?"

"No! But I'll tell you who."

"Who?"

"Lady Mountbatten."

"Really?"

"Yes, really. Her grandfather was the richest man in England, Ernest Cassel. And guess what else?"

"What?"

"He was Jewish."

"Good Lord." *Don't tell Lindbergh.*

"He's dead now, but she inherited the lot, and unlike some members of the royal family, she's got taste."

"Lord Mountbatten is quite a dashing figure, I must say."

"Well, don't run off with him, dear. Little Man misses Fluffy."

"Oh, Alfred! Not on the phone."

He giggled. Yes, Stieglitz could giggle. It always sounded halfway between a hiccup and a cough, but it was a genuine giggle.

"All right, this call is costing a lot of money." There was no way he could tell that she was calling from the police station. "Just one second. I heard that Lindbergh is out there. That true?"

"Unfortunately, yes."

"Ah-ha!" Stieglitz said.

"You know something?" Georgia asked.

"Probably the same thing you know—he hates Jews."

"How do you know this, Alfred?"

"Fritzy."

"Oh, Fritzy. I haven't thought about him in years."

Stieglitz was fascinated by spies. When she once asked him if Fritz Freihoff was one, he seemed to dither a bit, not characteristic of him. *"Well, not exactly a spy,"* he had said. *"Technically he was a cryptographer."* Fritzy Freihoff. He was too smart to be a spy, he had told her. He and Fritzy had met in elementary school in New Jersey, but it was when the Freihoffs told Stieglitz's parents that they were going back to Germany in 1881 for better schooling and the Stieglitzes also decided to return that Alfred and Fritzy became fast friends. "You think Einstein's a genius—I got news for you; this guy makes him look like a dolt," Alfred had once told her. Georgia had met Fritzy once. He had come to Stieglitz's gallery and bought one of Alfred's photographs.

There was a discreet knock on the door just as she was finishing the conversation. "Got to go, dear."

"All right, My Faraway One!" he replied.

"So?" Ryan said as he walked into his office. It took Georgia a minute to relocate herself. Stieglitz's voice still rang in her head. *Fluffy, Miss Fluffy.* She almost blushed. For a split second, although she was fully clothed, she felt that she was standing naked for Stieglitz's camera. The jutting pelvic bones. The dark mist of pubic hair. And then of course the terrible nude photograph of her breasts that had been slipped under the door. Should she tell Ryan McCaffrey? She couldn't. She simply couldn't. She composed herself quickly.

"Yes, Mr. Bowes called Stieglitz."

"And?"

"And he said he wanted to do an article on me, and Stieglitz said, well, that I was gone indefinitely, so he better just try and reach me out here."

"Did Stieglitz say he'd ever heard of the guy?"

"He hadn't heard of Bowes specifically, but he's certainly heard of the magazine *Colloquy*. He thinks it would be good. The market is coming back in London."

"I think you should see him too. Tell him to come on over here."

"Why?"

"Okay, let me put it this way. Do art magazines make a lot of money?"

"I doubt it. It's auction houses and art agents who make all the money."

"Exactly! And I don't know that much about art or auctions or art agents. But do you think this magazine, *Colloquy*, has the kind of budget for ship passage to New York, then a train to come out here?"

"You've got a point there."

"Absolutely—just like Franciscan priests don't have a lot of money and yet he had reserved one of the most expensive casitas at Ghost Ranch, and they don't usually carry guns or condoms."

"But comparing this—Simon Bowes—with that, well, isn't it just a kind of coincidence?" Georgia asked.

"I don't believe in coincidences. Coincidence is just a reason waiting to be revealed."

"Hmm …" Georgia poked at her hair, which was in a very loose bun that was threatening to come undone. Which it did a second later.

Ryan opened his eyes wide. A warmth seemed to flow from them. "You got nice hair, Georgia."

"Oh …" She paused as she tucked the hairpins back in. "So you think I should tell him to come out here? Travel all that way, miles and miles for an article on me?"

"Yeah. I want to meet this guy."

"You do, do you?"

"Yes, and you invite him for dinner."

"I have to make dinner for him? Why would I want to cook for this perfect stranger?" She paused. His dark blue eyes looked across the desk at her expectantly. "All right," she growled. "I guess I'll have to call him back."

"Do it from here. Put it on my tab"

"I suppose I could. I brought the number. What time would it be there?

"Let's see. It's nine a.m. here. So there it would be maybe five in the evening. He might be in still. He must be aware of the time difference."

"Don't you imagine he'll think it's weird, me calling from a police station?"

"He'll never know. Just say it was easier to call from town. Better connection. Tell him you're at a friend's house."

"A friend who happens to be a cop?"

Ryan smiled quizzically. "Or the order is more like a cop who became a friend."

"Oh," Georgia said softly, suppressing a small gasp. She could have first brought up Clara's terrible drawings, but somehow she couldn't face discussing them with the sheriff quite yet. It was so vile. So repugnant. She didn't want him to really ever see those drawings. It was a crime—molestation. A dirty little crime, but how to talk about it? Murder seemed so much easier.

Chapter 11

"Well, Mr. Bowes, yes, you can come and visit." The connection was a bit crackly. "You say you want to do an article about landscape painting from Turner to O'Keeffe?" More static. "A whale must be swimming over the lines of the transatlantic cable," she said as loud as she could.

There was a great guffaw from Mr. Bowes. "Yes, Miss O'Keeffe. You're in good company with J. M. W. Turner. Good company. Yes, he was a very fine painter."

"But gracious," Georgia replied. "He ended up living in squalor, and his gallery fell into disrepair ... very sad ending."

"Yes, very sad, Miss O'Keeffe. Very sad indeed."

"So you'll be arriving in New York seven days from tomorrow?" She rolled her eyes at Ryan, who was listening on the extension across the room. "You already got your reservations?"

There was some more innocuous chitchat. "Well, we got a lot of sun out here, so bring a broad-brimmed hat. Leave your trilby at home."

"Wouldn't be caught dead in one." *Let's hope not*, Georgia was tempted to say. "Yes ... Yes and cheerio to you." Georgia set down the phone. She looked at her hand that was still resting on the receiver. "What a silly word. How'd they ever come up with that?"

"So, when's he getting to New York ?"

"A week from Tuesday. Then in another three days here in Santa Fe. He's calling Carmelita now to book a casita." She sighed. "I suppose, as you said, I should invite him to dinner." She gave a mournful sigh.

"That's not so bad, is it?" Ryan asked. A slight frown crinkled her brow.

"It is if you planned on cooking only for yourself all summer."

"I'll help you out."

"You cook?"

"And sew."

A smile now replaced the incipient frown on Georgia's brow. "Well, I'll be!"

"Yeah, I'm quite the catch. And I can shoot straight."

"So can I. When my sister Claudie lived with me when I was teaching at a small art school in Texas, we used to shoot at tin cans in the evening. It was nice ..." She paused. "I don't know why, but I found it relaxing for some reason after teaching all day long."

"Where did you teach?"

"West Texas Normal College near Amarillo in the Panhandle. I fell in love with the light—the dust and the light. Could have eaten that dust. It saturated everything—your clothes, your underwear, cupboards, closets, my hair. Probably washed half a cup out of my hair every night." She sighed as she recalled those evenings with her sister Claudie. "That was years ago—B.S."

"B.S.?"

"Oh dear, not bullshit. Before Stieglitz."

"Sounds like that was a landmark event in your life, Stieglitz that is."

"Yes, it was ..." She paused and sighed deeply. "And still is. A marker."

Chapter 12

On her way back to Ghost Ranch, she began composing the dinner menu for Simon Bowes's visit and realized she was going to need some spices from Goetz's general store. There was an amazing range of items in that store—from tire patches to paint thinner and Mexican chili lime powder, a unique spice that absolutely made her lamb stew.

"Ah, Miss O'Keeffe. So nice to see you," Otto Mueller said. "How might I help you?"

"I need some of that wonderful chili lime powder. Just a bit. Maybe an ounce at most."

"Yes, strong stuff."

Nina Mueller came out from the back. "Have you heard our good news, Miss O'Keeffe?" Otto asked, smiling at his wife.

"The baby news?"

"I told her, Otto," Nina said.

He giggled a bit. "I'm so excited, you know. I tell everyone who walks in here," Mueller said, putting an arm around his wife's shoulders and giving her a hug.

"You must be so excited," Georgia replied as he handed her the small bag of spice.

"Yes!" Nina said in a high-pitched voice. Her eyes had a peculiar brightness as she stared straight ahead. Her pale cheeks flushed. "And if it's a girl, we shall name her Gerda! Isn't that a fine name?" She looked up into her husband's face. He towered over her. All color suddenly drained from his face, making the pink worm of the scar on his temple even brighter as it crept toward his eyebrow.

Something is happening here between this husband and wife, Georgia thought. This was not simply a couple talking about the name of a baby. It was a coded, perilous conversation of sorts that flashed with menace.

The unspeakable tension that filled the small store could not be ignored. It was as if winter had swept thought the room. Everything had been fine, had been spring or summer until Nina said the name *Gerda*. She hadn't just said it. She had blurted it out. Seconds later the screen door slammed, breaking the tension as Clara came into the store. Georgia was shaken as she saw her. She had to do something about this child. The Muellers had disappeared into the stockroom at the back of the store.

"Hey there, Clara, can I buy you and José there an ice-cream cone?" She nodded at the boy who was shelving some boxes. "You can scoop us some ice cream, right, José?"

"Yes! It's my specialty." His joy in comparison to Clara's soberness was striking.

"It's so nice having a real soda fountain. Wonderful improvement," Georgia said as she and Clara settled on two stools.

"José, since you work here, you should know about that big antenna I saw on the roof. What's that about?"

"Oh, that's for Mr. Mueller's shortwave radio. He just got it. He's always on it. Crazy for it."

"Who does he talk to?"

"I wouldn't know, but he always is talking in German, so probably his family, I guess, or his friends over there." He sighed. "I can speak English pretty good. And Spanish. Navajo the best. But no German."

"I guess it's cheaper than using the telephone to call Germany."

Clara wandered over with her ice-cream cone to a display case. José followed her.

"See those knives, Clara?" he said.

"Hmm ..." was all Clara said.

"See the one on the left? I'm saving for that. It's a commando knife."

Georgia sat up straighter on the stool. The words sent a chill down her back. *"These knives should be outlawed."* Dr. Bryce's comment came back to her. She walked over to the case and looked at the knife. It was an elegant piece of work.

"*Mira* …" José spoke softly. He was clearly in awe. "Very light. You see, the blade how it's beveled, even though it's so narrow? The forward thrust is incredible. Some people call these knives falcons."

"Why?" Clara asked.

"Because falcons, especially peregrine falcons, are the fastest flying birds in the world. They say that when they go in for the kill, they can fly as fast as eighty miles an hour!"

"Wow!" Georgia said.

She looked on in amazement. José obviously knew something about physics. Maybe the young man should be studying physics instead of lethal knives that could fly. The sheriff's words came back to her: *"It's a knife designed for throwing—very aerodynamic."*

She heard the screen door swing open again.

The sunshine fell on a curly blond head. Charles Lindbergh stepped through the doorway.

"Hallo, Herr Mueller," he called out. *"Ich bin hier für meine Zigarren."*

Mr. Mueller came out from the back of the store. "Ah, Charles … yes, yes, I have your cigars." Mueller turned to Georgia. "And, Miss O'Keeffe, have you met our illustrious visitor?"

"Yes," she replied curtly. "We've met." Lindbergh gave her a taut smile.

"Oh!" Lindbergh said suddenly as he glimpsed Clara coming back to the ice-cream counter. "You must be related to that gal Rosaria, the pretty girl up at the Hacienda."

Georgia felt her skin crawl as if a thousand ants had suddenly swarmed over her. She strode over to Clara and slipped her arm through the girl's. "Come with me. I think they're selling some melons down the road at that stand. I'll get some for you."

As she was driving back to the Hacienda, she could not get Clara out of her mind. She needed to tell Ryan about those charcoal images. She should have told him when she went to ask about Bowes. In truth, she had conveniently forgotten. She vowed that she would go to the police station the first thing the next morning. Now this seemed to be her world. Two crimes. Murder and possible molestation of a child.

As she pulled up to the Hacienda to collect her mail, she saw a large silvery sedan. It must be the film star Diego Sanchez and his new wife. She had heard they were coming. She couldn't remember the wife's name for the life of her, though she had met her four years or so ago in Taos.

Carmelita was standing on the portico with an enormous bouquet of flowers. Georgia decided to park a little bit away from the entrance and try to sneak in through the side door. These scenes of Carmelita greeting celebrity guests were unbearable. Carmelita was always at her most unctuous. Beyond unctuous. She was positively oleaginous, and she insisted that "her" staff line up on either side of her to greet the guests. If Georgia could now just slip in through the side door. She began walking down a small path when a high-pitched voice suddenly drilled the air.

"Georgia! Georgia O'Keeffe!"

The voice emanated from beneath the enormous hat the new wife was wearing. She began waving madly. "Come here, darling. Diego would love to meet you."

"Come along." Carmelita was now waving. "Miss O'Keeffe, come over and meet our new guests."

There was no escaping now. Georgia trudged over. A froth of blond curls tumbled from beneath the brim of the hat framing a delicate pear-shaped face. She wore round white-framed sunglasses. *But what the hell was this woman's name?*

A slender gentleman in an impeccably tailored pale cream suit stepped forward. "Señora O'Keeffe." With a sweeping gesture, he removed his white bolero hat. "Felicity has been telling me all about you."

Felicity, of course. Felicity Wilder—heiress to, what was it? Paper business. Yes, newsprint paper, pulp. And from that her father, one Edward

Wilder, got into tabloid news—yellow journalism. He had come full circle from pulpwood to pulp journalism. He had created an empire based on pulp.

Felicity clasped Georgia's hand. "I cannot tell you how wonderful it is to see you again. Not since Mabel's. It was a difficult time for me. I had just broken up with Harry Belford and I was so lonely. Mabel's place was such a ... a solace ... for me."

"Yes." Georgia nodded. A solace in the arms of Isadora Duncan and a cloud of peyote.

"Do you do portraits, Señora O'Keeffe?" Diego Sanchez asked.

"Never," Georgia snapped. She hadn't meant to answer so harshly. "Just landscapes, Mr. Sanchez, mostly."

"Landscapes, señora. Well, let me tell you about the most beautiful, luscious ..." Georgia didn't like where this was going. "Yes, the most luscious landscape on earth is my wife, Felicity, nude reclining on a chaise longue."

She heard a small shriek of laughter from Carmelita. *How she must be enjoying this*, Georgia thought.

"Matisse already has done it. No one better."

"But the background's too busy with all that, how do you say ... wallpaper with flowers."

Georgia was now truly straining to be civil. "I think not."

Then Carmelita piped up. "Señor Sanchez has promised to teach us all the tango one evening." She clapped her hands

"Tango, how nice. But you're not from Argentina—I thought Mexico," Georgia commented.

"My mama, she was from Argentina. I learned from her." He suddenly embraced his wife and began sliding into a musicless tango. Felicity squealed with delight. "You see what a good teacher I am. Look at my darling Felicity. She learned all that just in the short time since we've been married—three months! No more. And when did we meet?"

"April fifteenth!"

The very date I was sprung from the loony bin, Georgia thought.

"Well, thank you very much, but I must be going. Just stopped inside to pick up my mail." She turned to Carmelita. "I know Tomas is not here today. But when he gets back, can you give him a message that I need my cistern filled?"

"Yes, Miss O'Keeffe. And remember tango night. We're thinking of doing it the day after tomorrow."

Over my dead body, Georgia thought as she walked into the Hacienda to collect her mail. She quickly reminded herself not to use such language, even if it was not out loud. But tango was not on her priorities list. Clara was!

When she walked into the lobby, she noticed that the display case had a new display with the arts and crafts of many of the Ghost Ranch workers. She always liked to check the case out, as so many of the workers were quite talented beadworkers or potters and weavers.

She peered down and saw an adorable pair of little buckskin booties. "Oh, my goodness," she sighed. "Aren't those lovely!"

"Indeed, Miss O'Keeffe." Carmelita said, coming up to the case.

"Who made them?"

"Elena, her beadwork is the finest around."

"I think maybe I'll buy those for Nina Mueller. You know there is a baby on the way!"

"Yes, all the way from Germany!" Carmelita said with delight. "I'll wrap them up for you."

"Thank you, just put it on my bill. I have an errand to run in tomorrow in Santa Fe, so I'll pick them up in the morning and drop them off at Abiquiu on my way."

"They'll be ready for you." Carmelita smiled broadly.

The following morning, Georgia was just pulling out from her place in front of Goetz's as a Ghost Ranch jeep was pulling in. She was expecting someone like Joaquin or perhaps Tomas to step from the car. But it was Charles Lindbergh. Thankfully, this time she had missed him in the store and there would be no awkward encounters. She heard the door slam as he entered.

Behind the counter, Nina Mueller was admiring the tiny little beaded booties that Miss O'Keeffe had just dropped off. She was murmuring softly in the cooing voice that one would use to lullaby an infant to sleep when the slam of the screen door jolted her out of her reveries.

"Ah, Herr Lindbergh."

"I hope I'm not interrupting."

"*Nein, nein,* of course not. I'm here tending the store. Here to serve. What can I do for you, Herr Lindbergh?"

"Why, look at those little booties?" He came over and peered down at the tiny booties. Nina felt a surge of empathy. So sad for him and Frau Lindbergh. It was an awkward moment. She didn't know what to say.

"Is Otto in?" He nodded toward the back office?

"*Nein*; he went to Albuquerque today to pick up some supplies."

"Might I use … the …" He broke off his words then nodded toward the stairwell to the store's upper floors.

"Of course, of course. Otto says you are always welcome. You know how it works." She paused and laughed a bit. "Not me."

"Dear, I can talk on a radio and fly a plane at the same time."

"Of course! How silly of me."

"Not silly all. Thank you, dear. And I can't wait to hear when your good news arrives. What a blessing."

"Thank you, sir. Indeed a blessing." She forced a smile and watched him with narrowed eyes as he went to the back to go upstairs. She couldn't help but think, *What does Mrs. Lindbergh know? Is she a good sport about all this? Soll ich es einfach hinnehmen,* she thought. *"Just be a good sport,"* as the Americans say.

Chapter 13

The same morning she dropped off the booties, Georgia went to the police station. She had to admit that she was very nervous. She would have been much more comfortable discussing this with a woman. Emily Bryce! Why had she not thought of her to begin with? It would be easier to speak to a woman about the unspeakable. And Emily was a doctor. That would be helpful too. Maybe she had dealt with child molestation cases. But now she was here. And just as she was thinking that she might pull out and try the coroner's office, the sheriff walked out. He leaned into the car window.

"My, my. What brings you here—another crime?"

"Uh, sort of."

"Let's go in and talk about it," he said, opening the car door. As they entered the station and walked by Florence's desk, he turned to Georgia. "Coffee?"

She gave him a sharp look. The meaning was clear. *"Not in front of Florence."*

"No, thanks."

He sat down behind his desk. "Have a seat. From your face I'd say this looks serious." She took a deep breath.

"It is, Ryan."

He leaned across the desk. "You okay, Georgia?"

"Yes, but it's a difficult thing to explain to a man. I realized just as I parked out front that I really need to discuss it with a woman."

He didn't say "I understand." He didn't say anything. But it was the way he looked at her across the desk. He just barely nodded his head, and she saw a softness in his eyes.

"You see, I found evidence—nothing to do with the murder. I saw evidence for what I believe is a crime—a crime against a child."

"Abuse?"

"Uh, molestation."

"Same thing basically. That's what they call it now—sexual abuse."

"I can show you some of the drawings the child made if you want." The images swam up from some dark place inside her. She shut her eyes and began to whisper, "There were no eyes in the faces. No eyes," she repeated. "But lots of teeth. Terrible teeth like … like a shark's."

When she opened her eyes, the sheriff was quiet for several seconds. He sighed.

"I think you should talk with Emily."

Georgia felt a huge relief flood through her. "Yes, I think that's best."

"But Emily might be up in Albuquerque today consulting on a case. I can check for you."

He picked up the phone. "Florence, get me Irma over at the coroner's office…. Irma, Sheriff McCaffrey here. How ya' be? Great! Say, I'm trying to track down Dr. Bryce. Is she around … oh … okay." He put his hand over the mouthpiece. "You want to take the drawings over to her office and drop them off? I can put a sticker on that says, 'Sensitive Information for Dr. Bryce only.' And you can include a note."

"Yes! That would be good, very good." Georgia gave a sigh of relief.

"So, aside from that … how are the dinner plans going for our British guest?"

"Not well. Rosaria didn't show up today. So unlike her. I was counting on her to make dessert. I don't do desserts."

"No, it doesn't look like it." He chuckled and patted his own belly. "I do them, as you can see. So you're in luck. The first peaches on my tree are just about ripe. I'll make a peach pie."

"Thanks, Ryan."

Chapter 14

She slowed her car as she passed the hospital. There was scant traffic, but it was halted by roadwork in front of the hospital. "About time!" she muttered. What looked like a major piece of road equipment was backing out of the drive into the hospital. As she waited, two familiar figures caught her attention. "The Lindberghs," she murmured to herself, and they were arguing vehemently on the sidewalk. "My, my," she whispered. As she stopped, her car was just about ten feet away with her window down. She watched spellbound as Charles Lindbergh raised his hand. It was bandaged. And there were scratches visible on the side of his face.

"Yes, hit me, Charles!" Anne Lindbergh snarled. "Just hit me and pop those stitches open!" The couple appeared to back away from each other. She heard Mrs. Lindbergh emit a sob. "I can't take it. I can't take it anymore." Her husband leaned forward now and tried to pat her shoulder gently. "Get your hands off me." She stormed toward a car that was parked a few yards off. The road crew motioned the waiting traffic to move.

Georgia drove on to Emily's office, which was only a quarter mile from the hospital. A trim woman in a nurse's uniform sat behind a desk. The name plate said IRMA GREYEYES.

She stood up and came round the desk to shake hands. "Miss O'Keeffe, pleasure to meet you."

"Nice to meet you as well."

"I understand you have some sensitive information for Dr. Bryce."

"I do. Here it is." The scraps of paper were sealed in a special large envelope labeled Santa Fe County Office of the Coroner.

"Don't worry, no one will open this except Dr. Bryce. There are heavy fines if they do. Do you have a phone where she can reach you?"

"Uh … well, you know I'm out at Ghost Ranch." She hesitated. "Let me think about this." At that, a buzzer sounded.

"Excuse me just a second, Miss O'Keeffe. A delivery has arrived with some equipment we've been expecting. This will just take a minute or two."

While she was gone, Georgia looked around the office. There was a wilting plant on a table and a dish of what appeared to be wrapped mints, the kind a restaurant might have in a bowl for departing customers. Seemed like an unlikely touch in a place like this. On a large bulletin board were some photographs. She stepped up closer and rested her chin in the cup of her hand as she studied the photos labeled "ballistics." The first row showed close-up pictures of gunshot wounds. A label above the two pictures read "Small caliber 20 to 30 point." On each picture was a scale for calibrating the diameter in centimeters of the hole in the flesh. Some of the pictures were labeled as entrance or exit wounds.

Adjacent to this bulletin board was another with photos of all sorts of gruesome wounds that Georgia supposed were non-ballistic injuries. Bites, cuts and scratches. None of them a pretty sight. These could have been made by animals, but they hadn't been. Amazing what a human being could do when set on murder. What slashes did one inflict on their own humanness to sever their moral roots. She heard approaching footsteps.

"Ah, Miss O'Keeffe, studying up," Irma Greyeyes said. "Want to become a coroner?"

"Hardly." Georgia laughed. "I guess these are examples of non-gunshot wounds."

"Yes, more range here, really, depending on what's doing the slicing or the biting, scratching, or tearing."

Georgia turned about suddenly. "You don't by any chance have pictures from that murder out by the Ghost Ranch?"

"The priest fellow?"

"Yes."

"That's right; you're the one who found the body."

"That I am."

"I'll warn you, the knife wounds around his neck are very gruesome. You really up to those?" Irma asked.

"Actually, what I'm most interested in are the head wounds. Those damn vultures ripped quite a bit of his scalp off. Doctor Bryce said they have talons like scalpels."

"That they do."

"Do you have any photographs of those?"

"Yes; you want to see them?"

"I do if you don't mind."

"Not at all, Miss O'Keeffe." Irma Greyeyes went over to a cabinet and took out a file. "Got at least half a dozen here of just his head." She began to spread them on a table with a glass top and an overhead light. "They had themselves quite a feast. Pecky eaters, we call them. Not picky. Pecky. Actually, they don't really peck as much as tear ..." She paused. "Rip, flay ..."

"Yes, that would describe it, wouldn't it?" Georgia murmured as she looked down at the bloody patchwork of Father Castenada's once-perfect tonsure. As perfect as the almost intact tonsure of Father William, except of course for those marks, chicken scratches really. She caught her breath for a moment then turned and looked at Irma Greyeyes, whose eyes were not gray at all but black-brown, the same color as the wood shanty of Georgia's studio back at Lake George—a dismal, impenetrable color that reflected nothing. "May I ask you a question, Miss Greyeyes?"

"Certainly."

"What kind of a wound would a ... say, kitchen drawer make on a bare scalp?"

"A kitchen drawer?"

"Yes, you know, if you were down on your knees and got up suddenly and banged your head against a drawer that you left open?"

"The corner of the drawer?"

"Yes, possibly the corner."

"Maybe a little gouge, a kind of divot." Irma Greyeyes paused. "An abrasion of some sort. But not a tear or rip like this." She tapped her fingernail on the photo. "This is a tear, not simply an abrasion or a contusion."

"Pardon my ignorance, Miss Greyeyes, but what exactly is the difference between an abrasion and a contusion?"

"An abrasion is caused by rubbing or scraping tissue away. A contusion is a bruise, basically resulting from a direct blow. Capillaries leak under the skin and result in a bruise."

"Uh-huh." Georgia nodded. "And what other kinds of wounds can vultures make with their talons, aside from tearing skin?"

"Oh my goodness; I have a whole rogues gallery of lacerations made by vultures. As I said, they're not picky in the least. They'll rip anything metal, flesh, rubber, plastic, wood. It's that middle talon that gives them the edge, so to speak. That's the scalpel."

She went to another filing cabinet, brought out a new folder, and began to spread some pictures on the table. "First of all, their beaks are the … well … I guess you'd call it … the heavy artillery. It delivers the death blow to the prey. See how the beak is hooked at the end. It can actually penetrate the brain of a small animal. Of course, vultures are carrion eaters, so they let others do the killing work. But these vultures tore off most of the tonsure of the victim, who was already dead. From the wounds I saw, they had started on stabbing with their beaks through the skull to get to the goodies."

"The goodies? Georgia asked.

"The brains. They love brains. All animals do." *As do the French*, Georgia thought. Irma continued with the calm cheeriness of someone who knows their subject well and delights in sharing that information with an eager student, which apparently was how Georgia appeared to her. "The talons are also curved. Again, better for tearing. Three talons point forward, the other two backward. Widely spaced, you'll see; these scratches on Castenada's remaining scalp are what we call 'grip wounds,' made by the other four talons. The flanking talons of the central one—the scalpel—

help anchor the victim's head while the scalpel tears. The marks vultures leave aren't parallel, unlike the kind of scratches made by fingers."

"Uh-huh." Georgia looked up now. "I think I've seen enough now. I'll be on my way, Miss Greyeyes." Irma Greyeyes last remark echoed in her head. *"But vultures of course deal with carrion. They aren't the murderers. They aren't guilty. No moral roots severed there."*

"Anytime, Miss O'Keeffe, and I'll be sure to get that envelope to Doctor Bryce as soon as she returns."

"Thank you, dear. I'll call you back to find out what Doctor Bryce says." She'd call from Abiquiu. She simply didn't trust Carmelita. She was sure she listened in on calls. "If for some reason Dr. Bryce is out my way, I am up the Rio Azul. Only house on the right."

"Okay, Miss O'Keeffe. I'll tell her all this." Irma scratched her head as she watched Georgia leave. Georgia could tell she was wondering why this woman, this painter, would have taken such an interest in the forensics of murder.

On her way out of town, Georgia decided to take a shortcut behind La Fonda hotel to the main road. "Good grief!" she gasped as she spotted Rosaria walking into the back entrance of the hotel. She pulled over and tooted her horn. Rosaria turned around. Her shoulders sank, and she gave Georgia a mournful look. It was as if she were carrying the whole weight of the world on her shoulders. Rosaria began to walk toward her. Georgia got out of the car.

"Where were you this morning? I was worried." Rosaria would not meet her eyes. "I checked at the Hacienda on my way. You usually leave messages for me there."

"They didn't tell you."

"No, I only saw Carmelita."

A sneer scrolled across her face—an expression Georgia had never seen on Rosaria before. "She wouldn't have told you."

"Told me what?"

She looked straight into Georgia's eyes. "Carmelita fired me."

"Fired you! What for?"

"Ask her." She glanced toward La Fonda. "But I got a new job now. Chambermaid here and helping out in the kitchen. So I won't be able to work but one day a week for you now, Miss O'Keeffe."

"Forget about that. That's nothing, but how are you going to get into work every day?"

"I'll figure it out. Don't worry about me."

"Rosaria, I will worry about you." Rosaria gave her an odd look. But Georgia could read it clearly: *"Oh, you white people with your worries!"*

It was useless. Rosaria had clammed up, and there was no breaking through. Her silence had a strange power. One dared not challenge it.

"All right, dear." She touched Rosaria lightly on her shoulder. "You let me know if you need anything. Anything I can do." But Rosaria was already walking away.

Georgia looked at her watch. It wasn't even one o'clock yet. God, the day was half gone. No dawn. No rattlesnakes to look out for. No bones in the broiling sun. She was about to say no painting. Normally she would have said it was a wasted day. But she didn't. Something had happened. She'd taken her first step, perhaps, in helping Clara. She had begun to name the unnamable. Now what she really had to do was get back to clean up the casita herself, because Rosaria would be cleaning guest rooms at La Fonda. She wasn't particularly good at cleaning, but she did like a clean house. She could think better in a tidy space.

The more she thought about Rosaria's situation, the angrier she got. How could Carmelita just fire her like that? What could Rosaria have done to incur her wrath? She had to admit that she really couldn't stand Carmelita. *She was a sycophant, a gossipy, condescending bitch.* Georgia searched for another noun or adjective—*treacherous*! Yes! Carmelita's love—call it lust—for gossip combined with her almost desperate manipulations to be accepted as a social equal rather than just staff made for a very unpleasant person, in Georgia's mind. Her unpleasantness, well camouflaged as it was, actually was somewhat ironic, seeing as her main job was to be pleasant and accommodate every wish of the Ghost Ranch's wealthy and often storied guests. Her cloying obsequiousness could almost make one vomit. She was the desert version of Uriah Heep.

By the time Georgia drove up to the Hacienda, she was in a fine froth. Striding into the lobby, she went directly to the desk. Joaquin was tending to a newly arrived guest. "Is Carmelita in her office?"

"Yes, Miss O'Keeffe. Do you want me to tell her you're here?"

"No need. I'll go right in."

She heard excited whispers behind her. "Was that really Georgia O'Keeffe—the painter?"

"I heard she was quite ill last year."

Georgia was tempted to turn around and say, *"Yes, I was in a mental hospital because my husband, renowned photographer Alfred Stieglitz, was screwing a young thing—Dorothy Norman, a photographer of mediocre talent. In fact, the previous year he was taking a few tumbles in the hay with our cook. Ample cause for a mental breakdown, don't you think?"*

But she said nothing and walked straight into Carmelita's office. She was on the phone, speaking in Spanish. Something about a plumbing issue in the laundry room. She flashed Georgia a big smile and held up a finger to indicate *Just a minute.* "*Bueno, Miguel ... hasta.*" Then she set down the phone. "What can I do for you?" Her voice dwindled as she saw the expression on Georgia's face.

"Why did you fire Rosaria?"

"Uh ... Georgia, this is Hacienda business."

"That's not an explanation. The question is why? You know as well as I do how important jobs are for the people in this community. Rosaria is, what? Seventeen years old? She's taking full care of her little sister, Clara."

"She's late—a lot. We're getting more and more guests each season now. We're even booked through the fall."

"Late? Rosaria is never late, and you know that."

"Well, she's rude."

"Rude! That's outrageous. She's anything but rude. You are creating this out of thin air."

"Look, I'm the manager. Carson leaves all personnel decisions to me." She rose from her desk. "Now, if you'll excuse me."

"You're lying, Carmelita, and I'm going to get to the bottom of this."

"There is no bottom. This is it, and I'll thank you for not interfering."

"Is that a threat, Carmelita?"

Carmelita shifted her eyes.

Georgia began to leave, but just before exiting, she stopped. "Oh, and by the way, did Mr. Lindbergh have some sort of accident?"

Though her back was turned to Carmelita, she heard her gasp. She kept her back turned. "When I was in town I saw him with his wife just leaving Saint Michael's Hospital. His hand was bandaged."

"Just a bad cut. That's all." She was taking her pocketbook down from a hook behind the desk. "I'm in a hurry, Miss O'Keeffe. Today is the day I go to Albuquerque to stay the evening with my mother. I can't be late. Goodbye!" She sailed out from behind the front desk and headed toward her car that was in the drive.

The hinge screeched as she opened the door. *What is it with me that I can't remember to buy Hennessey oil whenever I go into town? Early-onset senility?* But as soon as she stepped inside, she gasped. She pressed her hands to her mouth and felt the strength leak from her. She'd rather see a rattlesnake than this envelope. Her hands shook as she bent over to pick it up. She walked toward the stove, took a sharp knife from the rack on the wall, then walked to the kitchen table. She sat down and looked out at the Red Hills and the shivering green lace of the cottonwood trees. She closed her eyes briefly as if to cling to these images before she slit open the envelope.

It was just her breasts this time, pressed together, deepening the cleavage. She emitted a small shriek. A sliver had been cut from the paper just where the cyst had been removed from her actual breast. Panic flooded through her. "Oh God! Oh God!" she gasped.

She was unsure how long—not more than a few minutes, maybe not even five—she sat there staring at the mutilated picture. She took several deep breaths. She closed her eyes then opened them and tried to focus on the cottonwoods the way she might have if she were going to paint them. It wasn't working. *Take a seltzer. Take a seltzer.* That was the Stieglitz family's cure for everything from the common cold to cancer. "Seltzer!" She muttered "But they don't have seltzer out here." She got up, went to the sink, and splashed cold water on her face. How could anyone have gotten that picture? Of course it wasn't the original. But somebody somehow made a copy. Or photographed the original. That was when the idea came to her. Fritzy! Fritzy Freihoff had told Stieglitz about the tiny cameras that were being developed for spycraft.

She realized that since Carmelita had just left as she usually did on Wednesday to see her aging mother, it was the ideal time to call Stieglitz. She wondered if Stieglitz had brought Dorothy Norman to the lake. Would Selma approve? Probably not. His sister would put her on the third floor, as far as possible from Stieglitz's bedroom. But Stieglitz had been known to creep around on nightly prowls. Heavens, when he was sleeping with that cook, he went all the way to the dilapidated little guest cottage.

Fifteen minutes later she was sitting in Carmelita's office placing the call. It rang four times before someone picked up. "Selma! It's Georgia."

"Oh, my God, how are you doing out there? I bet you're broiling to death. You need to come back here and swim in the lake."

"I'm fine where I am for now, Selma. How's Alfred?" She could hear Selma's irascible terrier yapping in the background. Stieglitz's sister moved in a cumulous of chiffon accompanied by an ill-trained dog nicknamed Rippy.

"Fine, but he misses you. I can tell." Selma was the majordomo of the lake house since Hedwig, Stieglitz's mother, had died twelve years before. To Georgia she was everything that she disliked in a woman—high-handed and pretentious as she lorded over this family retreat. Perhaps this was a natural inclination for some talentless women. "Hush, Rippy, hush. I'm talking to Auntie Georgia." Georgia cringed. She hated when

Stieglitz's nieces and nephews called her "Auntie," and now the dog was supposed to?

She could just picture Selma in the swirling vortex of chiffon, a plethora of garish beads draping over her impressive bosom, scolding the damn dog.

"Well is he around? I need to talk to him about something."

"Oh dear, Georgia, I hope nothing's the matter."

"No, no; everything's fine. I just have a question for him." She knew Selma was dying to ask what. But she didn't.

"I'll get him. It might take a few minutes."

It did. But five minutes later she heard the familiar voice. It still excited her. The tinge of a German accent mixed with a New York one.

"What's up, kiddo?"

She told him about Lindbergh's comment and then about Carson Powell's nickname for Roosevelt. She did not tell him about the photographs. If she did, he'd probably come out here on his own and drag her back East.

Stieglitz gasped as she finished. "Georgia dear, you have to get out of there."

"Calm down, Alfred. I just want to talk to Fritzy. That's all. I'm not in any danger."

"But you even said you had to call me now, while this Carmel … what the devil is her name?"

"Carmelita."

"When she's away…. Oh, and by the way, when you went out there those first couple of weeks, she was very snippy with me whenever I called. You think she hates Jews too?"

"Oh God, Alfred, she wouldn't know a Jew from a … a Presbyterian. All of us white people out here are just that—white blobs. Anglos."

"Wait … wait a minute, dear. I think I might have his office phone. Can you call me back in five minutes? Will the beast still be away?"

"Yes. I'll call back."

They said goodbye and she set down the receiver, very thankful that Carmelita was on her way to Albuquerque and nowhere near. In those brief moments she had come to a decision. She would not tell Fritzy about the photographs either, at least not yet. There was no way he would not tell Stieglitz about that. But she would ask about the miniature spy camera. She sensed that the photos were perhaps simply a distraction as a part of something larger. To distract her attention from the murder of Castenada. She could inch into that conversation of the miniature camera by way of Simon Bowes; after all, he was an art journalist. Or so he said. But suppose he was an art thief? A crooked dealer of some sort?

In any case, she was beginning to feel that she was a relatively insignificant figure on this chessboard. The anti-Semitism seemed suddenly rampant. There was not simply Lindbergh, but now Carson Powell. And did that include Howard Hughes? Was this about Stieglitz being Jewish? The image he had made of her breasts had been vandalized. What part of her would be attacked next? Was this Carson Powell's notion of how to get rid of her? Prevent her from buying the casita? Instinct told her that she was small potatoes. Whether she bought the casita or not was immaterial to what was going on at Ghost Ranch.

Stieglitz call back with the number, and five minutes later Georgia was on the phone with Fritz Freihoff.

"Georgia, what a delightful surprise."

"Well yes, Fritzy. Very nice to hear your voice. Although I'm not sure if you'll find this so delightful."

She quickly summarized what she had told Stieglitz.

"Well, this is no surprise to us. We've had our eye on him because of his possible involvement with a group of isolationists, a bunch of Yalies, actually, who seem less concerned about Hitler than the rest of us. It could border on sedition. They might be involved with a network that is spreading across the country. There could be as many as forty members in what is now called the Lutzen ring after one Ludwig Lutzen. Whether these Yale isolationists are part of that group, I'm not sure. I actually doubt it. But they might be, or they might be aiding it in some way."

"One more question, Fritzy."

"Anything, my dear. Although I can't promise to answer everything."

"There's this fellow out here—Simon Bowes, a Brit."

"Never heard of the fellow," Fritzy said quickly, a little too quickly.

"You know I can't help but worry a bit. You hear about these crooked art dealers, and now I've heard that there are these tiny cameras that spies use. Not sure if I should let him in my studio."

"Oh, I wouldn't worry about that." Again, Georgia found his dismissal a little too quick. "But I'm very glad you called, dear. Keep your eyes open, and do not under any circumstances hesitate to call me again." He paused. "And as for Mr. Lindbergh—very unpleasant fellow."

"You've met him?"

"Unfortunately, yes. In the Oval Office. Thought he was going to wash his hands after he shook mine."

Fritzy Freihoff replaced the receiver and reflected for several minutes on what Georgia had just told him. His instincts suggested that she had not told him everything. Which meant she, herself, might feel threatened in some way. This was often the course an informant took in the beginning. One couldn't push, but it was always better that the person gain some confidence and come on their own. However, one thing was certain. The Lutzen ring was expanding rapidly. He got up quickly and walked to "the slot," as it was called. It was an electronically shielded room with a dozen receivers. He pressed a code and entered. Twelve people sat at long tables, each at a Hartley receiver breaking code. An efficient looking woman in her mid-forties stood up.

"Dr. Freihoff, what timing!"

"Something special?"

"Call it a rash. An outbreak," a bald man said. "But the numbers have doubled in the last week.

"Are you going to tell me that the Lutzen disease is spreading?" Fritzy asked.
"Yes, sir."

"And what about that bird in the Irish Sea?"

"Sparrow?"

"Yes, that one. He's confirming this?"

"Been quiet of late. He's a cautious type. He's often gone for longer than this without transmitting. But should I call Crypto in London, sir?"

"Not yet. You know Sparrow's got a damn good listening post out there. Who knows? He might be onto something big."

"Yes, sir," the woman said. "They claim that it's so good out there because of some geographic and atmospheric anomalies."

"And are the coordinates out there?" Fritz Freihoff asked.

"53° 46' N / 005° 47' W," the bald man replied.

"And it always rains in the Irish Sea?" Fritzy said. "Never very good sailing weather."

He scratched his head. And what was Berghof, Hitler's mountain retreat? 47° 38' 01" N / 12° 56' 31" E. What were they all doing up there—the lot of them: Goebbels, Himmler, Goering? Listening to Wagner with their dirndl-clad wives. Meanwhile, the first concentration camps were being built. The Nuremberg laws were rapidly being passed. *All in a day's work leading up to another great war*, Fritz Freihoff mused.

He could call his British counterpart, Cedric Barkley, at Crypto in London, but he knew that would be just a bit out of the line of protocol. First he had to call the Bureau and that bastard Hoover. He went back to his office for this unpleasant task. *All in a day's work*, the thought echoed.

Five minute later, Hoover picked up the special phone.

"Freihoff," he growled.

"It's spreading."

"Not surprising."

"Howard Hughes might be involved."

"Fuck."

"Any ideas on how to proceed?"

There was a deep sigh, then a brief silence. "Just one," Hoover replied. "I got a nigger agent here, Linc Stone." The word lingered noxiously in Fritzy's head. What a vile human being this man was. If it was "spreading," why would Hoover only put one agent on it? Fritzy wondered. But now was not the time to ask.

Chapter 15

That same evening, Nina watched her husband carefully. He appeared to be trying hard to be jocular. He also was not drinking. Not at all. Otto seemed to have recovered from her blurting out the name Gerda in the store. In fact, he was more solicitous than ever. "You really like that name, my dear, 'Gerda'?"

"Oh, yes," she had said, mustering all the enthusiasm she could. "I had a very good friend as a child whose mother was named Gerda, and she was so lovely and kind and made the best streusel." *What an actress I am*, thought Nina. And suddenly she realized that she had been an actress for most of their fifteen years of marriage.

When they went to bed that evening, he tried to make love to her but couldn't. She sensed that he was waiting for something. She had often heard him stirring in the middle of the night, especially those nights when he had not drunk himself into a stupor. Hearing the creak on the stairs, she knew he'd gone up to the second floor, most likely to connect to his old friends in Germany via the ham radio. So much cheaper than a trunk call.

She pretended to be asleep, then waited at least twenty minutes before creeping up the stairs. Pressing her ear to a crack in the door, she could hear that he was speaking again in Swabian. But she was confused. There was only one person he spoke to regularly in Swabian, and that was his uncle Willy Goetz in Stuttgart. The accent, the sounds, were not familiar to her ears, but two names emerged clearly: "Gerda" and "Lindbergh."

Stealthily she made her way back down the stairs. The hem of her night-gown snagged on something. Carefully she removed the fabric and, holding up the hem, made it down the rest of the stairs.

If it weren't this time of the night, she would have sought out Father William. Otto did not like the idea of her attending church. But she, like many from southern Germany, was a devout Catholic. Otto, from northern Germany, was an indifferent Protestant. However, she had found solace in her faith and in her friendship with Father William. She could talk to him about so many things: Otto's drinking. The longed-for child, although she did not tell Father William the full truth about *Lebensborn* and the Fount of Life program. She had stuck to the story of their niece, young and irresponsible, and how in order to save the family honor, they had enthusiastically offered to adopt the child.

Just a month before, however, Nina Mueller had heard that her local parish priest in Germany, Father Erich, had been slain during the Night of the Long Knives, when Hitler moved against what he perceived as his opposition, which included prominent church leaders. She was devas-tated and rushed into Father William's study, collapsing in his arms. He was so kind. She told him that her husband was not a Catholic. "He is not anything," she said, sobbing. "He has no faith. He's not unkind, but I think because he has no faith … that is why he drinks."

"Perhaps when the child comes, he will find faith. Remember, dear Nina: 'The wolf shall dwell with the lamb, and the shepherd shall lie down with the young goat, and the calf with the lion, and so a child shall lead them.' Isaiah, chapter eleven, verse six. Have faith, dear Nina."

What would the good Father William think if she told him how this child was really conceived? She couldn't risk telling him. He would be horrified, as most people would be. And she … well, Otto would kill her if she told anyone.

Their courtship was almost unimaginable now. It had begun in 1919. Otto had just returned from the war to finish his studies. He had earned his first dueling scar in his second year at the university. He'd received his second scar on the battlefield at Ypres, just hours before the wind shifted and the gas attack that was supposed to be aimed at the enemy came back and ruined his lungs. It could have been worse, of course. He was already in a field hospital with the bayonet wound to his belly. He was proud of both wounds, both scars. And his lungs back then had not seemed to be too badly damaged. It was only five or six years after the war that they began to wear thin. At least that was how he thought of it. Wearing thin. And then, two years ago, this particular opportunity came along in America—in a region that was supposed to be healing for weak lungs, no less.

But when Nina had met him in his last year at university, he was her dream. Tall, slender then, with azure eyes and the alluring dueling scar. He had thick, almost-white blond hair. He might have been Siegfried just stepping out of Wagner's *Ring* cycle. And she, Nina Alholtz, could have been Brunhilda. She had even grown her own blond hair long and had worn it in braids that flopped over her shoulders. Now, at thirty-five, she felt that she was a little too old for such braids, so she wound them atop her head in what was called the Gretchen style. She'd grown skinnier as Otto had grown fatter. She remembered when she took an English class after the war. The teacher had given them the rhyme about Jack Sprat. She thought of that now as she rose from crouching on the stairs. She had to stifle a giggle. How did it go? "Jack Sprat will eat no fat; and Jill doth love no lean. Yet betwixt them both, they lick the platter clean." Well, it was the opposite now. She was growing thinner and thinner and he fatter and fatter, but they both licked the dishes clean. They had never been richer. Yet, without a baby of her own, she felt oh so lean. She sighed and climbed back into her bed—to feign sleep, to feign life.

When Otto came down half an hour later, he held a small pink pearl in his hand. He looked down at his wife. Sleeping soundly. He rolled the pink pearl in his hand. The same as was on the hem of her nightgown. This was not good. Should he report it to his uncle on their next call?

Chapter 16

Only later that evening, after she had called Fritzy, did Georgia wonder about Lindbergh's cut. Had it been an accident, or had he too been cut by the commando knife? Earlier that morning, she had begun marinating the meat for the lamb stew she planned to serve at the dinner for Bowes, and the redolent aroma was filling the casita. This whole affair of the murdered friar was a stew—a stew of knives, clergy, fancy condoms, and those terrible images. The charcoal lines on the paper. The jagged teeth, the eyeless figures. She wondered when Emily Bryce would be back and open that envelope.

Georgia felt the electricity of agitation coursing through her body. Too many images were crowding her mind. It was not just Castenada's torn scalp, the bloody patchwork of that tonsure left by the vultures. She remembered the slash of their wings against the flawless sky when she had first caught sight of them that dawn, diving in to rake their talons on flesh. Little did she know then that it was not animal carrion, but human. She leaned on the kitchen counter and clamped her eyes shut. Their wings angled as they plunged. Images circled her then swam away, then drifted close enough to snag. Something twitched in her like phantom fingers.

She walked to her studio and took out the watercolors, then a pad of hot-press watercolor paper. Hot press, not cold press. She wanted as smooth a surface texture as possible. She poured a small amount of water into a shallow dish and took out an array of sable brushes. Someone once told her that sables were vicious creatures and possessed razor-sharp teeth curved like small scimitars. *Well, sables*, she thought, *you've met your match here with the vultures and their scalpels.* She dampened the paper with a sponge, careful not to make the surface too wet. Then, barely wetting the tip of a brush, she began to make a quick series of slashes across the surface. The marks pleased her. They were derived from quick warm-up exercises she had practiced as a student at Columbia Teachers College. Alon Bement, the teacher, often played recordings of harp concertos—"a liquid sound," Bement said.

A peculiar calligraphy began to emerge on the paper. Slashes and dashes poured down, and then fragmented shapes, as if torn from a patchwork, began to float ominously, looking like they had been stirred by an invisible wind. She recalled vividly now the gruesome flap of skin that fluttered in the draft of the vulture's wings as it took off. She pressed her eyes shut for a moment. Another image stirred behind her eyelids. She began to make short parallel strokes with the tip of her brush. She wasn't sure why, but they fitted with the design that was emerging on the paper.

As soon as she had made the next marks, she was finished. What had she accomplished? It didn't matter. She had cleared her head, at least momentarily. *Good for you*, she thought. She had learned to nurture herself a bit.

When it came to nurturing, Stieglitz was actually a very good nurse. He excelled in convalescent food. When she had first arrived in New York from Texas years before, she had been quite ill with pneumonia. Stieglitz had nursed her back to health with coddled eggs and plates of cut-up fruit, oatmeal, toast, and the chicken soup he picked up from a nearby deli or the Automat, which became her favorite restaurant. He was a skilled convalescent attendant, but now she realized that she could do it herself. No Automat or coddled eggs required. She was growing stronger. Stronger without him.

She decided to bake some bread. She found the whole process of making bread quite soothing.

She walked into the pantry and from the canister of wheat scooped out three cups to put in the mill in the kitchen. She began grinding, about three-quarters of a cup at a time. There was something calming about the sound of the mill and the motion of turning the handle. In a strange way, it was the same tranquility she experienced when preparing a canvas or mixing paint colors on a palette. These preparations were so fulfilling in their own way. Was it like an orchestra tuning up? While she ground the wheat, she looked out the window at the Red Hills and the piñon trees to the north.

Three hours later, after a second rising of the dough, the fragrance of the baking bread mingled with the pungent odor of the marinade for the lamb. This long day was finally coming to a close. She'd make herself some mint tea and sit on her patio. It wasn't roof time yet. She took some mail with her that she had neglected to open and settled into a chair. Nothing very interesting, but there was a letter from her sister and then one from Stieglitz. She opened that first.

My dearest Pumpkin …

Georgia gasped and slapped her hand to her mouth. Pumpkin! "Oh, Mr. Stieglitz!" she murmured to herself. Pumpkin was his pet name for Dorothy Norman. She'd heard him call her this so many times as she bustled around the gallery, supposedly doing her four hours of office work a week. Of course Dorothy could hardly type or figure up a column of numbers. Georgia didn't need to read any more. Any lover that Stieglitz called Pumpkin wasn't worth the distraction. She folded the letter and walked into the kitchen, where she took a match to the letter and lit it over the sink. She watched it burn, then washed the ashes down the drain with the slightly amber-colored water that came from the faucet on occasion. This was the third time she had washed the ashes of burnt paper down the drain. A convoluted paper trail that could encompass murder? She watched the burnt fragments swirl down the drain. But why was she at the vortex of this swirling gyre? Ashes to ashes?

She returned to the patio. The sun had been brutal. It was sinking below the scorching horizon until the low clouds began to glow like hot coals. As she sipped her tea, she heard the Angelus chimes of the twin bell towers begin to toll when the wind blew from this direction. They tolled three times every day. A call to prayer. The evening tolling was a signal that the workday was over and now it was time to turn to God. The shadow of those black crosses would drop like a veil and spread across the New Mexico landscape. She hadn't painted the shadows of the crosses in years. Not since she had come out to New Mexico that first time. That had been five years ago, to be exact, when she was staying with Mabel Dodge Luhan in Taos.

In her imagination she could almost see the shadow stretching out from the cross atop Saint Francis's Church in Abiquiu, engulfing the sagebrush and the small statue of Saint Francis feeding the birds in the spreading darkness.

She watched as the purple light began to soak into the land. She was just about to climb the ladder onto her roof when she heard the engine of a car approaching.

Who could that be at this hour? The engine cut. Then a car door slammed. Would it be Ryan?

"Hello!" a woman's voice called out.

Georgia got up and walked around the corner of the house. A woman stepped away from the car.

"Dr. Bryce!"

She could tell instantly from the creases that seemed to pull at the sides of the coroner's mouth that she had something unpleasant to discuss.

"The drawings—right?"

"Yes, yes, indeed."

"Come inside." She sighed. "Goodness, you're quick."

"There is no time to lose in these child abuse cases." Georgia felt a shudder rack her body. *Edna! Lemonade and whiskey with a full bottle of weed killer.*

"I'm afraid I'm going to have to ask you to look at these again."

"That's all right. So you think ... ?" Georgia couldn't finish the sentence.

"Yes, I think this child has been abused."

For the next half hour, Emily Bryce explained what she saw and what she considered incontrovertible proof.

"But what can be done?"

"I'm not sure. The law is not exactly on our side. Some cities and some states have child protection programs. They are mostly oriented toward labor—child labor laws. But sexual abuse is hushed up or discounted." Emily sighed. "This country is far from ready to confront that dirty little secret."

"And you're sure that Clara ... that this happened to Clara? That she is a victim?"

"Positive."

"How can you be positive?"

Emily Bryce straightened up and looked directly at Georgia. "Because as a child, I was a victim of sexual abuse." Georgia clamped her eyes shut. One thought seared through her brain: *There are so many ways to murder a child.* She felt something tearing inside herself. Those words the doctor had spoken to her after her abortion: *"You are no longer pregnant."*

"Oh, Emily, I am so—"

"What we have to do is try to get her away from whatever her situation is. Who does she live with?"

"Her parents are gone. Well, her father left the family years ago. Her mother died not even a year ago. She is being raised by her older sister, Rosaria. She's about seventeen or eighteen."

"That's her only relative?"

"No, there's a brother—Tomas. But he works as a wrangler and lives mostly up at the bunkhouse on Ghost Ranch and rides the rodeo circuit. I ... I don't think he would do anything like that to her."

"You never know, Miss O'Keeffe. You never know. You can't count anyone out."

Then Georgia remembered. "Rosaria was just fired from Ghost Ranch, where she worked as well as doing housekeeping for me."

"Fired?"

"Yes, for no particular reason. She's a fine young woman, but Carmelita got it into her head that she was rude to people and often late. The whole thing is made up. I know Rosaria. She's lovely. Hardworking. But she got a new job at La Fonda. And that means a long trip for her each way. If anything, it means that Clara will be left alone more."

"Hmmph," Dr. Bryce said and hunched her shoulders. "Let me think about that. Maybe I can find a temporary place for them to live."

"Oh, that would be wonderful. And if you do, I don't mind footing the bill."

"Alright, but the main thing is that we have to try and remove the child. Get her as far from the situation as possible."

Emily Bryce began to gather up the scraps of drawings. "Where does she go to school? Our Lady of Grace, with the nuns?"

"Yes, too bad school's out for summer vacation. Maybe we could make an arrangement with them."

"Are you crazy?" Emily Bryce said with a sudden vehemence that was shocking. Georgia looked at the doctor blankly. She couldn't comprehend this reaction.

"Look, I left Ireland for England when I was barely fourteen to escape my second abuser."

"Second abuser?"

"Yes. A nun."

"Who was your first?"

"My father." She paused. "I killed him."

Georgia was aghast. "You killed your father?"

"I did." She paused. "With an H-W 12, a commando knife, or the Transvaal knife. This particular weapon was used in the Wreckers' Corps, an Irish brigade during the Boer War. My father joined right up." She sighed. "He came back with a Transvaal knife, an H-W 12. Some call it the Wreckers' knife, especially if you're Irish."

"So that's how you knew so quickly out there with the monsignor."

"Yes, you could say I had firsthand experience." She began to roll up the sleeve on her left arm. There was a scar. "Stopped about a quarter inch from the brachial artery. I would have died."

"Your dad did that?" Georgia stared down at the scar.

"Yeah. But I got him back. I got him with his own knife in the end—the Wreckers' knife. He took better care of the Wrecker than he did of me." She sighed deeply. "You see, Georgia, I'm a patient sort. I just had to wait for the right moment." Her eyes grew distant, as if looking into a faraway place. Then she began to speak again, her Cork accent now pronounced. "Oi had me choice after I murdered him: prison or a convent school. It wasn't a tough choice."

"And then what? How did you get here?"

"My second abuser, as I said, was a nun at the convent I was sent to. Sister Mary Catherine. I didn't kill her. I just ran."

"But now you're here—how?"

"Oh, my dear, 'tis a long story. But I did become a nurse's aide during the Great War at Endell Street Military Hospital in London. It was an extraordinary place. Staffed almost completely by women. Women doctors, pathologists, X-ray technicians. We treated the wounded men from no-man's-land, those strips of land in the Great War separated by barbed wire where the bloodiest battles often occurred. Nightmares of anguish, blood, and poison gas and, yes, commando knife wounds." She sighed deeply. "After the war ended, I began my medical training to become a doctor, and finally I came here. And here I am, the coroner of Santa Fe County and, before that, Albuquerque. I figured this was as far as I could get from Ireland. But this kind of crime …" She paused. "Well, it doesn't know anything from countries. No borders, no boundaries."

It was late by the time Emily Bryce left. Her story was overwhelming. Overwhelming yet inspiring. How wonderful if she could find a place for Clara to live. Georgia stood in the doorway and waved goodbye as the coroner pulled out to head back to Santa Fe. As Georgia went upstairs and undressed, she could not help but think of what an insulated life she had led in comparison to Emily Bryce. She judged Emily as being close to her in age, perhaps a few years older. When Emily was stitching up horrendous war wounds in Endell Street Military Hospital in London, say it was 1915, she herself had begun corresponding with Stieglitz after Anita Pollitzer had sent some of her drawings to him at 291, his gallery in New York. And when Emily was being raped by her father, Georgia was helping her parents with the dairy farm and taking art lessons that her mother had arranged in their home for her and her sisters. Life was so goddamn unfair. How had she been so lucky?

She stood in front of her bedroom window. Like a scythe, the thin scrap of moon cut the night right open. A blade of its light fell through the window onto the floor. The moon was barely a quarter. Enough for the jimsonweed to catch in their swirling flattened cups? There was no sleep in store for her tonight; why not go to the moon garden? She stripped off her nightgown, pulled on her pants and a black shirt so as not to distract the moon from the flowers, and laced up her boots. She went to her studio and packed up her satchel, this time with pastels and water-colors. In the kitchen she slung two canteens over her shoulder, one for the watercolors and one to drink. Then, grabbing her snake stick, she set off for the Camina de Oro. As she stepped out of her casita, she glanced up at the moon. It had fattened up just a bit—*all for me*, she thought and smiled. She felt like a thief in the night with the moon as her sidekick.

When she walked through the gate of the vacant casita, she wondered if this was the one Simon Bowes had reserved. There were only a few this expensive. Should she be nervous? She didn't care. It was as if the garden behind the adobe walls had been waiting for her. There were myriad night-blooming flowers that she had not been aware of on her previous visits. The air was heavy with the scent of night-blooming jasmine and evening primrose, all unimaginable shades of whiteness. Lacing through these fragrances was that of moonflowers. There was a rare night-blooming orchid that only opened for a scant two or three hours. It was tipping its mouth hungrily toward that slice of moon, as if negotiating with the man in the moon for just a bit more, like Oliver Twist—"Please, sir, may I have some more." If the man in the moon had been a woman, light would have poured down like milk in the night for this orchid.

She set up her small lapboard with its tray for watercolors and began to paint. First four very quick studies of the orchid with its deep whorl of inner complications—the sepals, the labellum, the outer petals. It felt as if the calla lilies, next door, were begging for attention but—*Hey, hold on dears; you'll be there in the morning. I have to catch your transient friends here.*

This is what she was doing when she made the watercolor of the queen of the night orchid. It wasn't the whole plant, not the prickly column of the cactus, just a fragment really, the blossom's ephemeral existence in the splinter of moonlight. But for that fleeting moment, it was her whole world. The flower itself was becoming something greater than it was. If later she painted it big, really big, it would become arresting, literally so, and people would fall into its opening blossom. They would be devoured. They would finally see a flower the way she wanted them to see it.

She looked up at the sky and saw that the moon was beginning to slide down the thinning darkness to the west. It would be the perfect light for the jimsonweed. She tried to push what Lupe had once told her from her mind. That women often used it to abort. *Come along, you deadly thing*, she thought. It was the pale shadings of the petals' green edges that intrigued her. In the darkness, of course, colors, particularly cooler colors like green, faded. The warmer colors too were quenched. But whites were startling in the moonlight. After a quarter of an hour, she moved on to the calla lilies. They were so persistent in their begging for attention, for light, even though they would bloom the next day. Their throats were tipped toward the moonlight, as if gasping for it before it dissolved into the west. Cygnus the swan constellation was escorting the remnant of that moon, sweeping her into a new day. The light was perfect. A sudden breeze blew through the garden. All the flowers began to tremble. "Settle down, ladies," Georgia whispered into the night. Thirty minutes later she began to pack up her gear. She didn't want to leave, but she'd be back again. By the time she walked out of the gate, the queen of the night orchid had closed its petals.

She decided to walk a bit more up the hill. She was soon near the casita of Diego Sanchez and Felicity Wilder. She cut down the small lane to peer into their garden. But suddenly the tranquility of the evening was shattered; so was a glass window. "Not this soon. We had a deal! Goddammit!" A *fight*. She turned around quickly and hurried back up the lane and then headed down the hill to her own casita. However, she couldn't help but wonder what kind of a deal Diego and Felicity had struck.

Fifty miles away in Santa Fe, the coroner was enduring a restless sleep. She was caught in a web of horrifying images from the drawings Georgia had given her. A face contorted with rage scratched her dreams. *You little bitch* ... Her father was screaming, clutching his crotch as it sprayed blood and semen. He had bled to death within twenty minutes. There was blood everywhere that night as she had miscarried.

But these dreams were followed by the good one of her escape from Saint Mary's of Mercy. Then, at last, after the war there was the salt breeze of the open sea as she left it all behind.

Chapter 17

Sleep would continue to be difficult for Georgia. Except for her time in the moon garden, if she took up a brush, those terrible charcoal images swirled through her head.

Music seemed to be her only respite. She put Beethoven's *Sonata no. 23* on the Victrola and sat down in her reclining chair. She let the music roll through her, over her. She was soon engulfed in waves of color—translucent, softly vibrating colors. They began to match things in her head—forms, shapes, not like anything she had been taught—but ideas came to her, companionable to her way of thinking, of being. When the sonata finished, she went into her studio and took out one of the canvases she had prepped three days before. She touched one with her fingertips and pressed lightly. It was ready. But was she? *"Never know 'til you try, Georgia."* The words of her mother whispered in her mind. She began.

She finally felt calmer than she had in days, and the next morning she slept through the dawn then rose and drove into Abiquiu. She needed to start the final preparations for this dinner that Ryan had so spontaneously proposed. The lamb had marinated. Now she needed to braise it before she put it in the adobe *horno* oven on the patio. That was the only way to cook lamb, as far as she was concerned. She loved going to bed with these pungent odors swirling through her house.

Her sleep had been dreamless, but when she woke, the first thing she thought of that disturbed the peace of the morning was Lindbergh. His bandaged hand raised, and the marks on that lean, tanned cheek. The snarling voice of Anne Lindbergh. *"Yes, hit me, Charles.... Just hit me and pop those stitches open.... I can't take it. I can't take it anymore."* What couldn't she take? And had perhaps she had hit him, or scratched him? What was it Irma had said? *"The marks vultures leave aren't parallel like the kind of scratches made by fingers."*

Those marks! Why did they haunt her? She immediately went to her studio and took the watercolor she had made from the folder. She studied the odd calligraphy composed from the various angles of the vulture's wings and then the cluster of parallel lines at the bottom. It was as if her mind's eye somehow sped ahead of her rather pedestrian brain. It flew as she toddled unevenly along, trying to catch up with what she was seeing. She felt she was attempting to unpack a scattering of moments and weave them into some sort of design.

She thought back to her encounter with Lindbergh when she was with Clara at the general store. What was it he had said to Clara? That she must be related to "that gal Rosaria" up at the Hacienda? Yes, his words had made her skin crawl. It was not quite the same, but still similar to his remarks about Jews. There was just something so essentially dreadful about this so-called hero. But it especially sent a chill through Georgia because Clara had been right there. All Georgia could think was *Predator, not hero.* But was he Clara's predator? No! Of course not—not Clara's, but possibly Rosaria's? That must be why she was fired. She hadn't scratched him, but had she cut him? In any case, the attack had to be the reason Carmelita had fired Rosaria. Some things were falling into place. Should she confront Carmelita with what she suspected? Not yet, she thought. She was reacting with pure instinct. She wasn't a card player. Stieglitz was, and he would often say about a deal he was trying to make with artists' agents, *"Never play all your cards."* For her this meant trying to stay out of the office at the Hacienda as much as possible. She would have to go for her mail sometime today, but she was going to have to act as if nothing was out of order. All would appear well, even though she was mad as hell at Carmelita for firing Rosaria. Nothing would have pleased her more than to confront Carmelita with her knowledge. But, of course, at this point it was all supposition.

Several hours later, she was leaving the lobby with half a dozen letters tucked in her handbag. She hadn't been out the door more than thirty seconds when Carmelita came rushing up to her. *All must be forgiven,* Georgia thought. *She must want something from me.*

"I didn't want to ask in the lobby, but is there anything more on the murder?"

"Not that I know of."

"I understand you have a guest coming all the way from London to stay here. A journalist for a very important art magazine."

"Oh, yes. Mr. Bowes." Georgia paused. "Just curious, Carmelita, but what casita is he staying in?"

"Oh, the same one the monsignor was to stay in."

Oh, Georgia thought. *He must have some money. Where were all these people getting all this money these days?*

"Well, I hope it's not bad luck!" Georgia said.

"Miss O'Keeffe! Of course not. I would never take you for a superstitious person."

"Generally, I'm not," she replied as sweetly as possible.

"Good. You realize it wouldn't be good for business. And we are in the hospitality business here at the ranch." Why was it, Georgia thought, that she so often caught just a whiff of a patronizing tone from Carmelita?

"I've got to get home now. Start cooking. This fellow Bowes is coming for dinner. Making lamb stew. It takes almost three days, what with the marinating and the slow cooking."

———

Cooking was a ritual—a ritual that Georgia usually enjoyed. But as she cut the marinated lamb shoulder into smaller pieces for braising, her hands began to tremble. The thought of the commando knife haunted her as she sliced the marinated meat into smaller chunks. The thought of the knife flying through the air as fast as a peregrine falcon was unnerving.

She felt beads of perspiration forming on her brow. She walked away from the cutting board to the sink, rinsed her hands, then splashed some water on her face. Cold water. Was it a growing addiction, this cold-water ritual? She had dumped how many buckets on her head after discovering the fragments of Clara's drawings. But there were some things you simply couldn't wash away with cold water. For it came back to you like a rising tide … a rising tide of blood.

On her way through her studio, she stopped and looked at the water-color of the plunging vultures. "Scratches," she whispered to herself. Scratches that fingers would make. This was like a piece of a jigsaw puzzle that you continually disregarded until close to the end—when you say, "Of course! That piece!" And then the puzzle quickly fills in and the fragments make a whole picture. But the picture was not quite complete yet. She would have to exclaim, "Ahh, the fragments of my disorderly mind."

She sighed softly. She remembered now a wonderful quote—had she read it, or was it one of her teachers who quoted Van Gogh? *"For the great doesn't happen through impulse alone … it is a succession of little things that are brought together."* Yes, little things. And then of course her own wonderful teacher, Arthur Wesley Dow, always emphasized that the artist does not "teach us to see facts, but rather to feel harmonies." Both were true, Georgia realized: The facts were scratches made by human fingers, or flayed skin torn by the talons of vultures. But where were the harmonies? She must be patient. She would find them. Listen for them.

By the time she went to bed that evening, she was drifting off to sleep with the help of a Schumann sonata. She would put the marinating lamb in the *horno* in the morning and would figure out the rest of the meal tomorrow. Ryan, of course, was taking care of dessert, with his home-grown peaches for a pie. He sews, he cooks, he solves crimes—well, this one not yet, but hey, what a guy! She didn't care about desserts in the least, but she supposed the meal might seem incomplete if she didn't have one for guests. At Lake George, desserts were de rigueur, and the Stieglitz family and their guests lingered over them interminably. She always left before dessert was served. But she could hardly do that here, when she was the hostess in her own home. *Own home*; she liked the sound of that. She really did want to buy this place.

After putting the lamb in the *horno*, she decided to take her sketching pad and go for a walk. Beyond the moon garden, she was curious about the casita on the Camina de Oro that Castenada had reserved and where Simon Bowes was supposed to stay. It was said to be lovely. If the maids were cleaning, she might be able to have a peek.

As she approached the casita, she noticed the door was open and a maid was just going in with a stack of linens.

"*Hola*, Señora O'Keeffe."

"*Hola*, Lupe. How's the baby?"

"Beautiful, almost two months old."

"Time flies." She peered in through the door.

"You want to see this casita, señora? So beautiful!"

"Really?"

"Of course. No *occupado* now, but soon."

"Yes, I know ... a friend ... well I really don't know him, but a gentleman is coming to interview me about my painting and will be staying here."

"Sure, sure. Come in and be sure to see the garden out back. *Muy bonito*."

Should she confess that she has sneaked into the garden to paint? She decided not to. She wandered through the casita. A bit cluttered for her taste, but still quite nice. Very modern bathroom features. She exited a side door to a garden, as Lupe suggested.

"Oh, my goodness," she whispered. She did not have to feign being mesmerized by this garden. It was as gorgeous in daylight as in moonlight. There was a burst of jimsonweed—white jimson, white hollyhock, climbing hydrangea, and lantern hydrangeas with their pale tint of green. Since Mr. Bowes was renting this particular casita, perhaps he would not mind if she came and painted sometime during his stay.

"You like, Señora O'Keeffe?" Lupe asked.

"Very much, Lupe! Do all the casitas on this road have such lovely gardens?"

"Yes, but this is my favorite."

"Just lovely; thank you for letting me see this. Thank you so much. I love jimson, and that is some of the prettiest I've ever seen"

"*De nada*, señora. The one where the movie star is, Diego Sanchez, that one is nice too. Lots of jimson. But you watch out for jimson tea. Bad."

"Poisonous, I heard."

"Can be. But can kill babies you know—unborn ones."

"You mean abortion?"

Lupe clamped her eyes shut, made the sign of the cross, and nodded her head. "The leaves and the seeds from the plant are very powerful," she whispered.

"Really?" Georgia said. She felt her heart race. *"You are no longer pregnant."* And once more thought of the time when Stieglitz had insisted she get an abortion. She did, did as she was told, like an idiot, and then fled to New Mexico, to Mabel's for the first time. What a fight they had about that. "Outrageous!" he had screamed when she told him her plans the day after the abortion. "No, needing your permission is outrageous, Alfred. I need to go someplace where the whole country isn't Stieglitz." The fight, their rage; it all came back to her now.

Lupe nodded again. "Just a little bit. Not enough to kill the mother."

Georgia coughed slightly. She wondered if Lupe herself had ever tried to self-abort with jimson. She had one other child, who was perhaps three years old. And she had seemed thrilled when this new baby arrived.

"Lupe, could I sit here for a while and sketch?"

"Sure. I have to lock up the front door, but you can leave through that little gate."

"Perfect."

She sat down in a chair and for the next thirty minutes sketched the jimson. A slightly frustrating activity, for while the sun rose, the colors began to surrender to the brightness of the day. She had been there at night before but now, in the morning, she wondered about painting the garden at twilight and then maybe beneath a half-moon. A full moon—

too much she thought. Just three quarters to half. She was gluttonous for this garden. She smiled a bit to herself as she recalled Stieglitz's obsession with "whiteness"—her whiteness that had nothing to do with either race or virginity. It had more to do with her clarity of vision. He once wrote to her that she was white but he was gray. He was awed by her "whiteness." What she was seeing now was not whiteness. It was gray. She would have to come back.

Just before she packed up her sketching pad, she took out her portable watercolor kit. In the corner of the garden was a lovely clump of ground cherry, small purple flowers with delicate cups less than an inch across. This is what she would paint for little Alma, Lupe's baby. The little cups tipped toward the sun. It took her no time at all. Across the bottom she wrote, *Good Morning, Alma, with love. G.*

She felt a slight tremor as she wrote the *G*, recalling the initials on the map.

She continued walking up the narrow road. This was a part of the Ghost Ranch she had never really explored. Every casita looked as if there might be a lovely garden tucked behind its adobe walls offering refuge for wildness, a scrap of the desert sequestered. She discovered narrow lanes between some of the casitas where the garden walls were lower and she could peek over. She was peeking over one such wall when she began to hear soft grunts and groans, mixed with gasps. This was the casita of Felicity and Diego Sanchez, where she had heard the shatter of breaking glass the night she had visited the moon garden. Someone was making love to someone. *They must have made up,* Georgia thought, and smiled to herself. Had she and Stieglitz once made love so obstreperously, so gutturally? She hurried on. She was a painter, not a voyeur.

The walk was lovely. It seemed to clear her head. She had gone perhaps another quarter of a mile when she heard the roar of a motorcycle. She should really turn around, but it was so lovely. Then she began to think about that damn dinner again. Well, it would be worth it if Simon Bowes would let her come some evening and paint by twilight, or moonlight again, just not too much moonlight. She would consult her almanac for the phases of the moon this week.

She turned around and headed back down the hill. She had not gone far before she saw a figure walking up the road toward her.

"Señora O'Keeffe." Diego Sanchez took off his hat and waved.

Oh dear, thought Georgia. It was slightly embarrassing that twenty minutes before she had heard him in the throes of making love. He strode up to her, still vigorous after his midmorning romp with Felicity.

"What brings you out, señora?" he asked, glancing at her sketch pad and satchel. "Art of course."

"Well, yes. The flowers up here, especially the walled garden ones, are beautiful. There's a vacant casita just down the road a piece, and Lupe, who cleans, let me in to look at it and sketch."

"Oh, you must come to our garden. It is so lovely!" He paused and held up a finger. "On one condition."

"A condition?" Georgia asked.

"Yes, you must come to tango night next Thursday evening at the Hacienda."

"Well, if you insist."

"I shall tell Felicity when she gets back. She'll be so excited."

"Back? Back from where? She's not here right now?"

"No, she went into Santa Fe for the mud baths at the spa. I believe the wrangler Tomas gave her a lift."

"Tomas! Oh, he's back? I'd been looking for him. He rides rodeo you know."

"So I hear." There was a mischievous twinkle in his eye. "Quite a favorite with the ladies."

"All the rodeo riders are." She paused. "They might even compete with movie stars like yourself."

"I'm an actor, Miss O'Keeffe. Stars are for ..." A sly grin crept across his face. "Dare I say—stars are for the tabloids?"

Georgia laughed nervously. "Well, I guess you should know all about that."

"I never read the tabloids. Nor does my dear wife, although her father publishes them. And she's very bold about it. She says 'Papa, you publish trash. I won't read that.' Felicity's a bit of an intellectual, you know. That's why she loved Mabel's place. More of her kind there."

"Yes," Georgia said hesitantly. *Her kind.* She recalled now that Isadora Duncan and Felicity were briefly each other's kind. Isadora loved Felicity's mons veneris, her pubic mound, which she compared to Mujercita, a geological mound outside Taos that archaeologists liked to study for artifacts from an old Anasazi settlement.

"That's why she so adores you, Miss O'Keeffe."

She hardly knows me, Georgia thought. She had done her best five years ago, when their visits overlapped, to avoid the silly creature at all costs.

"So we'll see you Thursday for tango night."

"Oh yes, absolutely." And she meant it absolutely. Things were getting very interesting—and it wasn't just painting jimson in the moonlight. Yet again she thought she might be getting drawn into something, something that was beyond murder or perhaps had sprung from the murder. In fact, it seemed almost unavoidable. If Sanchez had just been making love, as it had certainly sounded, but he had just told her that Tomas had taken Felicity to the mud bath in Santa Fe, then what were those grunts about? Lovemaking? Or something else? Hard labor? This guy, as far as Georgia could assess, had never labored a day in his life. If she did get drawn into this, was it really so at odds with her art—for what was art but seeing the unseen, making visible the invisible and what is around you? Isn't that what she did all the time?

Chapter 18

Georgia's mind was in a tangle. She was trying to sort through what she knew and she did not know. The dawn was just breaking, and Georgia decided not to drive into the desert to paint but to walk all the way into the new day. Walking always helped her think. To help her untangle things that did not fall into place into neat little piles, or like the spools of thread on her mother's spool tree. She would walk toward Mesa Pequena, a mesa studded with mica that glittered fiercely at this time of day.

However, an hour later the knots had not been untangled. She decided to get into her car and drive out to where she had found the body of Monsignor Castenada, the site where it had all begun. But what did she mean by *all*? Castenada? The farthing? Clara's terrible drawings? The sound of the shattering glass? The lovemaking that maybe wasn't lovemaking? Were these all disparate threads that had wandered out of a tapestry?

She parked the car by the side of the road and began to walk. As the wagon hub came into view, she wondered if there would be any other remnants of what had transpired here. A new hollyhock had burst into bloom—a lovely pink one. She really couldn't determine now the exact spot where she had found the body. The rain had wiped away any footprints from the sheriff and his team. No vultures circling. Everything had been erased. "Who were you, Mr. Castenada?" she whispered to herself. And why dress up as a Franciscan? She looked out toward the Red Hills. This land was so vast, so empty, and yet two separate but unspeakable crimes had happened. Could there be any connection?

Emily's words suddenly intruded on her thoughts.

"My second abuser."

"Second abuser?"

"Yes. A nun."

"Who was your first?"

"My father."

———————

As Georgia passed the Hacienda on her way back, Lupe came running out. "Miss O'Keeffe! Miss O'Keeffe, a message just came for you. A phone call. Miss Carmelita wanted me to take it up to you."

"Well, I'll save you a trip and come in."

As Georgia walked into the Hacienda, she saw Carmelita behind the front desk. She lifted her eyes. Did Georgia see perhaps just a shadow of contrition?

"Morning, Miss O'Keeffe."

"I understand there's a message for me."

"Yes, here. Dr. Bryce. Said call her. There's her number." Carmelita shoved a piece of paper toward Georgia and sighed. "You can use my office."

"Thank you, Carmelita." She spoke softly and managed a little smile. "We're still friends, I think."

"I think, Miss O'Keeffe." Carmelita replied and actually smiled.

Georgia walked into the office and picked up the phone. After several rings on the other end, she was about to hang up when Emily picked up.

"Dr. Bryce here."

"Yes, Emily. It's Georgia."

"Oh, happy to talk. I have good news. I think I have a place for Rosaria and her sister, Clara, to stay."

"Really?"

"Yes—the casita that I own behind my house. They'll have to clean it up a bit. I took a look at it today and feel it might work out nicely for them."

"Well, I'll have to ask them. I know Rosaria has an elderly aunt that she takes care of who lives next door to her."

"All right. But it's theirs if they want it. I might be able to find Clara something to do in the coroner's office at the hospital."

"Really? Lovely!" Georgia paused and gave a harsh laugh. "Tending to the dead?"

"No. You think I'm going to put a child in with the stiffs? You crazy? If the child can read, she can file. She can answer the phone. Take messages. Can she type?"

"Probably not."

"Well, she can learn."

"All right. Rosaria's in town already. I'll go over to Abiquiu and see if Clara wants me to drive her in, then she and Rosaria can take a look at it together."

"Try and move fast on this, Georgia. Every minute a child is in fear of a predator is a minute lost. You never know when things will turn and then someone gets killed ..." She paused a long time. "Or more." Georgia shut her eyes. Emily's earlier words came back: *first abuser ... second abuser.*

"All right, I'll pick up Clara and bring her to town."

Twenty-five minutes later, she was parking her car in Abiquiu.

She spied Clara and José sitting in the shade of Goetz's store, each drinking a cold soda pop.

"Hello, Miss O'Keeffe," José said brightly. But Clara kept her eyes cast down and said nothing.

"Clara, I'd like you to drive into Santa Fe with me."

"Something wrong? Is Rosaria all right?" Clara looked up, her face a tight knot of despair.

"Nothing wrong at all. I just need for you to come with me; we'll pick up Rosaria on our way at La Fonda if she can get away. I have something interesting to show you."

"Well, can we wait a half hour? I have to ring the Angelus with Father William."

"You ring the Angelus?" Georgia asked.

"Yes."

"Hey, I'll do it," said José. "He gives her fifty cents each time."

Clara bit her lip lightly. "Okay, José. You do it. Take the left bell tower to ring. It's easier. Father William actually likes the right one more."

Georgia followed Clara's gaze as she tipped her eyes up to the church steeple. At this time of day, the shadow of the cross on top was just slipping over the roof on the northern side. In an hour it would be sliding down the front, which faced east, until finally at sunset, when the next Angelus would ring, the shadow would be in the yard and stretch to the edge of the street.

There was a creak behind them and the slam of the screen door. "Ah, nice time for a break." Mr. Mueller came out. He had an orange soda pop in his hand. "Hello, Miss O'Keeffe." She had never noticed before, but his fleshy face was exactly the color of oatmeal. Pouches of flaccid skin beneath his pale gray eyes drooped like deflated balloons. There was not a flicker of light in those eyes. The C-shaped scar that crept like a pink segmented worm from his hairline to his left eyebrow stood out now more fiercely than ever. Georgia had assumed the scar was from the Great War.

"Hello, Mr. Mueller."

"Not painting today?"

"Oh, I'll paint. But getting on noon is not the best time. Harsh light, you know. Got to wait until the shadows begin to grow." She looked at the church again. A quote from a not very good play by William Butler Yeats came to mind: *The light of lights looks always on the motive, not the deed, the shadow of shadows on the deed alone.* She thought of the light on the bone of that horse skull the first time out on the desert the morning before she had found the body. When she had come back the next day, there was the strange disorder of that scene as she caught sight of the hat blown by the wind fetching up right on top of the horse's head. The jaunty angle of its perching there. Its shadow printed on the ground. And then there were the wing prints of the vultures against the sand and sagebrush as they pecked away at the man's skull. The coyote watching over it all like a silent sentry—a sentry of shadows.

The ride into Santa Fe was silent. Georgia liked that. It gave her space to think, actually to marvel at how within a very short time she had moved from resentment about her peace being violated, her unassailable isolation being trespassed by horrible events, tragic events, to being obsessed by these crimes. She no longer felt indignant, quite the reverse. She was compelled to find the answers. *What a selfish creature I am,* she thought. But so is Stieglitz. Now Ryan ... she wondered about Ryan. He didn't seem like the selfish kind, but one never knew.

"I think, Clara, this could really work out nicely for you and your sister—what with her new job," Georgia said as they drove into Santa Fe.

"I guess," Clara replied in barely a whisper.

"Dr. Bryce says that maybe you could help her do some filing, and who knows? Maybe there'd be some work at La Fonda too."

"But Tía Paloma? She needs us," Clara replied.

"I'll help you figure something out. Don't worry. And Rosaria gets Sundays and Mondays off. So you can go back for those two days and check in on her."

"Maybe."

"I think it's a nice idea, and come fall you can go to school here in Santa Fe. It's supposed to be a very good school." Georgia reached over and patted the girl's knee. She felt her flinch. *Damaged* was the word that floated through Georgia's mind. This child is damaged.

Fifteen minutes later, they entered the lobby of La Fonda. Clara shrank beside her and seemed a mere shadow as they approached the desk.

"Ah, Miss O'Keeffe." The desk clerk came out from behind the desk and greeted her warmly. She had no idea who the person was, but they obviously knew who she was. "What an honor. What can I do for you?"

"I believe my good friend Rosaria Benally has recently started working here, and this is her sister, Clara. We're here on a family matter. Might you find her for us?"

"Certainly. I hope nothing too serious."

Georgia ignored the question. "We just need to talk with her."

"It's her lunch break, so I'll check the kitchen."

"Thank you so much."

"Would you mind going to the rear entrance? There's the courtyard there, where she can meet you."

"Fine," Georgia replied.

Three minutes later, Rosaria rushed into the courtyard, obviously agitated.

"*¿Qué pasa? ¿Tía Paloma?*"

"*Nada*, Rosaria." Clara embraced her sister.

Georgia stepped forward. "I think I've found a living situation for you and Clara here in Santa Fe."

They walked over to a bench as Georgia began to explain.

There was a mixture of relief and apprehension on Rosaria's face. She clutched her sister's hand as Georgia spoke. "And in addition, there is the possibility of a job for Clara with Dr. Bryce. I think it's a wonderful opportunity."

"I ... I don't know ... I mean, Tía Paloma needs care and ... and ..."

"I'm going to help you figure that out."

There was a long silence. The Angelus began to sound from the cathedral in Santa Fe. José must at this same moment be ringing the bells at Saint Francis's in Abiquiu. The shadows of church crosses would begin to spread across New Mexico.

"Let's go over and meet Dr. Bryce. It might work out. Be good for both of you."

Clara slid her eyes to the side. "Come along. Worth a try."

———————

They had just completed the tour of the small house. To Georgia it looked perfect for Rosaria and Clara. They would certainly enjoy the bathroom; few houses in Abiquiu had indoor plumbing. But she hesitated to say anything.

"So it's all right?" Emily Bryce asked at the end of the tour she had given Clara and Rosaria of the casita.

"Very nice, Dr. Bryce," Rosaria said and smiled.

"Well, I am very pleased to have you both staying here. You'll bring your gear here tomorrow, right?"

"Yes, ma'am." Rosaria nodded. The relief that seemed to sweep her face was clearly evident.

"I'll drive you in tomorrow morning," Georgia said.

"Tomas can drive us," Rosaria replied. "He's going over to Santa Domingo."

"If he can't for any reason, let me know," Georgia said. They had begun to walk out toward her car.

"Oh, Georgia, can you stay a minute? I have something I wanted to mention," Emily said.

There was an opaqueness to her eyes as she spoke, and yet Georgia could tell this was meant to be a private conversation.

"Certainly, I'll meet you at the car," she said, nodding to Rosaria and Clara.

"Oh Rosaria! Just a moment," Emily said brightly. You mentioned that your aunt suffers from digestive problems."

"Yes, ma'am. She takes those blue tablets, but she's run out."

"Don't worry. I can give you a dozen packets, but to tell you the truth, the magnesia ones are better. Not as hard. They dissolve faster."

"Oh, that would be really nice, Dr. Bryce."

"No problem. I'll send them out with Georgia after we talk."

"Thank you so much."

Emily Bryce's eyes followed the two figures as they made their way to Georgia's car in the drive.

"So what's this all about, Emily?"

"Lindbergh."

"What about him?"

"Come on in the kitchen. I'll tell you there." As soon as they came into the kitchen, Emily turned around. There was a wintry look in her eyes.

"Did you know he was treated at the hospital two days ago for a cut?"

"Well, actually, yes; I saw him and his wife just outside Saint Michael's. His hand was all bandaged up. And he and his wife were having what appeared to be a fairly heated argument."

"Well, did you know that he's got about twenty stitches in his hand and that the cut was made by a commando knife?"

"What?" Georgia sat down immediately on a kitchen chair.

"Yep. Seems odd, doesn't it? Twice in what? Less than two weeks."

Georgia stared straight ahead. "You know they sell them at Goetz's store."

"No, I didn't know that."

"Well, they do." Georgia paused and looked at Emily. "Did you tell the sheriff?"

"Yep; called him just before you arrived. As I said before, those knives should be outlawed."

"How did you find out? Aren't medical records sealed?"

"Irma Greyeyes. She was the nurse who helped stitch Lindbergh up."

"That hardly explains it. How did she know what a commando knife cut looks like?"

"Irma does double duty. She helps me at the morgue. She worked on the examination of Castenada's body. She examined the wound with me. Very clean, very deep, deep enough to nick the bone. Yes, it went right between the tendon in the first and second metacarpal. He'll most likely need further surgery when he gets home. Irma's smart, she's observant, and she has the makings of a good medical examiner. She's going back to school and get certified as one."

"Gracious," was all Georgia could say. She looked up suddenly. "By the way, did Irma mention the scratches on Lindbergh's face?"

"No, not that I recall. I imagine she was too busy with the wound itself, stitching it up and all, to notice the scratches." Georgia sighed.

But one thing was certain. It was unlikely that Mrs. Lindbergh was responsible for either the scratches or the knife wound. There were no harmonies here.

That night her anxiety dreams returned. It was as though that knife, or the jagged wound made by that knife, had sliced through her dreams and was bleeding into her sleep. In the dream she is seeking colors, but everything is red—blood red—and then it begins to wash away, taking all the other colors with it. Her palette is dissolving before her eyes, as if it is not oil but watercolors. With her brush, she is reaching for just a scrap of some color, but it evaporates and there is no color at all. The palette is scrubbed, and she is left with this terrible yearning and a blank canvas.

When she would eventually wake, she would still have the shadows of those colors in her mind, lingering like a melody in her head. On some level, for the next few days, she would be groping for these colors—like a blind person trying to remember what she had once seen. The colors would be slipping behind a horizon just as she might grasp them, lurking just beyond her comprehension, and yet it was somewhat illuminating to wander in these shadows, these ghosts of color.

She startled in her sleep. "Gracious!" she gasped, and woke up. The air was redolent with the pungent odors of the lamb stew she had put in the adobe *horno* oven on the patio the night before. It smelled good. She was slowly mastering the art of cooking in the *horno*. Tonight was the night when Ryan McCaffrey would be bringing Simon Bowes for dinner. Oh God, she thought. She never liked talking much about her art. She wasn't even sure now why she had agreed. Stieglitz had said something about how it was important. The Brits needed to know more about her and her work. Oh well, she thought, at least the sheriff was coming.

Could there be any creature on Earth the more opposite of Stieglitz than the sheriff? No, not in five hundred years, or ... what was that terrible term Hitler used about the Reich? It was supposed to last one thousand years—*Tausendjähriges Reich*. Stieglitz spoke German. He had translated as they had listened to the madman on the radio up at Lake George. "God forbid," she muttered, thinking of that madman casting his shadow over the next one thousand years. A millennium!

Chapter 19

Ryan McCaffrey had just stepped into the Hacienda when Carmelita came out from behind the desk.

"Ah, Sheriff!" Carmelita greeted him warmly. "Our guest Mr. Bowes is expecting you, but I believe you're early."

"Yes, I got out of a meeting early and decided to drive on out."

"He's on the patio, having drinks with our illustrious guests—Mr. and Mrs. Charles Lindbergh." She almost crowed. "I'm sure they'd be happy for you to join them." It seemed implicit in her comment that he might add to the local color in some way. A slight embellishment—an Irish-Hispanic-Pueblo officer of the law.

"I'm off duty, so I suppose I might have a drink. Rosaria knows what I like."

Carmelita's face arranged itself into a mournful aspect. "I am afraid that Rosaria is no longer with us. Unfortunate."

"What?" The sheriff was surprised. There had always been Benallys at Ghost Ranch, even before it was Ghost Ranch and known as a hideout for outlaws. The Benallys had helped build most of the structures on the ranch. They had been not just builders but also wranglers, guides, cooks, and maids that served the occupants who now came here for solitude, inspiration, or perhaps their ailing lungs.

"Yes, it was unfortunate." She did not meet his eyes as she spoke. Ryan McCaffrey was a patient man. She said not a word. He would wait very still until she decided to look at him. She would. He took his time. She fussed with some papers. At least eight seconds passed before she glanced up. "What might I get you to drink?"

"Unfortunate." He repeated her word.

"Yes," she replied tersely.

He sighed deeply. It was the sigh of a patient man. "You may bring me two fingers of whiskey with ice." She seemed relieved and bustled off toward the bar.

He walked out onto the patio. It was hard to miss the handsome couple. Lanny Powell and Carson, her husband, were at the table with their children's tutor, Peter Wainwright. Next to Wainwright was the man McCaffrey assumed to be Simon Bowes.

"So you see," Carson Powell was explaining, "Ghost Ranch was originally called Rancho de los Brujos—Ranch of the Witches. A couple of fairly violent cattle rustlers, the Achuleta brothers, were getting away with not only cattle rustling but also murder. Stories grew up about spirits and winged monsters that terrorized any humans who trespassed. A convenient myth for the murdering cattle-rustling brothers." Carson Powell rose quickly as he saw McCaffrey approaching.

"Scaring guests with ghost stories, Carson?" Ryan said.

"Ah! I believe our esteemed sheriff has arrived for our esteemed guest from England." A fair man with pale hair that flopped over his brow rose quickly.

"Sheriff McCaffrey, so kind of you to escort me to Miss O'Keeffe's house for dinner this evening."

"Well, I'm bringing part of that dinner. So I'd better come along."

"Have time for a drink?" Carson asked.

"Believe so. I'm on the early side."

Carson Powell began the introductions. Lindbergh apologized: "Forgive me for not shaking hands—as you can see, I've had a bit of an accident."

"My goodness," the sheriff said. "Looks like you did yourself in."

"Well, unintentionally, but yes. I'm told that I might need further surgery."

Carmelita came with his drink. "Here you are, Sheriff. Two fingers of whiskey and lots of ice."

"Thank you, my dear." He lifted his glass "Well, here's to Prohibition being over—almost a year now." He paused. "And, yes, I'm off duty, so this is okay."

"Oh, glad you cleared that up!" Lanny said jovially. She gave Peter Wainwright's ribs a gentle poke with her elbow. The handsome young fellow blushed. It seemed like an odd gesture coming from Lanny, who was essentially his employer. Did they have some sort of private joke, the sheriff wondered.

Carson looked on glumly then quickly said, "Mr. Bowes was telling us that Georgia O'Keeffe's work is becoming increasingly popular in England. He's writing an article for a magazine. It appears there might be an exhibit in the coming year. Collectors are lining up in anticipation."

"I don't know anything about that," Ryan McCaffrey said. "But she's a fine lady."

"I'm hoping she'll take me out to some of her favorite sites to paint," Bowes said.

"I'm sure she will. Be ready to get up early. She goes before the crack of dawn."

"The light, I suppose."

"Yes, she's particularly partial to the light on bones."

"Light on bones?"

Chapter 20

Fifteen minutes later, the sheriff and Mr. Bowes were jouncing up the dirt road toward Georgia's house. "They've got to do something about this road. Hang on to that pie, Mr. Bowes."

"I shall indeed, Sheriff. Are all the roads this rough?"

"For the most part. This one is especially bad, I think. Everything like basic public services takes time out here. Only got very limited telephone service about a year and a half ago."

"And Miss O'Keeffe, does she drive around out here?"

"You betcha. She's got a Model A. The back of it is set up as a kind of art studio for when the sun starts to scorch her and her canvas. She can sit in the back of the car, all nice and shady. Paint for a while. Take a nap, whatever."

"Have you known her a long time?"

"Oh, no; just met her a few weeks ago."

"You don't say. What brought you two together?"

"Murder," the sheriff said flatly.

"No!" Simon Bowes exclaimed. "Not the cow rustlers they were talking about?"

"Cattle, Mr. Bowes—cattle rustlers. *Cow* suggests dairy farming."

"Oh, sorry."

Ryan McCaffrey chuckled. "Don't worry. I'm just ragging on you."

Bowes laughed softly. "Ragging as in jesting. Interesting word."

"Words interest you, Mr. Bowes?"

"A bit. I was on a linguistics course of study at Cambridge but then switched to art history." The sheriff glanced at the fellow. His hair was flopping about. This must be a British style. Not to mention the apricot-colored bow tie with tiny daisies and a pocket square tucked into his well-tailored jacket.

"But what about this murder?" Bowes asked. "And how did Miss O'Keeffe come to be involved?"

"Well, she's not a suspect, if that's what you mean by being involved."

"Oh, heavens no! I ... I ... ," he stammered.

"She discovered the body."

"No! My God, the poor woman. What a shock."

"I have the feeling that very few things shock Miss O'Keeffe. But this did to a degree."

"To a degree?"

"She kept her wits. Enough to get back to the Hacienda and contact our office."

"But how did she come to discover his body?"

"'His'?" Ryan turned to his passenger. "Did I say—?"

"Oh, I mean ..." The Brit's knees began to jiggle.

"Hang on to that pie," the sheriff said as he turned into the short driveway and pulled up to the casita.

Now, there is a picture! Ryan said to himself as he saw Georgia leaning against the doorframe limned by the setting sun in that beautiful cream-colored dress with the tucked pleats. She wore a long white scarf on her head, tied bandana style, that almost covered her eyebrows. The tails of the scarf hung down over her left shoulder and stirred slightly in the wind. The effect? A bandito crossed with an angel.

"You got the pie?"

"Absolutely, Georgia. Mr. Bowes rode with it on his knees all the way here."

Georgia strode over to the car and opened the passenger door. "Thank you, Mr. Bowes, for your service. I can take custody of the pie now."

"Oh, Miss O'Keeffe, so kind of you to invite me for dinner."

She took the pie. "Mmm, smells good, Sheriff." She looked at Simon Bowes and gave him a wink. "We have many talents out here: Sheriffs bake pies, and I have learned how to make ice cream in the high desert, which we will eat with the pie."

"What an excellent woman you are!" Ryan McCaffrey clamped his hand down on her shoulder and gave it a firm squeeze. That touch stirred something so deep in Georgia, she almost gasped. *A delicious squeeze.* Had Stieglitz ever touched her in this way?

"Well, come on in, Mr. Bowes." She paused "Or, if you're game, we could ascend to the roof of my casita for a drink. I can bring up a bottle of wine. Or some beer, my preference. Or both." She looked slyly at the sheriff. "Now with Prohibition over, we get a little wild out here."

"Lovely," Simon Bowes exclaimed softly.

"Yes, lovely," the sheriff said. And Georgia had to stifle a giggle. The word *lovely* sounded simply ridiculous when Ryan McCaffrey said it. It was perhaps a word best uttered by a slightly effeminate Brit in a brightly colored bow tie.

"Sure you can climb in those shoes?" Georgia asked, looking down at the Brit's obviously bespoke shoes. Stieglitz had a pair of fancy shoes. He claimed it was because of his fallen arches, but in reality, the man did have his small vanities. "And for Lord's sake, don't step in any cow pies."

"Oh my, not cattle pies? I thought you called the bovines cattle out here."

"Cow pies are cow pies no matter where you are," Georgia answered.

"Might I quote you, Miss O'Keeffe? I feel that would make a lovely opening for my article."

Georgia laughed. "Of course. Why not!" She liked this man. She headed into the casita for the drinks and glasses. "I'll be up in a minute." The door squeaked loudly. "Forgive my door. Sounds like a chorus of crickets, doesn't it? I keep forgetting to oil it."

They proceeded to the roof, and Simon Bowes displayed an agility and readiness that his rather curated attire would never have suggested.

Twenty minutes later, after the cocktails, they descended to the kitchen, where they would eat. As they sat down at the table, Georgia looked out the window toward the sunset and sighed. "There's so much of it, isn't there?"

"So much?" Simon Bowes asked.

"So much of the sky out here. When I'm on the roof or if I just walk down the road, it never ceases to amaze me, this huge sky. Look now: blazing hot, simmering coals on the horizon. The hotness of it all. And the little adobe buildings crouching under it. Yet all so beautiful. And in the morning, when I go out in the desert—how can you not be a painter out here?"

Georgia turned from the window and began bringing bowls of lamb stew to the table. The conversation was pleasant. Simon Bowes did not try to limit the discussion to art. He was interested in the whole region, and then he asked her a question no one had ever posed to her before. It was about the emotion of color. This in turn led into a discussion of her Lake George paintings and how her palette altered dramatically when she came to New Mexico.

"And so Alfred Stieglitz introduced you to Lake George?"

"Oh, no, no. I went there years before I ever met him, when I was still in art school with my friends. There was something so perfect about it all. My art school friends talked about this place with its thousand shades of green. It was visually so stimulating. I painted fallen leaves, apples—the placidity of the lake. Not precisely serene but, yes, placid."

"And you left all that to come to this very different place."

"I haven't really left it. I've just left the greener place behind for now. The green can become ..." she paused. "Well, enfolding and, on occasion, even smothering. A smothering perfection. Sometimes, you know, something is so perfect that you want to tear it to pieces." She closed her eyes briefly, and the image of sixteen people or more crowded around the Lake George dining table came to mind. God, those family dinners were rowdy and exhausting. A gaggle of Glietzes, as she often thought of Alfred's extended family. His sisters, Selma and Agnes; the sulking daughter, Kitty; Elizabeth, his favorite niece; his brother, Lee, and his wife. And then there were any artists or literary types who happened to drop in—Paul and Rebecca Strand, Paul Rosenfeld, Marsden Hartley.

"And the flowers. The flower paintings?" Bowes asked

Oh, God, the endless flower questions! Would folks never stop asking these "gynecological" flower questions, as she thought of them?

She recalled the flowers in the walled garden of his casita that she had just painted. For some reason, she had no desire to share that she had been there. And yet she wanted to go back and had considered asking him. She was greedy. A miser with her stash of gold—the jimsonweed, the calla lilies, the orchid that only opened for scant hours in the night.

"I actually hate flowers. I paint them because they don't move and I don't have to pay them. They're cheaper than models."

Simon Bowes opened his eyes wide with a mixture of surprise and acute curiosity.

"Forgive me; I didn't mean to shock you. There are beautiful flowers out here, and they do hold still."

Ryan guffawed. "Miss O'Keeffe loves to shock."

Georgia gave him a sharp look. "What are you laughing at, Ryan?"

"Oh, nothing." He clamped his mouth shut. His eyes were merry with light.

Georgia pushed. "You disagree, Ryan?"

"About what? That flowers don't move?"

"No, that I like to shock."

"Well, I do think you have a bit of a history of that with me. Do I have to 'spell' it out for you?"

Oh, God, how had she forgotten the scene on the road from Albuquerque. She could hear her own voice now spelling out the word *M-E-N-S*...

She tucked her chin down and dared not look at Ryan. "Yes, I suppose I do sometimes." Then she looked up at him. "And I always regret it afterwards."

"I understand. I think it comes naturally to some people. To shock, that is." The sheriff said softly.

"Some like me, regrettably." She sighed.

Simon Bowes looked from one to the other as his two dinner companions indulged in this peculiar but cheerful volley.

He coughed slightly as a pause occurred when Georgia rose to get some more bread for the table. "I walked out briefly this afternoon to the walled garden of my casita. It was lovely."

"Even lovelier in the moonlight. Many of the flowers only open in the moonlight. Don't miss it."

"Not much of a moon tonight, I think."

"Oh, that's right." She was impressed that this dandy kept track of the phases of the moon.

"Anyhow, now you are here and not enfolded as you were at Lake George," Simon said.

"No, not at all enfolded."

"And what does this place mean to you, this country—aside from the change in your palette?"

"Everything!" She paused. "You know, Mr. Bowes, you're young. Decades younger than me. I am almost a half a century old. In a few years I shall turn fifty. I've come to a point in my life where I want to strip away stuff. You learn so much when you can begin stripping away. That's what it's like out here in a way. You strip away and find a new uncluttered world, an uncluttered sky. A land scraped by wind and the ages."

Ryan McCaffrey had just brought the pie to the table. It looked simply beautiful. The golden curves of the peaches peeked through the lattice crust topping. "Mmmm," Georgia said. He set the knife down beside the pie plate. Knives, she thought, knives. How they varied. The dull innocent blade of that pie knife, which was just slightly pitched down from the handle to pry the slice out. "You do the honors, Ryan," she said softy.

Simon Bowes took a bite. "Oh goodness, this pie is marvelous. And you made it, Sheriff?"

"Indeed, from peaches of my own tree."

They ate silently for a couple of minutes, savoring the pie with the side of vanilla ice cream Georgia had served.

"I have a question for you, Miss O'Keeffe."

"Well, that's what you're here for, I gather."

"Yes, I understand from the sheriff that you often walk out into the desert at dawn."

"I do."

"Would you allow me to walk with you?"

"I suppose so. I leave early, you know. Four-thirty in the morning. I drive usually a mile or two and park and then walk, say, another half mile or so."

"That would be wonderful. And might you allow me to take some photographs?"

"I suppose so." She looked at him directly over the peach pie. They were on their second helping by this time. "You think you can get up and be at the Hacienda gate by four-forty?"

"Absolutely!"

So it was set.

"Can we help you clean up?" Ryan asked as the evening was coming to an end.

"No, no. I can do it."

"I understand that Rosaria no longer works at the Hacienda," he said, "which means you don't have a housekeeper."

"Yes," Georgia said curtly. "I really miss her. Don't know what happened over there."

"Did you ask Carmelita?"

"I tried. She clammed up on me."

She walked to the door with the two men and watched as they climbed into the sheriff's car. She remembered that she had forgotten to tell Ryan that Lindy's hand had been cut by the same kind of knife the murderer had used. How could she have forgotten that? But then again, it would have been awkward to bring it up in front of Simon Bowes. She called out just as they were getting into the car. "Oh, Ryan, I think you forgot your ... your pie cutter."

"Oh ... uh, didn't realize I brought it."

"Yes, you did!" she said a bit too forcefully. He was now striding toward her.

"Come in."

"What's this all about? Not a pie cutter."

"Right, a commando knife. You mentioned you met Lindbergh this evening at cocktails down at the Hacienda."

"Yes."

"You noticed that his hand was bandaged?"

"Yes."

"Same knife. Or rather same kind of knife."

His eyes opened wide. "You don't say—an H-W commando?"

"I do say."

She quickly told him the story of Lindbergh's "accident" and Emily's findings, or rather her assistant Irma's findings.

"Yes, Irma, the one I sent you to over at Emily's office. Alright; thanks for this information."

"Don't forget your pie cutter." She shoved it into his hand.

It was as if an electrical energy crackled between them. She didn't want to let go of the pie cutter, the stupid pie cutter. His eyes wouldn't meet hers as they both clasped the pie cutter.

Then he looked at her and gave a wink. "I'll bring it back. Promise."

Georgia watched him as he turned and walked back to the car.

They pulled out onto the road. The dust kicked up behind them. Red dust in the darkening night.

Am I being foolish here? I'm almost fifty years old. I have a scar on my breast from the cyst. Georgia Totto O'Keeffe, have you lost your mind?

———

Later that same night, luckily a moonless night, Simon Bowes crept up onto the roof of his casita with his Grunow Teledial shortwave antenna. It was a complicated multiband system for transmissions and interceptions on a minimum of three different frequencies. It was going to be such a nuisance having to take it down each night just before dawn and then reassemble it the next. But there was no way he could risk leaving it on the roof. Thankfully, the next few nights would be dark as well. He rotated the antenna to the southeast.

The distance was less than ten miles. He'd had no trouble getting the signal. The signal was clear out here, and he'd had no problem picking up the code. It matched the code of the nine other coded messages they had determined that stretched from New Jersey to Los Angeles. That meant there were close to a dozen operatives in the United States. But tonight, as last night, things seemed to be silent. Nevertheless, he was patient. He tipped his head back and looked at the stars. Pegasus's wing tips were rising just over the clouds that broke on the backs of the mountains to the east.

When there was no moon, there were no shadows. Had there been even the tiniest sliver of a moon, a long shadow might have been cast on the ground below, alerting Simon Bowes that someone was watching the assembling of a receiving antenna for a Grunow Teledial shortwave radio. He had to admit that his alarm over Sparrow's silence was increasing. Crouching now, he donned his earphones to monitor a nearby station. There was still total silence. He didn't understand it. It was definitely what shortwave operators called a "numbers station." But now it too had gone silent. And in this moonless moment, the man with no shadow smiled. Sparrow.

Far away from the New Mexico desert, a man with just four minutes to live smiled into the dawn as the sun broke over the Irish Sea. The yacht rode on gentle swells as he heard the crackle of the receiver below. "Can you pick that up, darling? I believe the Sparrow is chirping. I know I've been out of touch for a while. All for a good reason, but Crypto is probably anxious. I think I can start transmitting again." But it was already too late. There was a thunderous boom and the yacht burst into pieces, sinking within two minutes.

Chapter 21

Georgia had hardly slept after handing Ryan the pie cutter. Notions of sleep grew increasingly futile. She finally gave up two hours before she was to pick up Simon Bowes. She went to the kitchen and ate the rest of the pie. At precisely 4:39 in the morning, she drew up in front of the gates of the Hacienda. Bowes was striding down the drive. He was more appropriately dressed now than he had been the previous evening. Not cowboy boots, but sturdy footwear. A light jacket over a checkered shirt. Not dungarees, but at least pants that weren't pressed with a sharp crease. A bag of some sort slung over one shoulder, presumably for his camera, and even a canteen, most likely supplied by Ghost Ranch.

"So you made it," Georgia said as he opened the door.

"Indeed, and so did you."

"I'm used to it."

Georgia took a deep breath and turned to him. "Let me tell you a bit about the land and where I'm heading today. We'll drive about three miles or so to, well … a sort of turnoff. The roads here are more or less implied than actual. But let me pull over here, as it's a good view, even though it's still pretty dark."

She stopped, and they both got out of the car. "You see the stars hanging over that flat black mesa?"

"Yes."

"But of course it's not really a black mesa. It's purple—isn't it?"

"Extraordinary." He had pulled out a set of binoculars from his bag to look at the mesa.

"No, you can't do that," she said with a chuckle buried beneath her words.

"Can't do what?"

"Look at the land, the sky, through binoculars. You're wrecking the emptiness. First you have to be overwhelmed by it, the space, the sheer emptiness. Only later can you look more, well, selectively. When you're more experienced, like me. I often hold a bone up to the sky. Pelvic bones of cattle are especially good. They have interesting cavities. But you're not ready for that yet. In the meantime, you have to wallow in this void. You haven't wallowed enough. You're trying to reduce it to a ridiculous human scale. So put those away, young man."

"Alright."

"Good. Now look out there, because in seconds, a minute at the longest, things are going to change. You see the mesa is purple against the darkness of the sky. Without the sky, you would think it was just plain black, but with the sky you begin to understand, and you would not truly comprehend how black the black is if it weren't for the stars. But the stars are slipping away, and then you won't grasp the color."

They climbed back into the car. Two miles later, the dawn was just beginning to break when they pulled to the side of the road, got out of the car, and began to walk straight out into the desert. There was sharp line of electric pink as the sun began to rise.

"See that blocklike mesa ahead?"

"Yes."

"They call it Mesa Huerfano—Orphan Mesa."

"And what is the significance of that? A story?"

She stared hard straight ahead at the mesa. It was light enough, so Bowes got his camera out and took a picture of her. She was riveted on that mesa. There was something disturbing about it to her now. Why had she never thought of this before? She began to talk almost as if in a trance.

"They told you, didn't they, about the *brujos*, the witches?"

"Yes, the cattle rustlers. Seemed to be a scheme they dreamed up to keep people away with tales of spirits and winged devils or whatever."

"Yes, very advantageous for keeping folks away."

Georgia remained silent for two minutes or more. She began to speak slowly. "There was a story, you know, that one of the two brothers killed the other one, who he thought knew where some gold was. The dead brother's wife and daughter became prisoners of the murderer. He thought he could get the secret of where the gold was from them. But they didn't know. The daughter had been told by her father and her uncle to watch out for 'earth babies,' long humanlike snakes that emerged from the ground to devour children. They would howl like babies to attract attention; then, when someone found them, they would emerge—anyone who saw an earth baby would die soon after. And one of the worst of these monsters lived right under that mesa—Orphan Mesa."

"Myths can be powerful." Bowes sighed. "So what happened?"

"According to the story, although the mother and daughter were imprisoned close to the Orphan Mesa, the little girl dared. She became the leader and led the mother out one evening when her uncle had drunk so much that he was in a stupor. They both fled."

"And didn't die? Where did they go?"

"Some say Abiquiu."

"The little village?"

"Yes. And she told the priest, who told the authorities—or what constituted authorities back then—where the uncle was."

"And did the little girl become a hero?"

"Not really. She remained rather anonymous, but I didn't realize until just now that her name was Clara. I … I have a friend, a young friend in the village, and her name is Clara."

"Surely not the same Clara."

"Oh, no; this Clara is just ten years old. The other Clara must be close to seventy-five or more by now."

"What made you think of it right now?"

"I really don't know, maybe just looking at that mesa. The Orphan Mesa. Maybe I was thinking about orphans. Clara, the Clara I know, is an orphan."

"So this is where you're going to paint today?"

"Yes, I think I might. I had originally planned to go a little farther, but I like the light right now."

"Would you mind if I took pictures not of you but the landscape?"

"Fine." She turned to the Model A and opened the back. "Sun's coming up fast. I'm going to paint from in here." She quickly set up her easel and from a special shelf that held canvases she drew out a blank one. She turned to Simon Bowes. "If you want to go for a walk, take my snake stick with you."

"Snake stick?"

"Yes, lots of rattlers out here. If one gets in your way, just give it a good poke like this." She stabbed the blade of the stick into the ground.

"Well, alright. Thanks for the demonstration," he said, taking the stick. "You're not painting the mesa, though?"

"No," she said, and offered no explanation but angled the painting and the small stool east, where the sun looked molten as it spread out on the horizon.

For the next hour there was complete silence. She was pleased that Mr. Bowes had not spoken a word. He seemed perfectly content to watch her, and then he would periodically wander off to take photographs of the landscape. There was something about the way he held the camera that made her think he was not a professional. She knew men and cameras. A professional would hold the camera closer to his chest, pressing his elbows close to his ribcage. His feet would be planted firmly a bit farther apart. But most telling of all was that Simon Bowes appeared to be carrying only one lens. One lens in a landscape as vast and spectacular as this desert country was shocking. He was no more a photographer than she was a symphony conductor. He looked as if he were out for a walk in the park.

It was getting on toward midmorning. The sun had begun to drain any color from the land. It was all becoming a harsh, impenetrable white.

"Getting hot out here. But I got to pick up that bone over there before we leave." She slapped a broad-brimmed black hat on her head.

"My word, you could be a friar!" Simon Bowes exclaimed.

"Hardly!" She laughed and walked off toward the pelvis of a large animal she had noticed about fifty feet from the car. But she had to wonder, how would a British gent like Simon Bowes—Church of England—know about friars? There was Friar Tuck, she thought. Did he know about the hat Mr. Castenada had worn? How would he?

As she walked back with the pelvis, she held it up toward the sky. "Perfect, isn't it? Pelvises are my favorite, as I said before. Just look through that oval, Mr. Bowes." She handed him the pelvic bone. "Now hold it up to the sky."

"Ah, yes."

"Tell me, is that not better than your binoculars."

"Miss O'Keeffe, I think you've just given me another opening line of my article about you."

"Better than cow pies?" She laughed. "Come along. Don't get too enthralled. I've got to go into Abiquiu. Have to get some paint thinner at Goetz's, and I'll buy you a soda pop."

"Well, thank you. That's really not necessary."

"Of course it's not necessary. I rarely do what's necessary."

They climbed into the car and drove off, leaving the Orphan Mesa behind them, but not Clara. Clara, it seemed, had invaded her thoughts once again. She was safe for now, at least for a few days, a week, at Emily's in Santa Fe. Georgia and Ryan had not really discussed the coincidence of a commando knife having been used to attack both Castenada and Lindbergh. But she could guess what he might have said about not believing in coincidences.

As Georgia and Bowes were driving into Abiquiu, Simon turned and looked at the church.

"Quite a substantial cross there, between the bell towers."

"Yes. There are only a handful of twin bell towers in this part of the state. So I guess they felt they had to build a larger cross to show up between them."

"Have you done any more paintings of the black crosses?"

"No, not really. That was five years ago, when I first came out to New Mexico. I was in Taos then."

"Any particular reason you quit painting them?"

"No. I might paint them again. I was just so entranced with shadows, the shadows of the crosses in particular, when I first came out here five years ago. Back East, especially at Lake George, where it is so cloudy and often rains, shadows are a rarity. Those church crosses were all painted either at sunset or sunrise. At those times of day, the crosses are backlit and appear black. Really black, not purple like the mesas appeared, as I pointed out earlier. Just black-black. When their shadows start to slide over the ground—well, that's interesting too. I noticed it the other day when I was in town just about sunset. Kind of like putting the lid over a coffin."

"Rather macabre."

"Maybe. I don't know. The shadows of crosses interest me more than the actual crosses. Who knows? I might someday start to paint just shadows of things."

A casual remark seemed almost prophetic a moment later as they both climbed out of the Model A and headed up the front steps of Goetz's store. She stopped suddenly. The shadow cast by her own broad hat collided with another coming down the steps, and sliding over each other, the two became one. It gave her a start. Had it been what Simon Bowes had said just a quarter of an hour ago. *"My word, you could be a friar!"*

"Miss O'Keeffe," a voice said.

"Brother William—I—I mean Father."

The priest laughed warmly. "As I said before when you and the sheriff visited me, a title is but a shroud for an occupation, as the body is simply a shroud for the soul. I don't care what you call me. How about Bill?"

"Well, Bill, look at that design our hats make on the boards of the porch."

"Ah, the eye of the artist never stops looking. Even at shadows."

"Yes, that's true; I never stop looking. I was just telling Mr. Bowes here about how shadows interest me. Mr. Bowes is an art journalist and came all the way from London to interview me." However, Mr. Bowes was not looking at the shadows on the ground but had his head tipped up.

"That's some rig he has on top of his roof. Antenna, I suppose."

"Yes, Mr. Mueller is a ham radio enthusiast. And I'm sure you know, Mr. Bowes, that Miss O'Keeffe is our treasure in New Mexico."

"Don't call me that," Georgia almost snapped. She immediately felt abashed.

"Sorry. Didn't mean to offend," he said quickly.

"Oh, don't worry," she mumbled. "I … I just don't like the word *treasure*—that's all." She felt Simon Bowes's attention fixed on her. His fascination seemed to go beyond that of a journalist. Good God, he couldn't be falling in love with her. She was probably twice his age. And besides, she thought he might be "a little light in his loafers," as Stieglitz would say. It could just be that he was so arty and British. She kept her eyes cast down and focused on the shadows as they slid together then apart with the slightest movements of her head and that of Father William. A slow tango of shadows. Why did this image affect her so? Again, Bowes's words came back to her: *My word, you could be a friar!* What did this fellow Bowes know about such accouterments of friars and such? Who was he really? She wasn't frightened. She was intrigued. She recalled the awkward way he had held that camera earlier. His elbows all stuck out at odd angles. He looked more like an ungainly bird than an experienced photographer.

"Come on, Mr. Bowes. I'll buy you a soda pop." Simon Bowes's head was still tipped up as he studied the antenna.

Just as they were coming into the store, José was coming out.

"Ah, José, where is my usual bell ringer?" Father William asked.

"Clara? She moved into town for a while with her sister."

"Really?" The voices drifted through the screen door behind them as Georgia walked up to the counter.

"Mr. Mueller, could I trouble you for a soda pop for my friend here, Simon Bowes?"

"Certainly, Miss O'Keeffe. And welcome, Mr. Bowes." At just that moment, a man came out of the stock room. "Ah, Miss O'Keeffe, Mr. Bowes, might I introduce you to my uncle, Willy Goetz. The previous owner."

"A pleasure!" The man stepped forward. There was absolutely no resemblance between Otto Mueller and his uncle Willy Goetz, who was a thin blade of a man. He reminded Georgia of a shard of flint. The kind used for arrowheads. He was perhaps in his mid-fifties, with sparse hair and a pencil-thin mustache. He wore spectacles. Had his mustache been a little thicker and his eyebrows a little bushier, he could have been Groucho Marx. Except there was nothing funny about him.

"And what brings you here Mr. Bowes?" Otto Mueller asked.

"Miss O'Keeffe, of course. I'm an art journalist for *Colloquy* magazine."

"Sorry to say, we only carry the almanac here, along with a couple of hunting and fishing magazines. And a lot of hunting and fishing gear—rods, ammo …"

"And some knives, Mr. Mueller. You know young José out there?" Georgia tipped her head toward where José was standing and talking to Father William. "He's quite taken with that special knife—the commando knife."

"Dangerous knife. You have to be experienced to use that one. I'd never sell it to a young kid," Otto Mueller replied.

Georgia swallowed. "Well, that's responsible of you, Mr. Mueller. I'm pleased to hear it."

"What brought you here, Mr. Mueller?" Bowes asked.

"The air! My lungs were damaged in the Great War." He quickly held up his hand. "Our fault, I admit it. We were the ones to use the mustard gas. One wind shift, and that did it to me and my platoon. I was one of the luckier ones. But, yes, we were wrong to use such weapons. I am very grateful to America for allowing me to come here. Yes, let bygones be bygones."

"That's quite fine of you, sir," Simon Bowes said, extending his hand to shake Otto Mueller's. The storekeeper looked slightly undone by the gesture; there was a split second's hesitation, then he shook Bowes's hand heartily.

A short time later, Georgia dropped Simon Bowes off at the Hacienda after they had driven out through the Red Hills to see the landscape she hoped to begin painting soon. It felt good to be alone. She hadn't spent so much continuous time in someone's company since she'd arrived here. But right now she did wish she could speak to Ryan about that strange tango of shadows that was sliding through her mind: the intersecting black disks made by the shadows of her and Father William's hats.

Could the murder have been a result of mistaken identity? Would someone actually have wanted to kill Father William? Why? Or perhaps that person wanted to kill someone else wearing the same hat. After all, there were variations of that hat all over the Southwest, and they were not solely worn by priests. Those were called the cappello romano, but they were almost indistinguishable from the bolero she wore and had picked up in Taos five years ago, or the saturno, named for the ringed planet, or the very prevalent gaucho hat. Friars' hats were broader brimmed and were more often dark brown than black. But shadows did not discriminate between colors. They were impervious. All shadows were black. She thought back yet again to that convergence of shadows on the steps of Goetz's store—the two shadows, seemingly identical, gliding together. "No, Sheriff," she murmured to herself, and thought, *Not a coincidence but a confluence of shadows.* Could there have been a mistake out there in the desert that night, a misapprehension, and the wrong friar killed? But, of course, one was not really a friar. One had presumed to be a "man of the cloth"—and of a hat, she thought. Who was this Alberto Castenada? Why was he posing as a friar? And had it gotten him killed?

A strong feeling began to grow in her. But for what reason? Why would anybody want to murder a man of the church in the first place? Was it really possible that Father William was the intended victim? Or maybe herself! She was tempted to drive straight into Santa Fe and tell Ryan that the wrong man had been murdered. *Dammit!* Tonight was tango night, and she had promised to be there. Good lord, it might as well be charades or bingo night at Lake George. The alarming thought came back to her. Had she, with her broad hat, been the intended victim? So many times she had taken that same path around sunset. It would be just twilight when she would return, when the longest shadows were cast, making her a perfect target. It could have been me! But why? Why would anyone want to kill me? To get at something else? But what? Was she just collateral?

Chapter 22

"Left—forward—one—two; back—one—two ... now open reverse." Diego and Felicity were sliding across the floor. Both of their backs arced, their chins lifted high. They now swirled to a stop. *What am I doing here?* Thought Georgia. But she knew. Pieces of a very diabolical puzzle had to be fitted together. There were the shadows of hats. The shattering glass. The sex, or what she thought was sex, and the Lindberghs and his sliced hand. The farthing, of course, and therefore Simon Bowes. And Clara! Rosaria fired on the same day that Lindbergh went to the hospital to have his hand stitched up.

Diego stepped forward in his tight-fitting vest. "Now, ladies and gentleman, that was just the briefest of demonstrations. Or maybe I should say ladies and ladies, for we seem to be short on men! Or maybe we just have a few very nice short men." He glanced over at Chuckie Powell and his twin brother, George, who both burst into giggles. "No *problema*. The children always learn the fastest." Diego clapped his hands together. Felicity beamed at him with a simpering gaze. "And soon there will be more!" He darted a loving glance at Felicity. Whatever the "deal" had been that caused her to shriek and for a pane of glass to shatter must have been resolved. She was dressed in a dazzling saffron gown with a vertical ruffle that started at the hem and climbed on a diagonal to one shoulder. The gown was designed to swirl.

"Diego! What a place to announce this." *Ahs* and *oohs* reverberated throughout the room. "Yes, a little bambino—a *bébé*, bambino, is on the way." Applause rang out. "*Sí, mi esposa* ... Felicity ..." He held his arm out toward Felicity, who blushed, gave a dazzling smile, and nodded to her husband. Diego cut a stunning figure, thin as a dark blade in his tight black pants and black shirt that was slit almost to his navel. From Felicity's hand a ring blazed with a diamond as big as the Ritz, thought Georgia, remembering the Scott Fitzgerald story of a dozen or so years before. But who was really the leader and the follower in the dance Felicity and Diego had just demonstrated? Was Felicity really the follower in that dance? She had a rather grim look on her face. A determined look more suitable for a leader.

"And before we start, a couple of things. You see in that dance that I was the leader and Felicity the follower. In the next dance, the follower will become the leader and the leader the follower. And secondly, let us give a thank-you to our band, our Orquesta Tipica, as we call a tango band. On guitars we have our own wranglers John Lopez and Pedro Garcia. And on the piano we have Lorenzo Juarez." He introduced the two violinists, who Georgia did not recognize.

"Now choose your partners please." Georgia looked around. She was surprised not to see Simon Bowes. But he had said that he wanted to start writing up his notes for the article.

Three or four minutes later, when the music stopped, it was time to change partners. The follower was instructed to choose a new partner and become the leader in the next dance.

"And remember when you dance—what we call the 'forbidden dance'— though there might be distance between you and your partner, your eyes are always locked. And finally, listen to the music. El Flaco, the greatest of all tango dancers, said that 'music goes in through your ears, then is filtered through one's heart and comes out through one's feet.'"

Georgia had already decided she was choosing one of the Powell twins, George or Chuckie. Two advantages—one, a child would be short and she could see over his head and keep her eyes on everyone in the room. She glanced around and spotted two very unhappy campers, Lanny and Peter Wainwright. They appeared to be glaring at each other. Elsie Powell came up to Peter and tapped him on the shoulder. "Me! Peter?"

"Delighted, Miss Elsie." Lanny seemed relieved. She buzzed over to Eduardo, one of the wranglers who had obviously been drafted to attend this gathering. Carmelita and Anne Morrow Lindbergh were paired. "Come on," said Anne; "we can do this, Carmelita." There was no sign of Anne's husband, but of course he was literally handicapped for this kind of evening.

"Alright now, here we go." Diego clapped his hands together. The band started up. Although, from the look on Anne Morrow Lindbergh's face, had she been dancing with her own husband, she might have wanted to squeeze that bandaged hand until it bled. Carmelita herself did not look too happy.

But it was Chuckie who yelped, "Ouch! Miss O'Keeffe you stepped on my foot."

"Oh, sorry there, Chuckie. I don't weigh that much. Hope no permanent damage."

"How much do you weigh, Miss O'Keeffe?"

"Oh, not sure. Around 118 pounds or so."

"I weigh eighty pounds and I'm almost five feet tall. You know how much that is per inch?"

"Can't say as I do."

"Well, I know. That is one point three pounds per inch." He paused. "I rounded down a little bit."

"Oh," Georgia replied. "I appreciate your honesty, Chuckie." Georgia realized that she had actually had less-fascinating conversations in her life than this one. The music had stopped.

Diego clapped his hands again. "Now. It is time to change partners. Whoever is the follower in your couple can now choose another person. And remember, we rarely clasp hands in the tango, for we do not want to interrupt the lovely flowing line of an arm by bending at the wrist."

Felicity was approaching Georgia.

"My turn." She smiled sweetly. The music began again.

After a minute or so, Diego called out over the music. "Now we're going to try out the dragging foot step where the lead's left foot drags toward the right foot and the follower of course follows. This slow drag you must make it sultry. And this is why they call tango the forbidden dance. It can lead to all kinds of trouble. Romantic trouble."

"Hey, you're pretty good at this, Felicity," Georgia said.

"Practice—after all, I'm married to the teacher." There was a grim note in her voice. Georgia followed Felicity's gaze. The teacher was now dancing with Peter Wainwright. Peter was exceedingly graceful. Perhaps it was because he no longer towered over his previous partner, Elsie.

"Wonderful news about your baby," Georgia said.

"Yes, isn't it though," Felicity replied. "Should we try the open reversal move?"

"That's pretty advanced."

"Trust me, I've done it a million times. Follow me."

Georgia's last partner for the evening was Peter Wainwright. "You're a fast learner, Peter. So good at this."

"Well, I had taken some lessons before."

"You had? Where?"

"Princeton."

"Really now. How interesting."

"Princeton Triangle Club. You've heard of it?"

"Yes, that theatrical club where men dress up as women."

"That's it. Great fun."

"I can imagine," she murmured inaudibly.

"Let's try that *corte* move, where I go backward in that lunge move," Peter suggested.

"I'm game."

"I bet you are, Miss O'Keeffe." They covered a lot of ground, with Peter gliding backward then reversing the move.

"Tell me, Peter, when Albert Einstein came to Princeton hardly a year ago, did he tango?"

"Yes, actually he loved to tango. And guess what, I had the pleasure to dance with him once. I was better at the tango than the relativity theory."

"So what was Einstein like?"

"I never took a course from him, but I'll tell you one thing."

"What's that?"

"He had dandruff on his collar, and he liked the ladies."

The music stopped. Lanny cut in on Peter. And this time Elsie cut in on Felicity.

"Miss Sanchez, do you think your husband could get me into the movies."

"Oh, shit," Felicity muttered. "That's all anyone ever asks me." She stomped off the dance floor. "Sorry, but I'm not feeling well. Pregnancy, you know."

Georgia almost gasped out loud. As if a kid would understand this. *What a selfish bitch*, Georgia thought. Elsie's face was a mixture of sadness and confusion. Eduardo was just approaching Georgia for the next dance.

"Eduardo, I think I'll sit this one out."

"Sure, Miss O'Keeffe."

Georgia made her way over to where Elsie was sitting chewing on her nails. She took her free hand and held it lightly. "People are stupid, aren't they?"

Elsie looked at her. There was a flicker of astonishment in her eyes.

Georgia could almost read her thoughts. "Yeah, I know; you thought only kids could behave badly."

"Not exactly true, but yeah."

"I heard what that dumb cluck said to you." Now a smile began to inscribe itself on the young girl's face. "Miss O'Keeffe," she giggled. "You called a grown-up a dumb cluck."

"I've called many grown-ups dumb clucks and worse." She was thinking of Stieglitz and the names she had called him after he had forced her to get an abortion.

"I think my parents are dumb clucks. They fight all the time. I think they might get a divorce."

Georgia wasn't sure how to answer this. She had heard the divorce rumors too. It was always the children who paid the price in these situations. Elsie turned and faced her squarely. "Aren't you going to tell me it will all be okay?"

"Why would I do that?"

"That's what grown-ups always say. That's what my grandma told me when I cried to her."

"Well, I can't tell you that. It wouldn't be honest."

"You're a very honest lady, Miss O'Keeffe." Elsie got up and walked away. Georgia looked toward Elsie's mother, Lanny, who was now gliding across the floor with Peter. Two more miserable creatures she'd never seen. Lanny seemed to exude bitterness from every pore.

She had expected to see Felicity in the lobby, but now there was only Joaquin, behind the desk.

"Señora Sanchez isn't here?" she asked.

"No, Miss O'Keeffe. She wasn't feeling well. Lupe drove her back to the casita."

"Oh!" A breathy voice gasped behind Georgia as she stood at the desk. She turned around and saw Anne Lindbergh. "Uh, Miss O'Keeffe, are you driving up toward my casita?" She didn't wait for an answer. "Would you mind dropping me first?"

"Uh …" Georgia was a little surprised by the request after how she had so thoroughly confronted her husband. A meek look filled her eyes. *This woman is beseeching me.* She looked as if she would drop to her knees and beg.

"Certainly. My car is right outside."

They walked together through the darkness to the Model A. No sooner had they seated themselves in the car than Anne turned to her. She grabbed Georgia's hand that was on the gear stick.

"You don't need to apologize, Mrs. Lindbergh."

"How could one apologize for my husband?" she said, with a sob threatening to break in her throat. "It was wrong what he said the other night."

"I feel it was more than wrong, Mrs. Lindbergh."

"More than wrong? How do you mean?" Her lovely blue eyes grew soft. A childlike innocence appeared to fill them.

"Mrs. Lindbergh, it was despicable what he said about Jews. "

"That is a strong word, Miss O'Keefe."

"What he said was strong and nasty. I can think of no other words."
Georgia took a deep breath and wondered why this woman was even
talking to her. Is this what she honestly considered an apology? Another
thought suddenly struck Georgia—was Anne Lindbergh trying to warn
her of something? Did she know about the initials *G.O.* on the map? *No!
Don't be a fool, Georgia.*

Anne Lindbergh had turned her head and was peering into the darkness
ahead. "When one is married to a hero, a golden boy, as he is so often
called, a flawless man, one might think …" Her voice dropped away.

"What might one think?" Georgia said in a low voice.

She sighed, "Our son—his murder was called the crime of the century.
But, Miss O'Keeffe, my husband might be the criminal of the century."

"I ,,, I really don't know what you are saying, Mrs. Lindbergh."

"I'm just saying what you already know. He hates Jews, and I'm saying
there will be a war. Maybe not this year, or next or even the year after
that, but it will come, and … and … and when it does come … well,
perhaps we will have to face fascism, let fascism take its course and learn
to live with it."

Georgia was aghast. What had started out as an apology of sorts had
turned into a warning that she would have to understand. That was what
Anne Morrow Lindbergh was saying. Georgia knew she would not sleep
tonight. She wished she could call Stieglitz, but it would be close to one
o'clock in the morning at Lake George. She'd wake the entire household.

That same night, Nina Mueller had been sleeping soundly until she rolled
over and realized that the space beside her on the mattress was empty
and that Otto was not next to her in bed. She heard footsteps above.
She looked at the baby booties on the dresser that Miss O'Keeffe had
given her. She knew she could never mother this child as she should
with the specter of that other woman. A sudden resolve flooded her body
and settled firmly somewhere deep inside her. She would confront Otto.
Even though he had warned her that she must never come into that

room when he was on the radio. That it was extremely official business he was conducting. Well, this was extremely personal business. Although it might be called "*Reich*" business, it was her body and that of another woman's body and a baby that would be entrusted to her, so this made it her business. Indeed, it was through the Party that they were able to adopt the coming baby. She would go quietly and then simply open the door, surprising him. She had a little speech prepared in her mind. She was halfway up the steps and could hear him speaking. Just as she was on the last step, the door opened and a wash of light flooded the narrow stairwell. The shadow of a man much thinner than Otto Mueller danced against the wall. *"Wilkommen wir haben Sie erwartet." Waiting for me? They were expecting me?* Nina thought. Then there was nothing, nothing except a sweet strong odor as something was pressed again her mouth and nose.

Chapter 23

"There will be a war ... I am saying ... he hates Jews ... let fascism take its course ..."

Anne Morrow Lindbergh's words haunted Georgia. They were all she could think of when she woke up the next day. She decided to take a walk while the sun was still low. She had some extra drawing paper and pastels. She had promised to take them to Peter Wainwright's for the children but kept forgetting. So she now set off to deliver them. He might be out, but she could leave them on his kitchen table. As she came out, she caught sight of Felicity Sanchez walking down the road. Felicity waved.

"Hello, Georgia."

"Hello, Felicity."

"Where you going?"

"Just to Peter's to deliver drawing paper and some pastels for the children."

"Want any company?"

"Sure. Glad to see you're feeling better."

"Oh yes, much better. They say you get over the morning sickness after a couple of months. But mine doesn't confine itself to morning. It seems it can be any time of the day."

"Well, it will be worth it, I'm sure."

"Yes, I'll have to put my acting on hold for a bit."

"Have you started acting?"

"Oh yes, and I was to have started shooting a film with Diego next month, *Sombrero Moon*. Not a big part, but they said I was perfect." She sighed. "But alas."

"Well, there'll be more movies in your future, I'm sure."

"I certainly hope so. But I'm also sure this baby will be worth it."

"Oh, absolutely."

They walked through the gate to Peter's casita. Georgia knocked on the door.

"Yoo-hoo!" She knocked again. "Well, no problem. I know where the key is. I've come over here often to give him some art supplies for the Powell children." Georgia walked over to a large ceramic tub that was spilling with bright nasturtiums. She reached into the mass of orange and yellow blossoms and pulled out a key and let them in. "Oh, a note in the planter!" She picked up an envelope with the distinctive Ghost Ranch logo. "Well, I'll put it on his desk. And here's the key."

"Oh, this is quite charming!" Felicity said in a somewhat distracted voice as they walked in. Georgia went directly to the desk and sat down to scribble a quick note to Peter about the supplies she had brought. Sitting at the desk writing, Georgia felt Felicity come close behind her. It was almost as if her eyes were drilling into her back. She turned around quickly. "Something wrong?"

"Oh, you know, just gazing out at the view." But there really wasn't a view from the desk. The nearest window was at least eight feet away. Felicity's face was pale except for the dabs of rouge on her cheeks that now stood out like a bad paint job. "Nothing at all wrong." Her mouth cracked into a smile.

She ran her hand along a shelf of books. "Shakespeare. My! My!"

"Peter was a student at Princeton until he graduated about a year or so ago."

A canteen hung on a set of antlers. "He mustn't be gone for long or going far, as he usually takes two canteens with him," Georgia commented. "Have to be careful in this desert, not just snakes. It can be scorching this time of year. But look, the sun is setting." She pointed in the direction of the Chama Valley. "There is a white rock formation, pillars really, over there that reflect the sunset. Must be gorgeous right now." She sighed.

"Wish you were there?" Felicity said.

"Oh, there are so many places one wishes one could be out here." Georgia laughed. "All at the same time!" She picked up a note on a pad of paper on the counter and scribbled a note for Peter, reminding him that she would happily come by and give the kids some drawing instruction. She and Felicity left. She replaced the key in the planter, and they walked for another quarter mile together until Felicity took the road leading to her own casita.

––––––––––

Across the valley, somewhere in the Chama hills, the sun had finished setting and a chill wind blew through. The sickening sweet smell still seemed to cling to the darkness where Nina Mueller lay hog-tied, *Händen und Füßen gefesselt sein,* on hard ground in a dark space. And like a pig, something was stuffed in her mouth. Not an apple, however, just a rag of some sort. She tried to move her feet and felt something sharp digging into her ankles. Her wrists and hands were bound as well. The binding was meticulous—even her fingers were tied so there was no possible movement. They were almost numb from the strictures of what seemed to be wire.

It might have been a cave she was in, but Nina Mueller was unsure how long she had been there. *Why? Why? Am I Gretel waiting to be fattened up for the oven? Who is the witch? Otto? Fat Otto?*

The place she lay was filled with small sounds—the skittering of mice, the whisper of wind against rock, the light footsteps of a small animal—a coyote or perhaps a deer. Might they find her? Help her as if in a good fairy tale.

Then she heard footsteps, human footsteps, not the pitter-patter of rodents or the delicate hooves of deer or pronghorn. She tried to call for help, but she only gagged.

Someone was bending over her, but their head was covered with a hood that had only two slits for eyes. Almost gently she felt a hand at the back of her neck, lifting her head slightly. A flicker of hope. She felt a wire tighten and cut into her neck … then nothing.

Later that same evening, a message came up to the stables from Carmelita at the Hacienda. *Tomas, we need your help at the bar this evening. Joaquin had a family emergency. Could you be a sweetheart and help us out?*

Let another wrangler mix their goddamn margaritas. This was about the last thing Tomas wanted to do. No favors for Carmelita. If he saw her, he'd be tempted to punch her in the face. He was furious about his sister's firing. He had decided to ride his pinto out to the Orphan Mesa. It was place he knew like the back of his hand. Maria Rosa, his sometimes girlfriend, had wanted to come with him, but he wanted to be alone. He needed to think. She chattered too much.

Rosaria had been fired. He had money, was making good money with this new job. But it was a job he couldn't talk about. And if he began throwing money around, people would become curious, too curious. It was a moonlit night, and the mesa cast a long shadow over the basin from which it rose. He had taken off the pinto's saddle, put it on the ground. He took some crushed marijuana leaves from a small pouch and stuffed his pipe. He was about to light up when an odd shadow caught his attention. How many times had he come to this place, the Orphan Mesa? But now there was the shadow of something that was not supposed to be here. He knew this instinctively. There was not a cactus around here. Not a boulder. Not a chunk off the mesa. Something immobile was casting that shadow. And then in the moonlight he saw another shadow—that of wings, vultures' wings—printed against the moon-glazed sand of the desert. *Something died out here.* He got up and walked the hundred yards or less to where the birds were just settling by a heap. Waving his arms he broke into a run. *¡Salid bastardos! ¡Salid!*

The birds took off. It wasn't an animal; it was a woman. He fell to his knees. "Oh, Holy Mother. Señora Mueller!" Her head was twisted at a very bizarre angle. Her eyes glared up at him, each one with a tiny reflection of the moon. A thin line of blood encircled her neck. Garroted. Nina Mueller had been garroted.

It had been a long day for Ryan, actually an endless day. He had not slept for two nights. Georgia seemed to fill his mind. Would they maybe have made love that night when he had come back with the pie cutter? How many years had it been since he had last made love? More than three, as Mattie had become sick nearly two years before she died. She had actually died in his arms in the hospital. He had defied every nurse and every rule and had just crawled into the bed beside her and held her for the last two hours as the breath went out of her. What would it have been like to hold Georgia, that lean woman in his arms who was pulsing with life? She appeared all tendons and muscle.

But now other thoughts crowded in. There was something wrong with this case. Who was Alberto Castenada? And who was Simon Bowes? Although his credentials checked out, Ryan didn't for one second believe that Bowes was an art journalist. He had called *Colloquy* magazine and confirmed Bowes was on the staff. A plummy voice on the other end, some English socialite, confirmed that and told him Bowes was not available, as he was traveling in America. Was there anything else she could do for him? When he asked where Bowes was in America, she seemed a bit cagey and replied that she thought New York most likely—then quickly added that she had no contact information.

She was dead-ending him. He knew that from the first airborne syllable of her crystalline voice. He could just picture her. Porcelain complexion. Teacup nose. Scent of roses. It all reeked. He needed to call Ray Phillips again at the BI—but then he had another idea. Three years or so ago, the BI had hired their first Negro, one Lincoln Stone, as a special agent. Not only that, but his brother Washington Stone was the third Negro to be a Texas Ranger. Why hadn't he thought of Linc? Although they had met only once, at a conference in DC, they had really hit it off. Both loved to fish, and they had decided to make plans to go fishing out West. Linc would try to get his brother Wash to join them. But then Mattie got sick and, well, there were no plans for anything fun.

Now that he thought of it, the dinner at Georgia's was the only social event he had gone to in three years. Couldn't count funerals and wakes, of course. And it wasn't like people hadn't invited him. He just hadn't wanted to go. He found work his only solace. At work no one asked him "How ya doin'? How ya gettin' along?" It was just work. A bank robbed in the next county. A painting or something stolen from that crazy millionaire lady in Taos, Mabel Dodge Luhan. She was actually married to a distant cousin of Mattie's, Tony Lujan, a Tewa from the Taos Pueblo. He had become Mabel Dodge's fourth or fifth husband. Functionally illiterate but a clever guy, Tony had helped Mabel build her sprawling house, which drew artists handpicked by Mabel to pursue their craft, as well as large amounts of peyote.

Before he was sheriff, Ryan had been a state trooper. He was called one time to search for two "missing guests" who had wandered off from Mabel's house. He found them in a ditch, babbling away. The woman was half naked. When he came home and told Mattie, she asked who they were. He had to think to remember their names. "Martha somebody and a man named Lawrence."

"Ryan!" Mattie exclaimed. "Not D. H. Lawrence and Martha Graham!"

"Yeah, that's the guy, and her last name was Graham."

Mattie read constantly. She was in fact a true intellectual. She found a beauty in words that was elusive to him. He preferred nonfiction, how-to books, fishing and hunting. He tried a few times to read a detective mystery and was so appalled by the manner in which evidence was handled that he usually gave up before the end of the book. He occasionally did read a children's book that Mattie had raved about. He preferred fantasy children's books—*The Wonderful Wizard of Oz, Peter Pan*—books so far from detective mysteries that he couldn't be appalled by any errors.

He took out his list of Bureau of Investigation numbers then dialed Linc Stone.

Three rings and the phone was picked up. "Lincoln Stone here."

"Hey, buddy, got some inquiries about a largemouth bass I sent your way. Hook in the gullet."

"Ryan! My friend. How you be?"

"I'm fine, but, well, that largemouth bass—even dead, he's given me a heck of a time."

"Bass are mighty rare in your neck of the woods. I go down to Florida to get mine."

"Yeah, that's just the problem. I don't think he's mine, and I don't think … uh, Morgan Smathers Funeral Home is the place to get him mounted for my wall."

"Oh …" There was a long silence. "I get you. That's what they told you, yeah?"

"Yeah, that's what that bald-headed guide told me."

"I'm reading you loud and clear. What kind of fly was used to catch him?"

"Commando, H-W." There was a low whistle from Lincoln Stone's end of the line.

They chatted on amiably in a mélange of fly-fishing language that afforded a fairly decent code for what they were really talking about. Why he had not thought of calling Linc right off the bat, he didn't know.

"Well, buddy," Linc continued, "I was planning to go down to the Potomac myself and try getting some stripers."

"They're running now?"

"You betcha."

"Okay, then, let me know if you have any luck. Maybe I'll come down."

"Or maybe I'll go out to New Mexico for a largemouth."

"You do that, Linc."

"I'll be back to you soon."

"Call me at home if you need to."

Chapter 24

Lincoln Stone did not relish this walk down the long corridor of the BI. J. Edgar had been in a foul mood all summer. Rumors—swamp rumors, as Linc had first thought them—had started to burble up from the muck of DC about an "unnatural relationship" between Hoover and Clyde Tolson, his deputy assistant director. In fact, it was said that this was the reason Hoover had gone light on the Mafia investigation. Meyer Lansky supposedly had compromising pictures of Hoover with Tolson. The director had been in a bad mood all summer. But maybe a Brit found dead in the desert would be a distraction. Some international intrigue.

"Hello, Miss Gandy," A wraithlike woman sat behind a desk outside Hoover's office. A name plaque read MISS HELEN W. GANDY. Beneath the name were the words EXECUTIVE ASSISTANT in smaller letters. Her face was taut and her eyes mirthless. It would be harder to imagine a grimmer person.

"Oh, hello, Mr. Stone." She blinked several times. Although Stone had been at the bureau for almost three years now, it took some people a while to get accustomed to seeing a Negro in the building in a position of relative stature—in short, not a janitor, a doorman, or a waiter in the lunchroom.

"I need to see the boss. It's about an international issue that has just come up that is of some urgency."

"International!" There was a new alertness in her eyes now that had nothing to do with the color of his skin.

"The United Kingdom," Linc replied.

"United Kingdom," she breathed more than spoke the two words.

Perhaps she was imagining crowns, tiaras, ermine-trimmed robes. He didn't know. He merely put his hand on her desk and tapped his fingers as if waiting for her to act. She did, plucking the telephone from its cradle and dialing one digit. She didn't like his fingers on her desk.

"Mr. Hoover, Agent Stone is here to see you regarding an international issue. Great Britain. Yes, sir. I'll send him right in."

He walked through the door. Hoover was standing with his back to his desk and gazing out his window onto Pennsylvania Avenue. He began to talk without turning around. No "Hello." No "What can I do for you?"

"You know, Lincoln, I've been thinking that here we are doing great work for this new president." The way he said "this new president" made Linc feel that Hoover didn't particularly care for Roosevelt. "And you know I don't cotton to sharing this building with the Justice Department." He kept his back to his visitor. "What do you think about that?"

Linc shifted the weight on his feet. "As an agent, what do I feel about it?"

"Yes," he said with his back still turned. "I think if we moved it would be good, good for morale, good for space."

Hoover finally turned around. There was just a hint of a startled look in his eye. As if he were thinking, *Why is this black man in my office? Why isn't he carrying a tray with a napkin over his forearm and his favorite drink, a fizz Cherry Heering with Jamaican rum, bourbon, and soda water?* He had started drinking them shortly after Prohibition ended. Discovered them at the fancy new nightclub in New York, the Stork Club. "So Stone, Agent Stone, what do you think of that idea?"

"I approve. We're a bit crowded in here."

"Absolutely." He paused. "And one more thing."

"What might that be, sir?"

"I think we need a name change."

"A name change?"

"Don't look surprised, Agent Stone. I think we need to be called the Federal Bureau of Investigation. It gives us more authority. Hell, anyplace could be a bureau of investigation. That's way too local. Too vague. Don't you agree?"

"Yes, sir. I think you're right."

"Oh, and by the way, how's the Old Hoot Owl investigation going?" A nasty little curl began at one corner of the director's mouth. Stone suspected it could turn into a snarl at any moment. "Old Hoot Owl" was Hoover's code name for Eleanor Roosevelt. "She's pink, I tell you. I'm hearing all sorts of things about her and her liberal causes. Got to nip that in the bud. I know you're on that detail. We put you on it because she likes your kind. Partial to your race."

Linc Stone wanted to say something, but the hardest part of his job was shutting up in moments like this.

"So, anyhow, what brings you here? International something with United Kingdom."

"Uh, yes, sir. A man dead, murdered out in the desert. Traveling under a false name and occupation."

"What was the occupation?"

"Catholic priest."

"So what does this have to do with England?"

"Police department in Albuquerque sent the body to Morgan Smathers," Lincoln Stone replied.

"Oh, well that settles it, doesn't it? Must be Britain or some place in Europe, I guess. Maybe I should contact Signal Intelligence Service here. What the devil is that man's name? Just talked to him the other day. A Jew, Fritz something or other." Hoover began scratching head. "Ask Miss Gandy on your way out. She'll know."

Miss Gandy did indeed know, but she didn't speak the name out loud. Instead, with nary a reply to Agent Stone, she got up and went into the director's office to tell him. Linc was left standing in front of her desk to ponder how many times in the course of less than ten minutes he had been insulted.

She looked surprised when she found him still standing there.

"Mr. Stone?"

"Agent Stone, Miss Gandy. You know I took an oath of office, didn't you?"

"What are you talking about?" She seemed genuinely perplexed.

"As an agent here, I took an oath and solemnly swore like every federal employee to support and defend the Constitution of the United States against all enemies, foreign and domestic. I did that. I swore to bear true faith and allegiance to the same. I took this oath and its obligation freely, without any mental reservation or purpose of evasion; and I promised that I will well and faithfully discharge the duties of the office on which I am about to enter. So help me God." He paused. "As secretary to Director Hoover, did you take such an oath? Are we on equal ground here?"

Miss Gandy was flustered. The word *equal* had upset her. And it was written all over her face, even though she didn't speak it out loud. *This uppity nigger!*

"Now, Miss Gandy, what is the name of the person at the Signal Intelligence Service?"

After Ryan had hung up from talking to Linc Stone, he was allowing himself some time to reflect on Linc, their friendship over the years, and how he was truly an exceptional person in DC aside from the color of his skin. He heard some commotion outside his office and, seconds later, Descheeni burst in. "Body found out by Orphan Mesa."

"What? Not another fake priest?"

"No, the wife of the fellow who owns the Abiquiu general store."

"Mueller?"

"Yeah. Nina Mueller."

"Have you alerted the coroner?"

"Yes, sir. She's driving right out."

Another commando knife? He had been about to ask when Descheeni raced out the door.

Chapter 25

In the coroner's office three hours later, masked and gowned, Emily Bryce bent over the body of Nina Mueller with a magnifying glass and began speaking in a monotone. "Note the following: This is not, I repeat, not manual strangulation. It is ligature asphyxiation. Evidence of hemorrhaging, petechiae around the neck, almost evenly. Conjunctiva of the eyes shows similar petechiae. No fingernail marks or fingerprint bruises on the skin. Assailant must have been wearing gloves. You getting all this?" She turned to Irma. The women had put Vicks VapoRub under their noses.

"Yes, ma'am."

"Good, now find me the needle-nose tweezers and we can lift out this garroting wire and see what the larynx damage is. I want to be careful with the wire, though. Don't know if we could ever get prints off this thin of a wire. But we can try, same for the wire around her hands and feet." She sighed.

Irma Greyeyes returned with the tweezers. Emily reached for her magnifying eyeglasses, which were somewhat like twin jeweler's loupes set in a frame with five changeable lenses and tiny lights. They were invaluable in this kind of work—picking out garroting wires, small caliber bullets, or fragments of hollow-point bullets from body tissue. It took her a quarter of an hour to extract the wire embedded in Nina Mueller's neck.

"Okay, got it. Send that over to forensics. After they're done looking for any prints—which I doubt they'll get—have them do a tensile strength test on the wire. This one looks to my unpracticed eye like piano wire, and I would guess that is what it is. As I recall, that has a ksi of around four hundred. You know that massacre in Germany that Herr Hitler is responsible for, Irma?"

"No, ma'am. I don't."

"Hitler ordered a purge just a month ago of his enemies. They called it the Night of the Long Knives. Well, guess what they used besides knives?

"Piano wire?" Irma said.

"You got it, Irma."

"You done here now?"

"Yeah, I think so. Let's wrap her up and put her in the cooler for now. Finish up the tissue samples, and you can send those to forensics. And that wire, let's ask if we can get Creighton on the case. He's in ballistics, but he knows more about metal than anyone else. And you have the nasal swabs with the chloroform tubed?"

"Yes, Doctor. They don't expire fast do they?"

"No. The odor evaporates a lot faster than the molecules. They can hang about for fifty days or more. Whoever it was gave her quite a dose too. And did you say some glass fragments were picked up at the crime scene?"

"Yes."

"I'll take a look at the glass fragments before I go."

"Holy Mother, what was the murderer doing, having a cocktail out there?"

"Don't always assume it was a 'he.' Sometimes females murder. I'm going to take a look at those under the high-power microscope before we file that evidence folder. See what kind of glass."

"You love that new microscope, don't you, Doctor Bryce?"

"I sure do. Very happy that the governor saw fit to spend the money. My guess is we should be thanking Mabel Dodge Luhan in Taos. She and the governor are friends. And of course *gracias* to Herr Max Knoll and Ernst Ruska for inventing this scope."

Five minutes later, Emily Bryce whispered "My, my" as she bent over the electron microscope.

"What is it, Doctor?"

"They weren't having a drink out there."

"What's the glass?"

"This is prescription glass, lenses for spectacles not martinis." She glanced at the clock now. "I've got to get home. Can you put make a note of this in the evidence file, Irma?"

"Sure thing." Irma paused. "I think you like being a mommy," Irma said and smiled.

"Clara's a nice little kid and smart as a whip, I'll tell you." She got up from the stool and began to gather her things.

"Good night, Doctor."

"Good night, Irma. I appreciate all you do here."

"Thank you, Doctor."

When Emily Bryce walked into the cottage where Clara and her mother were staying, she could hear the typewriter clattering away. Dr. Bryce had found an old Olivetti for her, and Clara had taken to typing immediately. She loved it. It seemed to Emily that this was the sound she always heard when she arrived. The girl's diligence was impressive. She had been there for ten days now. Her goal had been to type twenty words per minute. She surpassed that in her first five days of living at Dr. Bryce's and working at the coroner's office on Don Gaspar Avenue, which was just a block away. She loved the office and everything about office work. She had quickly learned the ins and outs of the filing system. There were the active files and then what Dr. Bryce called the closed-case files. Within each of those categories were autopsy reports, county by county, throughout the state. Then there were the monthly reports in the active files, which had to be filed with the police departments, district attorney's office, the mayors of various towns in the districts, as well as with the districts' medical examiners and coroners. This was all part of the business of death. Clara seemed to enjoy the work immensely. She loved straightening out the files. Perhaps, Emily thought, the child wishes her own life could be so orderly, so simple and tidy.

But now, as the Angelus began to toll, Emily saw the child's narrow back stiffen as she entered the room. The clatter of the typewriter ceased as Clara's fingers appeared to freeze over the keys. She clamped her eyes shut. Nine strokes tolled three times: *Angelus Domini nuntiavit Mariæ*, "The Angel of the Lord declared unto Mary." And then above that, a rather startling imprecation was hurled through the air. "Fuck Mary!" Clara blurted.

The tension in the young girl's narrow back seemed to reverberate through the room. When the Angelus ended, Emily saw her relax. It was as if a tide were retreating. The typing resumed. Clara was still unaware of Emily's presence, so she coughed and cleared her throat.

"Hey, Clara, tomorrow is the Corn Dances over in Santa Clara—your namesake pueblo. Don't you usually dance with the Corn Maidens?"

"Yes."

"So, will you go tomorrow?"

"Maybe."

"Oh, come on. It'll be fun."

"Okay," she said softly.

"Great!"

Clara turned back to her typewriter. She seemed more or less herself again. She had given a slight smile and made eye contact. It had taken her a while to make any eye contact with Dr. Bryce. The girl had actually opted not to go home with Rosaria on her two days off. Dr. Bryce felt this was a good sign. She was going to check into enrolling her in the Santa Fe public school.

Chapter 26

Georgia had asked Simon Bowes if she might come and paint the jimson-weed in the garden of his casita before the morning light became too harsh. "Please," he replied, "my pleasure! I'll even fix you breakfast."

"Not necessary, but I accept."

As she was setting up her easel in the garden, she thought she heard sirens in the distance. But she simply blocked them from her mind. This morning light was so limpid. The dew point was perfect, as so often happened out here and never back East. She didn't really understand dew point, but the same doctor who had explained the primitive nervous systems of rattlesnakes and why their mouths kept snapping after being decapitated had also explained dew points and why the New Mexico light was so perfect for painting. She had been painting for fewer than twenty minutes when Joaquin knocked on the garden gate door. "Miss O'Keeffe! Miss O'Keeffe. You in there? It's me, Joaquin. I have a message for you."

"Oh, of course, come in. What is it?"

"The sheriff wants you to call him?"

"The sheriff?"

"He says it's very important. Urgent." She now remembered the sirens she had heard earlier. "I'll drive you down to the Hacienda."

Five minutes later she was standing in Carmelita's office, her hand trembling as she held the receiver to her ear. Carmelita herself was collapsed in a chair, sobbing.

"What?" Georgia gasped.

"Nina Mueller is dead. Murdered. Tomas found her." The sheriff's voice was taut.

"What happened?"

"I don't know, Georgia; if I did, I wouldn't be so worried. Worried about you. You should move into town."

"No I shouldn't! This has nothing to do with … with those initials on the map."

"I don't know what this has to do with anything. If I did, I wouldn't be asking you to come to town."

In as calm a voice as she could manage she said, "I'm not coming to town. Let's … let's just see what happens."

"That's just the point, Georgia. I don't think we should just wait and see."

She knew she couldn't get rid of his idea so easily. "Let me think about it, Ryan. Just let me think about it." There was a long pause before he spoke again.

"Georgia, I care about you."

Tears sprang to her eyes. "I know, Ryan; I care for you too," she replied softly and hung up the phone.

Nina Mueller, the sweet, shy wife of Otto Mueller, had been murdered. Carmelita was beside herself and looked up at Georgia just as she hung up.

"I am so sorry, Carmelita. I know you were very close with Mrs. Mueller."

"Yes, yes. She and Herr Mueller treated me so nicely."

Georgia squinted at her. The way Carmelita framed that sentiment, and the word *Herr* coming out of her mouth, struck her as very peculiar. Had other people not treated her nicely? Perhaps the Muellers had treated her more as an equal than the guests at the Ghost Ranch, who, despite her position as manager, nevertheless thought of her as more of a high-end servant, a "domestic accessory." Carmelita's next words almost confirmed this. "They would sometimes invite me for dinner. I loved when Nina made that German dish spaetzle."

Would a guest at the Hacienda ever invite Carmelita to sit at the table with them, share a meal or anything else? Never.

Georgia thought about this on her way back to her casita. An hour later, she was just starting to make herself a sandwich when there was a knock on the door. She got up to answer it.

"Ryan." He looked fairly distraught.

"I don't know what the hell is going on out here. But I'm worried about you, Georgia. You sure you don't want to move into town."

Georgia felt some sort of defiance rising in her. "No, absolutely not. I came out here to work."

"I just want to protect you, not lock you up."

"I know that, Ryan. I don't want to be locked out either, locked out of this." She began to stammer. "This ... this world I find totally inspiring."

"You'll be locked out of it forever if you're dead."

"I'll take my chances."

"Georgia, you're a difficult woman."

"You aren't the first to tell me that. Come on, sit down and have a beer."

"I'm working. I don't drink on the job."

"Oh, baloney!" she said and went to the icebox, got him a beer, and opened it.

He took a swallow from the bottle. "So what do you think happened out there?"

"I don't know. Her throat was cut."

"I heard."

"A commando knife?"

"No, Emily says not."

"They were expecting a baby," Georgia said.

"Really? Emily didn't say anything about her being pregnant."

"They were adopting."

"Huh. How did you know?"

"Nina Mueller told me. They were so excited."

A long silence followed. It was actually a comfortable silence, and Georgia began to ponder something she thought she should share with Ryan. She reached across the table and squeezed his hand, then gave him a sweet, almost flirtatious smile.

"I've been thinking," she began.

"Yeah, me too." His face looked almost joyful, filled with some sort of anticipation.

She didn't want to disappoint him. Maybe he was thinking about that moment when she had handed him the pie cutter. She was about to spoil it she knew. But she had to tell him about the shadows, and that possibly the wrong person had been killed. "I've been thinking about murder."

"Uh, Georgia, before we discuss this, just for tonight would you like to come back to my house? We could have dinner. I've got some tortilla soup and … and, well … some peaches." That was all he could think of to say. It was probably outrageous that he had even suggested this to her now at this moment.

"That would be nice," she said quickly. They both seemed surprised at her answer. She wasn't sure why she had just blurted that out after she had so insistently refused his request to move into town. Now, in a split second, she had agreed to come to his house for dinner. She felt a tiny little thrill as she recalled their two hands on that pie cutter when he came back to the house. "And, by the way, I finished the pie."

"The whole thing?" Ryan's eyes registered surprise.

"Um-hm." She nodded. "Yes, the whole thing, but of course only half was left."

"Can we wait until then to discuss your murderous thoughts?"

"Sure."

The sheriff's house was out on Upper Canyon Road near an intersection with Delgado. It looked deceptively small when one walked through the turquoise gate in the center of the surrounding adobe wall. But Georgia could tell there was more as she followed him beneath a winding arbor as twilight was gathering and a pale magenta light was falling on the city. They came to a patio and entered the house directly into the kitchen.

There was a simple white metal table in the center. She'd seen a similar one in a Sears and Roebuck catalog and had considered buying it as an additional work surface for her studio back at Lake George. It apparently served as an eating table for the sheriff, as it had a set of salt and pepper shakers in the middle. She could see through a door to a dining room, which had a nice wooden table, but she immediately sensed that the room had been abandoned since Mattie had died. *Since Mattie died* was a phrase that had frequently popped up in some of their conversations.

"Here, have a seat." She looked at the metal table. He tipped his head toward the dining room. "Used to eat in there, but since Mattie died you know …" His voice dwindled off. But now, somehow, when he said that phrase it was slightly different. It seemed almost as if he were introducing Georgia to Mattie. She found something rather dear about it.

He caught her hesitation. "Oh, guess you're not that hungry. Would you rather sit out on the patio and have something to drink?"

"That would be nice."

"Follow me. I'll bring some of my peach elixir."

"Not a pie, an elixir?"

"Yes, no pie. Not as sweet, but made with just a touch of vermouth."

They passed through the kitchen and took a left into a hallway with a set of double doors that led to the patio.

"Oh my, this is lovely!" Georgia exclaimed. In the center of the patio was a perfectly beautiful peach tree. There were urns spilling with nasturtiums and then bordering beds of what appeared to be lavender trembling in a faint breeze.

Two bright-pink metal chairs were pulled up to a round turquoise table.

"What's that?" Georgia asked, pointing at a clump of bright yellow spheres.

"Yarrow—moonshine yarrow. Mattie swore by it for tummy problems." *Tummy problems?* Georgia thought. Would Stieglitz ever use the word *tummy?*

"So." He tipped the pitcher of peach elixir and filled two small glasses. "Here's to you, Georgia." They both raised their glasses and clinked. Then he leaned forward and gave her a peck on her cheek.

"Thank you, Ryan." There was a slight quaver in her voice. He set his own hand atop hers.

"Now, tell me. You said you've had some thoughts?" She had already decided she would not mention her conversation with Anne Morrow Lindbergh. Her ruminations about shadows ironically seemed more concrete than anything else at the moment.

"Yes, about shadows."

"Shadows." He was uncertain himself if it was a statement or a question.

"You see, as I was walking into Goetz's store, I was wearing my broad-brimmed hat and it cast a shadow—it actually collided with another shadow, the shadow of a similar hat." She continued to explain how Father William, in his full Franciscan habit, had been exiting. When she finished, he turned to her and spoke.

"So, you're thinking that it might have been easy to confuse the two friars—one apparently fake, or an impostor, and one real—in the night?" Georgia nodded. "In other words, the wrong man was killed."

"It's possible."

"But what was the motive? Who would want to kill Father William? And who the heck is this guy Castenada?"

The Angelus began to toll in the tower of San Sebastian Cathedral in Santa Fe. He looked at Georgia with a twinkle in his eye.

"Time to pray, I guess."

"I hope not," she replied and bent across the table and kissed him. He came around to her side of the table and, standing behind her, slipped his hand beneath her shirt and stroked her breast. She was so glad she had not told him about those photographs. So glad!

"This is why I shouldn't drink on the job."

"Don't blame yourself. I did the kissing."

Later, when they were finished, with his body curled around her, she thought of that view she had painted at least half a dozen times this summer—the Pedernal Changing Woman. *I am that Changing Woman.*

212

The following morning at five o'clock, Ryan rolled over in bed and shut off the alarm before it rang. He looked at Georgia as she slept. She was nude. She was a landscape unto herself, he thought. He liked her collarbones and the slight well between her breasts. And at this moment, he loved the way her long fingers splayed slightly as her hand lay on the space between those bones and her breasts. He liked the faded scar on her left breast and wondered about it but would not dare ask. She was a lovely soul with a body to match.

"Who would be calling this early?" He groaned and heaved himself from the bed to walk toward the phone.

Georgia watched him. "Hey, Sheriff, I like your butt."

He turned around and winked at her. *Gosh*, he thought. *We're getting pretty foolish here.*

"Hello, sheriff here … What? He's what?" There was a long pause. "You're telling me, Linc, that this guy is part of what? … British intelligence? Well, what the hell are they doing out here in New Mexico? Okay, I'll get right on it."

Georgia caught her breath. Had she heard him right—something about intelligence? Was this some sort of weird coincidence? No, according to the sheriff there were no such things as coincidences, just reasons waiting to be revealed. How long had it been since she'd talked to Fritzy? Not long. Not even a week. Her thoughts dwindled as Ryan came back into the room. She must not tell Ryan under any circumstances what she had done. Not now. Not yet. God knows what his reaction would be. She vividly recalled his reaction when she had "disturbed the crime scene."

"You're a nosy little thing aren't you?" She had been ready to smack him.

Georgia was sitting up in bed with the sheets pulled up to her chin when he walked back into the bedroom

"Sounded kind of interesting from my end," she said.

"Yeah, kind of. Would you believe that Simon Bowes is a British intelligence agent and so was Castenada?"

"Intelligence?" Georgia said. She hoped she sounded clueless. But none of what he started to say really surprised her.

"You know, the Secret Intelligence Service, like our Bureau of Investigation in Washington." She tried to affect a blank look in her eyes—*How could a nincompoop lady like me know about secret agencies?*

"But I thought he was an art critic–journalist—whatever."

"Yeah, it's the whatever that's the issue. Just like Castenada was a priest."

"But Bowes actually seemed to know a lot about art." Again, she was attempting to feign ignorance.

"Probably more than Castenada knew about being a priest."

Not so sure, Georgia thought, and wondered to herself why she had even had that thought. What did it mean? What was she trying to tell herself? It was almost as if she were trying to figure out the elusive nature of a particular pigment. For her it was like cracking a code as she experimented with resins, oils, and thinners—grinding and mulling them, seeking an essence that was the key to their translucency, their vibrancy. *Not so sure.* The three words reverberated in her head. Should she be mad at Simon Bowes? Should she feel used, misled? That of course was what spies did—misled people. But she was not inclined to think of this now. She wanted to remain enveloped in the memory of her night with Ryan. His touches lingered. His warmth. His body pressed to hers. Pressed to her bones. She was the only skinny one in this coupling. It was so unlike Stieglitz. Together, she and Stieglitz had been like two skeletons rattling around between the sheets. But not the sheriff.

Chapter 27

Four hours later, Georgia arrived at the Santa Clara pueblo after shopping in Santa Fe. She had planned to go, as Emily Bryce had told her that Clara would be in the Corn Maid dance. They both took this as a good sign. Ryan had already gone to the pueblo earlier with two deputies, as sometimes things could get rowdy at these corn festivals. At an entrance to the pueblo's plaza, she saw a woman pleading with two policemen.

"No cameras? Really?" The voice was familiar.

"Sorry, ma'am."

"But, b-b-but ..." Then, more softly: "Do you understand who we are?"

It was Anne Morrow Lindbergh. Her husband was looking the other way. "Charles! Charles, can you do something about this?" *Yes, Mrs. Lindbergh, use that husband of yours when you can*, Georgia thought.

The sheriff strode up to them. "Hello, Bert, Joe," he said to the officers who had stopped the Lindberghs. "Let me talk to Mrs. Lindbergh here."

Georgia quickly made her way to another entrance.

Five minutes later, Ryan came up to her.

"You didn't let that woman take her camera in, did you?" she asked.

"Of course not! I don't make exceptions, even for heroes." He scanned the crowd. "I'm afraid I have to stay to the bitter end. So it's good you brought your own car."

"I might stay too. I love the Eagle Dance. It's my favorite, and I don't think it's on the schedule until the end. Oh, look—things are about to start." She pointed to two long lines of Pueblo Indians issuing from a large kiva. They filed slowly onto the plaza. Their costumes were fantastic. The Koshares, sacred clowns, who led each line had their faces painted white. It was Georgia's understanding that these sacred clowns provided a benign way of venting community tensions through humor as well as reinforcing cautions against certain traditional taboos or prohibitions.

Georgia did not know much about the significance of the costumes or the dances. But she did know that the dances were a culmination of several weeks of rituals that non-Pueblo people were not privy to or invited to witness. The priest made peculiar spellbinding gestures with his hands. She had been told that these gestures were part of a ritual-istic language. However, she had also learned that many of the dances had been incorporated into the Catholic calendar of holy days and feast days. This was not all that surprising, as most of the Pueblo Indians were practicing Catholics. As if to confirm this, Georgia spotted Father William six feet away. Did she see him first, or was it once again the colliding shadows of their hats that gave her a start? She wondered how his tonsure was faring after his encounter with the kitchen drawer. *Bird poop,* as her father might have said. One of his strongest oaths. He only swore when he'd had too much to drink, and even then his cursing was of the mildest variety.

"Why, hello there," he said cheerily. "We meet again, Miss O'Keeffe."

"We meet? Or maybe the shadows of our hats meet first." She pointed to the silhouettes on the ground.

He chuckled.

"A nice design, I would say," Georgia added.

"Always the artist, I think." He smiled.

"Always the priest, I guess."

"It's a calling, I suppose." He paused. "For both of us."

"I think you're ennobling what I do. It's just what I do. That's all." She replied.

"I would hardly say that's all." He turned his head. "Oh, look, our English friend is over there, Mr. Bowes."

Agent Bowes, thought Georgia. This might be challenging. Georgia was not easily given to pretense. She realized that she would have made a miserable spy. And now she was going to have to pretend that this fellow in his truly dandy bow tie was a journalist, an art connoisseur for a magazine—pocket square and all—she thought as he approached. The bow tie was rather charming. It was a lovely azure color that matched the sky and had little balloons on it. He could have been on the banks of the Thames at Henley cheering on the rowers. "Lovely tie, Mr. Bowes."

"Well, I do love bow ties, and this is really my most festive one. I thought it appropriate for a festival day. But I'm so glad I ran into you. I was wondering about that place—the White Place, I believe you called it."

"Oh, the Plaza Blanca," Father William exclaimed. "Extraordinary rocks. Massive pillar-like cliffs."

"I'd love to see it, Miss O'Keeffe. You said you like to go out there often."

"Well, I can go out there with you, but I'm not going to paint. I made an exception for you the other day, but honestly, Mr. Bowes, I found that I was very self-conscious. Didn't much like what I painted that day."

His forehead was suddenly pleated with creases. "I am so sorry. I certainly did not mean to … to violate."

"Oh, no, Mr. Bowes; that is too dramatic a word. There was no violation at all. I just couldn't paint—that's all—or at least not in the way I wanted to."

She felt a wave of remorse. She was uncertain why. The fellow was a spy, after all. "Look," she said. "I'll pick you up and we can drive out there and take a look. I've been meaning to go out there for the last few weeks—not for painterly reasons at all. I'm interested in some land on the old Chama road going out from Abiquiu. There's a moldering old Spanish colonial compound I want to look at. It's right on the way to the White Place. Best to go late afternoon."

"Wonderful!" he exclaimed.

"And actually, Mr. Bowes, I wanted to take some pictures myself. Why don't you bring your camera and I'll take my camera? I'm sure your pictures will be better than mine. There's a photo lab in Santa Fe, so would you agree to give me copies of those I'd like?"

"Of course."

She looked down at his shoes. "You might want to wear some sturdier shoes and bring a canteen of water."

"I shall."

"Good," Georgia said. "I'll pick you up at the Hacienda. I'll leave a message at the Hacienda as to whether tomorrow or the next day will be the best." She began to walk toward the plaza in the center of the pueblo, where the drummer had started playing and the dancers would soon begin. Under the shade of cottonwood trees, tables were set up and Indians, Pueblos and Navajos, were selling various items—jewelry, woven rugs, ceramics, Navajo fry-bread, and of course the ubiquitous spirit dolls carved from wood known as kachinas. The dolls were popular as gifts for mothers, wives, and sisters. She walked by a table of silver and turquoise jewelry.

She saw that Felicity was with Anita Delmore, a guest at the lodge, and Lupe. "What do you think?" she said, turning to her friend. She was trying on a necklace made of miniature carved kachina dolls. These were quite popular with the tourists.

"I think it's lovely," Mrs. Delmore said.

"And you, Lupe?"

"Very pretty, señora."

"Well you know what, Lupe, I think we both need one of these."

"Oh no, Señora Sanchez. No *necessita*."

"Yes, it is *necessita*," she said crisply and turned to the woman selling them. "Two please."

They caught sight of her. Georgia smiled, but she could see that Lupe was very uncomfortable. Felicity turned to Georgia. "What do you think?" she asked, showing the necklace she had just tried on. "And I just bought one for Lupe."

"Lovely, stunning piece of jewelry," Georgia said, nodding toward the necklace. She quickly moved on through the crowd surging around the jewelry tables. Some of the dancing had begun. The spectacle was not just on the platform in the center of the plaza but also all around it. It was a vibrating throng of moving colors. Threading through the mass were the haunting white faces of the sacred clowns as they checked their costumes, securing feathers to the dancers' ankles or headdresses. One was admonishing a tourist who had a notebook in hand.

"No note taking. No photos. We are not museum artifacts. This is a living faith." The words resonated with Georgia both for the words being said and for who was saying them. The voice was familiar.

"Tomas!" Georgia took a step closer and peered into the face daubed with white paint. Tomas's lips were painted black, and a black horizontal stripe of paint stretched across his face from ear to ear. Black circles surrounded his eyes. Bands of paint encircled his legs from ankles to kneecaps. She realized that on top of his head he was wearing a hat nearly identical to that of a Franciscan friar, with one exception. Two holes had been made in the crown for his long braids to be threaded through. Small explosions of feathers had been intertwined with the braids. The effect was rather startling. He carried a sheaf of corn, and he wore corn husks around his ankles. From his belt hung both a trowel and a knife. The sacred and the profane? The priest and the tiller of soil?

"Tomas," Georgia repeated. "Look at you! Splendid! I'm sorry about your sister Rosaria, though."

"Yes, so am I," he said grimly. The drumming increased in volume. He began to move his feet and seemed to dissolve into some transcendent realm. His feet beat harder on the ground. On the platform two girls who Georgia thought were called Blue Corn Woman and White Corn Maiden began to dance. Beneath all the paint and the feathers, Georgia recognized Clara. Her slender body swayed softly, tender as a reed in a gentle breeze. She wore a wrapped, fringed white deerskin skirt. Her legs were painted green, which Georgia supposed represented the corn's husk. Feathery white plumes exploded from her shoulders and the turquoise headdress she was wearing.

Georgia heard voices behind her. One was the woman Tomas had cautioned about taking notes. "Look, Dina, you see how softly the women dance as compared to the men. That's always the way it is. See her feet? So light, it's almost as if she's softly kneading the earth with her feet."

What a beautiful image, Georgia thought. Something about the woman's words reminded Georgia of Sun Prairie, Wisconsin. The dust in Sun Prairie was bright yet soft, and never harsh. She remembered how it had always entranced her as a child. She once told someone that it looked so soft she wanted to get down into it. *"I was probably eating it as a two-year-old,"* she had said.

She turned toward the woman. "Those words you just said. So beautiful. 'Kneading the earth.'"

"You know the story?" the woman asked.

"No, I'm afraid I don't," Georgia said. "What is it?"

"Well, briefly: It's an old Tewa myth. Somewhat similar to the Greek myth of Orpheus and Eurydice. Remember? Orpheus falls in love with the beautiful Eurydice and then she dies. He follows her to the underworld, and Hades, god of that realm, promises Orpheus that Eurydice can return and follow him under one condition: He must not turn back to look at her. But he does, and therefore she is lost to him forever. In the Tewa myth, both the Deer Hunter and the White Corn Maiden die because of his violation, and they rise into the night sky as a pair of stars, the brighter one the Deer Hunter and the dimmer one the Corn Maiden."

"Lovely," the woman's companion said.

Georgia was left wordless, however, as she watched Clara crumple slowly to the ground in the very last part of the dance. "Oh, my goodness," Georgia murmured.

"Yes, very sad," the woman replied, "but beautiful."

Not really, Georgia thought. *Not really.* She didn't want White Corn Maiden to be a star, a dimmer star, in the sky. *What a lousy ending!* She was almost desperate to say it aloud. But she said nothing and moved on.

As she was heading into the parking lot, she heard the roar of a motorcycle. It startled her. An Ariel Red Hunter! Was Peter Wainwright here? When she turned around, she saw it was not a bright shiny red like Peter's but black and somewhat banged up. A rather grizzled old Indian was riding it. She recalled the sound of the motorcycle on that evening, the same evening she had heard the sounds of what she thought was lovemaking in the Sanchezes' garden.

Georgia wandered about for another hour or so. The festivities were dying down. She had just turned a corner and was seeking a trash can to dispose of the remnants of a rolled piki bread filled with beans and corn. It was delicious, but she could never eat the whole thing. Now, however, she stopped short. She glimpsed bright green legs emerging from the fringed white deerskin skirt of a figure bending over a trash can and violently pulling something apart. Georgia walked over.

"Clara?" The girl was so involved in her act of destruction that she didn't even pause or look up. "Clara!" Georgia said again. The girl froze. She held in her hands the remains of a shredded kachina doll. She looked up at Georgia. Her face was painted green but had a horizontal turquoise strip across the front; her eyes, like two black agates, looked out blankly.

"What are you doing?"

"Murder!" That was all she said, and stomped off.

Georgia lifted her hand to her mouth. She felt herself sway a bit. *Don't faint! Don't you dare faint.*

Murder! Georgia could still hear the word, shrill like a siren, in her ears. She had been on the road for close to an hour as she drove back from Santa Clara. Along with that word, the image of Clara bristled in her mind. Had someone given Clara the doll? Why would she take such offense at it? Had she not danced the part of the White Corn Maiden? Was this in fact a kind of suicide gesture? Nothing was making sense. But according to Emily Bryce, Clara was doing so well. There must be a link between this doll and the person who had abused her. Did that mean the abuser was at the Corn Dances? Had he approached her at the dance or after she had danced?

Instead of turning off for Ghost Ranch, she drove straight into Abiquiu. It was Sunday, Rosaria's day off from La Fonda. If she weren't at her own house, she'd likely be at her aunt's, next door. Georgia parked just past the general store. Coming toward her was Mr. Goetz.

"Good morning, Mr. Goetz. You're still here and not back in Germany?"

"Ah, Miss O'Keeffe. Forgive me." He squinted and gave a stiff little bow. He had what Stieglitz would have called a "Prussian courtliness." An immaculateness of dress, manner, and bearing. Quite unlike his nephew.

"For what should I forgive you?" Georgia asked.

"You see, I had an accident with my spectacles; without them I don't see very well and didn't recognize you." The left lens was partially taped over with a piece of adhesive that held what appeared to be two, perhaps three remaining fragments. He raised his finger toward the spectacles. "Better than nothing, I think," he chuckled. "But to answer your question. I shall be returning shortly. The climate here is so lovely, however. Better than Stuttgart, which tends to be rainy this time of year."

"Well, no need for apology. My husband manages to break at least three pairs a year. How long do you plan to stay?"

"Not long. I leave tomorrow."

"*Bon voyage* then."

"Thank you, Miss O'Keeffe."

They both walked on. Georgia turned left, winding her way down a dusty path toward a small adobe house. She knocked loudly on the door. There was no answer. She walked around to the back and heard voices from the patio next door. Rosaria was sitting with her aunt, Paloma.

"Hallo!" Georgia called out.

"Oh, Miss O'Keeffe. Come over. Just keeping Auntie company." They were speaking Tewa, a language of the Pueblo people, with dashes of Spanish and Navajo, as Auntie Paloma had been married to a Navajo man. Most of the Indians in the region spoke more than one language in addition to their own native one. Rosaria had a board across her lap and was slicing slivers off a chunk of yucca root.

"She makes tea for my legs." Paloma pointed at her bandaged calf. "I get sores, you know."

There was something darkly fascinating about the old woman's face. It was like a tight little knot, creased and with the deep reddish-brown tones of quartz sandstone. Her eyes glittered like mica chips. Her entire face was a landscape unto itself.

"It's not tea. It's a poultice, Tía. I boil it, then mash it and press it, all wet, into bandages and wrap her legs. It works. Heals sores. Makes the blood, you know ..." She lifted her hand and swirled her index finger.

"Circulate?" Georgia said.

"Yes, that's the word, Miss O'Keeffe."

The talk about the benefits of yucca became a blur in Georgia's ears as she caught the flash of the sunlight reflecting off the blade of the knife with which Rosaria was skinning the yucca tubers. A prickle ran up her spine. It was the same knife. She could hear Emily Bryce's voice identifying it. *"H-W commando knife ... should be outlawed."*

"Your knife."

"*¿Sí?*"

"You got to be careful with that."

Tía Paloma giggled. Georgia shifted her eyes to the old lady. The few stumpy teeth Paloma had looked like little tombstones leaning this way and that.

"Very good knife," Tía Paloma said.

"But a very dangerous tool," Georgia replied.

"Not if you know how to handle it. We grew up with them," Tía Paloma said. "I knew how to handle one by the time I was five years old." She nodded sagely as she watched Rosaria's deft hands.

Georgia remained very still. Rosaria sat grimly erect, expertly peeling the tubers and barely moving any other part of her body. Barely breathing. Something had shifted among the three women. Georgia let her gaze settle on a stalk of a pale pink hollyhock. The blossom appeared like a goblet of soft light in the growing twilight. The Angelus began to ring. Georgia looked to the west; there was a clear view from where the three women sat. The sun, swollen and red, trembled on the horizon like a wobbly balloon on an invisible string.

Georgia sat with Rosaria and her aunt for another ten minutes. It was all she could do to drag her eyes away from the knife that Rosaria was so deftly using to strip the tough skin from the yucca. They spoke idly about Clara and her progress in typing. How well she had adjusted to life in Santa Fe.

"It's good, her learning this kind of thing," Paloma said. "She's a smart girl. She don't need to live out here. I take care of myself when Rosaria's in town." It suddenly struck Georgia that she and Rosaria had never discussed the real reason for Clara's move beyond the convenience for Rosaria's working at La Fonda. Georgia had not found it within her to bring up the subject. It was so awful. It was not simply that she could not bring herself to discuss this with the one person she should have, Rosaria, but one didn't pry. There was a code of silence among the Indian people. A code of denial that brooked no trespassing. Denial was thick, thick as sediment. Her eyes settled on the corrugated landscape of Paloma's face. It seemed sealed now. But Georgia had a burning urge to tell Rosaria what she and Emily Bryce felt had happened to Clara.

Georgia got up to leave.

"You need me to come over and do anything for you on my days off, Miss O'Keeffe, just let me know."

Georgia glanced down at the knife. It was as if they were speaking to each other through masks—masks of deception, masks designed to sanitize what was on both their minds.

"No, I'm doing fine, but you be careful with that knife, Rosaria."

"Oh, Miss O'Keefe, I'm very good with this knife. We know how to handle knives." A grim little smile flashed across her face. But her eyes looked dead.

———

"I'm very good with this knife. We know how to handle knives." Rosaria's words echoed in her head as she drove back to Ghost Ranch. Coupled with the vivid scene of Clara's destruction of the corn doll, the pieces of a diabolical puzzle began to assemble themselves. But there were still pieces missing. There must be. She could not believe that either Rosaria or Clara was capable of murder. But then, again, Emily's words when she had asked who her first abuser was came back. *My father. I killed him. With an H-W 12, a commando knife.*

Georgia pulled up to her casita. A chill ran through her almost as soon as she stepped through the door. Her back stiffened. Something was different. She stood very still. It occurred to her that the door hadn't creaked. It always creaked. It was halfway between a chirp and a squeak. Like rusty crickets, she often thought. But now it was silent. Even though she had been meaning to oil those hinges, she never had. But it was not just the hinges. As soon as she stepped through the door, she knew something felt different. The scent of Hennessy lubricating oil? Not even close. There was something slightly sweet beneath the tang of the sagebrush that blew through the door behind her. She stepped hesitantly into the entry. A chill ran up her back. She looked about. Nothing seemed out of order. She had the urge to call out "yoo-hoo." But even the thought was somehow embarrassing. She took another step, and sniffed again. There was some sort of slightly odd odor. She wouldn't have realized it except that the scent of the sagebrush almost acted as a foil for it. No note from Carmelita on the kitchen table, where she usually left them. She walked into the living room. The last record she had listened to was still on the Victrola, the album cover on the table beside it. Was it turned a slightly different way? She walked over to the chair where she always listened. She liked to glance at the album cover as she listened. She was especially fond of this cover with the photo of Pablo Casals. He always had the dreamiest expression as he drew the bow across the strings of the cello. Even through his spectacles and with his eyes closed, you could feel his dreaming, and Georgia felt she could enter that dream. She sat down in the chair. She caught her breath. From this angle, the album was upside down. Skewed in a way that she could not see his eyes. Someone had been here in her house! Disturbed her dream!

She sat bolt upright for several minutes. It could have been a quarter of an hour, or perhaps it was just two minutes, but her mind was working methodically. What might she do to protect herself aside from sitting up in bed all night with her rattlesnake stick? She wasn't going to sleep, for one thing, but there were alternatives that might prove more constructive than simply waiting for a prowler. However, that was exactly what she did—except for the bed. She sat in her music chair and put on Beethoven's *Symphony No. 5*, the "Symphony of Fate," as it was called. Fate because of those crashing first chords that someone said was like Fate knocking on the door. "Not this door!" she muttered. She put the volume up full blast—enough to scare the rattlesnakes and send tremors through the cottonwood trees just beyond her terrace. But as she sat perfectly still in the vortex of this thundering music, she felt a pure strange silence in the center of her soul. The pitches and rhythms of those four notes began to anchor her being.

Chapter 28

Room 40, the cryptanalysis center at Century House at 100 Westminster Bridge Road, London, had served through the Great War as the very heart of the Secret Intelligence Signal service. Although some called it not the heart but the gizzard, because its function was similar to that of a bird's hind stomach that grinds food. Room 40 ground intelligence so it could become useful, strategically useful, for the armed services. Fewer than twenty years before, during the Great War, Room 40 had played an important role in detecting German naval sorties in the North Sea. It was through a network, the Y system, that the British navy was able to pinpoint the exact locations of enemy ships through a triangulation of intercepted coded messages and German wireless transmissions. The battle of Dogger Bank was won due to these intercepts. And it was Cedric Barkley who had decoded perhaps the most significant German communication of all—the Zimmerman telegram, a message to the German ambassador in Mexico about the expected resumption of submarine warfare by Germany on February 2, 1917.

Cedric Barkley, or Bark, as he was known, was barely thirty then. Now gray at the temples, closing in on fifty, he was the director of the team. And although the war was long over, the cryptologists—the code writers and decoders—had not stopped. They were an odd lot, addicted to this peculiar branch of spycraft since before the Great War. For the last seventeen years, they had worked as if there were still a war going on. They had advanced the wireless systems, the technology, the equipment—the transmitters, the receivers. SIGINTEL, as it was called, had been developed and refined to a level that was quite astonishing.

That was mainly because all the cryptologists, or cryptos, believed that another war was coming. Crypto communication had become not simply reliable but also scientifically elegant. And thus, when the signal from Sparrow on the William Fife–designed racing yacht went silent, it was cause for alarm. This was not the first time they had used the latest triangulation system, now called W. It had been used to great success in the Mediterranean between Gibraltar, Tunis, and the Canary Islands.

Cedric Barkley sighed heavily as he stood over the transcriptions of code that used the basic Polybius square for "fractionating," or substituting one letter for another or for a set of symbols. "So Sparrow has gone quiet," he said to one of the younger cryptologists. "For how long?" Bark took his pipe from his pocket. A light sprinkling of shag tobacco floated down onto his pant leg.

"Seventy-two hours, sir. Indeed, sir, agents Bowes and Marlowe both have reported in."

"So basically, one leg is missing in our triangulation? Any bad weather reported in the Irish Sea?"

"None, sir. Quite calm."

"Hmm ... perplexing." Bark clamped down harder on his pipe. A silence descended on Room 40. Cedric Barkley was rarely perplexed. Cryptologists thrived on puzzles, but they rarely if ever used a word like *perplexed*. It was a dire admission of sorts that could suggest that the game had blown up. But, of course, they would not know that for some time.

"And you've contacted SIS about the Lindbergh matter."

"Yes, sir, and that's become a bit problematic in just the last ten minutes."

Barkley closed his eyes and clamped down on his pipe. To his colleagues, this was a familiar gesture of despair. "Oh dear; break it to me gently, lads."

"Well, it involves Miss O'Keeffe; the painter, you know."

"Of course I know. Simon Bowes's excuse for going over there in the first place."

"Yes, yes, exactly."

"Exactly what?" A winter light crept into Cedric Barkley's eyes now.

"Well, she's become a bit more than an excuse for agent Bowes. Miss O'Keeffe seems to have possibly stumbled upon the Lindbergh connection with the Lutzen ring. She's called Fritz Freihoff at SIS."

"She what? Get Freihoff on the phone immediately."

Ten minutes later, the analyst came back.

"Got him, sir. He's on the line."

Cedric Barkley left Room 40 for another room that was unnumbered, unmarked, and not much bigger than a phone booth. He picked up the receiver.

"Cedric Barkley here."

"Yes, Cedric, hope all is well, or well as can be. Oddly enough, I was about to call you."

Fritz Freihoff spoke with just the trace of a Yiddish accent. Born Frederick Wolf Freihoff, he had emigrated with his family from Germany to New Jersey when he was still a baby but had grown up in a Yiddish-speaking family. By training, he was a geneticist. However, when the war broke out, he had developed an expertise in cryptanalysis. It was not such a far leap from genetic code to intelligence code. It was all mathematically based. He and his fellow cryptos essentially worked on anything to do with the US War Department's code systems, and their division evolved into the Signal Intelligence Service. It was actually his wife, Marian, who had first lured him into cryptanalysis. She had been fascinated by a rather abstruse project at the Riverbank Libraries in Chicago that focused on supposedly secret messages buried in Francis Bacon's poetry, as well as those found in Shakespeare's plays. A geneticist, of course, had to interpret biological codes. A cryptanalyst plumbed linguistic codes and ciphers. His and Marian's romance was a perfect match.

"What were you calling me about?" Fritzy asked.

"We now have a situation with one of our agents in the desert operations that are part of a triangulation scheme."

"Yes, so I have heard. As the bard who was not the Bard said, 'Time and the hour runs through the roughest day,' and I hear you've had a rough day and been waiting."

"Forty-six hours, to be precise."

"Well, I have some information for you that in a strange way might be related to your present situation. I recently got a call from one Miss Georgia O'Keeffe."

"Yes, I've just heard. She knows about Bowes."

"You have to admit, Cedric, that the fellow sticks out like well—the proverbial sore thumb."

"And I understand that this aspiring Miss Marple contacted you."

"Yes. She didn't know for sure if Bowes was an agent. But—and this is even more surprising—Lindbergh's wife suggested directly to O'Keeffe that her husband was involved in something bigger. As one might suspect of an artist, Miss O'Keeffe is very perceptive. She can read between the lines, or possibly the brushstrokes is a more appropriate figure of speech here. She certainly read Bowes as being more than an art connoisseur, a journalist. Anyhow for some time now, we've suspected the Golden Boy might qualify for your list of candidates for the Lutzen spy ring."

Fritzy gave a soft chuckle and seemed to be enjoying this a bit too much for Cedric Barkley's taste.

"Good God, man! But how did you and O'Keeffe get to each other?" Barkley asked.

"Hah! That's the beauty of this. My old friend, my high school class-mate, Alfred Stieglitz, is married to none other than Georgia O'Keeffe. She called him. Long story. No time to tell now. But we've just contacted our agent in DC. We have some sheriff out there picking our fellow, Bertram Welles, up today at the airport in Albuquerque. But the sheriff doesn't know the all of it. We're working this through Hoover."

"Hoover. That SOB?" Cedric groaned.

"They've got a good fellow on it. A Negro."

"A Negro in the BI?"

"Yeah, well, modern times, Bark. They say that Mrs. Roosevelt is going to invite Marian Anderson to the White House to sing. How about that?"

"My goodness," Cedric Barkley said softly. "And then maybe Buckingham Palace as her next engagement?"

"Could be. Could be. I'll keep you informed, and let's hope you get the W network up and running."

"Who needs the triangle when we've got Miss O'Keeffe over there."

"Oh, and by the way, the Negro's brother is a Texas Ranger."

"And what the devil is a Texas Ranger?"

"Cowboy cop. They got him in on it too."

"Sometimes I think you Yanks are too clever for your own good. But hey, what do I know?"

Fritzy laughed. "Right, what do you know? What do I know? Just a poor Jewish boy who emigrated from Germany to New Jersey when I was but a wee thing." He paused. "But I'll tell you one thing. We're going to get these Nazi bastards before they get us."

When Fritzy hung up, there was a knock on his door. "Come in," he called. A new young analyst strode through the door, one of the very best of the new crop.

"Maguire! Nice to see you. What's up?"

"Well, sir, you're not going to like this."

"Hoover, again?" Fritzy asked dully. Maguire nodded.

"You got to call him." Maguire handed the dispatch that had just come through. It had been translated from Code 46. *Call Hoover. Have Hoover stop Hughes flight to pick up Lindbergh.*

Jesus Christ, Fritzy thought. He hated calling Hoover. He was a miserable, deceitful bastard. There was something absolutely rancid about the man. One always wondered what he was storing up, harvesting from every encounter to use against you. Reluctantly he dialed the number, the one that went directly from the Blue Phone on his desk to the BI. No secretaries to answer. Any guest in that office would be summarily asked to leave. No explanation given. It rang three times. This meant there must have been a guest. Then he picked up.

"Yeah," came a growl through the receiver.

"Fritzy here. Hughes has sent his plane to Albuquerque to pick up Lindbergh. Got to stop the flight. Call Hughes and arrange it. Mechanical problems, whatever."

"Hah!" Hoover exclaimed.

Chapter 29

The following morning, Georgia had gone to Abiquiu to pick up some paint thinner and a loaf of Acoma bread, which was always delivered on Tuesdays and Saturdays. It was said to be the best Pueblo bread in New Mexico. She noticed that the black drapery was still over the door of Goetz's store. Father William was just leaving.

"Here for the bread, Father?" she called out the window.

"Of course! During my five years in Acoma, I am afraid I became addicted to this bread." He walked over to the window of her car. The shadow of his hat cast a dark puddle in her lap. The shadow quickly dissolved as he removed his hat when it bumped again the window frame. She was now staring at his tonsure. She was actually fixated.

"Healed, I see," Georgia said in a low voice.

"What's that?" he asked.

"Your occupational hazard—the encounter with the kitchen drawer."

His eyes seemed to go blank. "Oh yes ... yes." He patted his head. "As they say, time heals all wounds."

"Yes," Georgia replied tautly.

"So terrible about Nina Mueller," he said, glancing at the black drapery over the door.

"Yes, how is Mr. Mueller doing?" She tried to keep the panic out of her voice. She wasn't sure why she was panicking, but she was. Another instance perhaps of her mind's eye flying out ahead of her plodding brain.

"Not well. Not well at all. I am gently urging him to have a service for Nina. It doesn't have to be a full funeral Mass. She was Catholic, you know. He is not Catholic but Protestant. I can accommodate that."

"What about the baby they were expecting?" She tried to carry on this conversation as calmly as possible.

"I'm not sure. He talks about going back to Germany and raising the child there. He has an aunt over there. I think Gerda is her name. He's quite close to her. She might help out."

"I suppose that would make sense. It would be awful here for him caring for an infant and running the store."

"Yes, it would. But I told him what I tell all grieving parishioners when they lose a loved one: Don't make any big decisions right away. Wait."

"Yes." Georgia nodded. "Good advice."

"Well, take care, Miss O'Keeffe."

"You too, Father William."

Ten minutes later, with her bread and paint thinner, she climbed back into her car. She took a moment before pulling out. The healed tonsure of Father William's head haunted her. What was it about those scabs on his bald pate? She sighed and rolled out of the parking place. Five minutes later, as she came to the highway, an ambulance roared by. As she passed the turnoff for the road to Taos, the ambulance stayed on the main road. She was behind it, and when it passed Ole Caliente Road, she knew it must be heading toward the Ghost Ranch. "Oh dear," Georgia murmured to herself.

Four minutes later she pulled up in front of the Hacienda. It was a somewhat improbable scene. Two other wranglers were standing by a stretcher. Lanny was crumpled on the ground sobbing. Her husband, Carson, crouched beside her. Their three children huddled and hunched off to one side, looking terrified. A medical attendant for the ambulance was bent over the stretcher. He was pounding on a man's chest.

Georgia got out of her car and walked toward Joaquin, who'd just come from the front desk.

"What is it?"

"Mr. Wainwright—heart attack, it seems. He was with the children just over there collecting arrowheads, and Elsie came screaming in here. We thought maybe at first he'd been bitten by a rattlesnake. But she said no. She said he stood up, clutched his chest, and collapsed."

Why, Georgia wondered, *would a healthy young man not even thirty suffer a heart attack?*

"He's still breathing?" she asked.

"Seems so." And in that same second, the medical attendant ripped off the oxygen mask. Casting it to the side, he rocked back on his haunches and lifted his arms slightly. The message was clear. There was nothing more to be done. Carson put his arm around Lanny's shoulders, but she cast him off. "Get away! Get away from me!" she screeched. The children looked on, horrified.

Georgia raced over to them. "Come, children, come along." They seemed dazed, dazed and docile. Chuckie was whimpering. "Is he going to be all right, Miss O'Keeffe?"

"No, stupid," Elsie spat. "He's dead. Didn't you see how they took the oxygen mask from his face. Just ripped it off. No use 'cause he's D-E-A-D dead."

"Hush, Elsie; stop that," Georgia said.

"No fair," George whined. Elsie wheeled around and glared at her twin brothers.

"Nothing is fair, you idiots," Elsie yelled.

Georgia herded the children into the Hacienda and settled them on a couch in the lobby. Joaquin had followed them in.

"How about I get you children some lemonade, and I think there are some fresh cookies, Lupe's cookies. You know what a great baker she is."

Lupe herself returned with the cookies. "Here, children. All for you. I was supposed to take some up to Señora Sanchez. But I'll bring her something else."

"I never knew you provided room service, Lupe?"

"Señora Sanchez has not been not feeling well for the last few days," Lupe said softly, but she avoided looking at Georgia.

"Oh dear, hope all is well with her pregnancy. She's not miscarrying, is she?"

"Maybe," Lupe said. Her eyes were cast down as if she were trying to avoid looking at Georgia.

"I can drive you up."

"No bother, Miss O'Keeffe; Tomas will take me. He has to repair a broken window." The broken window, of course. The window she heard shattering that night as she walked up the Camina de Oro on her night-time painting expedition. She recalled the words scalding the night. *"We had a deal, Diego."* Then the sound of shattering glass. That must be the window that was being repaired. Or maybe it was a second window.

The temperature had climbed by the time she was back at her casita. It was too hot to work. So she took a pitcher of lemonade and settled onto her couch, where the breeze could enter from the east window and blow right through to the facing one. It was the coolest place. She shut her eyes and tried to think. There was the shattering glass, the bitter words—a deal. What kind of a deal was Felicity Wilder Sanchez trying to make? She was one of the richest women in the world. A movie deal? She along with tens of thousands of other young beautiful women wanted to be movie stars. She seemed reconciled, happy about the pregnancy. "I'm sure this baby will be worth it." She had said that as they had walked back from Peter Wainwright's place after Georgia had delivered the drawing paper.

But there were a few more words that had been shrieked that night. What were they? *"We had a deal ... we had a deal."* Georgia tried to recall the other words. *"Not this soon."* That was it. She must have gotten pregnant earlier than planned. Too soon, and now she couldn't be in the movie. *That must be it,* Georgia thought. And now if she wasn't feeling well, if she miscarried, her acting career might resume. But Peter Wainwright was beyond resuming anything. Poor Lanny. She recalled the tango night. How miserable Lanny and Peter both seemed that evening. For that matter, Felicity hadn't seemed that happy either. Perhaps it was because Diego had announced her pregnancy to the world at large that evening. And if she was truly miffed about being pregnant, she would have some justification. "The deal" had been broken, reneged on—her acting aspirations wrecked.

Chapter 30

As she tried to fall asleep, Georgia felt as though she were entangled in three deaths. One by knife, one by heart attack, and one—Nina Mueller—she hadn't heard yet how she was killed. She could not rid herself of the image of Rosaria's hands with that knife, so skillfully peeling the yucca. Her long slender fingers, nimble and dexterous. Dexterity and agility, however, were slightly different from force and accuracy. Could Rosaria have hurled that knife through the dark to hit a target some twenty feet away with enough force to kill a man? Emily Bryce had told her that the force was strong enough to have actually penetrated deeply through the bones of the trachea. Could Rosaria really have done that?

By ten o'clock that morning, she had decided she had to drive down to the Hacienda and call Ryan. Was it a knife that had killed Nina Mueller? Same knife? He would not come up here for Wainwright's death. Heart attacks did not demand police attention, even if the victim was healthy and thirty. Emily Bryce would be the one to determine what had happened to him. But she would have to tell Ryan about Rosaria and the knife. Lindbergh had been cut by such a knife. A priest—a fake priest, she corrected herself—had been murdered with one. Was it the same knife? Did that mean Rosaria had used it twice? Had she slashed Lindbergh's hand? As Georgia pulled up in front of the Hacienda, she caught sight of Lanny waving goodbye to the Lindberghs.

"So, where're they headed?" she asked Joaquin just as Lanny walked up looking rather pale. "Houston?"

"Yes, Houston," Lanny offered. "Going to see Howard Hughes." She sighed. "My, my; think of those two men together. Two geniuses."

Chilling! Georgia thought.

"How are you doing, Lanny?"

"Okay, considering. The children, however, are very upset."

"I know," Georgia replied. "I'm just heading in to make a phone call."

"I'm sure Mr. Stieglitz misses you."

Funny how she just assumed that she was calling Stieglitz. Well, she certainly wasn't going to tell her she was calling the sheriff. "Yes, but Alfred understands that this is not his kind of place—country." She thought of the blue glassy lake surrounded by billowing green hillocks and swelling knolls.

"Yes, but that's why it's important to keep in touch," Lanny said. There was a mother hen tone to her voice that Georgia found annoying.

Oh, yeah, you should know! What about you and Carson? Georgia thought, but said nothing. It was as if she were having two parallel conversations: one with Lanny and one with herself, which was a running commentary on Lanny's obfuscation of her affair with her children's tutor. She went in to make the call.

"Sheriff's not in right now, Miss O'Keeffe," Florence Gilbert said. "He got one of those trunk calls earlier. You know, from overseas. Came right through the Atlantic Ocean. I swear I heard the water sloshing about." She was positively garrulous. "You know, I've always had an interest in marine biology." *Oh, my goodness*, Georgia thought; *the desert could be inspirational in odd ways.*

"So, the sheriff is not there right now?"

"Not here, that's right. He set off just after he got the call. It was patched through Albuquerque. So I think he went to Albuquerque, but he didn't say."

"Did he say when he'd be back?"

"Nope. But he had that look on his face." Georgia was dying to ask, "What look?" But she restrained herself. "Can I give him a message if he calls in?"

Tell him I love him. Tell him I want to hold him. Tell him I'm worried about Rosaria and that knife—that knife that cut Lindbergh and killed the priest. She thought of all those shadows—the shadows of her and Father William's hats colliding on the front steps of Goetz's store. It was as if she had suddenly entered a troubling maze of shadows—shadows and distorting mirrors reflecting the dark broad-brimmed hats.

"Oh, just tell him I called." Then she added as an afterthought, "Nothing really urgent." She wondered why she had said "really." Was she thinking of the single word as some kind of a coded message? Did she actually have that kind of intimacy with him? Could he read her the way Stieglitz might have? Stieglitz, with whom she had lived for decades now. It shocked her that she had known Ryan for only a few weeks. Less than a month, and she was fancying that they had some sort of code. A presumed intimacy that would go far beyond sex. That only became real, or perhaps consummated, after years of knowing each other. She actually felt more than a tinge of guilt, as if she had tried to commandeer, to hijack, Ryan McCaffrey's nature or inner being. This was not good. *Shape up, Georgia. Don't behave like a goddamn fool!*

She set down the phone just as Carmelita walked into the office.

"Nobody told me you were here." Carmelita's tone was accusatory.

"I just came in," Georgia said. "Had to make a call. You've always told me I could." She paused. "Do you have a problem with that?"

"No, no, of course not." But her face told another story.

As Georgia was leaving, Simon Bowes was coming through the front door into the lobby. He looked tense. "Ah, Miss O'Keeffe." His face suddenly arranged itself into a perfectly calm and genial demeanor. *Well, he's a spy*, thought Georgia. *Of course he can fake it.* "I am so looking forward to our little expedition tomorrow."

"Oh, definitely," Georgia said. At that moment, Carmelita came out to greet him—rather effusively, Georgia thought.

"Oh, Mr. Bowes, a message came in for you from a Mr. Edward Spooner. He said no need to call back. The gentleman said they are working on three more points they would like you to include in your article and will get back to you with more details soon."

"Oh, wonderful!" A look of sheer delight crossed Simon Bowes's face. But Georgia noticed that Carmelita also seemed to have an inscrutable smile. She hurried to her office and shut the door firmly. *She's up to something.* Seconds later she questioned her own thinking. She cautioned herself to separate her dislike—yes, she'd admit it—her dislike for Carmelita with any notions of suspicion. She turned to Bowes.

"I'll see you tomorrow, right, Mr. Bowes, for our drive to the White Place?"

"I am so looking forward to it!"

Georgia was exhausted, but the day was hardly half over. It was hot, dreadfully hot. She decided to take a nap. Waking, she was uncertain how long she had slept. She decided to go down to the hacienda and try to telephone Ryan again. He should be back by now. But, again, Florence told her he had not yet returned.

Just as she was getting back into her car, another vehicle screeched to a halt.

"Hang on, Georgia!"

She turned around, opened the car door, and leaned out. It was Emily Bryce. The coroner got out of her car and walked over. She leaned in the window. Georgia had never seen a grimmer look, not even out in the desert when they had found Castenada's body.

"It was murder," the coroner said.

"Yeah, we know that, Emily," Georgia replied.

"Not Castenada or Nina Mueller."

"Wh … what?" Georgia stammered.

"Peter Wainwright was murdered. I just got the autopsy report."

"I don't understand. I thought it was a heart attack."

"Cardiac arrest due to poison."

"Uh … possible suicide?"

"I doubt it."

"It was a slow buildup. I won't go into the details of his digestive tract. But it had to have happened over the course of a couple of days."

"But what was the poison?"

"Jimsonweed."

"I thought that was only used for abortions."

"True. But a woman would never have to take this much. An eighth of a teaspoon would be enough to kick a fetus out of the womb. And this brew was made from the seeds—crushed—which are the most powerful. It was done, as I said, over time. I talked to the botany guy over at the University of Mexico. The seeds have no taste, even when pulverized. They could have been slipped into his food, his water, his booze … who knows?"

"Did you call the sheriff?"

"I did, but he's out."

"Oh yes, that's right. Just tried to reach him myself."

A silvery sedan came down the road. It slowed to a stop and Diego Sanchez leaned out. "*Hasta la vista,* Señora O'Keeffe. We're heading back to Los Angeles."

"Goodbye." She waved, and then turned to Emily. "Wait here a second."

She ran down to the passenger-side window of the Sanchez sedan and leaned in."

"Felicity, I hope you're feeling better and that all your dreams come true."

Felicity blinked. A shadow seemed to skim over her soft gray eyes. "Thank you, Georgia. Thank you so much."

They drove off.

Georgia began to walk back to her own car. In the shade of a cottonwood, she saw Lupe. Her face was hard, a dour look on it. Was it anger? Her eyes burned—burned with what could only be thought of as hatred. Pure hatred. She was wearing the kachina necklace, but as soon as the sedan turned out of the main gate, she tore the necklace off; the bright little kachina figures scattered at her feet.

Georgia walked back to her car, where Emily was still waiting.

"Want to come up to my place and have a drink?"

"Can't drink on the job. Two deputies are coming out here. We got to set up the crime scene or, I should say, the possible crime scene. I'm going to have to crawl all over Peter Wainwright's cabin looking for traces."

"You got the key?"

"I'll go in and ask for one."

"I know where one is. He keeps it in the planter outside his door."

"Very clever," Emily said snidely. "But no thanks. We have to do this according to the book. I have to show them my warrant at the Hacienda, and then they give me a key. All very official, you know."

"All right, but if you want to stop by after your visit up there, you can have some iced tea."

"Not jimson please." Emily laughed. She started to walk back to her car but then turned. "And, Georgia, don't go blabbing about any of this."

"I'm not a blabber, Emily. Do I look like a blabber to you?"

"No, of course not, but don't tell anyone that you know where Peter Wainwright hid his key. That could make you a suspect."

"Oh great!" she chuckled. "I won't."

Chapter 31

"Just keep drinking out of that canteen, Joseph. Keep hydrated."

Ryan McCaffrey felt bad about dragging his best deputy, Joseph Descheeni, out of bed. Descheeni had been laid up for a day and a half with a bad chest cold. But Ryan needed someone experienced for this run. Perhaps *experienced* wasn't the word, Ryan thought. Maybe a little more dignified and articulate than, say, Eddie Collins, who was a gum-chewing young fellow with poor grammar and a slight lisp. Joseph was very smart. He could read people. He was much too good to be just a regular beat cop. He was a great detective. Ryan knew he was gunning for it, and he'd do everything he could to make sure it happened.

"I'm not too bad, Sheriff. Way better than two days ago, I'll tell you that. So this guy we're meeting at the airport is a Brit, right?"

"Yes."

"Must be pretty important if they brought him all the way from London, England."

"I think he might have already been in the country."

"At the Bureau of Investigation?" Joseph asked.

"Maybe there. It was my buddy Lincoln Stone, who's the only smart one at the Bureau. The rest have hash for brains. Anyway, it was Linc Stone who told me he was coming. But somehow all this is connected with the—oh, Jesus Christ, what do they call it? The SIS?"

"SIS? That's Signal Intelligence Service."

"I think so, but I tell you, all these letters, these acronyms are going to be the death of me. The Brits also have an SIS, but for them it means Secret Intelligence Service."

"Sort of like the BI?"

"Seems so. Both SISs, ours and theirs, were in on the call. Came in as a trunk call from overseas with a multiway patch for us out here in the desert. Can you beat that? Amazing what they can do now. Florence swore she heard bubbles and fish talking when she picked up the phone. Anyhow, this fellow's cover is something with the Smithsonian Institution. British archaeologist interested in the Stone River cliff dwellings. Well, here we are." They turned into a long drive with a sign reading WELCOME TO OXNARD AIRPORT.

"Quite a crowd. Wonder what's going on?" Joseph Descheeni said, looking out at the close to one hundred people packed around the entrance to the main building of the rather small airport. The two men got out of the car and were about to ask where to go to meet incoming passengers when Ryan caught sight of an exceedingly tall Negro in cavalry-style military dress, pants tucked into his boots. He wore a crisp shirt and tie and a Western-style hat—not a ten-gallon.

Ryan McCaffrey stopped in his tracks. "Wash! Wash Stone!"

The man turned around. "Well, I'll be. Ryan McCaffrey."

"What the hell are you doing here?" Something tickled at the back of Ryan McCaffrey's mind. This could be a coincidence. *But I don't believe in coincidences.*

"Might ask the same of you? I'm here for Lucky Lindy."

"So that's why there's a crowd."

"I guess so, 'cause they sure ain't here for you or me. He's flying over to Houston. I'm on security detail."

Ryan was silent. This was a lot of information hitting him at once.

"And why are you here?" Wash asked.

"Yeah, what a coincidence." He hesitated a moment. "I think you might know."

"Maybe." Wash winked. "Well, got to go. Got to protect Lucky Lindy."

"Hey, Sheriff, you okay?" Joseph Descheeni said, coming up.

"Of course I'm okay. Why'd you ask?"

"You got a funny look on your face."

You would too, the sheriff wanted to say. Too many coincidences here. And damn, he was going to find that reason. "So long, Wash. Maybe see you 'round sometime."

"Maybe."

Ryan McCaffrey and the deputy headed toward the runway where one Bertram Welles would be disembarking. They came up to a fence that separated them from the landing area where the Transcontinental Air Transport flight was supposed to land. He saw Wash escorting Lindbergh and his wife onto the runway, where a very odd but sporty-looking plane was waiting for them. Lindbergh strode gracefully. His wife had to accelerate to keep up with him. She seemed like a puppy whose legs were not quite long enough. His blond head shimmered in the bright sun. They seemed the perfect couple.

"Ain't it something?" A mechanic was leaning up against the gate on the other side from Ryan and Joseph.

"The plane or Lindy?"

"Both, I guess. But I was talking about the Hughes plane. It's a prototype for one Hughes wants to build to fly around the world. He wants to break Wiley Post's record from last year. But guess what?"

"What?"

"That plane ain't going anyplace."

"Why not?"

"Bad oil leak. Going to take a few days to fix."

Another plane had just landed. "That'll be our fellow," Ryan said.

"What's his name again?" Joseph asked.

"Bertram Welles."

Five minutes later, a slender man was walking toward them.

The sheriff stepped forward to shake hands. "Dr. Welles. Ryan McCaffrey, and this is Joseph Descheeni." He had purposely not mentioned their official titles. There was a game to play here, as Lincoln Washington had told him. The sheriff had come in an unmarked car.

Welles was very thin, but just from the brief handshake, McCaffrey sensed he was deceptively wiry.

"Oh, don't call me 'Doctor.' My father was a real doctor. Heart surgeon, actually. I just muck around in the dirt, looking for wreckage from the ages, anything from old firepits and cooking gear to bones."

"Bones—well, there are a lot of bones out here. A friend of mine loves to paint pictures of them."

"You don't say!" Bertram Welles's eyes opened wide in mild surprise. What an actor he was, Ryan McCaffrey thought. He's here because one of the SIS's agents is here and something must be up—a bit more than what he had been told on the phone from those fellows in the Signal Intelligence Service.

"So you're staying at a place out on the old Abiquiu road, near what we call the White Place. Just about two miles from the White Place, actually."

"Yes, a fella's going to meet me there. Supposedly he's stocked some food and other necessities in the casita, as they call it. Even dropped off a car for me. Very kind of him. I'm hoping he might be interested in helping me at the site. Setting up the grid, you know."

There was definitely a stilted quality to the conversation. That was of course because they were all playing roles. Bertram Welles was what was called a case officer, the person who manages agents and runs operations. At the same time, he was an archaeologist who had traveled with the requisite tools—a bag full of chisels, hammers, and photography equipment, the basic equipment of his trade. He could talk the talk and walk the walk in the same way Simon Bowes could.

"Yes, I spent a great deal of time out at the Salmon Ruins during my graduate years along with Muskie Vanderhoven on his earliest excavations." He spoke while the landscape flew by them. Ryan did not have a light foot on the pedal. They had been on the road for the better part of an hour, chatting amiably about Welles's previous work in excavations around the Southwest, when Welles diverted the conversation to more practical matters.

"May I suggest that we make a gents' stop here?" Welles said.

It took a moment for his meaning to sink in. "Oh, a piss!" Ryan said. "Certainly."

Ryan pulled over to the side of the road. The three men got out of the car and walked to a spot overlooking a ravine, standing about five feet apart, each looking in a different direction.

"Ah, Bandelier." Bertram Welles sighed as he looked out at the cliff dwellings to the east. "I worked that site once upon a time in my misspent youth. The people of the Cochiti Pueblo are their most direct descendants. You can see it in the pottery. My wife is an expert on pottery of the Southwest."

Joseph was humming a soft tune as they stood there. When he finished, Bertram cleared his throat and gave two shakes. Then he recited:

"There once was a lady with sass
Who thought she'd squat in the grass.
She began to pee,
Then said, 'Oh me,
A rattler just bit my ass!'"

Ryan turned toward him as he began to tuck in. "Are you sure you're British?"

"Absolutely."

Joseph guffawed. "It's true. Got to be careful out here... . How come you did your archaeology study here and not England? They must have plenty of stuff to dig up back there."

"Too wet. Wet and dreary. Go west, young man! That was the call. I came to study at Harvard with Alfred Kidder, the foremost scholar of Southwestern archaeology. Got my doctorate. Went back to England. Fell in love with Mary, but she had bad lungs. So a perfect excuse to move here, especially when an offer came through from the Smithsonian."

And how, Ryan wondered, *did the Secret Service get hold of him?* Instead he asked another question.

"When did you come back?"

"Couple of years after the war. The Great War, as they have taken to calling it."

"Were you in that?"

"Indeed." Welles sighed. "Uh … not at Ypres, thank God. Farther south, in an SOF unit."

"SOF?" Joseph asked.

"Special Operation Forces—a commando unit."

"Yes," Ryan said as he began to button up his pants. "The Great War." He felt a chill run through him. Hitler was behaving badly. He could, most likely would, get worse. He recalled what Georgia had told him about Lindbergh's hideous remarks about Jews. What if the Great War was not the greatest war? What would they call the next war?

They drove on and three-quarters of an hour later pulled into the drive of a ramshackle adobe house where Bertram Welles would be staying, a discreet distance from both Abiquiu and the Ghost Ranch. And, perhaps most importantly, where he could put up an inconspicuous receiver in a new triangulation monitoring system to intercept the Lutzen spy ring.

Chapter 32

"*Hola*, Miss O'Keeffe; I'm here with your groceries."

"My goodness, Joaquin, that was so kind of you," she said as she was walking toward her car in front of the Hacienda. "Perfect timing. So lucky you were heading to Santa Fe today."

"Don't worry about it, Miss O'Keeffe. I had to get something for the Lindberghs."

"What? I thought they'd left today."

"I guess there was some plane trouble. They're coming back," Joaquin replied. "I better call up to the wranglers and see if Mrs. Lindbergh's favorite horse is okay. It had been lame."

"There's a phone at the bunkhouse?" Georgia asked.

"Yes, at the stable, just put in a week or so ago. Mr. Powell is modernizing this place."

Georgia heard the sound of another car pulling up. She was standing in the shadow of a cottonwood tree. Joaquin stood beside her. They watched as the Lindberghs stepped out of the car.

"A Texas Ranger is driving them," Joaquin commented.

"Is that what that man is?" She looked at the fellow, a negro in uniform, stepping from the car.

"Yep."

"What's a Texas Ranger doing in New Mexico?"

"They send the Rangers up sometimes for important things, important people."

"People like the Lindberghs."

"I guess."

Georgia walked out now from the shade of the cottonwood. Anne Lindbergh came right over to Carmelita. "We hope this won't inconvenience you, Carmelita."

"Oh no, not at all, never." She was clearly flustered. "The call came through that you were coming back. So I sent Joaquin into Santa Fe to get you a few things. Your casita has already been cleaned."

Then Anne Morrow Lindbergh caught sight of Georgia and cast her a mournful glance. It was not simply mournful but almost a cry for help. Georgia smiled at her as she left, then she turned to Joaquin.

"Joaquin, do me a favor."

"Certainly, anything, Miss O'Keeffe."

"Send Mrs. Lindbergh an invitation to come and have a drink with me at my casita."

"Yes, right away,"

"Try and be discreet. I would prefer that Mr. Lindbergh didn't know."

"Absolutely." There was a trace of bitterness in his voice.

Two hours later, Georgia opened the door. She was shocked by Anne's appearance. The woman looked as if she had shrunk. She stood there trembling in the doorway.

"Come in, come in." She led her to the living room. "Might I offer you a glass of wine?"

"Yes, that would … would help."

Georgia poured the wine. The poor woman was still visibly shaking.

"Now, what is it that's bothering you, Mrs. Lindbergh?"

"Please, just call me Anne." She took a sip of her wine. "I know too much." She peered directly into the glass, as if expecting an answer from it.

Georgia looked at her steadily. "You know too much about what?"

She closed her eyes for a few seconds, as if thinking about what she should say next.

"I … I could wind up dead like … like Nina Mueller."

Georgia gasped. "What?"

Anne tipped her head and looked off into the mid space, clearly reflecting. "You see, Miss O'Keeffe—"

"Georgia, please."

"You see, Georgia, I know where Nina Mueller's baby came from."

"The one they were planning to adopt?"

She nodded her head. "It was not a niece who accidentally got pregnant. The baby came from *Lebensborn*."

"'*Lebensborn*? What is *Lebensborn*?" It sounded to Georgia like a German spa where one might go to take the waters or such.

"It means Fount of Life. Something only Hitler could invent. The birth rate in Germany is falling. Women are selected to propagate the Aryan race. But men are selected as well. The babies are given away to selected families to raise, families where either the husband or wife is sterile."

Georgia was speechless.

"My husband was not simply 'selected'—he volunteered. You can imagine how thrilled they were. Charles Lindbergh's sperm! It was as if a god from a Wagner opera had descended from Valhalla and offered his powers. His semen." Her voice was dead as she uttered those two words.

Georgia was aghast. "Your husband did this?"

Anne Lindbergh nodded.

"But I don't understand why Nina would have been killed. He was not the father of the child the Muellers were expecting. Or was he?"

"Oh no; he was not the father of the Mueller child. Otto Mueller was. She must have known how the baby was conceived. And I knew about Charles too. He convinced me it was a good thing—after our son was murdered."

"But did you want to raise a child conceived this way?"

"No, and there was no talk of that. But Charles was so distraught, and I thought if this would help, it might be worth it. I knew I could get pregnant again, yet I really wasn't ready. I mean I will be someday, but not then, when *Lebensborn* started."

"But I still don't understand. Why was Nina Mueller murdered?"

"She knew too much." She paused. "And I do too."

"You know too much? What? What do you know?"

"The Lutzen ring."

Georgia offered to drop Anne Lindbergh off at the Hacienda, where her husband was waiting for her in the bar, undoubtedly indulging in the awe and admiration of newly arrived guests. As they pulled up, Anne Lindbergh turned to her. "Thank you, Georgia," she whispered in a quavering voice.

"I'm not sure what you're thanking me for."

She shook her head wearily. "Oh … oh …" she stammered. "I'm not sure myself, but what I told you tonight, it's like a terrible thing. And if you keep it inside, well, that terrible thing becomes like a cancer gnawing away at you. So maybe you saved my life." She gave a harsh laugh, opened the car door, and got out. Squaring her shoulders, she began to walk toward the entrance of the Hacienda. She reminded Georgia of a terrible photograph she once saw of a man about to face a firing squad. But she could not at the same time forget that this was the very same woman who had said, *"Let fascism take its course and learn to live with it."*

From the Hacienda, Georgia drove directly to the bunkhouse. How nice not to have to use Carmelita's phone and worry about her listening in.

But maybe she still could? If the wranglers' phone in the stable was just an extension of the one at the Hacienda? She supposed Carmelita could easily pick it up. She met up with Jack McKinley as she walked to the stable.

"Moonlight ride, Miss O'Keeffe?"

"No, not this evening. I just wanted to make a call, and this is a lot closer than the one at the Hacienda." She of course neglected to say that she had just dropped Anne Lindbergh off there. "Is this a separate line up here?"

"Yep, just ours. If we need to get the vet or whatever, we can do it. Tomas convinced Mr. Powell on that. We lost a colt in the spring that could have been saved if we could have reached the vet in time. But go in and help yourself."

It was of course later in Washington, but if Fritzy didn't pick up, she could call him at home. He'd given her his number. There was no answer on the DC office phone, so she called his home.

A woman picked up. "Allo," she said in a slightly accented voice.

"Yes, Mrs. Freihoff, this is Georgia O'Keeffe calling."

She heard a slight gasp from the other end. "Indeed!"

"I would like to talk to your husband, Fritzy."

"Certainly."

There was perhaps a fifteen-second gap. "My goodness, what a treat! I need not tell you that my wife, Marian, is delirious. Now she might think I'm buying her a painting." He laughed. Then all exuberance drained from his voice.

"Fritzy, Mrs. L. just visited me. She is afraid for her life. She's afraid that what happened to Nina Mueller will happen to her."

"This Nina Mueller was killed?"

"Yes. She knew too much, Mrs. L said."

"What?"

"Lutzen ring."

There was silence. "And Lindbergh's part of it?"

"She as much as implied. And you know about Fount of Life?"

"I do. Disgusting."

"He's donated."

"Good God!" Fritz Freihoff inhaled deeply. "You sure you don't want to go back home to New York."

Georgia took a deep breath before she spoke.

"Fritzy, my dear, I am not being kicked out or removed or dismissed, expelled or anything else from this desert. This is where I want to be, to paint. I shall not flee just because of a few Nazis."

When he hung up Fritzy turned to his wife, Marian, and said, "*Diese Frau hat Eier.*" "This woman has balls."

"Fritzy! Don't be coarse!" Marian Freihoff gasped.

Chapter 33

Just as Georgia was preparing to go to bed, she heard a knock on her door.

"Yes? Who is it?" *Hope nobody from the Lutzen ring*, she thought with cheerful defiance.

"It's me, Lupe."

She opened the door. "Lupe!" The small woman's eyes were filled with fear. She was trembling. "Help me!"

"Goodness gracious; come in, Lupe." She took her and led her to a couch.

"What is it dear?"

"Oh, Miss O'Keeffe ... I ... I ... did something bad."

"Whatever could you have done so bad?"

"I ... I ... I don't know where to start."

The image of Lupe tearing off the kachina necklace flared in Georgia's mind.

"This has something to do with Señora Sanchez, doesn't it?"

"Yes, Miss O'Keeffe."

"I'm listening, dear. Just start at the beginning and tell me."

Georgia was still holding her hand. She would hold it for the full ten minutes it took Lupe to tell the story.

"Well, Señora Sanchez she did not want that baby. She told me this was her chance to become a movie star ... wouldn't you want to be a movie star, Lupe? She said ... I guess, I said yes. Even though I didn't mean it. And then she said she had heard about the jimson flowers. She asked me if it was true … and I said yes. She asked me if I could show her where the weed was. And I said right in her garden. But she said she was worried that her husband would notice if all the jimson flowers were cut, and she didn't feel it was right to cut them, as the garden was really not theirs and the next guest should be able to enjoy the flowers. She asked me if there was any place just along the road where they grew wild. I said yes, and she asked me to show her the place. And I said the seeds in the pods were very strong. She should only use one, two at the most, and drink the potion once a day for two days and she would start to bleed. She asked me if I could brew up the first batch for her. So I did while she was sitting in my kitchen down in the little casita where I live with my mother and my baby. I put it in two mason jars, and she took it away."

"And did it work?"

"I thought so at first. She spent a day in bed. But then I start to wonder. You see, I clean all those casitas up on the Camino de Oro, every day except Wednesday. I never see any bloody rags, you know. I ask Elena, who cleans Wednesday, if she ever saw any bloody rags, and she says no. I can't figure it out. Señor Sanchez seems very sad."

"He really wanted this baby?"

Lupe hesitated. "I … I think so."

"But?" Georgia asked. She sensed there was more as Lupe, for the first time in the telling of the story, seemed to hesitate.

"Señor … Señor … he is *maricon.*"

"What … a …" Georgia started to say "butterfly."

Lupe clenched her fists and shut her eyes. "He likes the men … and … and I find part of love letter."

"Love letter?"

"Yes, torn up and put in trash can in courtyard where I should have found bloody rags from miscarriage but instead a love letter. I don't read English so well, but I can tell. It's man's handwriting to other man."

"What did it say?" Georgia could see the color rise in Lupe's copper cheeks. "It talk filthy … filthy."

"Filthy about what?"

"Sucking, you know, *pito* ... how big this *pito* was ..."

"And it wasn't Felicity who wrote these words?"

"No, not at all. I know her handwriting. She makes list for things for me to tell Joaquin to pick up when he goes to town."

The image of the letter in the planter where the key was hidden at Peter's had been from Sanchez to Wainwright. Had Felicity swiped it? She recalled Felicity standing behind her while she herself scribbled a note to Peter.

Suddenly it was as if the roar of that motorcycle tore through Georgia's brain again. At the same time, there was a harsh knock at the door.

"Police, Miss O'Keeffe."

Lupe shrieked.

"You sit, Lupe. I'll take care of this."

She got up and left Lupe sobbing on the couch.

"What's this about?"

"Sorry, ma'am." It was a young deputy that she might have remembered from the desert when she had led them to the body of Castenada. "But we're here to arrest Miss Lupe Badillo on suspicion of murder." Behind him stood the coroner, Dr. Bryce.

"Emily, they've got it all wrong." She heard something crash in the living room. The deputy pushed her aside. "Eddie, go round the other way to block her," the deputy said as he shoved Georgia aside.

"Sorry, Georgia, but we found evidence," Emily said.

"What evidence?"

"Two mason jars. Empty now, but still with traces in the kitchen and the same traces in Wainwright's canteens."

"That's wrong ... that's wrong. No! NO!"

Lupe fled to the patio. There was a crash as a deputy tackled her. Georgia watched in horror as they put her in handcuffs and then began to half drag, half carry her to the police car.

"Emily, you have to stop this."

"I can't, Georgia."

"Where's the sheriff?"

"He's gone for the day. Had business up in Albuquerque."

"But it's eight o'clock at night. He should be back. We have to stop this."

"You can't, Georgia."

"Yes, I can." She dashed for her car as the police car was pulling away.

She followed them all the way into Santa Fe. Parking in front of the police station she was just getting out of the car when she glimpsed a photograph on the passenger seat and froze. *Another one!* Another nude— her torso with her hips thrust forward, the dark triangle of pubic hair prominent. But with a fine-nibbed pen, someone had drawn the figure of a tiny child dropping between her thighs. She shoved it beneath the seat hopped out and bolted toward the door of the police station. A shrill scream split the air. The door framed Lupe face contorted and shrieking as two officers dragged her through the entry.

"Lupe! Lupe! I'll get you out of here!" She raced toward the high desk where the booking officer sat overlooking this scene of chaos. Lupe's shrieks lacerated the air as Georgia attempted to get around two other officers who were blocking her way.

"Ma'am, I'm going to have to arrest you for disorderly conduct if you don't leave immediately," one of the sergeants on duty said.

"I'm her lawyer."

"No you're not. You're Georgia O'Keeffe, the painter."

She began to collapse. She felt the officers now propelling her down a hallway. Any resistance fled from her body. Slowly it dawned on her as the shadows of bars latticed the floor. *I am being jailed.* She fought a peculiar urge to laugh.

The cot was narrow, the blanket thin and coarse. She felt a coldness steal through. She didn't care that she was in a cell. She could have been anyplace. Nothing mattered. Who could have done this? She tried to reconstruct her day. Where had she been? Abiquiu. The Hacienda. Who would have had access to her car? When could this have happened? Why had she not noticed it until now? Simon Bowes? When had he last been in her car? Carmelita? Joaquin? Could Father William have somehow put it there earlier when she was in the store? She could hear Lupe in the cell across from hers sobbing into the pillow. Crying for Alma. She felt as if her own heart was being torn out piece by piece.

Amazingly both women finally fell asleep. Georgia was unsure how many hours she had slept. But then, lost between the edges of a dream and the edges of a breaking dawn, she began to dream. A flawless blue sky with wings and strange markings. She felt as though she were wandering in this strange blue landscape, cloudless but for the dashes of the parallel lines that began to eclipse the wings. Those marks! Yes, the marks now scabbed over on Father William's head! Finally her plodding, pedestrian brain was catching up with her mind's eye. Something was becoming visible. For wasn't that what artists did, make visible the invisible? Those were scratches made by human fingernails—a little girl's fingernails. *Clara!* The name shrieked in her dream. And with it came the memory of the photo.

A shadow of bars was printed across the blanket. She turned her head slightly toward the wall. There was a high window she hadn't noticed when she entered the cell. She clearly remembered the sound of the lock clicking as the cell door shut, but now … now she was locked out of the sky! The window obviously faced east, and the sun was rising. She held up her hand a few inches in front of her face. It was striped with shadows of bars. She was sealed in completely, hermetically. She felt a compression on her chest and began to gasp. *Clara! Clara! I have to get to her.* But she was seeing other parts of this terrible jigsaw puzzle of murder as well. The murder of Nina, and this thing called the Lutzen ring and the obscene drawing on the nude photo of her torso.

"You okay, Miss O'Keeffe?" It was Lupe's voice. It brought her back to this world.

"Yes, yes, dear." She was trying to think back on her conversation with Lupe just before the police arrived at the casita.

"Lupe, last night at my casita you said that Señor Sanchez liked the men."

"Yes, Miss O'Keeffe."

"And you know this for sure?"

"Oh, yes. Ask Tomas. He was after Tomas." She giggled a bit. "But with Tomas, no dice, as gringos say."

"And you knew this?"

"Everyone up at the stable knew."

"How about at the Hacienda?"

"Maybe a few." Lupe shrugged. "But that a different world, Miss O'Keeffe."

"So no chance Carmelita would know?"

"Never! She never really mixed with the wranglers and all them workers up there. She likes rich people; she likes white people most. Especially the Germans."

A chill went up Georgia's spine.

"Why especially the Germans?"

"Well you know she and Mr. Goetz. They close. Very close."

"But he went back to Germany."

"Yes, but he got her the job at the Ghost Ranch few years back before the other owner sold it to Mr. Powell."

"Hmmm ..." was all Georgia could say.

"Miss O'Keeffe, you think I'll ever see my baby again?"

"Of course you will, dear. As soon as the sheriff comes, he'll get us out of here."

She sniffled again. "They made big mistake. I didn't kill Mr. Wainwright. If anyone killed him, it was Señora Sanchez. Though maybe Mrs. Powell wanted to."

"You don't say?"

"She like to try to make him jealous. Flirting, you know."

"I saw that. Did she know about him and the other men?"

"Maybe, I don't know. These people."

"What do you mean by 'these people'? White people?"

"*Sí*, but rich people. They are bored. They do anything for fun."

"Even murder?"

"Who knows?" Lupe shrugged. "You are not like them, Miss O'Keeffe. You rich. You white. You an artist. *Tienes alma.*"

"Alma? I'm like your Alma?" Georgia was thoroughly confused now.

Lupe laughed softly. "No, *alma* means 'soul.' You have a soul. Not like people at the ranch. They are just ghosts."

Ryan McCaffrey walked into the police station at eight o'clock in the morning.

"How you doing, Florence?" His casual query belied the tenseness he felt. Things seemed to have built up quickly. The cancelation of the Hughes flight for Lindbergh. The presence of Wash Stone. Suddenly, what had started as a murder was ballooning into something of international crisis proportions. He had to get on the phone with Linc Stone. No telling, of course, what Linc would say to him. But the fact that Wash Stone was here—a Texas Ranger—to take Lindbergh back to the Ghost Ranch was rather perplexing. Or just plain suspicious.

"Fine," Florence replied. "By the way, there's a surprise waiting for you in W section."

"I don't need another surprise. Good Lord, we haven't had any guests in the women's section since Lord knows when. Bonnie and Clyde were just killed, so what now? When they came to New Mexico a year or so ago, Carlsbad had the honor of giving them a guest suite in their jail."

"Well, just go see, Sheriff."

He had to walk through two security doors to reach the women's section. The light was dim, as it was on the west side of the building. In the first cell he saw a slight figure sleeping on a cot; in the cell across, another figure began to stir. There was an odd familiarity to the shape beneath the thin blanket.

"Georgia!" he gasped. Georgia sat up slowly and rested on one elbow. The dreams were still jangling in her head. But so much was becoming clear. Murderers and rapists were getting away, and their victims were in jail or paralyzed with fear like Clara.

"Surprise!" she croaked as she swung her legs over the side of the bed and held her head, which was now bursting with all that had been invisible now made visible.

"What?"

"Now please turn your back. I have to pee in this bucket."

"B-b-but ..."

"Turn your back."

He immediately spun around and faced the opposite cell. The figure on that cot was beginning to stir as well.

"Tell me when I can turn back around."

"Hold your horses, it takes me a while sometimes to prime this old pump."

As Georgia was turning around, new steps were heard coming down the corridor.

"Georgia O'Keeffe, what have you done?" It was Emily Bryce.

"I did not do this," Georgia roared. "And let me tell you who, by the way, murdered Peter Wainwright. It wasn't Lupe Badillio." She pointed at Lupe, who was clutching the bars of her cell.

"Bring me my baby. I must nurse my baby," she cried. The front of her dress was damp with milk.

"No, Emily," Georgia continued. "And it wasn't me, although I knew the hiding place for the key." She smacked her head. "Why didn't I think of this before? Proof! We've got the proof that Felicity did it." Georgia wheeled about. "Lupe, the letter you found."

"The letter!" Lupe gasped. She reached into her pocket for the fragments. "Here! Here! The *pito* letter." She held the scraps above her head triumphantly.

"*Pito* letter!" the sheriff gasped.

"He want to suck *pene, pito* ..." And this time Lupe didn't even blush.

"His dick!" Emily burst out.

The sheriff was looking from Georgia, to Emily, and then to Lupe. "Remember, you warned me, Emily, about not blabbing about how I knew where Peter hid his key. So it was someone aside from me who knew where Peter hid the key. It was Felicity Sanchez."

"Sergeant!" Ryan McCaffrey yelled. The same sergeant who had locked both Georgia and Lupe up came running down the corridor.

"Unlock these women immediately!" The fellow seemed to hesitate for a moment. "Do it! Now!" The door of Georgia's cell swung open. "Just curious, Sergeant, on what grounds did you arrest Miss O'Keefe?"

"Disorderly conduct and impersonating a lawyer."

"A lawyer, Georgia! That's really something." He tucked his chin into his chest as if suppressing a laugh.

"Oh, shut up, Ryan," Georgia barked.

"Yeah, that's what I said, Sheriff. I knew she was a painter and not a lawyer."

"You shut up too," Georgia hissed. "I have a date. I promised Simon Bowes I'd take him to the White Place. Although she didn't give a damn about Simon Bowes. For all she knew, he had planted that terrible photo in her car. It was Clara that she cared about. The Angelus would soon be ringing, and she had to get there. Clara was home today. She knew that. She did not want her ringing those bells with that priest.

"Get a deputy to take Lupe back to her baby, who's probably wailing her eyes out with hunger."

"I'll take care of that," Emily said.

"Emily, where is Clara?"

"Oh, she went home this weekend. Today's Sunday. She tries to make it out there to see her aunt and go to church."

Oh, God! Georgia tore out of the police station.

"Georgia, can't you wait a second?" the sheriff asked. "Why are you so sure it's this Felicity woman, Felicity Sanchez?"

"No time to explain," she yelled back.

Emily Bryce turned to the sheriff. "She's right, Ryan. Sanchez is your main suspect. It just didn't add up. And now that I spoke to the other maid, Elena, I know the poison was not used for terminating a pregnancy. Wainwright had four times the amount needed for that in his system."

"Okay, I'll put an APB out."

The photo was still on the floor of her car. She tore it into shreds and stuffed the pieces in her pocket. Then she drove out of town fast. Fast as a scalded cat, she thought—an expression her mother had often used when chasing after Georgia's baby sister, Catherine. "Cat! Cat! You're faster than a scalded cat." Georgia smiled to herself as she recalled the image of her little sister running through golden dust in Sun Prairie, the dust she had felt she wanted to eat when she was just a toddler like Catherine. Catherine the scalded cat. She pressed harder on the accelerator.

Twenty minutes later she pulled up in front of Goetz's store. She paused. The doorway was still draped in black crepe. José was languishing against the doorframe with a bottle of orange soda pop. A cold chill seized her, a moment of foreboding, as if the doorway itself was signaling her into a dark tunnel, a tunnel of betrayal and death.

"José, what are you doing here? It's almost time for the Angelus. Don't tell me you were fired."

"Not exactly. Clara came back."

Georgia's stomach seemed to drop. She looked at the twin bell towers. "She came back? She's up there"

"Yeah, she and Father William just went up."

"No! No! No!" she screamed, and in that same moment she caught sight of Rosaria marching toward the church. She was clutching something under the folds of her skirt. Her face was tight with pure hatred.

An awful design began to assemble itself in Georgia's mind. The terrible shapes on those scraps of paper blowing across the patio, the disembodied arm that was actually a phallus, the huge black teeth, and then the cowering smaller figure with no mouth but radiating wavy lines as if screaming silently. All of those images lacerated not just her mind but her heart.

It was all so clear now. Darkness brought clarity. The real intended target was Father William. He was Clara's abuser. And the murderer was Rosaria, who had somehow mistakenly killed Castenada. Georgia tore up the stairs.

Sunlight came through a side window of the bell tower. Clara was crouched on the floor. The priest's hand was firm on her head, pressing her down. "Come now, Clara; just this one last time. There is a taste of the wine, Communion wine. This is holy." He was fiddling with his robes, lifting them as his white drawers dropped to the floor. He was shoving harder on her head until the robes enveloped all but her thin shoulders. She was virtually headless. Just then, another shadow leaped forward. Three dark shapes spread across the floor in an unholy Trinity. It was Rosaria, with the knife in her hand.

"No, Rosaria! No!" Georgia cried. The sun glinted off the blade. Father William seemed to freeze for a moment then suddenly shoved Clara away just as Rosaria charged him, clutching the knife. He ran straight toward the bell tower's window, and in one magnificent gesture dived out, the cassock billowing like black wings against the turquoise sky. Then the thud of his body as it hit the ground.

Georgia, Clara, and Rosaria looked at one another in stunned silence, then raced toward the window. Father William lay spread-eagled on the ground. José, still framed by the black crepe, remained rigid on the front steps, clasping his soda pop bottle.

Georgia, Rosaria, and Clara raced down the stairs. Rosaria folded Clara into her arms, murmuring, "*No más, no más. Nunca más. Esta muerto.*" Georgia stared down at the crumpled figure.

She heard a shriek of tires and saw the sheriff's car halt in front of the store, with two other cop cars following. Sheriff Ryan McCaffrey got out and dashed across the dirt of the main street.

The sheriff glanced at the priest. "What happened here?"

"He jumped," Georgia said.

"Do we know why he jumped?"

Georgia looked at Clara, who was pale but with a new brightness in her eyes, as if she had just awakened at last from a terrible dream.

Ryan held her gaze, and Georgia saw that he understood.

"Eddie—Eddie Collins. Get over here," the sheriff yelled.

Eddie, a carrot-haired fellow who didn't look more than sixteen, raced up. "Medic needed?" Eddie Collins asked.

"No, no," Sheriff McCaffrey said.

"Any arrests?" he asked, pulling out his handcuffs.

"No. Put those away for now, Eddie," Ryan said firmly, and lifted his eyes toward Georgia. "So, I think you were right, Miss O'Keeffe. Wrong priest murdered. But it looks like some justice here." He looked down at the sprawled body of Father William.

But Georgia wasn't looking at the body. She had turned west toward the sunset, almost marveling at how two such disparate events—one so beautiful and one so deeply ugly—could be happening at the same time. She put her palm to her cheek in disbelief then emitted a small gasp.

"Gracious, I forgot all about Simon Bowes. I was supposed to pick him up at the Hacienda this morning to take him to the White Place." She shrugged. "Oh, well." She was more than ready to call his bluff. It might even give her some satisfaction—and to think of the time she had spent on that damn lamb stew!

José, who had been standing as if in a trance, looking down at the body of the priest, suddenly wheeled about. "Miss O'Keeffe—"

"Oh, José," Georgia gasped. "You needn't see all this. Poor child." She glanced over at Clara, who was folded in her sister's arms. "Nor you, Clara." It was as if stitches were pulling apart inside Georgia.

"But, Miss O'Keeffe," José said, "I saw Carmelita. I was trying to hitch-hike to Chama and she drove by, straight toward the White Place. She had one man in the car. I think it was Mr. Bowes, but she seemed in a hurry. Wouldn't stop."

"Out on the Old State Road?" the sheriff asked.

"Yes," José replied. "Carmelita wouldn't stop for me," he repeated with a tone of utter disbelief. "And she's my cousin, through the Towering House Clan on my mother's side." He sighed. "She wouldn't even stop for me!" he said softly with an almost mournful tone.

"This doesn't make sense at all," Georgia said. "I was supposed to pick him up and take him to the White Place. Why would Carmelita drive him?"

Five minutes before, she had thought she had just cast sunlight onto all the shadows. Now there was more light suffusing her. "Lutzen ring," Georgia gasped. "She's part of it!"

"What?" Ryan turned to her.

"Spy ring," she replied. He blinked and looked at her. "How do you know this?" he asked.

Georgia looked at him. It was as if he were putting pieces together. His expression was one of amazement. Ryan had sensed when Linc had talked to him, and then when he'd been sent to pick up Bertram Welles, that this involved international espionage. But how the hell had Georgia O'Keeffe become involved at the level she apparently was? And what the hell was the Lutzen ring? She continued to be full of surprises.

"How long ago was this, José?" Georgia asked.

"Oh, at least an hour ago."

"You don't say," Georgia murmured.

"We've got to get out there," the sheriff said.

"I'm going too," Georgia said.

"No, you can't go," the sheriff almost barked at her. She didn't bother to ask why not. She was done explaining to men.

"I'm going," Georgia replied, dashing for her own car. She saw in his face that he was more than miffed that she knew something that he obviously did not. *Oh, men!* she thought wearily as she stomped on the accelerator. She turned the Model A around and peeled around the first curve out of Abiquiu.

She could get to the White Place faster than they could. She knew a shortcut that could save her at least five minutes. It was by an old arroyo that could be dangerous to horses and cattle during the rainy season. The rancher there had blocked it off with fencing. But the rainy season had never really arrived in full force. Just a week or so ago, he had taken down the fence.

Within fifteen minutes, she saw the white spires of the White Place rising a quarter of a mile away. The spires often reminded her of solid cones of smoke. Now they were rearing against a blazing orange sky as the sun sank behind them. She saw a car just ahead. Two figures were frozen against the surreal landscape.

"Sie werden nie damit durchkommen." Simon Bowes was speaking German and holding his arm, which was bleeding badly. "You'll never get away with this. I got your knife here."

"You think I travel with only one knife, you bastard?" Otto Mueller spat out the words.

Georgia watched transfixed as she sat in her Model A.

Knife, she thought. *More knives.* She grasped the snake stick that she kept in the front seat. She got out of the car quietly. She would not shut the door, as both men seemed unaware of her presence. She walked down a narrow, sandy path. How often had she walked this same path this summer? Walked it at dawn, walked it at sunset. Walked it once at twilight and dusk.

"Why, look who's here!" The thick German accent split the silence. "Come to visit us, Miss O'Keeffe? A nice little party out here. But don't you dare come a step closer, or I'll have to kill you as well." He shrugged. "Probably will anyway. You're a Jew lover, aren't you? You and your Mr. Stieglitz."

I don't scare easy, you Nazi scum, Georgia thought. But of course she said none of this. Her thinking was interrupted by another sound, not her own voice but the sandy hiss of a snake as it slithered across her path.

Not two feet in front of her, a huge rattler was coiling up, ready to strike. Her mind went blank as its glittering unblinking eyes fixed on her. If the snake was coiled, it made it harder to hit. But what choice was there? She was hardly going to wait for this fat fellow to relax. She gripped the stick hard and, with all the force she could summon, jabbed the snake. She missed that crucial point just behind its head, where the blade would sever it. Nevertheless, the snake was stuck on the blade but writhing up. Without really thinking, she lifted the stick and flung the snake as far as she could. It sailed into the air, a beautiful dark design inscribed on the flawless blue of the sky. So beautiful, it caught her breath. It was as if the world had stopped for a moment—a moment of exquisite silence that was broken only when she heard the roar of cop cars.

She stepped forward, watching the design un-scroll as the snake landed in a loop onto Otto Mueller's shoulders—like a noose with fangs attached. He tried to rip the snake from his neck, but it was too late. There was a horrible shriek as he crumpled slowly to the ground.

"Bravo! Miss O'Keeffe."

Good Lord, Georgia thought. How British could one be? He might have been playing cricket. Simon Bowes began to walk toward Mueller. "Stay away, Simon!" Georgia yelled.

He stopped for a moment and regarded Mueller's body, which was less than ten feet from him. "Otto Mueller is dead, Miss O'Keeffe. Most definitely dead. Come take a look for yourself, and so is the snake."

She slowly walked over to the body.

"Got him right in the carotid artery." Bowes said. Indeed, the fangs were sunk deep into Mueller's neck. "Yes, he's very much dead," Simon continued as he stared down at the crumpled body of Otto Mueller with the dead snake in a loose coil around his neck. "Unfortunately his group, the Thule Society, which grew out of the Order of Teutons, is not," Bowes muttered.

"What the hell?" Ryan McCaffrey came running up the path.

"Death by snake," Simon Bowes answered calmly. "Bravo, Miss O'Keeffe!"

"You all right, Mr. Bowes?" the sheriff asked.

"Just a nick."

"Doesn't look like that to me. Joseph, get the first-aid kit."

"Yes, sir"

"You sure that snake's dead?" Joseph asked.

"Which one?" Ryan said.

Was that a joke? Georgia wondered. She felt dazed. "You know, I think I need to sit down."

"I bet you do." Ryan paused and put a hand on her shoulder. "There's a rock right there." He took her arm and led her to it. She sank onto the rock. "You know, we have to stop meeting like this, Miss O'Keeffe." There was a twinkle in his eyes.

"Yes, yes … over dead bodies." She sighed and looked up at him. His eyes were blue, navy blue. "Now, is this the point at which we all retreat to the library and the detective explains everything—like the butler did it."

"You've read too much Agatha Christie, Miss O'Keeffe."

"Actually, Ryan, it was Arthur Conan Doyle. 'The Musgrave Ritual.'"

"Or it could have been Mary Roberts Rinehart—*The Door*," he countered.

"Oh … haven't read that one." They were a fair distance from the other officers, who were now finishing up at the scene. Descheeni was tending Bowes with the first-aid kit.

"Well, why don't you ride back to Santa Fe with me and I'll lend you my copy."

"I don't have any pajamas."

The sheriff burst out laughing. "That's a helluva non sequitur. But you can wear mine. Come along. I'll give you a hand." And he took her hand.

As they walked up the path, a thin man made his way down.

"Oh, Sheriff, fancy meeting you here."

"Mr. Welles. We have much to thank you for."

"I was lucky I was able to set up my rig quick enough to intercept Mueller's message."

"What?" Georgia said.

"Sorry, Georgia. Mr. Welles, this is Georgia O'Keeffe. It's why I came in on the early side this morning. I got a call from Mr. Welles, actually Agent Welles. A tip on Mueller."

"You mean you didn't just come in to spring me from jail?"

"Sorry, didn't even know about it." He turned to Welles. "With all due respect, Mr. Welles, I think I have to give Miss O'Keeffe complete credit for taking down Mueller."

"My goodness, a woman of many talents. I never knew snake flinging was one. Just heard it from the deputy. Extraordinary story."

"Yes." Georgia exhaled loudly. "I can hardly believe it myself. Never able to hit a baseball. Not much hand-eye coordination except with a paintbrush."

"Well, dare I say you might have added a new string to your bow," Welles replied. "Not to mention your uncovering of the Lutzen ring."

"Oh yes, Fritzy. I did call him."

"Fritzy? Who's Fritzy?" Ryan asked. He appeared totally befuddled now. "Lutzen ring?"

Georgia answered. "I can't say anymore. And please don't accuse me of concealing evidence or disturbing a crime scene."

"All is forgiven. Let's get on the road, Georgia," Ryan said, touching her elbow gently. "Joseph, you drive Miss O'Keeffe's car back with Simon Bowes. Drop him at the hospital. But patch him up good before you set out. Georgia's riding with me. We'll see you tomorrow morning, Mr. Welles."

Georgia eased herself into the car. The last dot of the sun was spreading out like a single drop of blood between two of the limestone columns of the White Place. Soon it would be a river of blood against the dusky purple of the falling night.

Georgia felt as if she had aged twenty years in the last twenty minutes.

"The British are very chipper about death, aren't they?" she said as they drove off.

"Bertram Welles, you mean?"

"Well, Simon too. He shouted out 'Bravo!' when that snake landed on Mueller's neck."

"Bertram Welles was a commando. Saw a lot of action in the Great War. As a matter of fact, the commando knife originated in Britain. Since the war, the Germans got hold of it and redesigned it, making an even deadlier and more effective version. Otto Mueller had a fascination with knives and swords and daggers. He was a member of one of those Heidelberg dueling societies, and some of those evolved into these societies that are dedicated to the purity of the German race."

"Sounds like Lindbergh," Georgia said. "Yeah, they got their eye on him."

"Who's they?" Ryan asked.

"Fritzy."

"Huh?"

She exhaled and looked at him. "You're surprised that I know something you didn't. Let's not allow this to come between us," she said with a slight smile.

"What would come between us?" Ryan asked.

"That I know more than you do. Men are sometimes sensitive about that kind of stuff."

He let his right hand fall on her kneecap and gave it a squeeze. "Never, Georgia. Never."

They drove on silently for several minutes.

"Okay, but I'll be honest," Georgia said.

"Honest about what?" Ryan asked, his hand still on her knee.

"I'll tell you what I know that is more than what you know." She sighed. Hard to know where to begin. "It was one of those infernal agencies with all those letters."

"I know what you mean. The Brits have more of these letter agencies than you can shake a stick at."

"Yes, so I know that more than one of these intelligence agencies has Lindbergh in their crosshairs."

"So that explains why my old Bureau of Investigation buddy, Linc Stone, contacted his brother Wash, who is a Texas Ranger, to intercept Lindbergh in Albuquerque when he was about to fly to Houston and give him a ride back to the Ghost Ranch. The oil leak on the plane was a hoax! I wondered what that was all about. It must be the Bureau of Investigation that stopped the trip." Ryan sighed and tapped his fingers on the steering wheel. "Linc Stone and his brother Wash were, of course, the perfect choice for this job."

"What makes them so perfect?" Georgia asked.

"They're Negroes. White people treat them kind of like wallpaper. They're not accustomed to paying attention to them. Think of all the things that have been said in front of Negro servants. They are regarded as a powerless, less intelligent species. Perfect for undercover work."

The radio suddenly crackled to life. "Sheriff?"

"Yes, Florence?"

"Report just came in on that APB. Subject arrested in Los Angeles at MGM Studios. Taken into custody at eleven-thirty a.m. Charged with murder." He turned to Georgia. "They got her. Now let's hope her millionaire daddy can't get her out." Georgia closed her eyes and tried to imagine Felicity Wilder Sanchez trying to urinate in a bucket. Although she was sure the Los Angeles jails had fancier accommodations.

She turned to Ryan. "So, when do we have the session in the library? The one where you explain how the butler did it."

"I'd say after the session in bed. You know, some disorderly conduct."

"Oh yes. I'm very good with that. My specialty. Disorderly conduct."

Chapter 34

The fragrance of the peaches suffused the patio as Georgia and Ryan walked out to sit beside the tree. They were both in pajamas. She wore a sweater over hers, as the night was chilly. She took a sip of the peach elixir and tipped her head back. The stars were spectacular. It was as if a fishnet of stars had been flung across the night.

"What did you say you put in this drink?"

"Peach juice, gin, a touch of vermouth."

"Mmmm!" She set down the drink. "Now for the library part, although we can call it the patio. "You didn't know about the Lutzen ring, but why'd you come after Mueller? Did he murder Nina, his wife?"

"More like he was an accessory to her murder."

"Accessory but not the actual murderer?"

"No. The actual murderer was Willy Goetz, former owner of the general store. He left Germany right after the Night of the Long Knives. You remember that."

"Yes, just a month or so ago."

"Well, he was one of the big commanders of it. Now that you've told me about the Lutzen ring, I figure he must have come back here to recruit for them."

"How did you figure his connection with Nina Mueller's death?

"Doctor Bryce."

"Emily?"

"Yes. You see Nina Mueller was garroted …" He paused. "With German piano wire. But I guess he had become part of this Lutzen ring. He had moved back here just about three weeks ago. But I, of course, didn't know the details of this ring, at least not the way you seem to know. And there was one more significant clue."

"What was that?"

"A small fragment of glass at the scene of the crime. A piece of optical glass."

"Optical glass. Like glass from spectacles."

"Exactly."

"Of course!" Georgia spoke so softly that it was more like an exhalation than words.

"Why 'of course'?"

"I ran into Willy Goetz two days ago. He apologized for not recognizing me from a fairly short distance. He told me he had broken his glasses."

"Joseph Descheeni found the fragment of glass. Descheeni has the nose of a blood hound and the eyes of an eagle."

"But how did you figure it out about Goetz being a spy?"

"Tomas Benally."

"Rosaria's brother!" Georgia was aghast.

"Well, I'm glad I can surprise you with something," Ryan said with a laugh.

"Tomas Benally? But he's just a wrangler, a rodeo rider."

"Yes, he's all that but also something more. He's what the intelligence community calls an asset, my dear. Tomas Benally wrangles information. And if you recall, he was the one who found Nina Mueller's body, although quite by accident."

"It seems to me that these secret agencies, the BI and SIS, gave each of us about half the information, and hoped that somehow we'd fit the pieces together," Georgia said.

"Yep, they divided the pie between us." Ryan winked at Georgia. "However, you got more than half and ate it all!"

"But what was the motive for getting rid of Nina?" Georgia asked.

"She probably knew too much."

"And guess who's soon to be occupying your cell?"

"My cell—the Georgia O'Keeffe cell for obstreperous painters. Who?"

"Carmelita."

"What?"

"Yep. Just came through on the radio. I had Eddie Collins head right over there to arrest her as soon as we left Abiquiu to come here. Carmelita was an asset too, but for the wrong side."

"The Lutzen ring?"

"I guess so, now that I know it exists, thanks to you."

"They must have let down their guard of racial purity. She's hardly Aryan. But what on earth could she possibly have been doing for them?"

"Apparently, she was quite good a copying documents, top secret or whatever. She had one of those little spy cameras. They are the size of a matchbox. Have you heard of them?"

Georgia shut her eyes tight.

"You okay, Georgia."

"Yes. Yes. Just fine." She would not yet tell him about the photos. Not now. She couldn't. But things were beginning to come together in her mind. Carmelita had mentioned at one time during the summer having to go to Chicago to visit a relative. There was a gallery there that had several of Stieglitz's photos. And now the Chicago Art Institute had been in touch with him as well. Somehow she must have gained access to the pictures and photographed them.

"Are you sure you're all right? You look a little pale."

"Oh, I'm fine. Did you by any chance find out why she fired Rosaria?"

"Lindbergh made a pass at Rosaria. Several passes actually, and it was Rosaria who cut him with that knife."

"I saw her with that knife. She was cutting yucca root with it for some concoction for her aunt. But where did Rosaria get the knife? From Goetz's store?"

"She could have, but she didn't." Ryan sighed. "They're very popular out here, those knives. The wranglers really like them. You can get them cheap if you go across the border. They have a kind of mystique about them, especially since the war."

"The war …" Georgia paused for several seconds. "With Hitler rising up, it sounds like we might be going in that direction again."

"Yes, it does," he sighed. "But, Georgia, what direction might you be going in?"

"Oh dear … probably back East for a while." She turned to face Ryan. "You've got to understand, Ryan. Stieglitz is close to seventy-five years old. I just can't up and leave him. We've been together for almost thirty years. There's a thickness there. Yes, I'll admit it's made of scar tissue, but other things too."

"It's the other things, isn't it?"

"Yes, but I'll tell you this. I'll come back here. I promise. This place has gotten under my skin like nowhere else in the world. I have my eye on a piece of land up above Abiquiu. There's a wreck of a house up there. I'm thinking of buying it. If not next year, the next, but in the meantime I'm going to keep coming to Ghost Ranch. Every summer and maybe for longer."

"It's like that book."

"What book?" Georgia asked.

"Peter and Wendy."

"You mean *Peter Pan?*"

"Yes. You know, I told you Mattie was a librarian. She started the children's room at the library here."

"Of course. I read that book to my little sister, Claudie."

"Remember at the end of the book when Wendy's mother promises Peter that Wendy can go back to Neverland every year for spring cleaning?"

"A-a-a-h, yes; that was lovely."

"But then he forgets to come for her—just forgets, like kids do." Ryan McCaffrey took her hand and kissed it. "Don't forget to come back, Georgia. Don't forget."

"Never, Ryan, never." She tipped her head up.

"Looking for the second star to the right?"

She laughed softly. "This isn't Neverland, Ryan. This is my life out here. My real life."

Epilogue

Ghost Ranch,
Abiquiu, New Mexico, October 1934

A crisp wind slanted across Georgia's face as she climbed the ladder to her roof with the canvas in a sling across her back. Her easel was waiting for her. She gasped a bit as she glimpsed the first streak of tawny light spilling across the horizon. The low-lying clouds stretched like a bed of cooling embers as the sun rose. She was so glad she had delayed going back East by a month. To have missed this October light would have been criminal. She laughed softly at her word choice—*criminal.*

The canvas was primed and ready for her first stroke of paint, and so was the Pedernal, the birthplace of Changing Woman. Had she painted it enough to own it? What a disgusting word, *own.* She took up her brush. *Why not paint that long stretch of clouds upside down?*

She heard a creak on the ladder. Ryan's hand reached over the top rung and set down a cup of tea. "Roof service. I'm getting good at this, Georgia."

"Thank you, dear."

Author's Notes

While many of the characters in this book are fictional, some are based on real people.

Historical Figures

Helen Gandy (April 8, 1897–July 7, 1988) was the secretary to FBI director J. Edgar Hoover for fifty-four years.

Hermann Goering (January 12, 1893–October 15, 1946) was a German political and military leader, and a convicted war criminal. He was one of the most powerful figures in the Nazi Party, which ruled Germany from 1933 to 1945. A veteran World War I fighter pilot ace, he was tried at Nuremburg in 1946, found guilty of war crimes, and sentenced to death. He committed suicide the night before he was to be hanged.

Charles Lindbergh (February 4, 1902–August 26, 1974) was an American aviator, military officer, author, and activist. At the age of twenty-five in 1927, he went from obscurity as a US Air Mail pilot to instantaneous world fame by winning the Orteig Prize for making a nonstop flight from New York City to Paris on May 20–21. His first-born son was kidnapped and murdered in what became known as the "crime of the century." Lindbergh in the 1930s became a notorious anti-Semite. He and his wife were greatly impressed by how rising Nazism in Germany had seemingly revitalized the country. In 1936 he was asked by the American military attaché in Berlin to report on Germany's aviation program. That was his first recorded visit to Germany. For the purposes of my story, I had him make a more-clandestine visit in early 1934, where he met with Hermann Goering.

However, he did go to Germany in 1938 when he was awarded the Service Cross of the German Eagle ("Fallen Hero") by Goering. He and his wife were planning to buy a house in Berlin when Kristallnacht, the pogrom against Jews, was carried out. They immediately moved to Paris and eventually back to America, where he spoke widely, urging Americans to remain neutral as the tensions built toward the second world war.

In 1941 he made his "America First" speech, which identified "the British, the Jewish, and the Roosevelt administration" as "war agitators" who had used "misinformation" and "propaganda" to mislead and frighten the American public. During his long marriage to Anne Morrow Lindbergh, he had three secret mistresses in Germany with whom he had children.

Anne Morrow Lindbergh (June 22, 1906–February 7, 2001) attended Smith College. She married Charles in 1929. Anne largely followed her husband's beliefs and was enthusiastic in her admiration for the revitalization of Germany during the rise of Nazism. In 1940 she wrote "The Wave of the Future," in which she openly admired Hitler and called him "a very great man, like an inspired religious leader—and as such rather fanatical—but not scheming, not selfish, not greedy for power." She also wrote several books, the most famous being *The Gift from the Sea*.

J. Edgar Hoover (January 1, 1895–May 2, 1972) was an American law enforcement administrator who served as the first Director of the Federal Bureau of Investigation of the United States, beginning in 1924, when it was called the Bureau of Investigation. It was renamed the Federal Bureau of Investigation in 1935, and Hoover served as its director until his death in 1972.

Robert Wood (R. W.) Johnson II (April 4, 1893–January 30, 1968) was an American businessman and one of the sons of Robert Wood Johnson

I, cofounder of Johnson & Johnson. He turned the family business into one of the world's largest pharmaceutical companies. He was a frequent guest at Ghost Ranch.

Mabel Dodge Luhan (February 26, 1879–August 13, 1962) was a wealthy American patron of the arts and particularly associated with the Taos art colony She was a friend of Georgia O'Keeffe.

Dorothy Norman (March 28, 1905–April 12, 1997) was an American photographer. Alfred Stieglitz began photographing her when she was twenty-one, he was sixty-two. They were both married, she to the founders of Sears & Roebuck and he to Georgia O'Keeffe, when they began their affair. In 1932, with money from Norman's family, Stieglitz opened his final gallery, An American Place. Norman was a tireless advocate for many liberal groups and causes, including the American Civil Liberties Union, Planned Parenthood, and other endeavors.

Georgia Totto O'Keeffe (November 15, 1887–March 6, 1986) was an American artist, known for her paintings of enlarged flowers, New York City skyscrapers, and New Mexican landscapes. O'Keeffe has been recognized as the "Mother of American Modernism." When she was called the best woman painter, her response was: "The men liked to put me down as the best woman painter. I think I'm one of the best painters." She was married to Alfred Stieglitz from 1924 to 1946.

Franklin Delano Roosevelt (January 30, 1882–April 12, 1945) was an American politician who served as the thirty-second president of the United States from 1933 until his death in 1945.

Anna Eleanor Roosevelt (October 11, 1884–November 7, 1962) served as the First Lady of the United States from March 4, 1933, to April 12, 1945, during her husband President Franklin D. Roosevelt's four terms in office, making her the longest-serving First Lady of the United States. She was an activist and an early supporter of civil rights. Eleanor Roosevelt first met Marian Anderson in 1935, when the African-American opera singer was invited to perform at the White House. Four years later, Anderson was invited to sing at Constitution Hall. The Daughters of the American Revolution objected, as such venues were segregated. Eleanor Roosevelt, a member herself of the DAR, tried to change their minds but did not succeed and ultimately resigned from the organization.

Alfred Stieglitz (January 1, 1864–July 13, 1946) was an American photographer and modern art promoter who was instrumental over his fifty-year career in making photography an accepted art form. He supported such photographers as Paul Strand and Charles Sheeler. Georgia O'Keeffe and Stieglitz met for the first time in 1916. He was entranced with her work. In 1917 Stieglitz gave her first show at his gallery, 291 They fell in love. Stieglitz left his wife, Emmeline Obermeyer Stieglitz, and he and Georgia subsequently began living together. They married in 1924.

Katherine (Kitty) Stieglitz (September 27, 1898–November 20, 1971) was the daughter of Alfred and Emmeline Stieglitz.

Selma Stieglitz Schubart (1871–1957) was the younger sister of Alfred Stieglitz and considered somewhat flamboyant.

Further historical notes:

Lebensborn was also called the Fount of Life program. The program was launched officially in 1935, and its goal was to produce Aryan children. I did take some liberties in moving up the preliminary stages of the program to 1934.

The Duquesne Spy Ring is the largest espionage case in US history. A total of thirty-three members of a German espionage network were convicted by the FBI. Of those indicted, nineteen pleaded guilty. The remaining fourteen were brought to jury trial in Federal District Court, Brooklyn, New York, on September 3, 1941; all were found guilty on December 13, 1941. On January 2, 1942, the group members were sentenced to serve a total of more than three hundred years in prison.

The Duchesne ring formed the basis for the Lutzen ring in *Light on Bone*. I advanced its espionage to a few years earlier.

The **Special Intelligence Service** was a covert counterintelligence branch of the US Federal Bureau of Investigation during World War II. It was established to monitor the activities of Nazi and pro-Nazi groups in Central and South America. It was a predecessor to the **Central Intelligence Agency.**

The British at this time also had an **SIS** agency, the **Secret Intelligence Service,** which evolved into MI6, the present-day foreign intelligence service of the United Kingdom.

Special Operations Executive was a secret British World War II operation. Its purpose was to conduct espionage, sabotage, and reconnaissance in occupied Europe (and later, also in occupied Southeast Asia) against the Axis powers, and to aid local resistance movements.

Ghost Ranch was originally won in a poker game in 1928 by Roy Pfaffle. His wife, Carol Stanley, named it Ghost Ranch. They planned to develop it as an exclusive dude ranch. One of the guests in those early years was Arthur Newton Pack, an environmentalist and editor of *Nature Magazine*. He bought the ranch from Carol Stanley when she began to have financial problems. Georgia O'Keeffe first visited Ghost Ranch in 1934. In 1940 she convinced Arthur Pack to sell her a small house and seven acres of property on the ranch. Many famous people came to the ranch during those early years, including Charles Lindbergh and his wife, Ansel Adams, and John Wayne. In later years, distinguished scientists who worked at Los Alamos and others found their way there.

In 1955 Arthur Pack and his wife, Phoebe, gave the ranch to the Presbyterian Church with the express mandate that it be a place for "spiritual development, peace and justice, honoring the environment and exploring family through the celebration of art, culture and nature."

About the Author

Kathryn Lasky is the award-winning author of many children's books as well as several adult novels including *Night Gardening* and the *Calista Jacobs Mystery Series.* Her bestselling series *The Owls of Ga'Hoole* was made into a Warner Brothers movie *The Legend of The Guardians* directed by Zack Snyder. She is the recipient of a Newbery Honor award and twice winner of the National Jewish Book Award as well as recognition from Amnesty International for her novel *The Extra.* Her books have been published in twenty different countries including Germany, France, China, and Italy. She lives in Cambridge, Massachusetts.